D0475608

Mr. MacGregor

Mr. MacGregor

ALAN TITCHMARSH

SIMON & SCHUSTER
A VIACOM COMPANY

First published in Great Britain by Simon & Schuster UK Ltd, 1998
A Viacom Company

Copyright © Alan Titchmarsh, 1998

The right of Alan Titchmarsh to be identified as author of this work has
been asserted in accordance with sections 77 and 78 of the Copyright
Designs and Patents Act 1988

Extract from *The Garden* © Vita Sackville-West 1946,
reproduced by permission of Curtis Brown, London

This book is copyright under the Berne Convention
No reproduction without permission

Simon & Schuster UK Ltd
Africa House
64-78 Kingsway
London WC2B 6AH

Simon & Schuster Australia
Sydney

A CIP catalogue record for this book is available from the
British Library.

ISBN 0-684-81989-9

3 5 7 9 10 8 6 4

Typeset in Goudy by SX Composing DTP, Rayleigh, Essex
Printed and bound in Great Britain by
Butler & Tanner Ltd, Frome and London.

This book is a work of fiction. Names, characters, places and incidents
are either the product of the author's imagination or are used fictitiously.
Any resemblance to actual events or locales or persons, living or dead, is
entirely coincidental.

Acknowledgements

A number of people have gone beyond the call of duty in helping *Mr MacGregor* see the light of day. My grateful thanks go to Luigi Bonomi, Chris Beith, Jilly Cooper, Rosamunde Pilcher, Jo Frank, Clare Ledingham, Hazel Orme, William Spooner, Steve Alais and Dr Phil Cunliffe who have, in order, enthused, directed, inspired, encouraged, contracted, edited, copy-edited and advised me financially, legally and medically. Without any of them I simply could not have managed. Neither could I have coped without the help of the woman I love.

For Kats

Chapter 1

"Counting out: ten, nine, eight, seven . . ." The voice in Rob MacGregor's earpiece seeped into the back of his mind while his lips continued to deliver words unrelated to those he was hearing. The bright lights of the television studio shone on him from above and three large grey cameras stared at him – one on a wide angle, another on a mid-shot and the third on close-ups of the lily bulbs he was planting in a terracotta pot on the bench in front of him.

Over his shoulder were mock-ups of a potting-shed interior, a pastoral backdrop of an English country garden and a pale blue cyclorama of a summer's afternoon, although it was February. Beneath his welly-booted feet the wooden shed floor was laid over plastic grass.

"And when they've been potted up like that, water them in and stand them outside by the house wall . . ."

"Six, five, run VT," came the count in his ear.

". . . so that they're protected from the worst of the winter weather. It's as easy as that."

"Four, three, two, one . . . and cue the trail . . ."

Computer graphics whirled brilliant pictures of verdant lawns, bright flowers, lawn-mowers and garden views on to the monitor suspended from the lighting gallery above him as Rob went into the voice-over: "Next week I'll be showing you how to make a new lawn from turf, finding this year's best new seed varieties, looking for the kindest cut of all when it comes to lawn-mowers, and paying a visit to Pencarrick in Cornwall, a place where spring always comes early."

"Just loike Mr MacGregor," said a rustic voice off-screen. For a moment Rob froze, then turned to see the portly man with sandy-coloured hair advancing towards him. Bertie Lightfoot was wearing yellow corduroy trousers, a green waistcoat over a check shirt, and a scarlet handkerchief around his neck. The ruddiness of his cheeks was due more to Max Factor than Jack Frost. He smiled deviously at Rob, then sweetly at the camera, his gold filling (third on the right in the top set) twinkling in the bright light.

"Goodbye, all, and just remember that what goes in must come up," said Bertie, in his Somerset burr, looking at Rob then touching his forelock and winking at the viewers.

"Er, yes, until next week," said Rob, and then, recovering himself and smiling at the camera, "From Bertie and me, goodbye."

The upbeat signature tune for *Mr MacGregor's Garden* started, while the animated cartoon credits of Rob pushing a wheelbarrow appeared on the monitor, names flashing up in time with the music until the cartoon gardener closed the garden gate behind him and the producer's name came to rest on the watering-can.

"Thank you, studio." The voice of the floor manager cut through the final bars of the music and he wove among the cameras towards Rob before he had a chance to say anything to his portly co-presenter. "Thanks, Rob. See you again next week. Oh, and I'll bring you my fern. It's got brown fronds."

"Don't bring it in," said Rob, casting a nervous glance towards Bertie. "Just water it, and stand it on a tray of damp gravel so that it has a moist atmosphere around it – it's dry air that's burning it up. Your central heating's probably on full blast."

"Oh, I never thought of that. Simple when you know, isn't it?"

"Oh, yes, dear, a piece of cake . . . when you know," said Bertie. His Somerset burr had been replaced by camp, flattened Yorkshire vowels and a sour expression had taken the place of the smile that, moments ago, had creased his ruddy cheeks. He grunted, cast a sideways look at Rob, then turned on his heel and minced off into the shadows towards the distant yapping of a small dog.

Rob sighed distractedly, wiped his hands clean of compost and walked off in the opposite direction. Once through the hefty double doors of the studio, he went into Makeup, grabbed a handful of baby wipes from the plastic drum in front of the brightly lit mirror, smiled at the girl doing her best to pacify a neurotic newsreader, whose bald patch was taking more than the usual amount of black pancake to make it invisible, then wandered along the corridor to find his producer.

It was a strange environment for a lad who had begun his working life as a gardener in the Yorkshire Dales, but one in which Rob had always felt comfortable – at least, until Bertie had started being a problem. His first call to the studio had come out of the blue one summer three years ago. Greenfly had invaded gardens in their millions, blown over the North Sea and the English Channel by warm winds from Europe. Painters in coastal resorts had found thousands of fat little bodies stuck to their non-drip gloss. The newsroom of Northcountry Television, like those all over Britain, was peopled by eagle-eyed hacks who knew a quirky story when they saw one and they needed an 'expert' to tell gardeners what to do. Their resident gardening man, Bertie Lightfoot, was then on holiday in Tenerife, so an alternative had to be found at short notice. One of the news editors came across Rob's column in his local paper and put in a call, expecting some horny-handed old son of the soil to turn up. Instead, a man in his early twenties had put his head round the newsroom door, a man whose looks and build would have been perfectly at home modelling rugged outdoor wear in a Racing Green catalogue.

When he'd turned up at the studio, Rob's mind was whirling with information and excitement and he was fighting the desire to be sick.

"Don't panic," he'd said to himself. "You know the answers, it's your job. Just be bright and pleasant and try not to speak too fast."

The producer of the early-evening news programme had been very encouraging. "Don't worry," he'd said to Rob. "Be yourself and try to relax. The interviewer will ask all the right questions. He's handled people far more nervous than you are. Enjoy yourself!"

He'd felt as though he was on the threshold of something new that day. He wondered what his dad would make of it. He was anxious not to let him down. If he did a bad job it would reflect on Jock MacGregor and on the nursery where a father had taught his son all he knew about plants and gardening. He didn't want that. He knew his mum would think he was wonderful whatever he did, but if the old man grunted that he'd not done too badly then he'd be well pleased.

Jock had worried about a son learning his trade at the hands of his father. He needn't have done. Rob had the sense and the patience to make allowances for his dad, and for old Harry Hotchkiss who'd helped Jock since before Rob had been born.

Rob's five-year apprenticeship of boiler-stoking, pot-washing, cutting-taking and shrub-growing with his father was boosted by day-release classes at the tech in Bradford – a place as foreign to Rob as if it had been on the other side of the world, but by the time he came to the end of his indentures he was itching to get away. He left for York, for a year's full-time training at the county agricultural college, and then to the Royal Botanic Garden, Edinburgh, for three years, which made his Scottish father almost burst with pride.

Rob did well. He'd grown into a good-looking lad with a passion for gardening and an infectious enthusiasm for passing on his skills. Now a six-footer, he had green eyes and a mop of untameable curly brown hair that framed a face which, more often than not, sported a crooked grin. And Edinburgh had opened his eyes. There was the entertainment and culture provided by the Festival, and the entertainment and culture provided by the women. Leaving at the end of the three-year diploma course had been a bit of a wrench, for one girl in particular.

He'd come back to the nursery for a few months but was soon restless. Gardening and selling plants were no longer enough for him: he really wanted to pass on his passion.

He rang up the local paper, the *Nesfield Gazette*, and spoke to the editor – a young raven-haired beauty, Katherine Page. She called him in, looked him up and down, asked him a few tricky questions then took him on, first as a columnist and then as a boyfriend. She was sparky and opinionated, and gave Rob a good run for his money both professionally and personally. His column caught on quickly: he had a flair for turning out copy that came to life on the page.

Which was exactly what had caught the eye of the man in the newsroom at Northcountry Television. His first appearance, when he waxed lyrical about greenfly, had gone down well. He could remember that first moment of live television even now: the countdown on the hushed studio floor; the red light and the wave of the floor manager's arm that indicated they were on air; the thrill, the dryness in the mouth, the fluttering in the stomach and the strange sensation that the sensible words coming out of his mouth didn't belong to him. It was all over before it had begun and they were patting him on the back and saying, "You must come back, you must do more."

He'd left the studio light-headed, and come home with his feet barely touching the ground. He *wanted* to do more. This was what he had been born to – communicating his passion for gardening to a huge audience. Then he watched the video recording his parents had made and for the rest of the week he didn't want to think about television again. What a let-down. His voice sounded strangled. Why hadn't he known what to do with his hands? Why had he kept looking at the wrong camera?

But they did ask him back. Would he stand by if Bertie couldn't make it? There were several occasions when Bertie couldn't make it – due to gippy tummy, said Bertie (due to Johnnie Walker, said the newsroom).

Slowly but surely his camera technique improved, he gained confidence and began to present his own pieces. 'I don't think you need me any more,' said the interviewer, good-naturedly. By now he knew what to do with his hands: if he carried something they looked natural. He knew that the camera to look at was the one with the red light, and if ever you wanted to change cameras, look down or look away first and then come back to the new camera whose light would already be on. Simple when you knew how. He could even carry on talking when the voice of the production assistant was counting down the minutes and the seconds in his ear, though for the first few times he felt his eyes glazing over as he listened to her too intently. It was, he decided, a matter of practice and aptitude. If you had both, the technique would become secondary and you could concentrate on your style and the content of the programme.

Some time later Rob was given a short programme of his own, regional at first. It captured people's imagination, and just a year later it was expanded to half an hour and screened live right across the country – most other gardening programmes were recorded. Their viewers, so used to staid, sober television gardening, or Bertie's phoney Mummerset, had shown their approval by making *Mr MacGregor's Garden* one of the most popular programmes on the network, and almost before he knew it – if, indeed, he ever believed it – Rob MacGregor was a star, especially with the female viewers who found his drop-dead good looks and slightly off-hand charm irresistible.

His friends had teased him mercilessly and Katherine had refused to take his new status seriously and persisted in making him push the trolley whenever they shopped together in the supermarket. When people asked for his autograph, she would stand behind them while he signed, making faces at him over their shoulders.

Rob wouldn't have known how to be starstruck. He'd dealt with customers in the nursery since he was a boy, and this was just the same. Be nice, smile and answer questions. There was nothing insincere about his manner: he was open and at ease in company. It was only when female fans flattered him too much about his looks and his flower-bedside manner, or asked if they could see if his fingers were really green, that he coloured and fumbled for words. One woman who bumped into him at the nursery even went so far as to try to roll up the leg of his jeans, saying, "Ooh, Mr MacGregor, you've got the sexiest legs on the box." Katherine had had silent hysterics behind a very large hanging basket.

Rubbing off the last of his makeup with the baby wipe, Rob pushed open the wood-veneered door to the office at the end of the corridor and walked in. There were around twenty desks in this open-plan area, and he threaded his way between them. At each sat a man or a woman, gazing at a computer screen, and, more often than not, remonstrating with some caller on the phone. His own producer, Steve Taylor, was no exception.

Fresh out of the studio gallery, glasses on the end of his nose, lank black hair pushed back and the sleeves of his white shirt rolled back, he waved at Rob and raised his eyebrows as he continued his conversation. "Yes, I understand that but, you see, he gets so many requests like this . . . I know, I know . . . Yes, you're right, it *is* a good cause. I will put it to him. But if you could just send him a note." A flailing arm motioned Rob to sit on a tubular steel chair next to the desk. "Yes, that would be lovely. Thank you. Yes. OK. Goodbye." He dropped the receiver into its cradle and slumped back into his chair. "Aaah! Why did they put her through to me? I hope your ears are burning."

"Why?" asked Rob.

"I'm getting fed up of acting as your secretary. When are you going to get one?"

"When you give me one."

"Steady! The budget for your programme's large enough already."

"What? I did all that stuff at Pencarrick last week as a single camera shoot, and now I'm doing winter programmes on a studio set that looks as though it's been designed by Walt Disney."

"Oh, God, prima-donna temperament already and you've only been on telly for a couple of years."

"No, not really. It's just . . . Well . . ." He sighed a long sigh,

7

looked out of the window at the dark February sky, then back at Steve. "It's Bertie."

"Tell me about it." Steve leaned back in his chair, pulled off his glasses and rubbed his eyes. "'What goes in must come up'? I ask you."

When Rob had been given his own programme Bertie Lightfoot's nose had been put well out of joint. *Mr MacGregor's Garden* had replaced *Bertie's Beds and Borders*, and Bertie, yet again, had seen his career on the skids. Once a variety artiste – 'Bertie Lightfoot, a song, a dance and a merry quip' – Bertie had found his work on the boards diminishing and decided he needed to branch out to survive. His hobby had always been gardening, and his garden, in Myddleton-in-Wharfedale where he lived with his partner Terry and two King Charles Cavalier spaniels, was regularly open to the public and had given him something of a reputation as a green-fingered thespian.

He'd written occasional articles for glossy magazines, and eventually been given his own television programme, for which he had adopted a stage accent more suited to Shakespearean mechanicals or rustics in Restoration comedy than to a twentieth-century gardener.

"Makes the advice sound more authentic, dear," he'd said to Rob, off camera on their first meeting.

Eventually Bertie's television programme had been considered past its sell-by date, and his bulbous nose too purple to cover up with concealing cream. The up-and-coming Rob MacGregor had been earmarked as a suitable replacement.

At first, Bertie had decided that he'd go quietly, with just the odd tart retort aimed in the direction of the young up-and-coming star. It had all been made easier in that his usurper was a friendly sort with no overblown ego, and Steve had suggested that the old stager should have a small slot in *Mr MacGregor's Garden* each week as a kind of sop.

Rob had foreseen no difficulties with this, and for a time the two had rubbed along fine. But lately Bertie had been getting just a touch more venomous towards his successor, and Rob had felt uncomfortable. The once-witty asides were now verging on animosity, which was not lost on Steve Taylor.

"Look, I'm sorry, old son. I know it's a problem – I can see it is. The trouble is, he's got friends upstairs."

"I can believe it," said Rob.

"Now, don't be unkind."

"Oh, but come on, Steve. I hate making a fuss about this. It's not that I haven't got a sense of humour, it's just that it's getting so embarrassing."

"Leave it with me. I'll see what I can do."

"I don't know what the solution is," said Rob. "I don't want to see the old bugger pensioned off. It'd break his heart, even if it is pickled. Perhaps I'd better try and sort it out for myself. Look, don't say anything. I'll have a word with him."

"You know, sometimes I think you really are a star," said Steve, with a relieved smile. "I'll see if I can't get you a bit of help with your secretarial work. Perhaps Lottie could take you on. Only part-time, mind. She's got her work cut out with me, so don't get excited about it."

"Thanks, Steve. You're a star yourself. Anyway, I'd better dash. I'm off to see a lady about a garden."

"Oh-ho-ho."

"No, she's old enough to be my mother." A shadow crossed Rob's face and his words hung in the air.

"Well, just watch out. I've seen how these old biddies look at you."

Rob recovered himself. "Oh, not you as well! Why does everybody seem to think that every single woman over the age of thirty is about to pounce on me?"

"It's not just the single ones."

"Thank you! Even Katherine's got this bee in her bonnet that I'm easy prey for vultures."

"And are you?"

"I think I'd better go. This conversation's getting far too personal." He laughed.

9

"Cheers, then – and good luck with the old son of the soil."

"I'll need it!" Rob lobbed the now salmon-coloured wipe into Steve's waste-bin, went back through the desks towards the door and, as he pushed it open, almost bowled over a devastating blonde. "Sorry!" he stammered.

"Don't be," replied Lisa Drake, giving him a look of amused admiration. She and Rob had never met before, although they were two of Northcountry Television's most popular figures. Rob was regarded as the rustic hunk, but as the station's main newsreader, Lisa's reputation was anything but that of a blonde bimbo. Politicians took this girl seriously.

"I'm in a bit of a rush I'm afraid."

"Evidently." Perfectly enunciated by glossed lips, set off by the wide smile of even teeth. The two-piece navy blue suit, with a white silk blouse beneath it, was the ultimate in soft-edged power dressing.

Rob took her in at a glance. Rather too long a glance.

She tucked the script she was carrying under her arm and offered her hand. "I'm Lisa Drake." She looked him straight in the eye. The handshake was firm and sure. "You're Rob MacGregor, aren't you? I can't think why we haven't bumped into each other before."

"Nor me. Funny, really."

"Your programme's going really well. You must be pleased?" She leaned on the door frame, legs crossed, sizing him up.

Rob felt as though he were about to be given the sort of grilling that Lisa normally reserved for cabinet ministers. "Er, yes, very pleased. Lucky really."

"Oh, I don't think it's luck. You're very good. You must be. I've never watched a gardening programme before in my life but I try to catch yours. It's fun."

Rob looked at the floor, then became aware that Lisa might think he was looking at her legs, which were certainly worth looking at, so he lifted his eyes again, in time to see her flash a final smile, glance at her watch and say, "I must dash. I've a bulletin in a couple of minutes. Great to meet you, I'll see you again some time."

And she was gone. Only a whiff of Chanel remained.

The bonfire crackled and a plume of amber sparks spiralled upwards into the lowering February sky as Jock MacGregor, his flat cap protecting his watering eyes from the heat, hurled another young tree into the centre of the blaze. Through the shimmering haze above the flames he saw the youth retreating towards the nursery gate, his khaki lunch-bag slung over his shoulder and a young pot-grown tree in each hand.

"Oi!"

The lad stopped dead in his tracks and looked around sheepishly, the whites of his eyes almost luminous against his black skin.

"Where do you think you're going?"

"Home," said the lad.

"Not with those you're not," said the old man. "They're for the bonfire."

"Aw, go on. If they're going to be burned I might as well take 'em 'ome." He stood near the old wrought-iron gate, embarrassed at being caught out.

"And where will you say they came from?"

"From work."

"Oh, yes? And what will folk think of this nursery then? If the lad who works here takes home shapeless trees with half their branches missing, what kind of advert is that for a business?" Jock beckoned the lad over. "Do you really want two trees?"

"No, not really. One'd be enough. It's for the old lady's garden – you know, the one I do of a weekend."

The old man looked at the youth. His tightly curled hair was close-clipped into a spiral pattern above his wide, honest face, and three rings were spaced around his left ear. Not the way apprentice gardeners had looked in Jock MacGregor's day. Then they had worn green baize aprons, clogs and corduroy trousers, rather than the baggy jeans, gaping trainers and sloppy sweaters that oozed out from beneath Wayne Dibley's slogan-painted donkey-jacket.

"Get yourself over there." The old man pointed to the standing ground where container-grown maples and birches, rowans and limes stood in neat rows, their vigorous young trunks strapped to stout horizontal wires to stop them blowing over in the wind. "If you want a tree for your old lady take a decent one."

He shuffled back to the bonfire, poked it with his long-handled fork and sent another fountain of sparks dancing upwards into the darkening sky.

"Thanks," said the lad, his eyes widening. "Can I have a birch? They've got dead cool bark. She'll be chuffed wi' that."

The faintest glimmer of a smile came to the old man's lips, then he was serious again. "Just remember," he said, "it takes years to build up a reputation and seconds to destroy it. Folk come here for quality plants and I don't like them to be disappointed at what we turn out."

"Sorry. I didn't mean to -"

Jock MacGregor cut him short. "Go on. Get off home. I'll see you in the morning."

The old man watched him go, a spring in his step and a tree in his hand, whistling some God-awful tune. He looked up at the sky, now a dark blue-grey, and then back at the dying fire. He prodded again at the bright embers that lit his craggy old face with an orange glow. A sad face. The face of a man once happy with his lot but which now reflected a hollowness inside.

Wayne Dibley, for all his unruly appearance, was, Jock thought, a good lad. Jock had thought he was joking when he had arrived there a fortnight ago, looking like a refugee in his ill-fitting clothes. But something about his persistence had told the old man that he might be worth taking on. Harry Hotchkiss was approaching eighty and his muscle power was worth next to nothing. Jock could do with a couple of strong arms about the place, provided they didn't cost too much.

"I don't mind 'ard work," the youth had said.

"I should 'ope you don't," said Harry. "There's plenty of it 'ere."

The irony of Harry's response was not lost on Jock, an early riser who unlocked the nursery gates to let himself in at seven thirty every morning. Harry, with good luck and a following wind, could usually drag himself in by a quarter to nine, and would then sit in an old armchair in the corner of the dusty potting shed, downing sugary dark-brown tea from a stained pint pot. He had a smoker's cough that could rattle the roof tiles, and spent a good half-hour every morning ensconced in the toilet with a Capstan Full Strength hanging off his lower lip and a copy of the *Sun* on his lap. Jock made sure that he was watering in the greenhouses while Harry's routine was in full swing. Yes, he could do with some fresh company as well as fresh muscle power. It might help to take him out of himself.

Jock perched on the side of the wooden cart that held the trees he considered too inferior for his customers. The lad had thought him barmy for not selling them. Maybe he was. But his own training had left him with a carefulness that he recognized as truly Scots. How far away it all seemed now. Like another world. Another life.

Young Murgatroyd MacGregor – he'd been happy to let folk call him Jock – had left school in Perth at fourteen and gone straight into service like his parents before him. He'd never shone at school – for him the three Rs meant rambling, rabbiting and ratting – but give him a plant in a pot or let him loose in a garden and he felt instantly at home. He'd tried to work out why and had decided that quite simply you were born with an affinity to nature; it was not something you could acquire.

Looking at the nursery now, even in the dim twilight, Jock could see why he and Madge had known that this was their rightful place. It was a picturesque spot: the beer-coloured river flowed by at the bottom of a steep grassy bank. When Jock and Madge had come to view it on that warm May day it had been swathed in cow parsley and red campion. It was only a couple of acres, but lapped by the river on one side, and with the moorland rising above the small town of Nesfield behind it, it had seemed like a patch of paradise to the young couple.

On the opposite bank of the river, crossed by a small, hump-backed stone footbridge, was the nursery cottage, a simple affair of local sandstone with a purple slate roof and small sash windows. It was surrounded by its own garden and enclosed by a drystone wall. Over the wall leaned a green sign with gold lettering, though when Jock and Madge had come here its message had been faded and peeling: "Wharfeside Nursery. Prop: F. Armitage", it had said, with an arrow pointing across the river.

Fred Armitage, the bespectacled old Yorkshire nurseryman had quietly impressed on Jock the need to keep down weeds and produce good-quality stock, and asked if it would be possible for his "lad", Harry, to remain with the business. Harry had been in his thirties then, and willing to work, if a little slow. Gradually Jock turned round the flagging nursery and built up the business, with Harry doing the labouring, and Madge keeping the books and looking after the boy.

All things considered, he couldn't have wished for a better son. And now they called him a star. One newspaper had even dubbed him 'The King of Spades'.

Jock couldn't have been happier. And then it had happened. For a month or two Madge had not been feeling herself. Just dizzy spells, she had said, no point in seeing the doctor. Until Jock returned home from the nursery one night and found her on the kitchen floor. There had been no time to take it in; no chance to help her. She had waved him goodbye from the doorstep in the morning when he'd walked over the bridge to the nursery, and when he returned that evening she was lying dead by the kitchen table. A brain haemorrhage, the doctor had said. Instant and painless. But not for Jock. The loss was agonizing, bewildering. What was the point in going on?

He watched the embers of the bonfire turn from bright orange to dull red, and felt a tear trickle down his stubbly chin. It was six months since Madge had died and the fire had gone out in his heart. He turned towards the wrought-iron gate, walked through it, secured the padlock, pocketed the key and crossed the bridge for home.

Chapter 2

The slightly foxed pale green Ford Fiesta was tucked into a corner of the studio car park, salt from the winter roads caked on its sills. Rob unlocked the door and slid into the driver's seat through the narrow gap between it and the charcoal grey BMW. Lisa Drake's car went perfectly with her image. A rust-spotted Fiesta wasn't exactly a bird-puller but it had belonged to his mother and Rob had been reluctant to sell it straight away. As long as it remained, so did the memories of her driving him around. Her woolly hat remained in the glove compartment, not through sentimentality but because Rob felt happier to leave it there. To remove it would be to clear his mother from his life and he wasn't ready to do that. He doubted that he ever would be.

He turned the key in the ignition. The engine coughed reluctantly into action and a little orange light illuminated the dashboard. Nearly out of petrol. Still, there was enough to allow a detour on the way home to visit the one remaining older woman in his life. It was a fortnight since he'd last dropped by. She might think he'd forgotten her.

He'd known Lady Helena Sampson since he was sixteen, when lack of funds had necessitated an evening job. He thought of her now as he drove away from the studios in the city, up the dale towards his home town. The depressing dark grey of the tower blocks and the sooted deep red brickwork of Victorian Leeds eventually gave way to rolling green fields crisscrossed by drystone walls and speckled with black-faced sheep. The twilight deepened and the plum-purple moors disappeared into the mist above the river valley as he turned up the moorland road towards Helena's house. There were few women whose company he enjoyed more, and few people in whose company he felt so at ease. He swung the Fiesta over the cattle grid between the hefty stone gateposts and it growled up the gravel drive to Tarn House, its exhaust making even more of a din than usual.

As he got out of the car the lantern in the porch came on, and Helena, a tall, good-looking, grey-haired woman in a heather-coloured tweed skirt, grey polo-necked jumper and pearls came out to meet him. He pecked her on both cheeks and walked indoors.

"You know, I remember when it was only one," she said, as they walked through the print-lined hallway into the handsome Victorian drawing room.

"One what?"

"One cheek that got a peck."

"I remember when it was no cheek at all, and just, 'Will that be all, ma'am?'"

"I don't believe you've ever said that in however many years it is that I've known you." She laughed.

"It's this television lark, you see," said Rob. "Two cheeks get kissed all the time."

"Quite right, too," replied Helena. "As long as both parties know and there isn't that embarrassing mis-hit when you go for the second. Anyway, it's nice to see you. How have you been?" She motioned him to sit on the plump, chintz-covered sofa, planting herself on the padded arm of an overstuffed chair by the fire.

"Well enough," said Rob. "Apart from a little local difficulty with a short fat man called Bertie."

"Oh, yes. Vera's been telling me. Your Mr Lightfoot's been getting a bit shirty with you, hasn't he?"

"You could say that. And folk are beginning to notice."

"I see. Are you rattled by it?"

16

"Well, not so much rattled as uncomfortable. It's such a pain. It won't be long before people start tuning in just for the end of the programme so that they can see us at each other's throats."

"So what will you do about it?"

"I don't know. I've told my producer I'll handle it myself so he's off the hook, but I don't know where to begin."

Helena got up, went to the door of the drawing room and called to her housekeeper.

"Scotch?"

"After the day I've had I'll have a large one."

"And I'll join you."

As she poured two large Glenlivets from the decanter on a side table into two cut-glass tumblers a plump, pink-overalled figure put her head round the door.

"What was it, ma'am? It's nearly six o'clock. I'm just about to go." And then, much louder and bursting with enthusiasm, "Oh 'ello, Mr Rob, 'ow are you? It's lovely to see you," and without waiting for an invitation Mrs Ipplepen waddled across the room to where Rob stood on the Chinese rug in front of the log fire. She put both arms around him and reached up and planted a moist kiss on his cheek. Just one. Rob felt the prickle of her whiskers. In spite of her advanced years, Vera Ipplepen had something of a crush on the youth she'd watched grow up from apprentice gardener to TV star. She was old enough to be his granny (and frequently told him so) but thoroughly enjoyed basking in his reflected glory. "I was watching today. Old Fatty's getting a bit above 'imself, in't he?"

"Vera!" admonished Helena. "Don't be rude!"

"We-e-ell," said Vera, her pink nylon overall straining at its buttons, "my Cyril says that when it comes to gard'nin' he dun't know what he's talking about, that Bertie Lightfoot. The last time we saw him was at City Varieties in Leeds when he were with Robb Axminster."

"I think it was Robb Wilton," said Helena, trying hard to stop her mouth going up at the corners.

"'E was still better at that than 'e is at gardening, whatever 'is name was," answered Vera.

She was not the kind of daily you'd have expected to find looking after Helena Sampson. Where her mistress was tall and elegant, Vera Ipplepen was short and dumpy. Helena's grey hair had the sheen of silver and was sleek and elegantly coiffed; Mrs Ipplepen's grey locks had been tightly curled and rinsed with lavender blue at Sharon's near the station, and her lips were courtesy of Clara Bow, usually a shade of pink that came nowhere near matching her overall. Dame Edna Everage would have killed for her spectacles.

She might have had a mouth that, on occasion, said more than it should, but her heart was twenty-four carat and she would have defended Helena with her life, and with her Cyril's too.

"How's Cyril?" asked Rob, casting a glance at Helena, who shot him a withering look. Mrs Ipplepen could offer a graphic account of the precise workings of her husband's large intestine at the drop of a rubber glove. Rob knew this, and had only risked asking because Cyril's tea had to be on the table in front of him at six thirty every evening and there was no way Vera would stay more than a few minutes. The spuds would have to go on soon.

"We-e-ll. 'Is arm's still playin' 'im up.'

"Why's that?"

"Daft blighter went an' broke it. Fell over carryin't coal up from't cellar."

"Oh, I bet that's cramped his style."

"It's stopped 'im fillin' in 'is pools coupon. It were 'is right 'and. That's 'is writin' 'and. I've told 'im 'e'll 'ave to learn to use the other one and be amphibious, then it won't matter."

"Ambidextrous, you mean?"

"Yes, and that as well if 'e wants me to keep lookin' after 'im. I told 'im one bottle of Mackeson's enough for a man of 'is age. But will 'e listen? N-o-o-o. Anyway, I'll 'ave to go. Time to get the spuds on. I'll see you tomorrow, ma'am."

"All right, Vera. Take care going home, it's a bit frosty."

"I will. Nice to see you, Mr Rob. And don't let old Fatty get the better of you." She looked at Rob and gave him the sort of smile schoolgirls give to boys they fancy. "Ta-ra," and she sashayed out of the room in her pale blue mules to the whistle of nylon on corsetry.

Rob's and Helena's eyes met and they dissolved into silent laughter.

"Cheers!"

"Cheers! Here's to Cyril's arm," said Rob.

"And Fatty's sense of proportion," replied Helena, raising her glass and taking the first sip of the day. "So to go back to my earlier question, how have you been?"

"OK, apart from dear old Bertie. Except that I'm a bit worried about Dad. He soldiers on, tough as old boots, but he has these quiet spells. Kind of in a trance. I know what he's thinking about but I don't seem to be able to say anything."

"Has it ever occurred to you that he might not want you to say anything?" asked Helena.

"But I feel I should be able to help."

"You can help. And you do help – just by being there. But there are times when someone in that situation needs to be on their own and in their own mind. It has to be gone through."

"But when will he come out of it?"

Helena turned her eyes towards the fire. "Oh, there are those who say it takes a year to get over all the anniversaries. And when Jumbo died I found there was a lot of truth in that. But it doesn't end there. There's a whole new life to build from scratch. It's like being reborn as somebody else and not knowing who they are. Not knowing any of the rules. It takes longer than you'd imagine. And just when you think you're recovering you find yourself driving home and suddenly thinking, Oh, I must tell him about such and such, and it stops you in your tracks. It's like Snakes and Ladders – you think you're climbing out of the mire and in a moment you slide back down to square one. You start to climb up again sooner as the years go by. But it's never quite the same. Ever. It's different.

19

But bearable. Eventually. And then you feel guilty for being able to cope." She looked wistfully at the blazing logs. "Don't rush him. Six months isn't long."

"I know. I suppose the problem is mine as much as his. It would help *me* to think that I was helping *him* get over it, so I suppose there's a bit of selfishness in there somewhere."

"Don't blame yourself for that. Keep doing well and that will take his mind off things. He's very proud of you, you know. And so am I."

Rob turned his gaze from the fire to meet the eyes of his patron. The Glenlivet was helping him to unwind. "Well, you helped me to get there. Gave me the confidence."

"Nonsense. You're your own man. I just watched you grow."

"Keep watching."

"Oh, I will. Along with half the nation's women, I should think."

"Don't you start. I've already had a dig in the ribs from my producer and a close encounter of the newsroom kind, and that's quite enough for one day."

"A close encounter of what?"

"I bumped into Lisa Drake on the way out of the studio. Never met her before. And I did tonight."

"Oh. She's that rather sharp newsreader, isn't she? Bit of a reputation. What did you make of her?"

"Well, for the first time ever I knew what a hare must feel like when a fox looks it straight in the eye. A mixture of terror and the thrill of the impending chase."

"So you think there'll be a chase, do you?"

"Oh, I don't think so."

"I should hope not. Katherine positively dotes on you."

"Not so's you'd notice."

"Nonsense. She cares as much about you as I do and she's had even more of a hand in your career. It was Katherine who gave you your break into journalism, I'll have you remember."

"Yes, and I'm very grateful."

"Sorry, I didn't mean . . . well . . . you know."

"I know," said Rob. "A tricky patch, that's all. It'll be fine."

Helena took another sip from her glass.

"Oh, it's just that we seem to have been getting off on the wrong foot a lot lately. Silly things. Arguing more than we used to. She's been working hard on some story or other and I've been away filming. I really look forward to our time together and then when we actually manage to be home at the same time . . ."

"It's hard when you both have demanding careers. You end up being tired in tandem at the end of the day. Or one of you is raring to go and the other is whacked. I know. I've been there."

"Well, with any luck we'll get it together this weekend. All we need is for the rest of the world to go away for a while and give us some time to ourselves."

He drained his glass and looked at the clock. "Time I went. I don't want the old feller to start brooding. I told him I'd cook his supper tonight and if I don't get back soon he'll be sitting in front of an empty grate and I'll have a job to snap him out of it."

"Thank you for coming," she said, passing her empty glass from one hand to another. "It's good to see you."

"And you." He kissed her on both cheeks, then she walked him to the door and waved the pale green Fiesta goodbye.

Rob parked the car by the nursery fence and walked over the bridge towards Jock's cottage, pulling his duffel-coat around him to keep out the cold. The house was in darkness except for a dim light at the downstairs window to the right of the front door. Rob stopped on the brow of the bridge, leaned on the stone balustrade and gazed at the silhouette of the cottage, surrounded by a trim garden stuffed with all Jock's favourite plants.

It was in this small garden, as much as in the nursery, that Rob's passion for plants had been nurtured by his father, and it had given both of them pleasure to watch rare shrubs grow slowly, year after year, the ground below them carpeted with trilliums and wood anemones, snakeshead fritillaries and hardy cyclamen.

There was little sign of all these riches on this crisp February evening, as the dark water sped under the bridge, making glooping noises as it eddied in the shallows. The moon was almost full, and Rob looked up at the black velvet sky, studded with stars, and across at the slumbering moors, under which the lights of the town winked. Then he heaved a sigh, headed towards the cottage and opened the wicket gate that led into the garden. He walked the flagged path to the bottle-green front door and knocked three times before pressing down on the old sneck.

The door opened into an old kitchen with a stone-flagged floor. The ancient black range still stood against one wall, though there was no sign of a fire. The only light came from a small lamp standing on the kitchen table, at which Jock sat, his flat cap pushed to the back of his head, revealing a few damp strands of grey hair.

"Dad?"

"Aye?"

"Are you OK?"

"Huh!" The old man almost laughed.

Rob was uneasy. "What is it?"

"The last straw, that's what it is," said Jock, pushing a letter across the table towards his son. Rob picked up the envelope and looked at the address. It was neatly typed. He pulled out the crisp white letter, unfolded it and looked at the green letterhead: "Gro-land Garden Centres". Rob knew instantly why his father looked so low. The letter confirmed what he had suspected:

Dear Jock

For some time now I have, as you know, been wanting to expand my business with a view to extending the leisure side of my marketing.

We have talked in the past about the possibility of my acquiring Wharfeside Nursery, and I know that so far you have not looked favourably upon my offers. However, bearing in mind the events of the last few months, and the current economic climate, it occurs to me that the situation may have changed and

I am writing to enquire if you are now disposed to sell. We are, as you know, highly thought of in the horticultural retail trade locally, and feel sure that any reservations you have about selling up will be more than compensated for by the fact that your nursery will become part of a respected chain.

I would appreciate your reaction as soon as possible, so that we can start talking in more detail. In an ideal world I would like, if possible, to get things up and running this spring, rather than having to wait until the autumn.

Please reply at your earliest convenience.

Yours sincerely,

Dennis Wragg.

"Oh, God," said Rob. "That man only opens his mouth to change feet. What the hell's he thinking about at a time like this?"

"Money, that's what he's thinking about. That's all he's ever thought about. Your mother always said that Dennis Wragg had a one-track mind and that the track was papered with ten-pound notes."

"Well, this time he's gone too far. I'm off up the road to see him."

"Nay, son. Leave him be. I'll be damned if Dennis Wragg is going to see me off. There's no way your mother would have put up with that. I may be nigh on retirement age but I'm not giving up yet. What the hell else would I do?"

Rob looked at his father. Jock turned to meet his eyes. "This is a battle I'll have to fight on my own now, but maybe it'll give me something to think about, eh?" The corners of Jock's mouth flickered into a smile. "I've not been much in the way of company lately, have I?"

Rob lowered his eyes.

"No, I know," Jock went on. "It's tough. But then it's tough for you, too. I lost a wife, but you lost a mother and I shouldn't forget that."

The two men, one standing the other seated, neither moved nor spoke for what seemed like an age. Both were clinging tight to their emotions, neither wanting to let the other down. The old station clock on the wall ticked loudly and Rob felt his heart pounding in his chest.

"Come on," said Jock. "You promised me supper. It's time a fire was lit in that range. This kitchen is as cold as – Well, it could be warmer."

That evening Rob saw a glimmer of the old spirit beginning to return to his father, an indication that the old man had not given up.

By the time he reached Katherine's flat in the centre of town he was worn out. It was nine thirty when he parked the car in the cobbled yard at the side of Wellington Heights, a large Victorian building with a baker's, a 'Country Pine' shop and a florist's on the ground floor. He let himself in through the heavy glass-panelled side door and walked up the ornately banistered steps to the top floor, four storeys up. He rang the bell of Flat 5 and waited. From inside, he could hear the honeyed tones of James Taylor on the sound system, then a voice asked, "Who is it?"

"It's me!"

The door opened to reveal Katherine, her jet black shoulder-length hair gleaming in the lamplight. At the sight of him her dark brown eyes widened in welcome, and she smiled, revealing shining white teeth. "Where's your key?"

"I picked up the wrong bunch this morning."

"Dummy." She tugged him inside, and shut the door, then stood with her hands on her hips and looked quizzically at him.

"Where've you *been*?"

"Seeing Helena and seeing Dad."

"No time for me?"

"Loads of time for you." He looked at her wistfully.

She threw her arms round him, pulling herself up to plant her lips on his. "What took you so long?" she asked, eyes closed and the side of her face resting on his coat.

He stroked her hair with one hand, his other arm around her

shoulders. "Oh, I hadn't seen Helena for a couple of weeks, then I cooked Dad supper and then I came on here."

"So you've eaten?" There was a note of disappointment in her voice as her dark eyes looked up at him.

"Yes. But I'll have some cheese."

She turned from the tiny hall and went into the living room. Rob took off his coat and hung it on a peg by the front door, then crept up behind her and dropped a soft kiss on the nape of her neck.

"How's Jock?"

"If you'd asked me that question a couple of hours ago I'd have said that he was exactly as he was yesterday, and the day before that. Lost in a world he doesn't know. But now . . . Well, I think the mist might be beginning to clear from his eyes."

"Why?" asked Katherine, looking up from the CD player, whose volume she had lowered to a level that allowed more intimate conversation.

"Dennis Wragg has written to him again asking him if, 'bearing in mind the events of the last few months', he wants to sell."

Katherine spun round, her eyes flashing. "The bastard!"

"I couldn't agree with you more."

"It's obvious that he thinks Jock's defences are down and that he'll just give in and sell out."

"Dead right."

The fiery side of Katherine that leaped to the defence of what she considered to be a just cause drove her on. "His wife's even worse than he is – grasping woman. You know what they call her?"

"What?" enquired Rob.

"The Wragg Bag. She's a social-climbing cow with the dress sense of a colour-blind Tiller girl. I mean, aren't you furious?"

"I was. I'd every intention of going round to Dennis Wragg's nasty little bungalow and planting something very firm on the end of his crooked little nose."

"So what stopped you?" She was square on to him now, looking up demandingly into his face.

"The fact that for the first time since Mum died I saw a spark of fire in the old man's eyes. Maybe a fight is just what he needs to bring him back to life again."

She looked questioningly at him.

"I don't remember Dad ever looking at me like that before. We had supper together and he didn't talk about Mum, he talked about the nursery and how things were doing – the dogwood stems were especially bright this year, and how folk kept saying so."

Katherine watched his face change, as it always did when he talked about plants. She'd been irritated by him lately. He never seemed to be there when she was, barely had time to listen to her news, but when he spoke like this, with a faraway look in his eyes, she knew why she loved him and why she wanted so much to be a part of his life.

"Dad sold some Oriental hellebores to a woman who'd travelled here from the other side of Leeds because she'd heard that he had a good collection – yellows and pinks as well as the usual white and purple – and she'd gone away happy and promised to tell her friends. It was somehow as if the plants are dependent on him now and he shouldn't let them down. Almost like his children. Does that sound daft?"

"Oh, it would have done once," she said softly. "Before I knew you and your father and what plants could mean to people."

Rob grimaced. "Oh, God, I'm beginning to sound like an anorak. 'Plants are more interesting than people.' Wait a minute while I talk to my aspidistra."

Katherine uttered a peal of laughter. "No. You're just a passionate man, and there's nothing wrong with that. Not unless you suddenly start getting interested in diesel engines or removal lorries. Then *I'll* start getting worried."

"There are only two things I'm passionate about and one of them isn't Eddie Stobart," said Rob.

"Well, I'm relieved to hear it. Any clues as to what the second thing might be, assuming that the first thing has roots, leaves and flowers?"

"I'm looking at it."

"Well, about time, too," said Katherine, reaching for his hand. "I thought you'd never get round to me. I haven't seen my friend in ages." There was a twinkle in her eye as she pulled him towards the kitchen. "Red Leicester or Double Gloucester?"

"Oh, I'll have none of that foreign muck. Just give me a bit of Wensleydale and a couple of digestives and I'll do anything you like."

"Anything?" Her crooked grin almost matched his.

"Anything."

Chapter 3

When Rob woke the following morning the pillow next to his was empty. He tried focusing his eyes, but the brilliant sunlight streaming in from the tall sash windows made it difficult to see anything clearly except the blurred lines of a distant wooden wardrobe, the sweep of long oatmeal-coloured curtains, and two brass bedknobs.

As his vision began to clear, his nostrils flared in response to the aroma of newly baked bread and fresh coffee. The fragrance of warm loaves drifted up through the crack of the open window from the baker's below, but the coffee was being made in the kitchen. The large stripped-pine door with its crystal knob opened slowly to reveal Katherine with a tray in her hands and a newspaper between her teeth.

Rob looked at her as he raised his shoulders clear of the duvet and stretched out his arms to relieve her of the tray. She wore nothing except a sloppy white T-shirt, and her hair had been swept back and held in place with a watercolour brush pushed through its glossy black knot. Her face was fresh scrubbed, her lips bright pink. She planted a kiss on his cheek and sat on the end of the bed, opening the *Nesfield Gazette* and scrutinizing the front page.

"Yes!" She punched the air with her fist and let fall one half of the paper. "That'll get them going."

"What will?" said Rob, rubbing his eyes and reaching for the coffee jug.

"Today's headline."

"Have you been stirring it again, then?" he asked, raising an eyebrow.

"Well, it's a good job somebody has," she retorted. "Otherwise heaven knows what would be happening to this place we call home."

Rob squinted at the headline: "HOW GREEN IS OUR VALLEY?"

"What is it now?"

"Whitaker's cotton mills. They wanted to be allowed to set up a new plant five miles up the Wharfe from here on those water-meadows that used to be farmland."

"I thought they were *still* farmland?" said Rob, taking a sip of Katherine's decaffeinated but welcome brew.

"Well, technically they are, but they've been owned for years by Whitaker's and now they want to stop letting them to old Tom Hardisty and his herd of pedigree Friesians and make use of them."

"Oh, I see. And our editor in her 'Green Pages' is giving them what for, is she?"

"Too right I am."

"The words 'hobby' and 'horse' come to mind," said Rob teasingly. "What's the big problem?"

"The big problem is that a part of the dale which has always been regarded as a beauty spot will be swamped with buildings and plant and chimneys. The traffic levels will be unacceptable, the roads will be clogged and before we know where we are we'll look like Bradford."

"Oh, I see. We're being a nimby."

"We are not being a nimby!" she snapped back.

"Excuse me for a moment," said Rob. "There is no way that the local council will allow the setting up of a monstrosity that will change the face of the dale, and this plant will provide jobs that are badly needed locally."

"Just whose side are you on?" asked Katherine, kneeling over him on the bed and looking menacingly into his eyes.

Rob carried on, "What's more, people need clothes unless they're to go round stark naked. But you, because of your and your paper's stance on conservation will oppose it as a matter of course."

"You bet we will."

"Well, you can't simply oppose every kind of industrial development that comes along or the countryside will grind to a halt."

"I don't believe what I'm hearing!" she cried, shocked at his reaction.

"Poppet!"

"Don't call me Poppet!"

"You can't object to every single plan to build anything other than a farm shop."

"That's not fair. We haven't stood in the way of every development in this dale. What we have done is open people's eyes to the dangers of some of them. There would have been a bypass carved through here if we hadn't taken a stance on that, and now it's this. The green belt is not nearly so sacred as it was – and money talks."

She was warming to her subject now. "This development will not only ruin the landscape but it will also affect the river."

"Yes," responded Rob, "and the National Rivers Authority comes down like a ton of bricks on anyone who pollutes their water."

"I know they do, but by then it might be too late. Whitaker's have already been fined twice for polluting other Yorkshire rivers, and there are other things to take into account as well."

"Such as what?"

"Such as the temperature of the water returned to the river afterwards. What people don't realize is the delicacy of the balance in a river. Any tampering with the temperature and its depth and speed affects the fish, the insects, the growth of aquatic plants."

"And that, ladies and gentlemen, is the case for the prosecution," said Rob.

"Don't you take this seriously?" she asked.

"I take it very seriously. I just wanted to see if you really had done your homework or if this was a knee-jerk reaction."

"Thank *you*," she said indignantly.

"All right, I'm sorry. I just wanted to sort out in my mind why you're taking the angle you are taking."

"And do you understand now?"

"Perfectly."

"And do you agree?"

"I'm not sure. I'll think about it."

"Sometimes," muttered Katherine, "I wonder why I stick with you."

"You stick with me," said Rob, "because I'm the only person who'll listen to you shrieking about your causes."

Before he had time to draw breath, the pillow beside him had been snatched up and brought down on his head, sending a coffee cup skittering across the scrubbed wooden floor.

"Now look what you've done." Rob watched a rivulet of decaffeinated coffee seeping through a crack in the boards.

"Damn!" exclaimed Katherine, springing up from the bed and darting for the kitchen. She returned with a bowl and a J-cloth, wisps of dark hair framing her face as she knelt to mop up the coffee which had stained the boards a darker shade of brown. "Damn!"

"If it's not one kind of pollution it's another!" said Rob, realizing his mistake as soon as the words had left his mouth. "I'm sorry. I didn't mean it. I'm as concerned about the environment as you are – you know that – but as far as gardening is concerned I try to strike a balance."

"Well, I wish you'd balanced your coffee cup better. People will think I've got an incontinent cat with an addiction to gravy."

"Sorry," said Rob.

"My fault," she admitted, smiling at him gently. "But you do see why I get so worked up, don't you?"

"Yes, of course I do. It's just that sometimes it's difficult for me to be quite as green as you are. I try, but it's difficult."

"Only because you have to hobnob with unfriendly things like chemical companies."

"They're a large part of the horticultural industry. I can't pretend they don't exist." Rob groaned. "Anyway, enough of all this, it's Saturday. What are we going to do?"

"Didn't I tell you?" Katherine got up off the floor and sat on the edge of the bed. "I have to go to Yeadon Airport to meet the boss."

"On a *Saturday?*"

"He's dropping in on his private jet from Glasgow before he goes on to Plymouth. He wants to talk about circulation."

"So do I," said Rob. "Or the lack of it in my foot. Can you move?"

She eased herself to one side and Rob leaned forward and kissed her.

"So I have to amuse myself today, then, do I?"

"And tonight, I'm afraid. I have to have dinner with the boss and his wife before they fly off to sunny Devon."

"Couldn't they make it lunch?" asked Rob.

"Oh, no. Her ladyship has to visit Lord and Lady Myddleton for lunch, so I have to be on call for dinner."

"Can't I come?"

"'Fraid not. The boss likes to think he has my undivided attention."

"Bloody-minded, I call it. And a pain. Fancy asking you out to dinner on a Saturday night and expecting you to pretend you live the life of a nun."

"Well, over the past few weeks I might just as well have been in a convent, bearing in mind the number of times I've seen you," said Katherine.

"I've been away filming!" he said defensively.

"Oh, I know where you've been. The thing is, you haven't been *here*, and I didn't know whether or not you'd be here tonight, not that I could have done much about it."

Rob looked crestfallen.

"I have my own life to lead, Rob, and just occasionally I wonder if you remember that. Rob?" She lifted his chin with a forefinger and looked into his eyes. "I'll be here tomorrow and we can go off up the dale for the day. The forecast's good. We can have lunch at the Devonshire Arms in Grassington and I'll give you my undivided attention. Yes?" She looked at him as a mother would look at her small child: kindly and lovingly with the hint of tears in her eyes.

Rob raised his eyes to meet hers. "Yes, OK. I'll go and get some sandpaper and sort out your floor. It's time you put some sealer on it to stop it being stained every time you throw coffee over me."

He got up and went towards the bathroom. She watched him go, lowering her eyes from his tousled brown head, to his broad, freckled shoulders, trim waist, tight bottom and shapely legs.

"Oh, Mr MacGregor," she whispered, "I do love you."

While Rob MacGregor was brooding over the absent Katherine, Guy D'Arcy was letting himself into his town-house in Fulham. It was an early-morning return after a long night out.

Of the modern breed of gardening broadcasters Rob MacGregor and Guy D'Arcy were the two rising stars. They had replaced the old breed of television gardener with a brand of youthful enthusiasm that would once have been thought gimmicky, but which now appealed not only to householders under the age of forty but also to ladies of a certain age who enjoyed the glamour that was now coupled with their compost.

The new wave of television gardeners might have swept away many of the techniques of their predecessors, but one tradition they continued was the subterranean rivalry that has existed among sons of the soil since Adam turned the first sod in the Garden of Eden.

Where Rob was the earthy offspring of working-class parents, Guy D'Arcy was a scion of the aristocracy. And he looked it. His jaw had a patrician cut, his thick blond hair was trimmed so that he could throw it back with a flick of his head, and he wore his clothes with that casual yet studied elegance that comes of breeding.

Rob had first met Guy at the Chelsea Flower Shower a couple of years previously. He'd recognized him from the gossip-column pictures but, then, only a hermit would have failed to recognize Guy D'Arcy – the man who was seen with a duke's daughter on his arm one week, a wealthy socialite the next, a mixed assortment of A-list celebrities and even a European princess.

Guy had fallen out with his father and been asked to leave the family estate agency in the Cotswolds. He had decided that gardening was just the thing for him and set about redesigning the gardens of his well-to-do friends.

His notoriety had provided him with a few contacts in journalism, so it wasn't long before he had written a book or two and acquired a fat fee from the *Sunday Herald* for a weekly column, "Guy's Garden". A year or so later he landed his own programme on a rival television network and Rob had noticed that Guy D'Arcy now treated him rather differently than he had before. A cursory nod was all he could expect from the man who, a year or two previously, had been all over him.

Guy D'Arcy tried to push open the royal blue front door of his Victorian villa. "Oh, bugger!" He leaned on it with his shoulder, then stooped to free it from whatever was preventing it from swinging open smoothly. A pile of post like a large molehill spilled over the doormat. Padded envelopes, long white envelopes, pale blue envelopes, pink, crinkle-cut envelopes, manila envelopes – enough to open a small branch of W. H. Smith, thought Guy, scooping up the mound and carrying it across to the hall table. Every envelope was painstakingly readdressed from the newspaper office or the television studio. Why couldn't they simply lob them all into one hefty envelope and post that instead? he wondered. Stupid.

Two hundred letters a week was not Guy's idea of fun. He wanted the fame but could cheerfully have done without the by-products, and especially the postbag, which, every week, included putrefying apples, crisp foliage and assorted items of rotting vegetable matter. There were reams of Queen's Velvet, Basildon

Bond and scraps of paper torn from shorthand notebooks that carried queries about flowerless African violets and leafless weeping figs. Why was it that only the clinically insane and the terminally dyslexic chose to write to him?

The mail slithered in a miniature Niagara from the hall table on to the Afghan rug below and Guy kicked shut the door and walked to the kitchen. The answering-machine winked at him from a pine dresser. Nine messages. A chap had only to be away for a day and the world and his wife were breaking his door down by dusk.

He pressed the 'play' button and went over to the kitchen cupboard, took down a tube of Alka-Selzer, filled a tumbler with water, dropped in two tablets and slammed his hand over the top of the glass. The sound of the effervescence was not improving the state of his head, which throbbed.

"Beeeeep. Hello, Guy, it's Sophie. You muttered something about supper tonight. Is it still on or am I being stood up again? Give me a call. Please?"

"Oh! Bugger." He'd forgotten.

He put two slices of bread into the toaster.

"Beeeeep. This is Chelsea Roofing Contractors," said an East London accent, with more than a hint of the cowboy about it. "We're returning your call abaht your roof what wants fixin'. We'll call back liter."

Guy chuckled to himself, and then frowned when he remembered why it had been necessary to make the call in the first place. His house, though pleasingly proportioned and in a desirable street, had a roof that was the Welsh slate equivalent of a string vest. Two pictures and an Indian rug had been the price of the last downpour. He gulped down the fizzy medication in the glass, grimacing at the bitter taste.

"Beeeeep" . . . There were several messages related to his programme, an enquiry as to the whereabouts of his column for the *Herald* and then a message that made him pause as he was jamming two slices of bread into the toaster.

"Mr D'Arcy," exclaimed a somewhat inebriated man's voice

with flat Yorkshire vowels and the merest hint of sibilance, "it is a truth universally acknowledged that a single man in possession of a television programme must be in want of some information. I wonder if I might have a word with you?"

Good God! thought Guy. What the hell does he want?

"I'm sorry to bother you on this fine evening when you're probably getting ready to go out on the toot, but there are a few things I'd like to talk over that might be to your advantage. Cheerie-bye."

"That was your last message," said the unfeeling female voice of the answering-machine, as it clicked and whirred back to the beginning.

Guy caught the toast as it flipped up. He spread it with butter and a thick coating of Gentlemen's Relish before flopping down in a wheel-back chair at the side of the Aga and wondering what on earth a sozzled Bertie Lightfoot could have been warbling on about.

The brass doorknob clinked as Jock entered the old white-painted greenhouse at Wharfeside Nursery. He looked down at it and grunted. The ferrule needed a new screw. He went out, closed the door behind him and walked across to the potting-shed.

All his life he had been like this. Madge had teased him about it, but Jock had always said that if a job didn't get done the moment it needed doing it wouldn't get done at all. He pulled out a hefty green drawer from beneath the potting-bench and rummaged about until he found an old screwdriver. The screws were in an ancient tobacco tin. He took two – one to lose and one to use – and went back to the greenhouse, past the neat rows of tethered trees and pot-grown shrubs sparkling with ice on what was turning into a bright February morning. Frost patterned the glass on the old cold frame outside the greenhouse and Jock stood for a moment taking in the view.

He hardly heard the river nowadays for its comforting sound had been with him, day and night, for the better part of his life. This morning, below the frosted banks, the amber water glittered as it flowed past. A blackbird sang loudly from a naked sycamore, whose silver-grey trunk leaned out over the water. The moors that rose up as a backdrop to the scene seemed sprinkled with icing sugar.

Jock breathed in deeply and the cold air stung his nostrils. For the first time in months he felt glad to be alive. It was a novel sensation. He looked round at the trim nursery. To many folk it was a dead time of year, nothing moved, nothing grew, few things were in flower, but Jock saw the promise of things to come in the primroses, snowdrops and hellebores, and the wintersweet, which decorated the old brick wall alongside the lean-to greenhouse with its waxy pale yellow bells, which, when you looked up into them, showed themselves to be stained with blood.

He was not, as a rule, given to flights of fancy, but he remembered a poem that Madge used to quote on days like this at this time of year:

> Gardener, if you listen, listen well:
> Plant for your winter pleasure, when the months
> Dishearten; plant to find a fragile note
> Touched from the brittle violin of frost.

He loved the last line in particular.

"Morning, Dad!" Jock snapped out of his reverie at the sound of his son's greeting and turned to see Rob walking up the nursery path towards the greenhouse.

"Morning, son! All right?"

"Fine. And yourself?"

"Well, you know, I'm all right."

Rob smiled at him, relieved at his relatively light-hearted response. The blackbird darted from the sycamore branch, shrieking its alarm call and burying itself in the bushes. "Thought I'd just call in to see how you were – after last night and all. What are you up to?"

"Fixing the door. A screw loose. Good as new now, though. And there's no need to worry about me. I'm fine."

"No Harry? No – whatsisname . . . Wayne?"

"It's Saturday. Harry'll be in the Legion by lunch-time and Wayne's doing his gardening job. He'll be here by eleven. I've told him I probably won't be rushed off my feet this morning so he's planting a tree for his old lady. Mind you, he'll have a job getting through this frost."

"Yes, it's a hard one, isn't it?"

"So what are you doing with yourself?" enquired Jock of the son who didn't usually spend his Saturdays at his father's nursery.

"Oh, I said I'd varnish Katherine's floor for her."

"On a day like this?" Jock raised his eyes to the sky, which was now a clear forget-me-not blue.

"Yes, shame, isn't it? I just thought I'd call in and see what you'd got planned."

"Oh, the usual. A spot of watering in the greenhouses, a bit of leaf-picking, and I thought I'd spend the next couple of hours sowing a few tender perennials in the propagator, if too many folk don't come and distract me."

There was a twinkle in his eye as he said it, but Rob knew that his father was happiest in his own company, and that of his plants. Not that his customers would ever guess.

"You know, there are times, Dad, when I think you'd rather you didn't have any customers."

"Oh, I don't know. One of them's just sent me some rose-bushes. Or, rather, his widow has."

"What do you mean?"

"Old Professor Wilberforce from over the moor. Keen rosarian. Dabbled a bit in breeding. You remember him – he worked at that research station the other side of Leeds – gave you a fiver once for rooting some rose cuttings for him. Good at the science but not so hot at the practical gardening."

"Nice chap," Rob remarked. "Roman nose and bald dome of a head."

"That's the one. His missus came round here yesterday with these bushes in a sack, pruned to within an inch of their lives and said that the Professor would have liked me to have them. I think she just wanted an excuse for a natter. I suppose I'd better try to break the ground and heel them in."

Jock's nursery was something of a rarity in an age of massive garden centres with five-acre car parks and lines of school-leavers at the check-outs. The takings went first into his dark blue apron pocket, then into an old wooden drawer. He ran the nursery more or less single-handed (you couldn't really count Harry now as part of any labour force, and Wayne was a newcomer) but somehow he eked out a living by selling unusual plants as well as his bread-and-butter lines. The customers who came here were assured of sound advice and well-grown plants that were not overpriced. Jock had little time for Dennis Wragg's Crystal Palace half a mile away where the girls on the tills knew as much about plants, he said, as he knew about the top ten, and where the rule of sales seemed to be that if you slapped something into a larger pot you could add a nought to the price.

"Cup of coffee?" Rob asked.

Jock glanced at his watch. "Aye, there's just time before I open the gate to the masses. Come on then, look sharp!" He turned and walked towards the potting-shed, his son following.

Over coffee and a digestive biscuit or two, they chewed the fat about this and that – the state of the nursery, the promise shown by young Wayne.

"You like him, don't you?" said Rob.

"I suppose I do. It takes a bit of determination to drag yourself out of the kind of place he's grown up in and come and ask for a job. I bet his mates take the mickey out of him."

"Oh, I know what it feels like. I remember when I decided to do it myself," said Rob, gazing at the mound of compost on the wooden bench then out through the cobwebby windows. "I took some stick from the lads at school. Whenever any of them walked past the nursery I used to head for the greenhouse so they couldn't see me."

"I know," said Jock.

"You noticed?"

"I was beginning to wonder what you were growing in there until I rumbled you. I felt a bit sorry for you, really."

"Oh, I got over it," said Rob. "Once they realized that there was a career to be had in gardening and that I wasn't destined to spend the rest of my life weeding they accepted it. But I did have to call it horticulture and not gardening, to give myself a bit of respectability."

"And look at you now," said Jock.

"Yes, look at me," said Rob, draining his cup. "I'd better be off or that floor won't get varnished."

"How's Katherine?" asked Jock.

"OK. She's meeting her boss today. No time for a gardener's boy. High-powered discussions and all that. I'll see her tomorrow when she's back down to earth."

Jock detected a faint note of discontent in Rob's voice but chose to ignore it. "Well, remember me to her."

"I will." He turned for the door. "See you soon."

From the potting-shed doorway Jock watched his son go down the path to the old wrought-iron gate where he flipped the 'Closed' sign to 'Open' on the green notice-board, waved, turned and was gone. Jock walked back to the bench, pulled out the drawer and dropped the spare brass screw into the tobacco tin. He gathered up a fistful of seed packets and headed, once more, for the greenhouse.

It was six o'clock by the time Rob made it back to his own place. He had never moved in with Katherine, they had both felt it important to hang on to their independence. He lived at End Cottage – the last dwelling that qualified as being in Nesfield, up at the top end of the valley. It had cost him next to nothing a couple of years ago, but then it had been little more than a shell, unlived-in for ten years or more.

He never imagined that he'd be able to either find or afford a house by the river, so when the dilapidated two-up and two-down had come on the market he was first on the phone and there with his deposit before the yuppie estate agent could say negative equity. Rob had spent all his spare time doing the place up. He'd always been good with his hands and enjoyed turning this one-time farmhand's cottage into a home.

He'd converted the outside privy into a bathroom, and done up the rest of the house to make the most of what little space there was. A tiny conservatory, more of a porch, really, was tacked on to the back and when the sun streamed in through the sash windows the place came alive. Rob loved it, which was another reason for not moving into Katherine's flat.

Outside, there was an old stone path and the riverbank. He had only a tiny garden, bounded by a low stone wall and surrounded by field, and though, at first, this had seemed a disadvantage, Rob had grown used to having the riverbank instead of a herbaceous border. It was scarcely less colourful: in spring it erupted first with orange coltsfoot and the weird pink drumheads of butterbur, then came cow parsley and red campion and bright yellow buttercups. The garden itself was just big enough to allow him to keep his hand in and try new plants. It was all he could want.

Rob let himself in by the door that went straight into the kitchen and dumped his car keys on the table alongside the *Daily Post*. He flipped through it to check his column. He'd been poached from the *Nesfield Gazette* a year ago now. He'd worried at first that Katherine would be miffed at his departure. Instead, she'd been genuinely delighted for him, making the move from a local to a national paper. "Don't be stupid!" she'd said. "It's what every hack wants."

"But I'm not a hack!" he'd replied.

"Oh, yes, you are, a horticultural hack. The subject may be rustic and rural but you're a hack just the same."

She'd taken him out to dinner that night, and he'd always thought she must have been more disappointed than she let on.

Page forty-two. They always put gardening fairly near the back, and there was no guaranteeing that your copy would not be cut to bits. If advertisements came in it had to be reduced. If there was a

big story, it would be squeezed. This week it had survived almost
intact. A large piece on winter-flowering shrubs, a smaller panel on
a garden famous for its snowdrops, and a list of topical tips. It was
a difficult time of year. Three weeks of snowfall and the gardening
public would forget their plants to slump in front of the TV. You
couldn't blame them, but it did exercise a gardening writer's
ingenuity.

Rob folded up the paper and went to put the kettle on. Then the
phone rang. He picked it up.

"Hello, is that Rob MacGregor?"

"Yes."

"Hi! This is Lisa Drake."

For a moment Rob couldn't think what to say. He felt himself
flush.

"Er . . . hello! How – how are you?" He managed to get the words
out without too much of a stammer.

"I'm fine. I just wondered if you fancied a drink tonight. It seems
stupid that we both work for the same TV station and that we've
only just met. I thought it was about time we put things right. Are
you free?"

All manner of thoughts flew across Rob's mind: Lisa Drake's
reputation; how she got hold of his number; the fact that what she
said was absolutely right – it was ridiculous that they had only just
met; the fact that he found her more than slightly attractive; and
the fact that she undoubtedly fancied him. Then there was his
loyalty to Katherine, and the fact that Katherine was out all
evening, but most of all there was the fact that Lisa Drake had
caught him off his guard.

"Yes, I'm free and I'd love to come for a drink."

"Great. Look, why don't we make it supper? There's a new
restaurant opened in Myddleton and I've been promised a free
meal on the strength of a news item I did. Why don't I ring them
and book a table for two and you could pick me up at eightish? It
should be fun."

There was little Rob could say except, "Fine."

She gave him the address – a flat in a smart Edwardian block in Harrogate – and said, "Ciao," before she put the phone down.

"Ciao," muttered Rob under his breath, as he replaced the receiver. He felt strangely unnerved as he unscrewed the cap from the whisky bottle, poured himself a tot and threw it back in one. "Ciao," he repeated as he walked, trance-like, upstairs to his bedroom.

He took more than his usual care in getting ready over the next hour and a half. Bathing, shaving, deciding what to wear. This is ridiculous! he thought, as he towelled dry his hair and tried to make up his mind whether he should go for navy-blue trousers or chinos. He chose the chinos, a pair of Timberland shoes, and a white T-shirt underneath a blue linen shirt. He looked at his watch – a quarter to eight. "Oh, shit!" He grabbed his wallet, car keys and duffel-coat, glanced in the mirror as he left and locked the door of End Cottage behind him.

She'd been waiting on the pavement stamping her feet to keep warm when he'd drawn up outside the grand Edwardian pile. She said she'd thought she'd better come down and keep a look-out just in case he couldn't find it. He'd confessed that he wasn't too familiar with Harrogate, except for the Valley Gardens, the green common known as The Stray, and Betty's Café, where his mother had taken him for toasted teacakes when he was a child.

She didn't seem to mind having been kept waiting, and Rob felt his stomach lurch as she got into the car beside him, and he took in the waft of Chanel as she pecked him on the cheek. Don't blush, don't blush, he thought. With his colouring it had always been a problem.

The conversation in the car was polite – studio and weather-orientated – and she'd broken off every now and again to offer directions he didn't need – the restaurant was in the next village to Nesfield – but which he was too polite to mention.

She was wearing dark brown trousers and a coffee-coloured jacket with a figure-hugging Lycra top under it. Her blonde hair shone and her skin seemed to be a soft shade of peach.

When they arrived at the restaurant they were seated at a table in the far corner where they had a good view of everyone else, and where everyone else had a good view of them. The restaurant had clearly become popular quickly: there was hardly a table spare. The white damask-covered tables were barely visible among the bodies. The branded ends of wine cases decorated the bare brick walls and candles flickered from bottles on the tables and black iron sconces on the walls. Rafters was really an old Victorian conservatory, sandwiched between high Victorian houses, that had once been a flower shop.

"I thought it was particularly appropriate that I came here with you," she said.

Rob said that he remembered what it had been like when it was still a flower shop. "In those days it smelled of mimosa and Longiflorum lilies, and great galvanized buckets were dotted around this damp stone floor and stuffed with cherry blossom and forsythia. I remember the scent of the freesias that I used to come and buy for my mum and she said how nice it was to have flowers that hadn't been grown at home. It made them more special."

"It's all a bit different now," said Lisa, looking around.

"Yes. I don't suppose they sell nicotine shreds any more."

"Nicotine what?"

"Shreds. Bits of shredded cardboard soaked in nicotine. We'd set fire to little piles of them in the greenhouses and the fumes would kill off greenfly and whitefly. We used to buy them in tins and we had to sign a poison book before we were allowed to take them away. The bar over there was once the shop counter with a wooden till that pinged when it was opened."

"You're a great story-teller, you know," she said, gazing at him across the table with her head resting on her hands.

He looked across at her and felt himself colouring again. "Oh, I don't know, it's just memories," he said, taking a sip of wine.

"Yes, but they're lovely memories. Tell me more about this place – the way it was before."

They dined on ciabatta and sun-dried tomatoes, sea bass and fresh vegetables, and drank a bottle of Chablis that Lisa said she particularly liked. She dropped questions into the conversation, about Rob's childhood, why he had followed his father into gardening, and as he answered she appeared to hang on his every word. Rob was enjoying himself. His audience was attractive and he was flattered by her rapt attention. Lisa continued to play him gently, like a speckled trout on the end of a line. She was, after all, a professional.

The waiter cleared away their sorbet glasses and asked if they wanted coffee. Before Rob had time to say anything Lisa had already shaken her head and dismissed the young man.

"I thought we could go back to my place for coffee. OK?"

"Fine. Lovely." He felt so stupid. What else could he say? The waiter brought Rob's coat, indicated that there was nothing to pay, said he hoped that they'd enjoyed their meal and that they'd come back again.

As they walked towards the door, just a few tables away Rob caught sight of the back of a familiar head. Its hair was dark and held back with an ebony skewer. Seated across the table from it was a tall, handsome man with a tanned complexion and a grey pin-striped suit. The fork, raised in one brown hand, stabbed the air. The other brown hand was clamped on that of his dining companion and his eyes gazed deeply into hers. He was holding forth in a loud voice about the importance of circulation, and he was not a doctor.

Chapter 4

"Are you all right?" asked Lisa, as they got to the car.

"Yes, fine," said Rob, fumbling to get the key in the passenger door. He let her in, shut the door and walked round the car, breathing deeply.

She leaned over and pulled the inside handle to let him in. "You look as though you've seen a ghost," she said.

"Do I?" Rob slid into the driving seat and tried to pull himself together. A dozen thoughts ran through his head. Had Katherine seen him? Why was her boss young and handsome rather than old and fat, the way she had described him? She *had* described him like that, hadn't she? Rob had certainly pictured him pasty and plump, not tanned and trim. And where was his wife? Katherine had said she was dining with her boss and his wife. Had she lied to him? Was there more to this relationship than just business? His mind reeled.

"Do you want me to drive?" asked Lisa.

"Sorry?" Rob's mind was elsewhere.

"Do you want me to drive?"

"No . . . No, I'm fine, sorry. Just felt a bit strange. All right now. Home?"

"If you're sure."

"Yes. Yes, I'm sure. A cup of coffee would be great." Rob started up the car, shot a reassuring smile across at her, then leaned over and deliberately kissed her cheek. She smiled back at him and settled down for the short journey to Harrogate.

The atmosphere in Rafters was getting smokier by the minute and Katherine's eyes were beginning to water. She sipped at the still mineral water the waiter had just poured over a mountain of ice and a slice of lemon in the thick-bottomed glass, and surreptitiously sniffed at the sleeve of her jacket. It stank of tobacco. Charles Wormald, her boss, was half-way down the fat cigar he had ordered with his brandy, and more than half-way up her arm with his sun-tanned hand.

His wife, he said, had not felt too well after her visit to Lord and Lady Myddleton and had gone back to their hotel for a lie-down.

It had not come as a surprise to Katherine. The evening had degenerated into the usual run of sexist innuendo for which Charlie Wormald was well known among the women he employed. "Wormy" had no time for male editors in his thriving stable of regional papers. He liked sparky women who would look good across the dinner table from him on occasions like this, but experience had taught him that the women who had the backbone to produce the best newspapers would seldom allow him even a glimpse of their vertebrae. So it was with Katherine.

She found the dinner ritual tedious, but although she was an idealist she had an equally strong streak of realism. If being nice to Wormy two or three times a year over the dinner table was all it took to keep him happy, then who was she to throw in the napkin?

As he rattled on about her talents and the great job she was doing with the *Nesfield Gazette*, she smiled absent-mindedly, looked out of the window into the dark night and wondered what Rob would be doing now.

The journey back to Harrogate had been silent but highly charged. Lisa could hardly take her eyes off the broad-shouldered man next to her. They wandered from the dark brown curls at the back of his neck and the muscles pulsating in his cheek, to his strong legs and the gentle-looking, fine-boned hands that gripped the wheel of the little car.

Rob agonized over Katherine's apparent lack of loyalty and Lisa's evident sensuality.

Lisa Drake's apartment block was everything that Katherine's Victorian flat above the baker's was not. It had a wide pavement outside, beside which Lisa suggested Rob leave his car. As he was locking the door, distractedly, he saw her looking at the rust-spotted Fiesta with a gentle smile.

"Go on, say it. It's not what you'd have expected."

"Well, no. I don't suppose it is," she replied.

"What *would* you have expected then?"

"Oh, a Range Rover, or a Discovery at the very least."

"Oh, please!" said Rob. "Credit me with some taste. It would be a battered Land Rover or nothing, not one of those posey Harrogate-housewife jobs."

"Yes, you're not pretentious. That's what's so nice about you."

Rob was losing count of the number of times she'd made him blush.

"Come here, Mr MacGregor. My turn now." She planted a soft kiss on his cheek, put her arm through his and walked him towards the glistening plate-glass doors of Richmond House. As they mounted the final polished marble step, she produced a swipe card from her pocket and deftly passed it through the steel jaws mounted on the wall. They entered a large marble-floored atrium, dotted with weeping figs and modern art. The soft peach walls were lit with brass up-lighters and a uniformed security man sat behind a light oak counter, listening to a radio with the volume set low.

He stood up as they walked in. "Good evening, Miss Drake, sir." He nodded at Rob and recognition flashed across his face as they walked over to the open lift. The doors closed behind them and Lisa pressed the top button, marked 4.

"Go on, say it," she said, turning towards him and smiling again.

"Say what?" he asked.

"That it's all a bit grand."

"Well, it is. But this is exactly what I would have expected."

"Yes, but it's also secure and it's private. George down there is the soul of discretion, and he and his mates have eyes like hawks. I don't have to live in fear of burglars or stalkers – well, not as much as I would if I lived anywhere else."

Rob's mind swam. Why was he here? What would Katherine think? But her mind was clearly on other things. She should have been out with him, not the tanned tycoon. And he was here with Lisa Drake who was . . . well . . . gorgeous. And fascinating. Lame word. But she was. And she had asked him back for coffee. He liked her. She listened. She liked him. The lift stopped and the doors slid open. They walked out on to a wide landing with cream carpet, more peach walls and brass up-lighters, and Lisa fished a bunch of keys out of her handbag, slipping the largest into the brass lock on the door opposite.

As they walked into her apartment the faint scent of Chanel that Rob had noticed earlier seemed stronger. She dropped the keys on a small glass-topped table inside the door, where they landed with a clank, and flipped a couple of switches. Several table lamps came on and Rob saw in front of him a stylish but sparsely furnished apartment in pale primrose yellow with two blue sofas facing each other across a low oak table. A massive oak chest was pushed against one wall and a folding screen stood in a corner. There was a carved mirror over the chest and three or four enormous black-and-white photographs on the other walls – views of mountains and rivers and towering trees.

"Coffee? Or a proper drink?" asked Lisa, slipping off her jacket, dropping it on to the sofa and walking towards him.

"Um. What are you having?" asked Rob.

"Oh, I don't know that I feel like anything . . . to drink," she said, looking up at him. Suddenly she seemed so still, so quiet and so much smaller than she had before. Rob's heart beat faster and, with unanswered questions echoing inside his head, he found his arms around her and his lips on hers. She was so soft, so sweet, so tender.

She drew away from him a little, and looking all the while into his eyes, she took his hand and led him towards another door, to one side of the folding screen. Opening it with one hand, she softly pulled him into the shadowy bedroom.

Without saying a word, she picked up a box of matches and lit half a dozen candles set in brass candlesticks on top of the chest of drawers. Then she came back to his arms and raised her lips once more to his, at the same time undoing the buttons on his pale blue shirt.

His hands stroked her shoulders and her arms, then slid the Lycra top down to her waist, revealing her perfectly formed breasts. By the time they had slipped naked under the duvet and wound around one another like the ivy embroidered on its cover, his doubts and worries had slipped away and he was lost in the warm and fragrant passion of Lisa Drake.

It was midnight by the time Katherine had extricated herself from the clutches of Charlie Wormald. She could still feel his clumsy kiss and smell the fetid mixture of Havana cigars and Issey Miyake aftershave that would take ages to evaporate from her jacket.

She drove back to Wellington Heights determined to shower away the unwanted aromas of the evening and to dump her clothes into a bin liner until they could be cleaned on Monday.

Her hair fresh washed and her face scrubbed clean of any trace of the lingering aftershave, she pulled the fluffy white towel around her and looked at the clock, which said that it was a quarter to one. It was late. Never mind. She would ring him and wake him. Her varnished floor shone like a conker and she wanted to tell him how pleased she was and to thank him for the bar stepping-stone patches he had left for her to get into bed. She dialled his number. It rang for ages but he didn't answer.

Chapter 5

Sunday morning in Bertie Lightfoot's cottage at Myddleton-in-Wharfedale was always the same: while Bertie walked the King Charles's, Alhambra and Palladium (or Ally and Pally for short), Terry would prepare breakfast of devilled kidneys and kedgeree. Bertie was the gardener; Terry was the cook. Well, chef, really. Terry Bean ran a little restaurant in the town based on traditional English cooking of the Michael Smith school. Plates were presented on brass chargers, glass was Old English, napkins were double damask, pies came with paper frills and, as Bertie would say of Terry's efforts when it came to poultry and game, "Every orifice is stuffed."

The two had met when Terry became Bertie's dresser in variety at Stockport. They'd lived together for nearly twenty years now, and seemed to complement one another perfectly in the garden and the kitchen: when Bertie grew it, Terry cooked it. Their dinner parties were the talk of the village, and no one had any problem in reconciling Bertie's on-screen image with the off-screen reality.

Bertie's everyday attire bore little resemblance to his 'costume'. He favoured pastel-coloured cashmere sweaters, pale slacks and soft Italian shoes, but always with a silk handkerchief around his neck – a nod in the direction of his rustic on-screen trademark, the red spotted kerchief. Outdoors, on the edge of the moor with Ally and Pally yapping at his heels, he wore a tweed trilby and a long sheepskin coat, and on this particular Sunday morning he had worked up quite a sweat in the wintry sun, trying to drag Pally backwards out of a rabbit hole and preventing Ally from feasting on sheep muck.

Finally he hauled them back down the moorland lane, only to have Pally start to gnaw her lead and Ally decide that she would prefer to travel on her bottom, just as the vicar's wife came round the corner from church. "Morning, Mrs Cunnington!" said Bertie, raising his hat and pulling the two dogs along with difficulty. "Lovely day for a walk." The woman crossed the lane, her face now set in a rictus grin.

"It's worming tablets for you, my girl." Mrs Cunnington darted a glance over her shoulder to check that he was no longer addressing her.

Bertie opened his garden gate and walked down the gravel path to the front door of the long low stone cottage. Just as he was wiping his boots on the scraper by the stone-roofed porch, the door opened and Terry, in a crisp, white shirt, canary yellow V-necked sweater and William Morris floral apron, opened the door.

"You're back. It's just as well – the kidneys have been to the devil and back and there's Pride and Prejudice on the phone for you."

"Who?" asked Bertie.

"D'Arcy. Says you rang him yesterday. You didn't tell me." Terry looked a bit peeved, his toupee a touch lopsided.

"You were in bed with one of your heads," said Bertie, slipping the two dogs off their leads. They bolted between Terry's legs, knocking him momentarily off-balance but straightening his toupee.

"That's better," said Bertie, tapping him fondly on the head with the palm of his hand. "I can't be doing with rugs that aren't straight." At the same time he used his toe to square up the doormat that the dogs had sent skidding across the parquet. He smiled sweetly at Terry and went into the tiny study by the front door. There, among the black-and-white photographs of past theatrical triumphs, he picked up the phone.

"Mr D'Arcy?"

Guy had not had a good Saturday evening. His features editor had played hell with him for being late with his copy and seemed hardly impressed with Guy's witty title for the piece on choosing the best varieties of witch hazel. "Which Hazel?" was, he said, hardly Booker Prize material. And he'd had to take a different sort of witch out to supper.

Sophie, the Sloane Ranger who had left the message on his answering-machine, was as horsy as Harvey Smith and not all that different in appearance. She had a pair of thighs, thought Guy, each of which could feed a Third World country for a week. But he needed to get on the right side of her father, who wanted his garden in Gloucestershire completely redesigning. It was Guy or royal favourite Edward Siggs-Baddeley, already rumoured to be lined up for redevelopments at one of the palaces, and Guy viewed the prospect of a commission on that scale with a watering mouth. He'd stop at nothing short of an engagement to clinch this deal.

He'd managed to drop her off at her Hampstead home by half past eleven and get home to Fulham for what he considered was a well-earned rest. In the morning he woke bright-eyed and raring for a little sport. He would ring Bertie Lightfoot and find out just what was to his advantage.

"Bertie, you old soak, how are you?"

It was not a response guaranteed to get on the right side of Bertie, who was beginning to be irritated that folk were remarking on his predilection for bottles from north of the border.

"Guy D'Arcy, you are a wicked boy and you don't deserve any friends."

"I haven't got any," quipped Guy. "What's all this about information that could be to my advantage?"

"Oh, wouldn't you just like to know?" replied the Yorkshire voice.

"Well, yes, I would rather. Come on, Bertie, dish the dirt."

"I just happened to be having a drink the other day with Sir

Freddie Roper who, as you might know, is chairman of the board of a well-known chemical company."

"Oh, yes, shooting pal of Pa's," said Guy.

"Oh, I thought he'd be a bit down-market for your father, being a working-class boy made good," rejoined Bertie, tartly.

"Now don't be unkind, Bertie. I'm a working-class boy myself nowadays. What were you talking to Freddie about?"

"Does the name BLITZ mean anything to you?"

"No, I don't think so. Other than the war and some old musical by Lionel Bart. Should it?"

"It soon will. Sir Freddie's company are promoting it as what they call 'a revolutionary new product'. It's some special pesticide, guaranteed to kill off loads of bad things and leave loads of good things unharmed."

"Oh, you mean ghastly to greenfly and lovely to ladybirds?" teased Guy.

"Something like that, except that it also bumps off whitefly, scale insects and all sorts of creepy crawlies that other pesticides don't."

"But you *can* kill whitefly and scale insects with other pesticides," said Guy, dredging up the knowledge he'd acquired from reading the right magazines.

"Yes; but they come back after a week or two. BLITZ is supposed to finish them off for the whole season."

"Sounds lethal," said Guy.

"Ah, but that's the thing. It isn't. It's as near to being organic as you can get – kind to hands, bees, butterflies and flowers, just lousy to lice."

"And why are you telling me all this?" There was a note of distrust in Guy's voice.

"Because Sir Freddie told me that they'll be looking for someone to spearhead their advertising campaign. Someone well known with a bit of gardening street cred."

"And you thought of me?"

"To tell you the truth, I thought of Rob MacGregor. You might be well known, Mr D'Arcy, but your street cred isn't quite up to his.

But, then again, I thought you might appreciate it more than he would."

"And why not you, Bertie?" asked Guy, well aware of Bertie's growing antipathy towards his young usurper.

"Don't be daft," said Bertie. "I might be old but I've not lost me marbles. I know I went to school with old Freddie Roper but I'm not the sort of image they want. They want a macho male who's young and thrusting. I might thrust every now and again, but the years aren't on my side. And neither is Terry at the moment," he added, as an afterthought.

"Sorry?"

Terry walked past the study door, carrying a silver salver with a domed lid, from under which a wisp of steam gently seeped, redolent of devilled kidneys. He looked sideways, and rather sourly, at Bertie then mouthed "BREAKFAST", in large, silent letters.

"Just a witty aside. You wouldn't understand."

"So what am I supposed to do with this knowledge?" asked Guy.

"Use it to your advantage," said Bertie. "Just make sure you're in the right place at the right time. There's a press conference next week to do the usual yearly PR bit for Amalgamated Agricultural Chemicals."

"Yes, I know. Deadly boring those dos. I never go to them."

"Well, if you've any sense you'll go to this one, and you'll pay attention, too, unless you want someone else to carry off the glittering prize. With careful negotiation you could be talking about a six-figure sum here – TV advertising and all."

Guy whistled. "Right," he said, suddenly serious, the cogs in his brain almost audible. "I'll be there."

"Just don't forget that when that one great scorer comes, in the shape of your accountant, it was old Bertie who put you right."

"Oh, I won't forget. Love to the old Bean, and I'll see you at the AAC do. In the meantime, take care of yourself," said Guy absently.

"Oh, I will," said Bertie. "Ta-ta." He put the handset back in the cradle and set off towards the aroma of the offal.

The fragrance that drifted into Rob's sensibilities on this Sunday morning was of a gentler nature. He came round slowly, conscious of soft, warm skin next to his and a delicate perfume that brought back in detail the events of the night before. He drifted on this heavenly cloud for a while before other thoughts trickled into his mind.

Lisa Drake's warm breath wafted across his chest where her head lay, her tousled fair hair falling across her face. His arm rested across her naked shoulders and his eyes gradually took in the green and white canopy, the collection of guttered candles on the painted chest of drawers and the shafts of silvery light that darted beneath the linen blind at the window.

She felt warm and perfectly comfortable. So did he, at first, but then his conscience pricked and hollow feelings of guilt and discomfort made him turn to one side.

She stirred, murmured softly and put her arms around him, drawing herself up close behind him.

"Hello," she whispered sleepily, running her finger up his spine and twisting the hair at the back of his head around it.

"Morning," he replied, his eyes focused in the middle distance.

"Coffee?" she asked.

"Mmm," he said.

"Black or white?"

"Sorry?"

"Your coffee. Black or white?"

"Oh, black, please." He came to and turned to see her slipping out of the ivy-covered bed. Her body was even more perfect unclothed, honey-coloured all over, finely toned and slender. She moved noiselessly across the room and took down a cream silk robe from the back of the door, fastening it around her in one circular movement.

She came back to the bed and bent forward to kiss his lips. Again his nostrils caught the warmth and fragrance that made his stomach flutter. Again he couldn't quite believe where he was. His eyes darted down the front of her loosely fastened robe and something inside him stirred again.

She turned and was gone, leaving him alone with his thoughts. Why had he come here? Because he'd felt let down by Katherine. Was that all? Or was he trying to prove to Katherine that he didn't need her? And had Lisa really fallen for him or was she just out to amuse herself? It hadn't seemed that way last night. What did he feel about her? Where was Katherine now?

He buzzed alternately with anger, pain, profound pleasure, confusion, lust – but, above all, guilt.

His soul-searching was interrupted by the door opening and the return of Lisa with a tray loaded with coffee and warm croissants.

She slid it on to the side of the bed, untied the robe and let it fall to the floor before she slipped under the duvet and nestled alongside him.

"How soon do you have to go?" she asked.

"Soon," he said, remembering Katherine's promise of a day out in the Dales and lunch at their favourite pub. "I have some writing to do," he lied, hearing his words echo hollowly in the room.

"Well, don't go just yet." She kissed his shoulders and neck, then his mouth, and ran her hand down his body until she found what she was looking for. She stroked him softly until once more he gave himself to her, then lay peacefully in her arms.

Eventually he slid out of bed, scooped up the crumpled heap of his clothes and made his way to the bathroom. He washed, dressed and returned to the bedroom, unshaven, to kiss her goodbye.

"Don't be gone too long," murmured Lisa, as he drew away from her. "We must do this again."

He smiled as brave a smile as he could manage, took a sip of the now cold coffee, and backed towards the bedroom door.

From the window she watched as he left the luxurious apartment block that had, for an evening, ensnared him in gossamer.

Chapter 6

By the time Rob reached End Cottage it had begun to rain. The skies were leaden grey; rivulets of muddy water ran from the side of the road and down the riverbank. The dull purple moors were almost invisible, shrouded in a veil of thick, wet mist, and the tall, naked branches of the riverside alders and willows flailed about the cottage, tossed by an increasingly brutal wind. The weather matched his mood. His feelings of the night before had refined themselves now. The elation seemed far away, only the confusion and guilt remained. And Katherine. What could he say to Katherine? And what would Katherine say to him?

He did not have to wait long to find out. As he slid the key into the lock of the green front door he heard the phone ringing. He glanced at the kitchen clock. It was a quarter to ten.

"Hello?"

"It's me."

"Hi, how are you?" he asked, trying to sound natural.

"I'm fine. How are you?"

"Fine." He felt the heat rising within his cheeks. The last time he had blushed it had been out of embarrassment; now it was generated by fear.

"Where've you been?" asked Katherine's voice, with a hint of hurt behind irritation.

"Oh, just out for a paper." A lame reply – he hoped it would be good enough.

"But last night? I rang you when I got back. I know it was late but you didn't answer. It rang and rang and rang. Were you asleep?"

"Must have been," muttered Rob. His blood was reaching what felt like boiling point. His forehead had broken out in a sweat. He struggled to take off his jacket and also to change the subject. "How's the floor?"

Katherine softened. In the mixture of worry and annoyance at his apparent absence she had forgotten about it. "It's lovely. And thank you for the note."

"The note? Oh . . ." He remembered with a little relief. He'd left it propped up against the tin of varnish with a clean paintbrush: "Please paint over the stepping stones in the morning when you get out of bed, working backwards towards the door. Then your floor will sparkle like your eyes. Love you, R x.'

He began to cool down. At least he knew now that she hadn't seen him at the restaurant. Hadn't seen him leave with Lisa Drake.

"And how about you?" he asked, chancing his arm. "How was your evening?"

"Oh, pretty deadly," she said. "My boss was as charming as ever. A real chauvinistic pain in the arse."

"And his wife?" he went on, trying hard to sound casual. "How was she?" He waited with a mixture of pain and pleasure for the expected lie.

"She didn't come. She was ill. At least, that's what he said. Though I don't believe him for one minute."

A sense of rising panic gripped him. Now he felt a chill breeze sweep across his skin.

There was only one question left to ask. "What does your boss look like? I've always had this image of him being fat and pink."

"Charlie Wormald? Oh, no. Tanned and trim. A martyr to his bullworker and a real ladykiller, he thinks. But his aftershave is too strong, his technique is far too obvious and he's about as sexy as a pot-bellied pig. It took me an hour just to get the smell of him out of my hair."

There was silence at the other end of the phone. Had a Dulux colour chart been to hand, Rob would have noticed that his face was 'white with a hint of lemon'.

"Are you all right?" she asked. She was the second person to ask him that in the space of twelve hours. He was far from "all right". He was all wrong. Entirely wrong. Katherine had done exactly what she had said she would do. She was as honest as the day was long. He, in a fit of misplaced jealousy, had blown it. And she didn't suspect a thing. It should have come as a relief that she didn't know. Instead, it made his guilt harder to bear.

"Anyway, why are you so interested in Charlie Wormald all of a sudden? You've never bothered about him before."

He floundered. "Oh, just curious. I had this mental picture of him being old and fat and unattractive and . . ." His words petered out. He wished that the earth would swallow him up. It didn't.

"So when are you coming round?" she asked.

"Er . . . I'm not sure." Confusion verging on panic. He needed time to sort himself out.

"What do you mean?"

"Well, the weather's so foul it's going to be miserable up the Dales. There'll be no chance of sitting outside at Grassington in this." Clutching at straws. "Have you seen the rain? It's coming down like stair-rods. I thought I'd knuckle down and get some writing done. Do you mind?"

A long pause. "No – no, fine. If you want to write then you write." She sounded angry, but he could hear bewilderment, disappointment too. Bad weather had never put them off before. They'd often sat in the car while the rain lashed down, eating doorstep cheese and tomato sandwiches and watching sodden sheep turn their backs to the rain-laden moorland wind as the windows steamed up.

Normally Katherine would have bullied him into it, but a note in his voice told her not to. She knew that something was wrong and yet for the first time she didn't want to ask what it was.

"Give me a ring later," she said, trying to sound as if she didn't mind.

"OK." There was an uncomfortable pause. "Er . . . sorry," he said.

"And me," she said softly.

She put the phone down and curled her legs up underneath her in the large armchair. As she gazed at her shining floor, the tears began to roll down her cheeks.

Jock MacGregor had been at Wharfeside Nursery since half past seven, even though it was Sunday. He didn't open on a Sunday: his Calvinistic Scottish upbringing would never allow him to consider Sunday trading, but plants needed watering and nurturing every day of the week, and while he could not allow himself to make money directly on the Lord's Day he had no compunction about tending his charges.

Through the potting-shed window, over the steam rising from his mug of tea, he could see storm-tossed branches and hear the wind whistling even louder. Twigs were snapping off and being hurled down among the plants below.

He took his coat from a hook at the back of the door, pulled it on and walked out, hanging on to his cap. Dense grey clouds, heavy with rain, lumbered across the sky as Jock walked nearer to the river. No longer were its waters clear amber, instead they were rich brown gravy, laced with sticks and soggy leaves and whipping up into a cream froth where they hit the rocks and boulders at the edges of the bank.

"Now, you just stay where you are," said Jock under his breath to the waters. He knew how quickly they could rise, given enough rain and the wind in the right direction. There had been a couple of occasions over the last thirty-odd years when the nursery had come perilously close to being flooded, but the water had always gone down before the banks had been breached. Old Fred Armitage had said that the nursery had been awash only once and that was back in the 1920s. Jock had been careful to ask about this: his love of the picturesque had not totally overcome his common sense.

Now he looked at the violently swirling waters with unease, and then up at the sky to confirm his suspicions that more rain was to come. He pulled his coat about him and headed back to the shed. As he did so he heard the tooting of a car horn in the lane outside the nursery. He leaned over the old stone wall in time to see a brand new wine-red Jaguar splashing its way towards the gate. It drew to a halt, its wipers still beating time to the music he could hear from inside, the door opened and a slight, stooping man with a short grey raincoat got out. He had a shiny pate with a few wisps of black hair snaking over its surface. Almost bent double, he slammed the door shut and scuttled towards the gate.

Dennis Wragg resembled nothing more than a red-faced tortoise with beady eyes and a hooked nose. His manner, though, was more hearty than that of your average Testudo.

"Now then, Jock," he bellowed as he executed an informal minuet in trying to dodge the puddles that would wreak havoc with his soft, shiny shoes.

"Shall we go in?" He nodded in the direction of the potting-shed.

"I don't open on a Sunday, Dennis," said Jock. "Unlike you."

Had Dennis Wragg really been a tortoise, he would have pulled his head inside his shell by now, but as he wasn't he tried, ineffectually, to pull his head inside his collar to shelter from the rain. Jock watched the water trickle down his skull dragging the strands of hair with it.

"I thought we might have a natter," offered Dennis, half closing his eyes to keep out the rain.

"Well, you thought wrong, I'm afraid," countered Jock, standing solid as a rock inside the nursery gate while the other man hopped from one foot to the other outside.

"Did you get my letter?" he asked.

"I did," said Jock, "and there's no need for a reply. You know what my answer is."

"Come on, Jock," snapped Dennis, as a rivulet of water ran down the back of his neck and under the collar of his pale yellow shirt. "Be realistic. How long can you afford to stay here? Take my offer. It'll give you a good retirement."

"I've no intention of retiring, Dennis. This is what I do. I like doing it and I don't want to see a plantsman's nursery turned into a small branch of your empire with padded sun-loungers in the greenhouse and concrete gnomes in the potting-shed."

"Oh, the buildings won't be here. We'd redevelop the entire site. It'd be modern and tasteful, it wouldn't look like your nursery at all," said Dennis, hoping that this information would make Jock feel better about selling up. Not surprisingly, it had quite the reverse effect.

"Dennis, I'm getting wet, you're getting wetter, and there is no way that I'm selling up. Now, I'd be grateful if you'd go back down the road and listen to your cash registers ring and let me get on. I don't want to be rude, but you're forcing my hand. I want to hear no more about your offer."

The horn of the Jaguar gave an irritated 'parp-parp' and Jock could faintly make out the image of a woman in the passenger seat. The blonde meringue of hair that was Gladys Wragg was getting impatient. Dennis looked over his shoulder and gestured that he wouldn't be long, then turned back to Jock for one final tirade. "You're mad. You can't manage this place on your own. You should pack it in while you've still got your health. And that won't last long. There's no future in this kind of business. People want a day out when they go to buy something for the garden. They want a tea shop and a kiddies' playground. They want to be able to buy everything from jam and honey to garden furniture and barbecues. Plants are just a tiny part of this business, MacGregor, and you're better off buying them in bulk from a specialist supplier. The money's to be made on all the other things."

Jock had heard more than enough. He pulled his cap down over his eyes to keep out the rain. "It might come as a surprise to you,

Dennis, to know that in my life money is not the most important thing. It might sound old-fashioned, and I know you think I'm as doomed as the dodo, but you should know that I do what I do for love. I love my plants. They don't let me down, they don't argue and they don't answer back. I earn just enough money out of growing them to make a living, and the pleasure I get from sharing my love of them is something that you could no more understand than fly. You're a lucky man, Dennis. You're a successful businessman who's made a lot of money. Whether or not you're a happy man I don't know and, to be perfectly frank, I don't really care. But I *am* happy here, Dennis. I've made a small success out of this patch of land, thanks to my wife and a grand lad who's done all right for himself, and I'm not giving it up for a lump of money that will sit in the bank and earn interest, because there's absolutely no interest in it for me. Have you got that?"

Dennis Wragg looked Jock straight in the eye, a drip of water on the end of his hooked nose and another on his curled upper lip. As he drew breath, the horn of the Jaguar sounded once more. He turned towards the car and waved, then turned back to Jock. He was too late. The old Scot was now half-way down the path to the potting-shed.

Dennis cursed under his breath as the insistent tone of the horn resumed. "I'm coming, I'm coming!" he shouted angrily into the wind, and picked his way through the puddles and back to the car to face his wife. She would doubtless be less than pleased at her husband's failure to land this particular catch on the riverbank, and she would not relish the prospect of pools of water on her nice cream leather upholstery.

Chapter 7

The news studio of Northcountry Television was compact and purpose-built, situated right next door to the hangar-like studio that was used for drama and the winter editions of *Mr MacGregor's Garden*. With a wide blue screen behind her and a massive monitor to her right, Lisa Drake sat in one of two padded chairs behind the curving crimson counter that was the newsdesk. Her freshly cut bobbed blonde hair just reached the top of the cream polo-necked sweater that rose above her deep green jacket, and the soft-toned face that had so captivated Rob the night before was now enhanced with a crisp makeup that meant business.

The Sunday early-evening news was two minutes from transmission, and a blue light shone over the heavy door in the blackened corner opposite her. In two minutes' time it would change to red. Three large grey cameras pointed at the desk; two were locked-off remote cameras that produced the standard mid-shot, which made every newsreader look as though they were born without legs. The man behind the other camera, rather strangely, seemed to have legs but no body. At least, that's how it appeared from where Lisa was sitting. Once on air a cameraman's face was a rare sight; usually all she could see were his arms adjusting shot size and focus, and his legs spread wide for balance and comfort.

She checked her watch, leafed through the pastel-coloured script in front of her, and pushed the top of her Mont Blanc ballpoint pen in and out nervously. Where was he?

There was a commotion over in the dark corner by the door and a loud apology as a huge man ambled out of the darkness towards the newsdesk, a disorganized script in his hands and a pen clenched between his teeth. He hauled on the second sleeve of his light grey suit jacket, aided by a nylon-coated makeup girl, who dabbed at the rivulets of perspiration on his forehead. A man from the sound department scuttled behind him, slipped the transmitter into his back pocket, then dashed round to fix the tiny microphone at the other end of the wire to his lurid tie, all as Frank continued to make a bee-line for the seat next to Lisa.

"Darring, shorry I'm rate," he mumbled through the pen, then took it out to make himself clearer. "Bloody subs. When will they find someone who has the remotest grasp of syntax? I said to one of them this morning, 'Where's your grammar?' and he said, 'At home with my grandad.' I ask you!"

Frank Burbage flapped his arms to get rid of both the makeup girl and the soundman as though he were shooing away flies. He had been anchoring *Northcountry News* since the station had been granted the franchise umpteen years ago. A huge Yorkshireman with grey hair that looked like steel wool, he had the stature, the booming voice and the right accent for this neck of the woods, and it was not put on.

He had come to Northcountry Television on the understanding that as well as being anchorman of their news programmes he could also cover Leeds United matches every Saturday in the season. Frank could bore for Britain when it came to football, but he was also a force to be reckoned with in the newsroom. Not that he cared much now for the goings-on in the broader political scene. It was a case of "been there, done that, read the script" as far as he was concerned. But he still had a mind as sharp as a rapier when he chose to unsheath it. Most of the time he didn't. Except when Lisa kept him on his toes and tried to poach some of his more choice interviewees. Then he would shake off the torpor borne of boredom and Tetley's bitter and do something about it.

Most of the time they rubbed along pretty well as a pair. It wasn't long after Lisa joined the station that Frank had realized she was no airhead. He'd tried to butt in on one of her interviews during her first week on the desk and been classily put in his place with one waspish line. He'd not done it again. Instead they'd forged a relationship based on mutual tolerance and professional envy, as is the custom with all newsreaders. These characteristics evinced themselves in wrangling for the opening and closing words of the bulletin, the seat to camera left, which indicated seniority, and being the first named in the credits, regardless of alphabetical order. Frank Burbage clearly beat Lisa Drake by a margin of two in the alphabet stakes, but nowadays they tended to take it in turns for the main story or interview and for opening and closing the programme.

"Why the hell they need two of us for a Sunday bulletin beats me," he grumbled. It was a remark that could be taken in one of two ways: either he didn't need Lisa to be there muscling in on his act, or he'd rather be in the bar while she got on with it. In fairness, it was probably the latter.

"Fifteen seconds, studio," the floor manager's voice rang out.

"Good weekend, love?" enquired Frank, shuffling his papers into some semblance of order.

"Not bad."

"Get yourself laid?"

His robust familiarity was, as usual, like water off a duck's back. "Yes, thank you. And you?"

"Only laid out legless last night after United lost to some God-awful team from over the Pennines. Three bloody nil. It'll be Millwall next. It's time I started doing the snooker. At least Steve Davis has more balls."

"Even if he doesn't know what to do with them," added Lisa, smiling, as the stirring signature tune of the lunch-time news boomed out its clarion call.

Frank took a deep breath: "In today's news, Helmingdale's biggest woollen mill goes up in flames, local farmers complain

67

about the Government's attitude to beef, and the chief executive of Yorkshire Water warns of possible flooding as the weather worsens."

The picture illustrating all three stories faded and Frank Burbage came into vision on television screens throughout the region.

"Good afternoon . . ." The first story was his, and Lisa watched him read the autocue with polished professionalism. Funny how people thought it was easy. "Oh, all he does is read the autocue," they'd say, but there was a technique to it, just as there was with any other skill. Get the camera too close and the viewers can see your eyeballs moving from side to side. Lift your chin too high and you appear to be talking down to the viewer. Stare too intently at the words rolling up in the lens and you look like a frightened rabbit. Get the camera too far away and you can't see the words. Find the right distance and move your head occasionally without getting 'the nods' and nobody would guess you were reading, provided that the emphasis on the words was natural and your technique polished.

Lisa's mind wandered idly as she watched Frank drawing in the Yorkshire viewers with his avuncular style. The second story – the one about local cattle – would be hers, and then they'd alternate until the end of the five-minute bulletin.

Frank was right: it was pointless having the two of them here for this cough-and-a-spit of news. There were seldom any interviews to conduct on a Sunday; it was nearly always a straightforward read. Boring, really. Her mind drifted back to the previous night, and the man who, in a few days' time, would be back in the cavernous studio next to the one in which she now found herself. She suspected the worst – that he'd wished their meeting had never happened.

Something roused her from her thoughts. It was a silence. Only a fractional one, but long enough to shake her wide awake: Frank had finished his item on the mill fire and it was time for the beef. She caught his eye as she launched into her own autocue script; his mouth was turned up at the corners and he was grinning. For the first time since he had begun working with her he had seen Lisa Drake caught off her guard. Perhaps she had feet of clay, after all.

As far as Rob's feelings were concerned, Lisa's assessment of the situation was only partially accurate. He did wish that the whole thing had never happened, that it had not presented him with such a crisis of conscience, and yet he could not pretend that he was not enormously attracted to Lisa. All through Sunday morning he swung between wretched guilt and high exhilaration, the screen of the word-processor staring blankly at him as he tried to pen something that would pass for a column in the *Daily Post* the following Saturday. By early afternoon a few uninspired sentences were all he had produced. He couldn't bear to be cooped up in End Cottage any longer.

He pulled on an ancient Barbour, a pair of tough fell boots, and walked out of the door and along the riverbank, eyeing the churning waters. He crossed the river by an old plank footbridge and struck out across the winter meadows, upwards towards the moor on a narrow, winding track, carpeted with silver sand. Soon the sheep-cropped tufts of grass at the side of the path were replaced by a thick rug of heather and the coppery fronds of dead bracken. As his boots bruised and crushed the plants that spilled in front of him, the true aroma of the moors reached his nostrils. It was a rich, earthy scent, a combination of sodden peat and the fruitily fragrant sap of heather and crowberry. The rain flattened his curly brown hair to his head, and ran off his chin and the end of his nose, washing his face as it poured over his skin and dripped from his fingertips.

He stopped for breath every now and again, gazing down into the valley that was obscured by thick mist, reinforced with the rain that moved sideways in great swathes. He gulped in the fresh, watery air, and still his head refused to clear. On he walked, eventually stumbling upon a vast black rock. A huge lump of millstone grit, it looked familiar, along with the wind-ravaged pine tree that arched over it. He remembered it now. Moving forward to the edge he found the spot he had discovered as a child. Part of the rock had fallen away, centuries ago most likely, and created a flat area a few feet below the upper surface. It was hardly visible from above, but as an exploring child he had found that it offered a fine view of the valley below and invisibility from parents walking above. He scrambled down to the ledge. Thanks to the overhang it was barely dampened by the rain that was driving away from it and out across the valley. Carefully he lowered himself into the hole, only just large enough for a grown man, and sat, panting for breath. He looked at his watch. He had been walking for three hours. Soon the light would fade, but not for an hour or two yet. He could sit for a while, and think, or try to stop thinking, or do anything that would rid his head of the miasma that seemed to have overtaken his mind.

He thought of Katherine and the hurt in her voice when he had made excuses not to go up the Dales. They could be sitting in the car now, eating and drinking and watching the water tumbling in milky veins down the sides of the fells of Upper Wharfedale. He thought of Lisa and the tenderness and sensuality of Saturday night. He thought of Katherine's encouragement at the start of his career, of her caring, her patience, her quick temper and her vital spark.

What if Katherine found out? The cold hand of panic gripped at his stomach and he felt momentarily sick. What if they lost everything they had because of one night of passion brought on by misplaced jealousy?

Occasionally the sun would shine weakly through a faint break in the clouds, allowing him a clear glimpse of a patch of the valley. In the same way he could momentarily see clearly what he knew was the only way forward. Lisa had been a flash in the pan, nothing more. He had been flattered by the attentions of someone so attractive, so highly rated. Katherine was a good friend, a good companion and a good lover, too. And he loved her, perhaps more deeply than he had realized of late. Maybe they had known each other too long; taken each other too much for granted. Familiarity had made them both careless. He must somehow retrieve what he had briefly lost. As the wind slackened a little he began to understand why the events of Saturday night had had such an effect on him. It was hardly surprising that he had tumbled into bed with the delicious Lisa: she had offered him a safety valve. But now he felt wretched on two counts. He would make it up to Katherine. Somehow. Without her knowing it had ever happened. But what about Lisa?

The light started to fade. He heaved himself out of the hole, stiff and damp from sitting too long, and picked up the track that led downwards into the valley towards another familiar landmark – Tarn House.

Helena had been surprised to see him. "Bless you! How nice of you to come on a Sunday. Of all the days of the week to be on your own I always think that Sunday is the worst." Then, recovering herself, "Where on earth have you been? You look like a drowned rat!"

She eased Rob's saturated Barbour from his back, "You do have to reproof these things from time to time, you know," and hung it by the Aga to dry, along with the sweater that smelled of wet sheep. Then she made tea, and they sat in her kitchen, eating shortbread, sipping Earl Grey and talking about this and that.

"There've been flood warnings on the television, you know."

"Mmm?" He hardly seemed to register.

"It's Katherine, isn't it? What's the matter?"

Rob was cagy at first. Opening up never came naturally to him. It was only lately, since his mother's death and his father's low spirits, that he had begun to share some of his thoughts with Helena. She never pried, simply listened and only offered advice where it was asked for. Rob didn't know how much he wanted to reveal; didn't know whether he wanted to reveal anything at all. Why should he tell anyone what was going on in his mind? It was up to him to sort it out himself. But the events of the last few months had lowered his defences. He ended up giving Helena the bare bones of the case without mentioning any names and without going into graphic detail.

"And now you don't know what to do?"

"Oh, yes, I know what I have to do."

"But it must be difficult."

"Yep." He gazed out of the window, preoccupied.

"The grand passion versus the comfortable, caring love?"

He hesitated slightly and inclined his head. "Yes. You've no idea what it's like.'

'Oh, I think I have."

Rob turned his head towards her.

"It happened to Jumbo and me," she said softly. Now it was Helena who looked away. "It was a long time ago. When we were in our forties. I thought it was the end of everything."

"And it wasn't?"

"No. Things changed. But it wasn't the end. Far from it. You can't turn off love like a tap. But I always remember one thing that Jumbo said to me." She faced him now. "He said that a man with two houses loses his mind, and a man with two women loses his soul."

Chapter 8

Now it was Rob's turn to find his telephone call unanswered. It was seven o'clock on Monday evening when he rang Katherine, only to find her answering-machine switched on. There were more than a couple of beeps at the end of her recorded message so he knew he wasn't the first person to ring that evening. He wondered who had left the other messages, then stopped himself from travelling down that unfruitful track. Jealousy had caused him enough problems over the last few days. It was probably her mother. Bunty Page had to speak to her daughter daily or she didn't feel she was on top of the scandal in the dale. He didn't leave a message. When he had put the phone down, he flipped on the television with the remote control and walked into the kitchen to get a beer from the fridge.

It was the end of the weather forecast. ". . . so there we are, dull in the south and west, but strong winds in the north with heavy rain. A very good evening to you." The weatherman smiled and winked, and Rob switched off the set.

He flipped off the cap with a bottle opener and put the ice-cold Beck's to his lips. Strange weather to be having an ice-cold beer, he thought, until the bubbles hit the back of his throat and he knew it was exactly what he wanted after a wearying day. He had, at last, crafted something reasonable for the *Daily Post*, although it had taken him the best part of four hours, thanks to a phone that wouldn't stop ringing. He'd settled on a piece about coping with cats in the garden – recommending his readers to use mothballs or lengths of hosepipe that looked like snakes to myopic feline eyes – had sung the praises of a garden famed for its daffodils and narcissi, given a plug to the *Plant Finder* directory in the hope that it might help reduce the size of his postbag, and jotted down yet another list of gardening tips for the week ahead. God, February was a bloody awful month to get excited about. He hoped there would be enough to fill the half-page he seemed to be getting at this time of year, and punched the buttons on his word-processor that sent it scooting off through a modem directly on to the paper's computer in London.

He had hoped for a call from Katherine, but it hadn't come. Instead he had heard from Steve Taylor about this week's programme in general, and Bertie's contribution in particular, which was to be about sprouting seed potatoes. Rob could hear Bertie's voice in his ear now and prepared himself for the *double-entendre* that was bound to hit the airwaves when it came to the word 'chitting'.

There'd been a call from some PR woman to check that he was going to the Amalgamated Agricultural Chemicals press briefing at the Dorchester on Wednesday, which he thought was odd since he'd already confirmed that he was, and a call from his agent to say she had some exciting news and that as he was coming up to London on Wednesday could he pop in and see her.

Rob had been with Liz Cooper for a year now. He'd always hated negotiating his own fees but had been terrified of being dictated to by some harridan from London who knew nothing about him or about gardening. And yet there was always the feeing that you were working in the dark when you did your own haggling. Nobody else in the television-gardening business ever breathed a word about what they were paid, in case they should be seen as coining it or, worse still, earning far less than everybody else. The fiscal pecking order was a closely guarded secret. Guy D'Arcy, with his aristocratic bare-faced cheek, had tried to tease out of Rob the

details of his fees when they had lunched together, but Rob had
stonewalled him and muttered something about everybody doing
their own thing. He was damned if he was going to tell Guy D'Arcy
how much he earned.

Liz had been recommended to him by the weatherman at
Northcountry Television, Archie Salt, who was more famed for his
bright waistcoats than his accurate predictions. In spite of Archie's
relatively regional appeal, Liz had managed to get him quite decent
fees in the after-dinner speaking line, secure him a longer contract
at Northcountry Television, and had persuaded one clothing
company to produce a range of all-weather garments marketed as
'Salt of the Earth'. Rob and Liz had hit it off from the first and he
had never regretted signing up with her.

After a couple more swigs of beer, he sifted through the post that
had arrived by courier in a large, fat, manila envelope from Lottie
Pym. Steve had been true to his word and first thing on Monday
morning the bustling, deep-voiced Lottie had endeavoured to
make some sense of the fruit and vegetable post that had winged its
way to the studios addressed to Mr MacGregor. Alas, she could not
help him at all with the stuff that came through from the *Daily Post*.

Rob sighed over a couple of wizened apples that fell out of a
cardboard box with a spidery note requesting to know their variety.
He remembered one of his college lecturers who could identify any
variety of plum simply by looking at its stone. A lovely old chap he
was, passionate about fruit. Well, you'd have to be to go to those
lengths. Rob took his beer with him to the window and looked out
through the rain-lashed panes. He shuddered and lowered the
blind to cut out the sight of the hurtling rain and at least some of
the sound of the wind. Then the phone rang.

Jock had finished his tea and had not been able to settle down to
anything that evening. He couldn't concentrate on his book, his
mind wandered when he tried to do the crossword in the paper, and
with the wind howling around the cottage he felt a need to check
that everything was all right in the nursery. He had to cling to the

parapet as he crossed the bridge, so strong was the wind, and the sound of water thundering under the old stone arches was deafening.

He unlocked the nursery gate and let himself in. The young trees tethered to the strong horizontal wires were straining to be free like young colts tugging at their reins. Evergreen shrubs shook and rattled in the wind and the branches of the sycamores by the river were hurling themselves around at an alarming rate. Fallen leaves fled across the ground, chased this way and that by the icy blast, which would occasionally whip them up into the sky before letting them fall in a cascade of damp confetti. Jock made for the green-houses. Their fragile panes would be the first to go, and as soon as one pane of glass popped the wind would get in and wreak havoc. Jock examined them as best he could from the outside, not wanting to open the doors for fear that the wind would take them out of his hands. As yet all seemed to be well. He struggled across to the potting-shed, almost bent double to butt his way through the gale.

He'd left some seedlings and trays on the potting-bench, half-way through a spot of pricking out. He might as well carry on for half an hour. The light above the bench would be bright enough to let him see what he was doing. He needed to do something.

He'd been working for barely ten minutes when he began to feel cold. His body was chilled and his feet were frozen. He looked down and saw the floor of the shed was awash. Brown water was seeping in under the door. He dropped a pan of seedlings, swore and made for the telephone in the cubby-hole. His hand shaking, he dialled Rob's number.

Rob would have been there faster had not Tom Hardisty been herding his Friesians down the riverside lane, away from the meadows where, half an hour later, they would have been cut off. End Cottage was higher up the riverbank than the nursery and, hopefully, might escape. He parked a few yards up the lane for safety, and then ran for all he was worth towards the gate and down the path to the potting-shed, cursing himself for not thinking of his father and the nursery when he heard the weather forecast earlier.

Jock was standing outside the potting-shed, his cap pulled down over his eyes, but not far enough to prevent Rob seeing the look of fear. His long black oilskin ran with water and his sodden boots were submerged in the eddying water of the river that was now creeping across the nursery.

"What shall we do?" shouted Rob, trying to make himself heard above the wind.

"We'll have to try and stop the water coming over the bank behind the shed. I've been heaving some sacks of compost over there but I'm just about done in," bellowed Jock, using up what little breath he had left.

"Mr MacGregor!" shouted a voice through the wind. The two men turned round to see Wayne running down the path, his open donkey jacket flapping in the gale. "I was on my way to youth club. I wanted to see if everything was all right. What's 'appened?"

"The river's breached its bank," said Jock. "We need to try and shore it up. Help Rob bring some of those sacks of compost over here. We'll have to use them like sandbags."

Rob cast his eye across at the river. By the light of the old street lamp at the corner of the bridge he could see a wide, heavy torrent of water gliding weightily by. It argued noisily with the bridge before tumbling over the rougher riverbed below and erupting into an angry cream spume. Just behind the potting-shed it was seeping into the nursery. The sacks of compost laid on top of the bank were containing it for now, but Rob did not hold out much hope for their continued success.

Furiously, by the light of the lamp, Rob and Wayne ferried the heavy sacks across to the low stone wall that capped the grassy embankment and piled them on top. Jock did his best to help, but the strain was beginning to tell and his face looked white and drawn. When the supply of compost ran out, he brought an armful of hessian sacks from the still swimming potting-shed.

"What are those for?" asked Rob, straightening up, his hair matted with sweat and rain.

"There's no compost left. We'll have to start bagging up sand."

Jock's voice cracked and his eyes darted around the nursery. Rob could see him checking up on his plants like the mother of a large family counting her children.

"OK. Give them here."

"The sand's underneath the old lean-to by the shed."

"I know, Dad, I haven't forgotten." And then, anxious that he might have sounded too sharp, "Don't worry.

"Wayne!" Rob called him over from the corner of the nursery where he had been searching in vain for more sacks of compost. The lad looked up, his face a mixture of fear and fatigue. "Over here!"

Wayne came running, his oversized black wellingtons splashing in the large puddles of water that lay on the path, the rain glistening like mercury in his tight curly hair.

"Grab a shovel from the shed and meet me in the lean-to. We need to fill these bags with sand."

"Right." Wayne hovered for a moment, as if unable to believe what was really happening, then turned on his heel and ran off. In seconds he was back and followed Rob into the darkness of the lean-to. "I can't really see what I'm doing," he said.

"Over here," shouted Rob. "Follow my voice. Your eyes will get used to the dark in a minute."

Rob held the sacks while Wayne shovelled sand into them, his aim improving as his eyes got used to the darkness. All the while the wind rattled at the corrugated iron roofing like some malevolent percussionist, until they were half deafened by the din.

A dozen sacks filled, Wayne put down the shovel and the two of them took each sack between them, carrying it like a dead body and trying not to let the sand spill out of the open end, and struggled towards the river. The damp sand weighed far more than the compost they'd been heaving around before. As they approached, the noise of the river was unnerving, like some grumbling, threatening giant lumbering by.

After a couple of journeys, Rob shouted, "We need to do it

faster! Let's try carrying one each," though in his heart he knew it would really slow them down. He staggered towards the riverbank with a third sandbag, his knees buckling beneath him, and heaved it into place on top of the long snake of plastic compost sacks. But the weight of water behind was making the whole construction unstable. As he turned to go for another sack, Rob heard a dull thud and whooshing sound. He spun round to see a tumbling Niagara of water coming straight for him.

"Get out of the way, Dad!" he shouted. Then he turned back to face the water, but lost his footing on the greasy mud. As he slipped sideways the gush of brown water knocked his feet from under him and bowled him along like a rubber ball. A three-foot section of compost sacks had collapsed. The water poured through in a narrow torrent with all the force of the river behind it. He put out his arms and grabbed at a tree trunk, pulling himself upright and spitting out filthy water. It was almost up to his waist and racing past him into the nursery, scooping up flower-pots and tubs and ripping newly planted shrubs from the now viscous earth.

On it swept, like an army of brown rats, slithering its way around cold frames and kerbstone and picking up the wheelbarrow as though it were a small boat being tossed on a foaming sea.

Wayne was retreating up the path, pulling at Jock's arm. Rob waded up the path towards them, watching the water swirl and gush past him along one side of the nursery. When it reached the wall at the other end it would start to back up and fill the enclosure, drowning the plants and undermining the greenhouses.

Jock, Rob and Wayne looked on helplessly for a few minutes as the light from the lamp glistened on an ever-increasing lake. A dull-coloured broth swirled over the ground, scooping up the dark earth and mixing it into an all-enveloping organic soup. The lights in the potting-shed went out, fused by the incoming water.

Rob looked up at the sky. The clouds were beginning to clear and the moon highlighted their deep blue-greyness as it leered between their fringes.

"What's that sound?" asked Wayne.

Rob listened. The rattling had stopped. Now there was only the deep bass roar of the water.

"It's the river. The wind's dropped." The noise was so loud, Rob could almost feel the vibrations in his chest.

He looked at his father. Jock stood, trance-like.

Rob racked his brains for inspiration. The sacks. They could move the sacks of sand and compost. Although the water covered more ground now, it was shallower and they should be able to wade further up the nursery with some of them to stop the water spreading to the fractionally higher ground. If they had the energy.

"Are you still OK?" Rob asked Wayne.

"Yeah. Fine." Wayne had little breath to spare but seemed willing.

"Could you help me get some of those sacks in a line across the nursery? That way we might be able to save the greenhouses."

"Course," replied Wayne, the vital spark returning to his eye.

Half wading, half running, the two scooped around in the slowly swirling water near the riverbank, delving into it as far as they dared to retrieve those bags that had not burst or been swept downriver by the raging torrent. Their legs sank into the mire, sometimes knee deep, which hampered their progress and made balancing difficult. Slowly at first, and then more speedily, they built a low wall half-way up the nursery like some fall-back position in a pitched battle. After half an hour they had achieved a knee-high barrier, which was now only a few yards from the advancing water.

By the time they had finished they were panting and bent double. All they could do now was hope and pray as nature took its course. Rob turned to Wayne and his silent father. "There's nothing we can do here now. Come on." It was only then that the thought struck. What had happened to Jock's cottage? He hardly wanted to look. He strode swiftly ahead of the others and climbed over the bridge. The wind had dropped completely now, but the water below raged on.

The cottage sat calm and still, in a garden that held not a trace of water. The ground on the opposite bank was clearly a fraction higher than the nursery, and yet the threat was still there.

Rob turned to his father. "The cottage is fine, but you're not staying there tonight. Come with me." Jock said not a word, but followed his son to his car.

Helena Sampson had taken in the silent Jock with no fuss, just as Rob had known she would. Then he drove straight back to the nursery and met up with Wayne, who had been able to do nothing except lean on the wall and watch the water's progress. "It seems to be slowing down. I've watched it for 'alf an hour and it's coming up much slower now. You see that row of young trees over there? It's been just below their lowest branches for ten minutes now and it doesn't seem to be getting any higher. Maybe it's because the wind's dropped."

Rob cast an eye over the nursery and tried to estimate the extent of the coverage. Water had submerged about half of the ground but was being held back by the line of sandbags and compost, which now looked like the Kariba dam. The greenhouses sat like great white swans on the edge of a lake but the potting-shed was probably about three feet deep in water. The branches of young trees sprouted like reeds from the water, but the upper reaches of the nursery, where container-grown plants were spaced out on the standing ground, was untouched. Thank God for that, thought Rob. At least he'll still have something to sell, although it occurred to him then that his father might never want to sell anything again.

"Come on," he said to Wayne, nudging his arm, "let's have another look at the cottage." They crossed the bridge once more and went through the front gate. The squat stone dwelling crouched peacefully in its plant-filled garden. All was well. At least it had the protection of a stout wall, should the river rise higher. Only the wicket gate provided a weak point of entry. "Do you think we could find a few more of those bags of compost and fill the gateway with them?"

"Course," replied Wayne, already loping up the hump of the

bridge. Rob watched him set off. His dad was right. What a find.

They waded once more into the muddy waters of the nursery, kicking to find what they were looking for.

"I didn't think TV stars did jobs like this," said Wayne ingenuously, as he passed Rob with a sodden sack on his shoulder.

"I'm just a gardener, really," replied Rob, puffing under the weight of his saturated load.

Slowly they hauled the last half-dozen sacks over the bridge and dumped them in the gateway of the cottage, before leaning on the wall to gasp in the chill night air, their chests heaving. Sweat poured from them, their legs were weak and shaking, but the gateway was, hopefully, impassable to water. Only now did Rob feel the deep cold of the evening and realize that he was soaked to the skin.

"I think you'd better go home and get dry," he said to Wayne. "There's nothing we can do now until the morning."

Wayne nodded. He had no energy left to speak, just raised his hand and turned to cross the bridge in the direction of home.

"And, Wayne . . ." shouted Rob, summoning up all his remaining strength. The lad turned round. "Thanks. *You're* the star."

A flash of white teeth, another wave, a shrug, and Wayne had disappeared into the darkness, leaving Rob alone and at the beginning of what he suspected would be an uphill struggle with his shattered father.

Slowly he stood upright, his head spinning and his lungs feeling as though someone had plunged a red-hot poker into them. He dragged himself towards the bridge, searching for his car keys in his saturated pocket. As he began to climb he saw, at its crest, the silhouette of a small figure, clad in black and muffled against the cold. For a long time the two of them stood still and stared at each other while the river thundered beneath their feet.

"I thought you might need help," Katherine said. He looked hard at her, then walked slowly towards her and wrapped her in his arms, resting his head on her shoulder. His body shook and she held him tighter than she had ever held him before.

"Hey," she said soothingly, stroking his sodden, stinking clothes, "come on. Let's get you into something warm."

He straightened his stiffening back. "What made you come?" he asked, softly.

She put her arm around his waist and led him over the bridge. "Because," she said. "Just because."

Chapter 9

Katherine didn't say much that night. She didn't need to. She undressed him and took him to her bed, cradling him in her arms until he slept.

When he woke in the morning the bed was empty and there was no sign of her. He forced his naked, aching body out from under the covers and made his way to the kitchen where the clock on the wall said ten to ten. No wonder she'd gone. He stretched his arms over his head and arched his back to relieve the stiffness in his muscles. Then he saw the note propped up against the toaster. 'Love K x' was all it said. No message, no indication of a return time, just 'Love K x'.

Rob shaved and showered with the stuff he always kept in a sponge bag in her bathroom, and slipped on clean underwear, a pair of old jeans and a sweat shirt that lived in her wardrobe. He found a pair of her socks and pushed his feet into the damp wellies that sat by the radiator in her kitchen, before leaving the flat for Helena's.

Half-way there he changed his mind. It would be better to go to the nursery first and size up the damage, see if the cottage had escaped the flood waters.

He parked in the same spot that he had used the night before, pulled an old waterproof out of the back of the Fiesta and walked down the lane. It was one of those classic 'calm after the storm' mornings. The sky was clear, washed a bright borage blue by the rain of the day before, and the blackbird with the strong survival instinct sang from the still branches of the riverside sycamore.

Rob reached the nursery gate and found it unlocked. He shouldn't have been surprised. How could he have expected his father to have waited this long before coming to see the state of the place? He looked further along the lane and caught a glimpse of Helena's car, then turned to take in a full view of the nursery. Amazingly the water had gone down. Now there were just a few large pools on the more heavily compacted areas of ground – the paths and lower areas of hard standing. The greenhouses, thank God, had survived without one broken pane, but the scene of devastation in the lower half of the nursery was heartbreaking. Everywhere was coated in a thick layer of silt, into which were mixed broken twigs, fallen leaves and litter. The once-neat rows of plants were submerged under a confection of mud and rotting vegetation.

The door of the potting-shed was open and Rob could hear voices from within as he walked down the path. He stuck his head round the door and saw Helena, Jock, Harry and Wayne standing inside in a semi-circle, each holding a plastic cup of coffee that had been dispensed from a large flask that stood on the bench where a tray of seedlings remained from the previous night's pricking out. The water had stopped about three inches below the level of the bench.

"Good morning." He greeted them with a note of enquiry in his voice.

"Good morning," they chorused, though, to be strictly accurate, Harry just coughed his usual bronchial greeting.

"Well," he said, "what a night." He looked across at Wayne, who stared at his trainers. "How are you feeling, Dad?"

"I've been better." Jock drew in breath slowly. "But I suppose it could have been worse. At least the greenhouses are still standing, and it didn't reach the cottage. It would have swamped both, except that somebody had the sense to block its path with sandbags."

"Well, you've got a crack labour force, haven't you?" said Rob, glancing at Wayne, who now raised his eyes from his mud-spattered footwear and grinned at him.

"God, it's bloody 'orrible out there," offered Harry, dragging on his fag but at least having the presence of mind to blow out the smoke in the opposite direction to Helena.

"Thanks for looking after him," said Rob.

"Oh, it was no problem at all. It was a pleasure. I'm only sorry it was in such rotten circumstances," she replied. "It is a bit of a mess, isn't it?" she said, walking out of the potting-shed. The others followed and, once again, took in the scene of devastation that lay before them.

"Dad," asked Rob, "are you insured?"

Jock shook his head. "The premiums were too high, being near the river. I know it's against my nature but with old Armitage saying that it hadn't happened very often I thought it was a risk I had to take."

"Have you any idea how much you've lost?" asked Helena, with real concern in her voice.

"All the shrubs and perennials down there are goners," Jock nodded in the direction of the lower part of the nursery next to the river, "though some of those over the other side we might save."

"How much were they worth?"

"Oh, a few hundred." Jock turned to Wayne and Rob. "But we were lucky. It's not the end of the world, thanks to you two. It's just the time it will take to clean up that's the problem. With the start of the season looming we're just going to have to knuckle down and crack on. Yes. We were lucky," he muttered again, pushing the toe of his boot through the thick film of mud that lay on the path.

Harry grunted, depressed by the amount of slave labour that loomed large on the horizon.

"So what do we do now?" asked Rob. Before anyone could answer they heard the wrought-iron gate clang against its catch. They turned and saw a small black-clad figure in woollen tights and a short skirt with a black woollen jacket. She was walking down the nursery path and picking her way between the puddles and the mud.

"Hello," said Katherine, tentatively. "Would you mind if I came in?" And then, without pausing for an answer, "I'm so sorry about the flood, Mr MacGregor, but do you think I might be able to write a piece for the paper? Or would you rather I came back later? Is it a bit too soon?"

"No, it's fine, lassie," said Jock. "I've just been saying that it could have been worse. I've still got a house."

Katherine looked at Rob to check that he didn't mind her intruding. Rob raised his eyebrows, surprised at his father's equability. Katherine pulled her shorthand pad and pencil from the pocket of her jacket and pushed a stray wisp of hair behind her ear. It shone in the sunlight, and Rob noticed that her face was shining, too, her cheeks flushed pink from the walk down the lane.

"You're sure you don't mind?"

"No, you carry on."

"I'll just need a few facts first about how long you've been here and that sort of thing . . ." Rob watched Katherine go to work. He'd never seen her operating professionally before. She was firm but, thankfully, sensitive. Rob had got used to newspaper reporters over the last couple of years: as a breed they were accomplished at feigning an interest in the basic facts as they cunningly picked their way towards the intimate or prying question that had been their aim all along. Katherine had a rare sincerity about her, and she cared passionately about justice and about people's well-being, especially in the dale, her home; their last argument had proved that. He found himself spellbound as he watched her win Jock's confidence. Even though his father knew Katherine quite well, here was a different kind of relationship in the making – that of inquisitor and respondent. She asked about Jock's background, about his passion for plants and about how long he thought it would take to get the nursery back in shape. And then she asked about the son who had become a famous television gardener. It seemed odd to hear Katherine asking questions about him. He wondered what she would say in her piece. She'd never had to write about him before, had never wanted to mix business with – well . . . love.

Her questioning completed, she turned to Rob. "Can I say that you helped save the nursery and the house?"

"Well, er, Wayne and I did what we could to . . . er . . ."

Katherine looked across at Wayne, whose head was bowed.

"What's your surname, Wayne?"

"Dibley." Wayne fidgeted and made circles on the ground with his welly.

Rob stepped in. "You can say that if it hadn't been for Wayne the nursery would probably not have survived. He stacked sandbags until he could barely walk and he's a star."

Wayne blushed, and grinned sheepishly, then loped off down the nursery to start the clear-up operation. Harry, too, shuffled off, coughing.

"All right, you two, enough of this," said Jock. "Do you want a cup of coffee before we start shovelling mud?" As Helena poured Rob and Katherine some of the steaming brew, they all heard cars coming down the lane rather faster than normal, splashing through the deep puddles that dotted its surface. The first was a Renault Espace with Northcountry Television emblazoned on its side, and the second was a charcoal grey BMW with a blonde at the wheel.

During the next few moments of Rob's life he contemplated many things: the proximity of Katherine, the state of his wellingtons, the colour of the sky and suicide, though not necessarily in that order.

Two men climbed out of the Espace and proceeded to heave camera equipment through its side door. Lisa Drake slid out of the charcoal grey BMW in a long camel coat and shiny brown boots. She pushed open the gate of the nursery and trod a path that was quite clearly about to lead to an interesting situation.

As far as Rob could see, several alternatives were open to him: he could pretend to faint; he could run away; he could sneak into the potting-shed lavatory and lock the door; or he could call upon all the experience he had accrued at the local amateur dramatic society and bluff his way out. If he tried the first he might hurt himself, if he tried the second they'd think he'd flipped, and the third scenario was out of the question since Harry had beaten him to it.

"Good morning," shouted Lisa from the top of the path. Jock, Helena, Rob and Katherine stared at her. Drawing her expensive coat around her she tiptoed gingerly down the path between the silt-swamped beds and came towards them. Rob thought his heart was going to burst through his chest. He was convinced that his face must be the colour of pickled beetroot and that, any second now, his head would probably explode.

Thankfully, Jock was the first person Lisa addressed in the bright but brusque manner that had become her trademark. "Mr MacGregor, Lisa Drake, Northcountry Television." She reached out a well-tailored arm that ended in a brown leather glove and shook his hand. "Terribly sorry about the flood. Do you think we could take some shots of the nursery and have a brief interview?" She flashed Jock a devastating smile. He opened his mouth to reply, but before he could say anything she'd turned to address the two men walking down the path behind her. "Martin, set up over there on a wide shot and I'll walk up the path towards you for the intro. This is *so* kind of you, Mr MacGregor. I realize it must be a bit of a morning. We'll do our best to get it over with in no time. Morning, Rob. How are you?" She felled him with another smile and walked towards her two-man crew, who were setting up the camera as bidden.

Her style was breathtaking. Rob glanced at Katherine, whose mouth was partially open and whose eyebrows, had they not been attached to her skin, would otherwise have been hovering somewhere above her head. Jock looked as though he had been run over by a velvet-covered steamroller, and Helena's brow was knitted as though she were trying to solve a particularly tricky crossword puzzle. Rob himself was in shock.

After a moment's consultation with the cameraman Lisa returned to the stunned group. "Where shall we do the interview? In the potting-shed?" She stuck her head round the door. "No, perhaps not. Bit of a smell in there. Must be the river water." She turned away and walked down the path. "Would you mind if we got the piece to camera out of the way first, Mr MacGregor?"

Jock, unsure of whether or not he wanted his nursery shown on television in its current state, was about to ask her a question, but she breezed past him and set herself up in front of the cameraman, who adjusted his shot size, and the soundman who, earphones in place, was twiddling a row of dials and holding a furry sausage on a pole in front of her as if he were trying to tempt a donkey to eat a large, hairy carrot.

Rob looked again at Katherine. She seemed mesmerized. She had seen some smooth operators in her time, but none with quite as much bottle and charisma as Lisa Drake. He wished he was anywhere but there. Perhaps if he kept quiet and still nobody would notice him. Lisa was ready to perform.

Another smile at her small audience and then, "Quiet, please!" It wasn't necessary. The rest of the assembled company was speechless.

"After last night's floods, the worst in forty years according to the locals, the residents of Wharfedale are piecing together their lives and assessing the damage that the flood waters have left behind. Farmland has been drowned, and gardens swamped. Thousands of pounds' worth of destruction has been caused by the Wharfe in full spate." As she talked earnestly to the camera she walked forward in her elegant coat, casting a leather-gloved hand sideways as she went, her shiny boots ploughing through the soft black sludge. "Most houses in the community escaped unscathed, but among the few low-lying properties that were damaged is the delightful riverside nursery of Jock MacGregor, father of television's 'Mr Gardening', Rob MacGregor. Just how will he and his nursery recover from the dramatic deluge which has left this scene of devastation in its wake? And cut. OK for you, Martin?" The cameraman nodded his approval. "Right, let's do the interview."

By now Jock was powerless to stop her. Helena and Katherine were hypnotized, and Rob was one step nearer to heart failure. Lisa carefully positioned Jock on the path, with the flood-damaged potting-shed and a few of the largest pools of water visible over his shoulder. "Do those pools of water read, Martin?"

The cameraman screwed up his face. "Well, they're OK."

"Yes, it's a shame there isn't more water here, really. Still, never mind." She turned back to Jock and massaged him with another smile. "Running?" she enquired of the cameraman.

Martin nodded and said, "Speed." The soundman, without lifting his eyes from his dials, nodded too. "OK. Mr MacGregor, what was your reaction to the flood?"

Jock endeavoured to convey his feelings, though he felt like a rabbit being sized up by a fox. "Will you be able to open again or will this mean the end for Wharfeside Nursery?"

At least she got the name right, thought Rob. But he didn't like her line of questioning.

"Whose fault do you think it is that the banks of the Wharfe were breached by the flood waters?"

Jock was beginning to find his feet. "You can't blame anyone for a flood. It's part of nature. I work with nature every day and I understand that sometimes it can be cruel."

"You don't think that the Yorkshire water authority is at fault because of its tampering with water levels in the river?"

"I'm afraid that's out of my province. You'd have to ask them what they feel about that," said Jock.

"Meanwhile, there's talk of you being taken over by a local chain of garden centres. Will they still want to buy you out now that they know the nursery is subject to flooding?"

The question came as a hammer blow. There was an audible intake of breath from Katherine, and Helena muttered, "Good God."

"This nursery has never been for sale," Jock replied evenly, "so the flood makes little difference to the situation. We'll tidy up and then get on with our work. And now, young lady, if you don't mind, we have rather a lot of clearing up to do." Jock raised his cap to Lisa and indicated that the interview was over.

"Thank you, Mr MacGregor. That was very kind of you. I'm so

sorry I had to ask those questions but I'm afraid that's my job." And then, turning to her cameraman, "Martin, is the first half of that last answer usable?" The cameraman gave a thumbs-up.

She turned to Rob. He watched her eyeing him. He could see in front of him the devastatingly attractive woman whose bed he had shared just three nights before and he could also see a hard-nosed reporter stalking her quarry. The scent of Chanel caught his nostrils for the first time that morning and he felt the fluttering in his stomach.

Lisa said directly, and for all to hear, "Can I ask you how you feel? This is where you grew up, isn't it?"

Rob nodded, as yet unable to find words.

"Just a snatch about what it means to you, how it will affect your father and . . ." she waved her arm around her, taking in the assembled company, "and how it will change your life." On this line she darted a flicker of a smile in Katherine's direction, and a broad one back at him.

She knows, thought Rob. She bloody well knows. What would she do now? Nothing. She wouldn't do anything. She'd just make him sweat.

"Er, can we do it quickly? As Dad said, there's a lot to do."

"Yes, of course. Sorry. I don't want to make this any more uncomfortable for you than it is already. Ready, Martin?"

Martin grunted in assent.

"Rob MacGregor, you grew up here on your father's nursery. It must be sad to see it looking like this?"

"Yes, very sad, but we'll cope. It won't be long before the nursery is back to normal."

"It must be a terrible blow to your father, coming as it does in a year that has held more than its fair share of tragedy for him, with the loss of his wife?"

Rob felt his colour rising. "Yes, it's been a hard time, but thankfully we've had lots of support from our friends," he looked at Helena and Katherine, "and we're pulling through." He fought to control himself, aware that she would not give up until she had what she wanted. He'd have done better to have declined the interview, but what would she have done then, with Katherine only a few yards away?

"And the takeover bid by Gro-land Garden Centres. Has it never been on the cards? Your father is, after all, not a young man."

"No, he's not young, and he's had a hell of a year. But my father has never ceased to surprise me." Jock was standing just outside the potting-shed, looking grimly at the muddy earth. He raised his eyes as Rob talked, and glanced across at him.

Rob continued, looking Lisa straight in the eye, "You see, what I think you have to grasp is that gardeners are not normal people. They don't give in easily because ever since they learned how to grow things they've coped with the failures as well as the successes. They rise to a challenge. My father taught me most of what I know about gardening, and the one thing he taught me more than any other is that you don't fight nature, you work with her. She doesn't let you down in the same way that people let you down. She's never disloyal, but she is sometimes fickle." Lisa backed off an inch.

Rob carried on, fixing her with a burning stare. "She's flexed her muscles a bit, but now, with any luck, she'll start to be a bit kinder." And then, more gently, "Wharfeside Nursery will soon be back in business, selling the sort of well-grown plants that only a good nurseryman like my father can produce."

Lisa stood still, looking at him. There was a long pause. "Rob MacGregor, thank you very much."

"My pleasure," said Rob, holding her eye. "And now I'm afraid we'll have to get on."

"Yes, of course. I'll get out of your hair." She turned to the rest of them. "Thank you, Mr MacGregor," she said to Jock, "and good luck. I'm sure everything will soon be back to normal." She nodded at Helena, then shot a glance at Katherine.

"Goodbye, Katherine. It seems you've beaten me to it. Today, anyway." She walked swiftly down the path, got into her BMW and splashed away down the lane, leaving her camera crew to pick up the pieces.

Chapter 10

The 7.38 pulled out of Leeds City station on time, with Rob slumped in a forward-facing seat in a non-smoking first-class carriage. Ordinarily he felt a pricking of conscience if he travelled first class, his canny father having instilled in him a keen sense of economy, but today he felt in need of as much privacy as he could get. First-class passengers might be more reticent about asking gardening questions than those in second class, and the events of the previous few days had left him longing for the peace and quiet of his own company. The train journey to the AAC press briefing in London would offer him that – for the next two hours and seven minutes anyway.

Big junkets like this never appealed to him, and neither did London, but he felt a duty to keep his finger on the pulse, even though the rest of the day always seemed to be wasted and the same old characters would crawl out of the horticultural woodwork, happy to enjoy a free buffet and drinks at the Dorchester.

The flood had given him yet another reason for abandoning the trip, but Jock had insisted that his "little local difficulties" should not get in the way of Rob's work.

He flipped through the *Daily Post*, not his favourite paper but he felt obliged to scan it daily, and kept the *Daily Telegraph* and its crossword for later in the journey. There was also the added treat of a cooked breakfast to look forward to in the dining car.

There had been barely time for a cup of coffee before he'd left End Cottage. In the excitement and confusion of the flood the day before he had almost forgotten about his own home. As Lisa had swept away in her BMW, and Helena had left, making him promise to come and see her soon, he had tried to follow a few minutes later in the Fiesta, with the excuse that he hadn't seen his cottage since the flood, before the questions from Katherine became embarrassing. He almost got away with it.

"Do you want me to come?" Katherine had asked, but he'd assured her that he would be OK on his own.

"Some lady," she had said, looking down the road where the puddles were still settling after the disturbance from Lisa's radials.

"I didn't know you knew her," said Rob, nervously.

"I don't," replied Katherine.

"But she called you by your Christian name," he countered.

"Well, we sometimes see each other across a crowded room at press briefings or, like today, when there's a story that we're both after, but I wouldn't say I knew her, and I've never seen her operate before. That came as a bit of a surprise. Talk about sharp."

"Well, you're not so dull yourself," Rob pointed out.

"Yes, but wading in like that as though she were Jeremy Paxman on *Newsnight* when she's interviewing a local nurseryman who's had his livelihood threatened by a flood. Bloody insensitive, I call it. Anyway, I thought you were great." She smiled at him, a proud, proprietorial smile, and rubbed her hand up and down his back. "You put her in her place rather well, I thought. Showed her what you're made of." Then her brow knitted a little. "How well do *you* know her? Do you ever bump into her at the studios?"

Rob tried to look casual, and hoped he succeeded. "Oh, now and again. Our studios are next door to one another." He paused. "But I couldn't honestly say I know her." He looked down the lane. "No. I hardly know her at all." That much, at least, appeared to be true. And then, changing the subject, he said, "Something puzzles me."

"Mmm?"

"Why all this interest in Dad's little nursery, first from Dennis

Wragg, then the television newsroom, and you here reporting on it?"

"Why it's interesting to Dennis Wragg I've no idea. He obviously has something up his sleeve. Or did have. I don't know how he'll feel after the flood. But as far as the newspaper and the television go, I'm afraid you're being a bit naïve."

"What do you mean?" He looked down at her.

"Rob, you're probably the most famous gardener on British TV and when the nursery where you grew up and which is still run by your dad gets flooded it's news. People want to know."

Rob blushed. Would he ever learn to cope with, or even remember, his fame? Katherine hoped not, she said. She rather liked him the way he was. If only he liked himself the way he was. Having to lie to Katherine was not something he wanted to become a habit. He hugged her, promised to ring her later and kissed her goodbye.

His car splashed down the lane to End Cottage and his heart beat faster as he approached, wondering what kind of scene would meet his eyes. The lane was sprinkled with twigs, leaves and other debris that the river had left behind, but the tidemark came to just below his doorstep. Someone had been watching over him. He looked skyward and mouthed a silent 'Thank you', at whoever was up there.

He had checked that all was well, grabbed a larger pair of socks – those he had borrowed from Katherine had bobbles on the back that dug into his heels in his wellies – then went back to the nursery to help with the clean-up operation.

Only when it was becoming dark had they stopped shovelling the silt and barrowing it back into the river, to carry on its journey down the dale. Paths were hosed clean, greenhouse walls and floors scrubbed down and the nursery was returning to some semblance of order under the direction of Jock, the muscle power of Rob and Wayne and the grumbling of Harry.

"Never remember it like this when old Armitage was 'ere," said Harry, who was using his yard broom as a leaning post and occasionally poking it in the direction of the malodorous mulch that adorned the path.

"Old Armitage was lucky," said Jock.

Rob had watched his father during the day for any tell-tale signs that he was slipping back into introspection. But the disaster seemed to have strengthened his resolve. Some folk needed sympathy to get out of their depression, thought Rob, others needed a challenge. His father clearly fell into the last category.

Wakefield. Ten to eight. The train sped on. It would soon be time for breakfast. His appetite was sharpening. He'd spent last night at home in his own bed, needing to change into smarter clothes for the briefing, and not wanting to wake Katherine when he got up at six. He left End Cottage at a quarter to seven and drove to Leeds, leaving the Fiesta in the station car park before boarding the train.

An announcement came over the loudspeaker system: breakfast was ready. Rob grabbed the *Telegraph* and walked down the train, the aroma of bacon and eggs becoming stronger. He planted himself in a seat half-way down the dining car and examined the menu, though he knew already that it was the complete works or nothing.

Five across: 'Effeminate gathering of boy scouts (4)'. He was just starting on the crossword when the voice he knew so well asked a steward if breakfast was being served. He might have guessed that his journey was not destined to be a relaxing one. Bertie Lightfoot was travelling to London, too.

He had swaggered into the dining car looking to left and right to see if anyone recognized him. He was difficult to miss in the outfit he had chosen for this particular trip to the big city. His baggy corduroy trousers were corn-coloured and his brogues shone with Cherry Blossom oxblood polish. Beneath the brown tweed jacket, with its leather elbow patches, he wore a check shirt, maroon tie and primrose yellow V-necked sweater. Nobody raised an eyebrow, however, as he made his regal progress.

Interesting, Rob thought, that when Bertie was out for the day on official business he adopted his official accent and not the flat, rather fey northern tones he used at home. At least this thought helped him with his crossword. Four across: 'Effeminate gathering of boy scouts' – CAMP.

He buried his head in the paper, hoping that Bertie might choose a seat further up the dining car. One down: 'French bread in English gullet induces irritation (4, 2, 3, 4)'.

Bertie spotted him and lapsed into his native tongue, *sotto voce*, as he bent down level with Rob's paper-hidden face. "Oh, Mr MacGregor. Going up to London to see the Queen?"

Rob looked up and tried to feign surprise. "Oh, hello, Bertie. You too?"

"I thought you hated these dos," said Bertie, settling himself in the seat opposite Rob without waiting for an invitation.

"I'm not mad on them, but you know what it's like, you have to keep in touch with new developments," replied Rob, determined to be pleasant. He filled in the answer to one down: PAIN IN THE NECK.

Bertie kept to his northern tones, several decibels lower than his fortissimo Mummerset burr. "Oh, it'll be full of those boring old farts as usual. Just tell me why most gardening experts are such dreary old sods. Except for the ones that think they're Brad Pitt in wellies."

Rob raised his eyes, but Bertie was now scanning the menu. "You having the lot?"

"Mmm," answered Rob. Eight across: 'Celebrity queen becomes snake (5)'.

"No devilled kidneys today," moaned Bertie. "Why is it that all the chefs on British Rail were trained at the Lucretia Borgia school of cookery?"

Rob put down the crossword. If he was going to keep his word and take Bertie to task about his asides, this was as good a time as any. "Bertie."

"Mmm?" He looked up from his menu.

"What's the problem?" asked Rob, trying to put it as gently as he could.

"What do you mean?"

"Your problem. I know it's a pain for you, this programme. I mean, having to share it, after you having your own programme. But we've got to sort this out."

"I don't know what you're talking about."

"These asides at the end of the programme. Folk are beginning to notice."

"I should hope they are. Just little rays of sunshine designed to bring light relief to an otherwise dreary landscape."

"They were at first. Don't you think they're getting a bit . . . well . . . strong?"

"Oh, for God's sake. You've been on telly for half an hour and you think you know the lot." Bertie's cheeks coloured until they almost matched his nose. "I've been doing this gardening lark since you were in your pram and you come along with your college education thinking you can wipe me off the face of the earth. Well, you can't, you little shit."

Rob sat back in his seat, stunned at the outburst. But Bertie was in full spate now. "Just because someone upstairs thinks you're the new face of gardening you think you can walk your little welly-booted feet all over me." He was raising his voice now, stage accent forgotten. "But I'll tell you this, young Mr MacGregor. I'll see you off. Oh, yes. You might think you're God's gift to your lady viewers in your tight jeans and your rugby shirt, but just remember that the higher up the gardening tree you go, the bigger the drop when you fall."

He was leaning across the table, pushing his face closer to Rob's now, and almost spitting. "You can't have it all your own way. There are others just as good as you and who are hot on your tail, even if you *have* caught the eye of a certain lady newsreader." At which he flung down the menu and stomped off to the bar at the end of the dining car where Rob heard him order, in his Yorkshire accent, a large malt whisky.

It was a few moments before the dining-car steward could drag Rob from his troubled trance and take his breakfast order.

Suddenly his appetite had gone. "Coffee, please. Black. And a slice of toast."

"It'll have to be the full Continental breakfast, sir."

"Fine. That's fine." He stared absently at the steward, who retreated with his order.

He looked out of the window at the industrial landscape of South Yorkshire as Bertie's words echoed in his ears, ". . . even if you have caught the eye of a certain lady newsreader."

His eyes drifted down to the crossword again. Eight across: 'Celebrity queen becomes snake (5)'. He filled in the letters slowly: VIPER.

Chapter 11

The large reception room at the Dorchester was already teeming with people, mainly men in sports jackets or suits, mainly middle-aged. Underneath the glittering crystal chandeliers, waiters glided among the guests, plying them with drinks. Rob stopped at the check-in table near the door and was given his lapel badge by a pretty girl who made a great fuss of pinning it to his jacket.

This was the moment he hated most, when, just inside the door, you had to hover and spot a familiar face and head for it as quickly as you could before you were buttonholed either by someone you knew you didn't want to talk to, or by a company executive who had a legitimate excuse to cut off your exit and extol the virtues of his latest range of products. God, how he hated these dos.

From where he stood he could see Bertie holding court conspiratorially in a corner with Guy D'Arcy and a couple of regional hacks. He wondered what they were talking about. He also wondered again just what Bertie knew about Lisa Drake, but convinced himself that it was nothing more than malicious speculation. Lisa wasn't the only person at Northcountry Television who gave him the eye – it was something he was learning to live with. But why should Bertie pick on her?

He tried to banish all these thoughts from his mind as he turned to enter the mêlée, but his arm caught someone standing directly behind him. In the fraction of a second it takes fizzy mineral water to leave an upturned glass Rob felt liquid soaking through his shirt for the second time in less than twenty-four hours.

"Oh, God, I'm so sorry."

Rob looked up from brushing the water off his clothes to see a bright-faced girl with open features and freckles, her fair hair tied neatly into a French plait that reached her shoulders. She had the clearest cornflower blue eyes he'd ever seen and wore a checked jacket over a cream top and dark brown trousers.

"No. Don't worry, it was my fault. I should have looked where I was going. And it's only water, not red wine. I'll dry out in a minute." He grinned at her and took a glass of orange juice from a passing tray, along with another glass of mineral water.

"You'd better have this – there's nothing much left in yours now." Then he thought he'd better introduce himself. "Rob MacGregor from Northcountry Television."

"I think I know that already. In fact, you're the only person here that I do know – by sight I mean."

Rob smiled. "It's good to meet you . . ." he glanced down at the badge on her lapel ". . . Rebecca."

"Rebecca Fleming. My friends call me Bex. I write for the *Worcester Star* and I do a bit of TV in Birmingham. I don't normally come to these things. Well, to tell you the truth, I'm not normally invited. This is my first biggie." She looked around the room, uneasily. "They're a bit daunting, aren't they? A bit grand."

"To be honest I can't stand them. The trouble is, you feel you've got to come or it looks as though you don't care," admitted Rob.

"Anyway it's good to meet you," she said. "I like your stuff."

"I'm very flattered."

"Well, we needed someone of our generation to give gardening a decent image. It's been dusty for too long."

"So how did *you* get into this lark?" Rob asked.

"Oh, the usual way." They were interrupted by a waiter carrying a tray of glasses that held champagne and Buck's fizz. Bex shook her head. "Champagne at this time in the morning and I'll be asleep by lunch-time," she said. "In answer to your question, I got into this lark when I started work on my dad's nursery in Somerset."

"That's funny. I did the same only in Yorkshire," said Rob. "What then?"

"Oh, the usual thing – college, then Kew Gardens."

"Well, I really shouldn't be speaking to you," said Rob.

"Why?"

"Edinburgh man."

She laughed, an easy relaxed laugh, and he noticed that, as she did, two deep dimples appeared in her cheeks. "Oh, well, in gatherings like this we botanic-garden lot had better stick together," she said cheerfully.

"Are you still working for your father?"

"No, I manage a local garden centre now apart from the bits of writing and local telly."

"Do you enjoy it?" he asked.

"Oh, it's fun, but I could do with a bit of a change in the day job."

"You've never thought of doing the writing and the telly full-time?" asked Rob.

"Never had enough of it to earn a living," said Bex. "I'd love to if I could. Maybe one day."

Rob liked her. She was easy company, light-hearted and with no apparent hang-ups.

"Well, most of this lot manage to do it," he said, looking around the room. "How ambitious are you?"

"Oh, I'm keen to do what I want to do, but I'm not driven. I think that's my problem. I love the work, I love the plants, but I've no career plan."

"Don't apologize," said Rob. "There's enough naked ambition in this room to make up for your lack of it. But you really should think about it. Someone like you, I mean someone as good-looking as you, could make a killing in this business. Sorry. Was that a bit offensive?"

"My turn to be flattered," she said, with a giggle. "Are you ambitious, then?" she added, looking up at him.

"I suppose I am." He paused. "But I can't be doing with all the backbiting that goes on. I've been lucky so far. I love my job and I'm doing exactly what I want to do, but I couldn't say I was ruthlessly single-minded. I'm still too crazy about plants to be bothered with meeting the right people and being in the right place at the right time. Stupid, really, isn't it?"

"Level-headed I call it," replied Bex. "Anyway, who are all these people?"

"You don't know any of them?" he asked.

"Well, I see Guy D'Arcy's over there. A real womanizer."

Rob raised his eyebrows.

"All right, so *I'm* being offensive now, but he does rather fancy himself, doesn't he?"

"You might say that but I couldn't possibly comment." Rob's mouth stretched in its crooked grin. "So who else *don't* you recognize?"

"Well, I've seen Bertie Lightfoot before, but I'm not a fan. When you've grown up with a father who had a real Somerset accent Bertie Lightfoot's rolling Rs are a bit hard to take. And, anyway, he keeps having digs at you on screen and I don't like that."

"You've noticed."

"Hard not to. Does he have a bit of a problem with you?"

"Yes, I think he does, but I'm blowed if I know why."

"I'd have thought it was pretty obvious, really. You've taken his programme from under his nose. I suppose you've put it out of joint."

"Yes, but he was OK at the beginning. It's only lately that he's been a bit sharp."

"Seen the writing on the wall, I suppose."

"Do you know that little group, over there in the corner?"

Bex craned her neck to see. "Mmm . . . nope. Not at all."

"They're the radio lot. The stars of *Up the Garden Path*, or, as it's come to be known lately, *Gardeners' Ego Time*."

She laughed. "Why?"

"Well, if you think Bertie Lightfoot has a bit of a problem with me, then you've clearly never heard about what goes on in *Up the*

Garden Path. They stick together at dos like this but they all hate one another. There's the fellow with the white hair for a start."

"The one with the bristly moustache?"

"That's him. Conrad Mecklenburg. One-time biochemist with an ego the size of a nuclear reactor. Cultivates the image of a mad scientist. His father was a Moravian prince so he expects every man to bow to him and every woman to . . . Well, you can guess. He can't stand the fellow on his left, Sid Garside, vegetable grower from Blackpool. Famous for his parsnips. His recipe for liquid manure is a closely guarded secret."

She chortled. "You're not serious."

"Deadly. You see the woman next to Sid?"

She nodded.

"Wendy Wooster. The only woman Conrad wouldn't make a pass at. He's very unkind about her. Refers to her as Miss Menopause. No one's ever seen her legs. Greenhouse expert at that difficult time of life."

"Oh dear," said Bex.

"Who else?" he asked himself, scanning the room. "Ah, well, there's the fellow over there with the headband in the linen suit and canvas shoes – Dave Philimore, the organic king. You've heard of him?"

"Only that he pees on his compost heap every night."

"And morning, even when there's a nip in the air. Wendy Wooster has a crush on him. Dying to get him into her conservatory. She's having trouble with her melons and thinks he's the only man who can sort her out."

Bex gave him a withering look. "Do you think he'd like to try?" She turned in the direction of Dave Philimore. "No, probably not. Anyway, if he's the organic king why is he here at a chemical bash?"

"Well, they're supposed to be launching some new product that's as good as organic so I expect they want his approval. Bet you anything he won't give it. No one's won him over yet."

"Who are the ladies over there?" She pointed to a small group of grey-haired women in tweeds and pearls.

"They're referred to as the Trust Fund. All very big in the National Trust – upmarket bunch."

"Aren't you a fan of the National Trust, then?" asked Bex.

"I'm the biggest fan they've got. I think they do a great job, but they've still got a bit of an image problem because they always seem to be represented by county types. You know the sort, Colonel and Mrs Satin-Buttocks."

"So who are those three?"

"Felicity Fortescue runs Dickers, the garden in Devon that's had all the publicity lately – mainly because it's just reopened after restoration, but partly because the head gardener ran off with the female landscape architect to set up a nursery on the Isle of Skye. Felicity is a bit yock-yock, but she can root anything."

"And the short dumpy one?"

"Emma Coalport. Writes the sort of books middle-class ladies adore. Something of an expert on colour. A Vita Sackville-West disciple. Knew her, too. In the biblical sense, some say. Has breath that could fell a Gladiator. Why am I telling you all this? I sound worse than Nigel Dempster."

"I'm beginning to think you *are* Nigel Dempster. And I thought you were such a nice man!"

"You mustn't believe all you read. I'm dreadful, really. If you breathe a word about any of this I'll be shot."

"Who by?"

"My girlfriend, for a start. She edits the local paper and she's taught me to be very careful about what I say and to whom I say it."

"Well, you're safe with me. It's been great fun. Do you think we ought to go through? They seem to be moving into the room next door."

"Come on, then," said Rob, and walked with his new-found friend into the large room that led off the reception area. Here they would be regaled with the latest exciting developments of Amalgamated Agricultural Chemicals. He could hardly wait.

*

Guy, Bertie and the coterie that had surrounded them sat on the front row of padded and gilded seats in the elegant room, whose great swags of turquoise velvet curtains had been drawn to keep out the weak winter sun. Spotlights illuminated five men and a scarlet-suited middle-aged woman seated behind the long table at the far end, whose pure white damask cloth was dotted with bottles of Buxton spring mineral water. An ironic touch, thought Rob, bearing in mind the company's less than sparkling track record when it came to river pollution.

He and Bex slid in at the back of the room at the end of a row, but in spite of their surreptitious entry Rob noticed that the largest of the five men had looked over in his direction and nodded at him. Rob had not met Sir Freddie Roper before, but he acknowledged him with a weak smile.

Guy looked over his shoulder to identify the recipient of Sir Freddie's greeting, saw that it had been Rob and, without any change of expression, turned his eyes once more to the front, running his hand through his thick fair hair to pull it back, temporarily, from his high forehead.

The chandeliers above them dimmed, allowing the spotlights to highlight the five grey suits, and Sir Freddie, as chairman of the proceedings, and of the company, rose to speak. The lady in red looked at him admiringly.

"Ladies and gentlemen, welcome to the Dorchester Hotel. It's my pleasure, as chairman of AAC, to pave the way for the announcement of what I'm sure you will find to be an exciting and quite unique breakthrough in the world of plant protection . . ." Rob sighed and glanced sideways at Bex, who looked back at him and raised her eyebrows.

Sir Freddie, his index fingers now pushed into the pockets of his ample pin-striped waistcoat like a farmer boasting about his prize pig, warmed to his subject and continued in a northern accent that had had the corners knocked off it in the interests of deputy lord-lieutenantship (West Yorkshire). Every now and again, he let himself down by falling over a vowel. Here, thought Rob, was the big-business equivalent of Helena Sampson's Mrs Ipplepen. Woe betide Sir Freddie if he had to say the word 'pluck' or 'duck', or ask a neighbour for a cup of sugar. Bearing in mind the subject of today's speech, the first two words were unlikely to feature, and the latter request had probably never been uttered since Sir Freddie had made his fortune with the abattoir he had founded back in the fifties. Rob brought his eyes down from the gilt and stuccoed ceiling and back to the man.

"For many years now AAC has been at the cutting edge of pesticide manufacture. In fact, I think I can say that our name stands out in the chemical business . . ."

"You can say that again," whispered Rob, softly in the direction of Bex's ear. She grinned and put her finger to her lips.

"Our scientists have been deeply conscious of the public's concern with the environment, and we at AAC have endeavoured to match that concern with our own painstaking research into more ecologically friendly products."

Sir Freddie's round, rosy face beamed a touch too smugly in the direction of the Trust Fund, but this was a man who enjoyed an audience and whose inability to embarrass himself was matched only by his ability to cause unease in others. The three ladies exchanged self-conscious glances. Bex looked at the floor. Rob looked again at the ceiling, and then remembered that he ought to try to look politely interested even if he was becoming slightly irritated.

Sir Freddie, his platitudinous preliminaries finished, proceeded to hand over "to one of our boffins – the lads who have been beavering away in the backroom" to explain the "exciting and quite unique breakthrough".

A thin, pale-faced man with a pale tweed suit and a pale grey moustache lurched nervously to his feet, coughed and riffled through the papers in front of him. "Er, thank you, Sir Freddie," he muttered, staring through his wire-rimmed spectacles to left and right across the room, as though he were a child looking for a lost parent. "The world of plant protection is complex and ever changing." He shifted his weight from one foot to another. "To stay at the forefront in such a volatile business it is necessary for research to be continuous and on-going." A dry cough. "New products need to be developed to cater for the ever more sophisticated needs of a growing market, not only on a commercial scale but also within the domestic scene. It is in this particular area that our latest product will make its mark."

Rob noticed that the man hardly looked up from his notes, such was his discomfort.

"For many years now we have been searching for a product that will satisfy three basic criteria – a broad spectrum of control over pests and diseases, and an environmentally friendly approach to those insects that are beneficial to the gardener. Added to this, it is important, from the gardener's point of view, that control is long-lasting. This new product fulfils all three of these requirements. It will kill a broad range of pests – from aphids and whitefly, to red spider mite, mealy bug and scale insects – as well as fungal and bacterial diseases. It will then keep them all under control for an entire season, while leaving beneficial insects, such as ladybirds and bees, unharmed."

There was an audible murmur about the room. Rob looked quizzically at Bex. "Sounds interesting," he whispered.

"I didn't think it was possible," she replied. "Not for years yet, anyway."

The edgy scientist proceeded to regale his audience with the chemical components of the new product, in terms vague enough to put other companies off the scent, and gave details of the comprehensive tests that had been carried out to prove its efficacy.

"This new product will be available to gardeners this spring. In May, in fact. It will transform pest and disease control as we know it, rendering obsolete a whole armoury of pesticides and fungicides. From this spring onwards the gardener will need only one product to make sure that his flowers, fruits and vegetables remain pest- and disease-free throughout the year. Thank you." He sat down, relieved, and wiped his now glistening forehead with an off-white handkerchief.

The room hummed with the muttered asides of the assembled company. Guy cast a conspiratorial sideways look at Bertie, while the *Up the Garden Path* team swapped anxious glances, aware that half their questions about pest problems were going to evaporate in the face of the new product.

Sir Freddie Roper rose to his feet. "Yes, ladies and gentlemen, I can understand your excitement. Such developments occur only rarely in the field of plant protection and it is understandable that you should be so enthusiastic about our new product. As you can imagine, we're pretty excited about it ourselves -"

"Can I ask a question?"

Sir Freddie was cut off in mid-flood. "I'm sorry?" His eyes scanned the room and lighted, eventually, on David Philimore, the organic king.

"Yes, Mr Philimore?"

"This new product."

"Yes?"

"Is it organic?"

"Well, it's been tested thoroughly and been found to be perfectly safe and reliable and, as you've heard, it's -"

"Yes, but is it organic?"

"Not exactly, but then, as we've explained -"

"Bloody typical. Another cop-out. Spraying your noxious crap around as though there's no tomorrow. You'll realize one day that the only way forward is with nature. I can't believe you lot can carry on being so irresponsible."

He leaped to his feet, stormed to the back of the room and out of the door. Wendy Wooster looked wistfully in his direction, not sure whether to follow. She thought better of it, stayed put, crossed her legs and bit her lip.

Sir Freddie, endeavouring to pour oil on the troubled waters, carried on. "Well, well, Mr Philimore will put his point, won't he?"

(At this point Bertie turned to Guy and whispered in his ear,

"Stupid little sod. Does it every year just to make sure he gets the coverage in his paper. I wouldn't mind but he'll be driving back to Essex in his V12 Jaguar with bugger all thought for the environment.")

Rob said, "Oh, Lord," and buried his head in his hands. Bex looked bewildered. "Don't take any notice," he said. "He only does it to attract attention," then smirked to let her know that they were all used to Philimore's outbursts, even if Sir Freddie did not quite know how to deal with them.

Sir Freddie motored on with his speech, endeavouring to make up for the hesitancy of the scientist. "Such a product needs to be brought to the attention of the public in a manner befitting its importance. To give you details of the specially planned campaign, here is our PR adviser Simon Clay." He sat down, happy, for once, to let someone else step into the spotlight.

A thirty-something arty type in green-framed frog-like glasses with a nattily cut navy-blue suit and lemon waistcoat got up – the exact opposite of the pale-suited boffin who was now examining the contents of his handkerchief.

"Hi. Well, folks, it promises to be the development of the century for gardeners. One spray that will take care of their garden for a whole season. Handily packed, easy to apply and competitively priced, it makes for peace of mind in every gardening family. No more epidemics while the family are away on holiday. No more ruined crops. Goodbye, greenfly, so-long, scale insects, *auf wiedersehen*, aphids, and bye-bye, blackspot."

Rob winced and Bex giggled quietly. The lady in red shot Simon Clay a withering look.

"With your help," he continued, "by the start of this year's growing season every British gardener will be clamouring to get their hands on this panacea for plants. As you can imagine, the launch for this new product will be high-profile. We plan a combined TV, radio and national press campaign that will leave no one in any doubt that our new product is the one thing they can't be without. But what to call it? We thought long and hard about

111

this, and came to the conclusion that there was really only one name that could be applied to a product that promises long-term control of all these garden problems."

The advertising man turned to the shrouded pyramid behind him and placed his hand on the corner of the green fabric that, as yet, hid the logo of the new product. As he spoke he grasped the corner and pulled away the concealing folds to reveal the name in all its glory, emblazoned on a mountain of red and green cartons. "Ladies and gentlemen, we proudly present the answer to a gardener's prayer – BLITZ."

The mixture of oohs and ahs that greeted his announcement was more muted than that provided by the audience of a TV quiz show who have just been told about tonight's star prize, but as everyone overcame their professional restraint, the gentle clapping that followed quickly built into a crescendo of applause – for most people, that is. The Trust Fund ladies were restrained, while Wendy Wooster sat guiltily silent, and the *Up the Garden Path* team were stern-faced, yet clapping robustly.

For the third time, Sir Freddie heaved his body to its feet and indicated that a buffet lunch and drinks would be served in the adjacent room where the company executives would be pleased to answer any questions informally. A press release would be available to everyone before they left.

Chairs rumbled backwards and the horticultural hacks spoke excitedly as they made their way towards the longed-for refreshments.

Rob drew breath to speak to Bex but was prevented from saying anything because a large hand slapped down on his shoulder. He turned round to identify its owner and came nose to bibulous nose with Sir Freddie.

"Mr MacGregor. Do you mind if we have a word?"

"No, not at all," responded Rob. And then, to Bex, "I'll see you in a minute. OK?"

"OK," she said, and turned to join the exiting masses.

*

Half an hour later Rob had still not appeared from the adjacent room and Bex, who had devoured enough canapés to assure the puff-pastry industry of a healthy future, decided she would slip out of the hotel and home to reality.

She squeezed past Bertie Lightfoot who, glass in hand, was swaying perilously from side to side and holding forth on the benefits of facelifts for men, and noticed that Guy D'Arcy had now distanced himself from his erstwhile companion and was chatting up another executive. He seemed to be working his way through them. She saw that his eyes kept raking the room for a person he evidently could not see. He smiled vaguely in her direction as a reflex reaction but his mind was clearly on business, not pleasure.

Bex remembered she still had a few questions she wanted to ask about this revolutionary new product. She couldn't leave yet. She looked around for the back-room boffin. There were half a dozen grey-suited men full of bonhomie who were singing the praises of BLITZ to anyone who would listen, but the scientist seemed to have left early. Shame. Clearly not a people person. She retrieved her Barbour from the cloakroom and glanced around once more, in the hope now of saying goodbye to her new-found acquaintance. He was nowhere to be seen.

She walked down the Dorchester's steps and caught a cab to Euston.

Chapter 12

Soft amber light flooded from the lower windows of End Cottage as Rob parked his car alongside the old stone wall by the riverbank and walked through the rickety front gate. He was glad. The thought of spending the rest of the evening on his own with the events of the day milling around in his head did not appeal. His spirits rose as he clicked open the ancient iron sneck and breathed in the aroma of warm bread and eastern spices.

"Hi!" he called, poking his head round the door.

"Hi!" she replied, and came towards him, smiling, with flour on her nose.

He wiped it off with his finger, licked it, said, "Mmmmm!" and took her in his arms, pressing his face into her soft, warm, fragrant neck. "I missed you," he mumbled.

"And I missed you, too," she said, her upturned face, eyes closed, wearing an ecstatic smile.

They squeezed one another, forgetting their recent troubles, and then he stepped back to look at her – shiny dark hair pulled back from her face, cheeks flushed from the heat of the kitchen, and her body encased in a black woollen sweater and white jeans. Her neat bare feet sported scarlet nail polish that made him smile.

"What is it?" she asked.

"Just looking at your cherries," he said.

"What's the matter with them?"

"Nothing at all, they're very pretty."

"Well, I did them especially for you."

"I'm glad. Is there anything to drink?"

"That's it, then, is it? Loving bit over, thank you very much, now where's my supper?" She turned away in mock disgust and walked towards the dresser.

"Oh, I'll make it up to you later – I've got stuff to tell you. What a day. You wouldn't believe it."

"Try me," she replied, returning with a bottle of Fleurie and a corkscrew, and pushing both into his outstretched hands.

Without taking off his coat he attacked the cork, pulled it out with a squeak and a plop, and poured two large glasses of the deep ruby wine. Giving one to Katherine and raising his own in the air, he said, "Here's to . . . whatever."

"Us," she said. He clinked her glass with his own before they both took a sip. They sighed in unison.

"Mmm," said Katherine. "I needed that. What took you so long? And what do you mean by 'What a day'?"

Rob put down his glass, slipped off his coat and jacket and pulled off his tie. "Where do I start?"

"Well," said Katherine, "let's follow Julie Andrews's recommendation. At the very beginning."

They sat at the scrubbed-pine table with a cluster of candles in the centre as Rob unfolded the events of the day, including his encounter with Bertie on the train and his acquaintanceship with Bex Fleming.

"Pretty?" asked Katherine.

"Very," replied Rob.

"Watch it!" she warned.

Rob laughed a touch too loudly and assured Katherine that a Torvill and Dean relationship was all that this friendship promised.

He recounted the events of the press briefing, told her who had been there, described the amazing claims being made for the new product, and then paused.

"Is that it?" she asked.

"Not quite. I was just about to push off when Sir Freddie Roper and a couple of his cronies collared me and took me into a room next door."

"What for?"

"They want me to front the advertising campaign for BLITZ."

"What?" Katherine's eyes widened in disbelief, then narrowed as her face hardened. "You said no, of course."

"I said very little. Except that I'd think about it."

"You said you'd think about it? Putting yourself in the pocket of a chemical company whose environmental record is second only to Attila the Hun?" The vibration of the table when she got up almost registered on the Richter scale and her pink cheeks turned carmine.

"Steady. I just wanted to talk to you about it before I did anything."

"Well, you knew what I'd say." She crossed to the stove and stirred a saucepan.

"Yes, I did. But I wanted you to be *able* to say it before I did anything."

She turned to face him, with a wooden spoon in her hand, looking chastened. "Sorry. I'm sorry." Then she became inquisitive. "But what will you do?"

"I'll run everything over in my mind, including the amount of money it would have made me, and then I'll . . . gracefully decline."

"Are you sure?" she asked.

"No. Not at all." He took another sip of the warm red wine and let it run over his tongue.

"Why?"

He swallowed. "It's a real quandary. Point number one: I am being offered a ludicrous sum of money by a chemical company who have done enough damage to the environment already. Answer: Turn them down flat."

"And point number two?" Katherine looked up from her stirring.

"My dad's nursery has just been flooded and he has lost more than he can afford. Answer: Accept the offer. Point number three:

If I took the job, how can I be an impartial TV gardener and recommend whatever I want to recommend if I'm in the pocket of some commercial company? Even if they are paying me a mint."

"How much?" she asked gently, walking back to the table and sitting next to him.

"Well, Liz reckons we'd be talking about a six-figure sum."

"No!" She pushed back her chair, which scraped on the stone-flagged floor.

"'Fraid so. I nipped in to see her after the meeting. With TV and newspaper adverts she reckoned it would come to about a quarter of a million." Rob took another reflective sip.

"Holy shit." Katherine looked stunned and stared into the middle distance, then she looked back again at Rob. "Does Liz think you should do it?"

"Oh, you know Liz."

"No, I don't."

"Well, you can guess her reaction. Very excited. 'Darling, sit down and listen. We're talking about a lot of money. Think very carefully before you turn it down.' But she did see my point when it came to keeping my nose clean. If I took it on, before I knew where I was I'd be advertising double-glazing and doing voice-overs for washing powder. What would happen to my gardening street cred?"

"But a quarter of a million . . ." Her voice trailed off.

"Just a minute Miss Green Pages, are you saying I should do it?"

She got up from her chair, walked round behind him, put her arms round his neck and bent down to whisper in his ear. "I'm saying, Mr MacGregor, that I think you're an absolute star for turning it down. I'm very proud of you. I know that sometimes when I go off at the deep end and don't give you a chance to get a word in edgewise you must think that I claim to have a monopoly on principles. Well, I don't. You're just about to turn down a quarter of a million quid, and if that's not a case of putting your money where your mouth is I don't know what is. I know I rattle on about my principles, but I've never been put to the test and I've never had to make that choice. You're a mega-star. And I'm sorry."

She kissed him gently on the top of his head and he leaned back towards her and smiled. "You're very kind, but I haven't yet put their money where my mouth is."

"Well, talking of mouths, what would you say to some curried prawns?" she asked.

"Hello, curried prawns," he said.

"You silly boy," she said, giggling.

Then he pulled her head down and kissed her softly on the lips.

It was midnight before they went to bed. She slid under the duvet next to him and listened to the sound of the river through the open window. Lying naked, enfolded in his arms and with her head on his chest, she felt warm and secure and wondered why they did not spend every night like this.

"Oh, there was something else," he murmured, stroking the sleek black strands of her hair which fell over her pale shoulders.

"Mmm? What's that?" she whispered.

"Liz had some more news."

"What sort of news?" Her eyes were closed, her arms wrapped round him, and she was beginning to drift off.

"They want me to present this year's Chelsea Flower Show programme."

She squeezed him and tried, vainly, to open her eyes. "There you are, you see. I told you you were a star."

He looked down at her, and noticed the contented smile spread right across her face. He could just hear her whispered words: "Who needs a quarter of a million when you've got all those lovely flowers?" And then she sighed and slid into a deep sleep.

Guy D'Arcy had not had a very good day. No one had come up and spoken to him at the Dorchester – at least, no one of any importance – and Rob MacGregor looked as though he was going to carry off the glittering prize. Added to which, Guy was stuck in a lumpy bed with Miss Pony Club 1975, in the hope of keeping his head above water and landing the contract to do her father's garden.

He would have to think of some way to make them see that *he* was the right man for the job. The only man for the job. But how? His present situation was hardly conducive to him coming up with a brilliant idea.

He looked across the pillow at her, snoring. Hair the colour of marmalade and the face of a Welsh cob. God! What a sight. He heaved her weighty leg off his body, eased the leather riding crop from her now relaxed hand and dropped it to the floor before he fell asleep.

Chapter 13

"Make those letters neat, now. I want to be able to read it when you've finished." Wayne Dibley was kneeling in front of the potting-shed door painting on it a black horizontal line and the date to mark the level of the flood water. Jock passed by with a watering-can on his way to the greenhouses.

The black line was half-way up the door, and there were other reminders all around of the river's recent misbehaviour. Mud, Wayne had discovered, was not easy to deal with. When it was wet it ran with the unpredictability of quicksilver, and when it began to dry it stuck like the proverbial shit to a blanket. The trick was to catch it with your shovel when it was half-way between the two extremes.

He stood up and admired his brushwork. Not bad. Even Jock wouldn't grumble at his printing now – pretty readable and every letter the same size.

"There's another R in February," said a voice over his shoulder. Wayne looked round to identify his critic and discovered a small man in a grey mac with crinkly grey hair and a briefcase under his arm.

Wayne turned back to the lettering. "Oh, bugger!" and then, "Sorry! I've been ages at that."

"Well, you can probably just squeeze it in between your B and your U if you don't put too big a top on it," said the man, sympathetically. "Is Jock around?"

"Yeah, he's in the far greenhouse," said Wayne, now preoccupied with his calligraphy and dipping his brush carefully into the can of black gloss paint that had an impressive row of runny drips around its rim.

"I'll go and find him, then. You must be Wayne."

Wayne looked up from his kneeling position. "Yeah, that's right."

"I'm Stan Halfpenny, Jock's accountant."

"Oh. Great name for an accountant," said Wayne, his face at last breaking into a grin.

"And it's not the first time I've been told that," said Stan, moving off in the direction of the greenhouses. "See you later."

Wayne took up his brush once more and, tongue poking out from between his teeth, he crafted his final letter.

Jock was tapping the clay pots of some cinerarias with a wooden cotton reel fastened to the end of a piece of bamboo when Stan opened the door of the old greenhouse and walked down the flagstone path. "What are you doing? Testing them for dry rot?" he asked.

"No. I'm seeing if they're dry."

"With a hammer?"

"Tricky blighters. Keep them too dry and the leaves start to curl and crisp. Keep them too wet and they'll wilt and die. This way, when the compost is damp enough you hear a dull thud, and when it's dry the pot rings – like this." He rapped the cotton-reel mallet against a pot that sported a green dome of leaves covered in a rash of blue and white daisy flowers. It rang out as though it were made of bone china.

"Clear as a bell," said Jock, and he pushed the narrow spout of the watering can up under the rosette of downy leaves and tipped out the water.

"I thought you didn't go in for things as common as house plants?" remarked Stan.

"I don't. I just like to grow a few cinerarias because they're tricky. I like to prove to myself that I've still got the knack."

Stan saw his opening. "Yes, well, you've definitely got the knack of growing plants. It's the other knacks of the business that I'm worried about."

Jock looked up from his watering. "What do you mean?"

"I've just been doing the books."

"I know you have. What's the problem?"

"The problem, old chap," said Stan, knitting the bushy grey eyebrows that matched his hair and his mac, "is that you have what people in this day and age call a cash-flow problem."

"I don't owe anybody anything," snapped Jock, defensively. "You know I always pay my bills the day they come in."

"Yes, you do – in spite of the fact that I've suggested, time and again, that you wait thirty days before settling any account."

"Madge always paid on the nail and I've continued to do the same. Is that why I've got a problem?"

"Not exactly. The main cause of it is that not much seems to have been coming in lately. Your bank accounts are in the black but they're on the low side and you don't seem to have much put by. When Madge was doing your books it was easy to see just what was happening. Your incomings and outgoings were set in columns, but all I get from you is this." He clicked open the brass clasp on his fat leather briefcase and pulled out a battered buff envelope stuffed with receipts. "It doesn't seem to add up."

Jock put down his watering-can and the mallet. "Well, Madge had the time to do all the book-keeping. I don't. But I give you all the receipts."

"Yes, but judging by what's left at the end of every month you must have more outgoings than I can see from the bills. I know you have to pay young Wayne's wages now, but they're not excessive. It seems to me that your takings have been drastically lower this year than they have previously."

"Stan, are you suggesting I'm on the fiddle?"

"My dear chap, that's the last thing I'd suggest. If I had to choose between you and George Washington in the honesty stakes he'd come a poor second. It's just that I'm a bit baffled as to why your funds are so low."

"It's the middle of winter. Trade's always slack in February. You'll have to bear with me. Things will look up," said Jock, picking up his mallet and tapping at his cinerarias once more.

Stan watched the old man at his work, a cloth cap on his head and a faded denim apron covering his old brown cardigan and baggy corduroy trousers. His feet were encased in an ancient pair of black leather boots. He was fond of Jock. They'd never socialized over the years, but his occasional visits to the nursery had resulted in an easy-going relationship, which seemed, now, to be under some strain. Stan smoothed his soft clean hand over his hair. "I was speaking to Dennis Wragg yesterday."

Jock cleared his throat warningly then carried on with his mallet, refusing to look up at the mention of a name that, in his mind, ranked on a par with Himmler or Dr Crippen.

Stan braved the iciness of the atmosphere, fishing for clues. "He still wants to buy you out, in spite of the flood."

"Does he now?" muttered Jock, tapping even more ferociously.

"He says that once in sixty years is not very frequent for a river to burst its banks, and a protective wall would be easy to build."

Jock didn't answer, but bent down and dunked the watering-can into a large tank of rainwater beneath the bench. It gurgled and glugged as the cool, clear water filled to its galvanized brim. Jock hauled it out, with some difficulty, and resumed his task as though he were alone.

Stan refused to be beaten and sought an olive branch. "I know you can't stand him, but he might be offering you a way out of this situation."

"Yes, and on what terms?" retorted Jock, still not meeting the eye of his questioner.

"Well, I know he'll expect a reduction in price due to the flood damage but it would get you out of a tricky spot."

"No, thanks." Jock's reply was brief. Dennis Wragg's reaction to the flood was as insensitive as he had expected – and Jock's response was exactly what Stan had expected. He knew that he'd taken this conversation as far as he could.

"Well, I'll be off, then. I'll leave you to your tapping."

Jock set his jaw and carried on with his work.

Stan walked back down the path of the old Victorian greenhouse, admiring the cinerarias on the gravel-covered benches to left and right and wondering how a man who was so good at the difficult job of growing plants could be so hopeless at understanding the simple workings of a profit-and-loss account. He paused at the door of the white-painted greenhouse, wrapped his fingers around the shiny brass knob and turned back with the intention of bidding his client, and friend, farewell. But the right words failed him.

Jock heard the door close, put down his watering-can and mallet, and looked through the condensation on the glass to see his accountant walking back up the nursery path.

Katherine had left End Cottage at half past eight, having shared a shower with Rob and torn herself away for her editorial meeting at nine. Rob had wolfed down a bowl of cereal and worked out the contents of the following day's programme before ringing up Steve Taylor to confirm the running order. He'd had an hour in his garden – enough to get it sorted at this time of year – another hour and a half at his word-processor, tapping out his weekly piece for the paper, and then decided to nip over and see the old man.

Stan Halfpenny greeted him at the gate of the nursery. "Hello, Rob. Nice day for a change."

"Hello, Stan. Great, isn't it? Good to see a bit of blue sky after all that rain."

"Yes. Blue sky. Lovely," said Stan, raising his eyes absent-mindedly to the heavens. "Lovely."

Rob saw the accountant's distracted look and felt the need to probe further. "What's the problem?"

Like father, like son, thought the accountant. He'd faced that question twice in ten minutes. He hesitated, unsure what to say.

"You would tell me if everything wasn't OK, wouldn't you?" asked Rob.

"What do you mean?"

"Stan, you've been Dad's accountant longer than I've been his son."

"I know." Stan reflected as he looked around at the familiar nursery. He'd been coming here since the days of one old greenhouse and a potting-shed in the days when S. W. Halfpenny FCA had just had the windows of his new office in town painted with gilded initials.

"I know you pride yourself on your confidentiality, but I am the old man's son and if something was bothering you you would tell me, wouldn't you?"

Stan looked him in the eye. "If something was bothering me I wouldn't know whether to tell you or not."

"If it meant the difference between Dad sinking or swimming, then I think you probably should."

Stan rested his briefcase on the wall and gave Rob a succinct, if circumspectly vague, indication of the state of his father's accounts, before apologetically picking up his case and walking back to his car.

Rob looked after the small, grey-macked figure as it trudged up the lane, then he turned through the gate and walked down the mud-spattered path to the potting-shed, where Wayne was blowing hard at the paint on the door.

"Oh, very neat," said Rob. "Won't it dry?"

"I just don't want it to drip or Mr MacGregor will give me a right earful," Wayne confessed.

Mr MacGregor probably has his mind on other things right now, thought Rob.

"Well, at least you've spelt February correctly," he offered encouragingly, eyeing Wayne's artistry. Wayne looked suitably smug. "Crikey, the mud's still a bit whiffy."

"Er, I don't think it's all down to the mud," said Wayne, tilting his head in the direction of the small room next door to the potting-shed.

They looked at each other and muttered, in unison, "Harry." Then laughed.

"Where's Dad?" asked Rob.

"He's in the far greenhouse," said Wayne.

"I gather he's just had a visitor."

"Yeah," answered Wayne. "He didn't stay long, though. Only here for a few minutes."

"So I gather. I'll go and see how the old man is."

Rob walked across the nursery in the direction of the greenhouses, looking to left and right at the gradually improving scene. Most of the clearing up had been down to Wayne, he reckoned. Harry might have shaken a broom at the mud now and again but he would have been unlikely to have made much of an impact on the devastation. But perhaps this devastation was only a taste of things to come.

He looked down towards the river, friendly and docile now, though the flotsam of dried grass and leaves in the branches of the trees showed how high the water had been. A pied wagtail hopped from stone to stone at the water's edge, its tail flicking up and down as it foraged for food.

He opened the door of the greenhouse. His father was at the far end, restaging the cinerarias.

"Every plant has a front and a back," offered Rob.

"I'm glad you haven't forgotten," said his father, without looking up.

"Some things you never forget. How are you doing?"

"I'm fine."

Jock still didn't meet his eye.

"I've just bumped into Stan Halfpenny," said Rob, as casually as he could.

"Nice for you."

Rob was surprised at the ice in his father's reply.

Jock went on, "And what did he have to say? Has he told you about the state of the business?"

"He didn't want to, but I think he understood why I needed to know."

"So he told you what he advised me, did he? That's it's time I sold out to Dennis Wragg and got this old liability off my back. Told you I haven't got a cash-flow, or whatever it is. Mentioned that the books aren't done like your mother used to do them."

Rob felt a churning in the pit of his stomach. Just as he thought his father had turned the corner another blow had been landed on him and he was beginning to buckle.

"This is my business. It's always been my business – mine and your mother's."

The old man's voice broke. A cineraria slipped from his hands on to the flagged path, its pot smashing into a hundred shards of terracotta and its perfect dome of velvety green leaves crumpling under the weight of the damp compost.

"Damn!" Jock turned away and held on to the edge of the staging, then pushed his cap to the back of his head before removing it and wiping his eyes with his forearm.

"I'm sorry, Dad. Dad?" Rob walked slowly towards his father. "I just wanted to help." Jock's shoulders heaved and he stuffed his hand silently into his pocket for a large white handkerchief, which he shook out then used to blow his nose loudly. Rob stood next to him, waiting, his hand on the old man's shoulder.

"Oh dear," murmured Jock, trying to hold back an old man's tears. "Oh dear, oh dear. What a mess. What a bloody mess." He blew his nose again, then gazed out through the glass of the greenhouse at the nursery beyond, stuffing the lump of damp linen back into his pocket. "I've got so wound up in this place that I can't see the light sometimes."

"What's happened?" asked Rob.

Jock fought to pull himself together, aware of the panic that might be rising in his son. "Oh, don't worry. It's nothing dishonest.

127

I've just been less than careful, which is not something you'd ever expect a Scot to admit."

"What do you mean?" asked Rob, gently.

Jock wiped his eyes with the back of his gnarled hand, then turned to look at his son. "It's Harry."

"What do you mean?"

"Oh, he's been having problems."

Rob's mind went blank. "What sort of problems?"

"He's been living with his sister for years now. She's even older than he is. Their house is rented. A fairly modest amount. Or rather it was. The lease came up for renewal and the landlord decided to increase the rent. He wanted to bring it in line with the rest of his property. A small fortune. Harry knew he couldn't afford to pay it so he told his sister they would have to move. The old lady went doolally. She kept waking up at nights and started rambling, went off her food."

Jock rubbed his hand across his stubbly chin to wipe it dry and Rob heard the rasp of his grey whiskers. "The doctor warned Harry that she couldn't take this kind of upheaval at her age. Some folk in their eighties are adaptable and some aren't, he said. Harry's sister fell into the last group. Harry came and asked me about it. He didn't know what to do. I told him not to worry and said that I'd pay the increased rent but he wouldn't hear of it. Even Harry has his pride."

"So what happened?"

"I went round to see the landlord. Explained what effect it was having on the old lady."

"And what did he say?"

"Not much. Tough as old boots. Heartless bugger. Said it wasn't his problem. Didn't seem to care if they ended up on the streets. As far as he was concerned the house was part of his income and he wasn't a charity. Life was tough, he said. If they paid the new rent they could stay, if they didn't, they'd have to leave. Simple as that."

"I think I know the rest," said Rob. "You pay their extra rent without Harry knowing, don't you?"

"It was the only way round it. The only way that Harry could save face and his sister could live out the rest of her days in peace. She's eighty-six, for God's sake. Eighty-six! I told Harry that the landlord had said that the two of them could have another five years at the same rent and then he'd think again. Harry seemed happy with that. I just put the money aside from the takings in my apron pocket. It doesn't leave me much at the end of the week but I can manage. I keep all my receipts and everything's declared."

"Except the rent?"

"Except the rent."

"Oh, Dad," said Rob. "What am I going to do with you? You're so kind." His eyes filled. "And I wouldn't have anybody else for a dad."

"Now don't start that," said Jock, clearing his throat. "We've had enough emotion over the last few weeks to last us a lifetime. Let's just try and get on with things and hope we come out the other side OK. It's been a long, hard winter but spring's coming and trade will quicken up. The money will start coming in soon. It's nothing to worry about. I'll go and put the kettle on," and with that he walked out of the greenhouse towards the smell of new paint.

Rob bent down to pick up the shattered cineraria. The plant was beyond recovery; its stem had snapped clean in two and its pot seemed to have shattered into a quarter of a million pieces. At least a quarter of a million.

Chapter 14

Rob wound down the Fiesta's windows to allow the fresh morning air to whistle through his hair. With any luck it might help to clear his head. He'd said nothing to his father about the offer he would now find it hard to refuse, knowing what the old man's reaction would be. But if things were as bad as Stan Halfpenny had suggested, it wouldn't be long before some kind of action had to be taken. Jock couldn't fund Harry and his sister indefinitely, and Rob couldn't stand by and watch his father bleed himself dry.

He took the moorland road. The damp tarmac glistened in the morning sun and black-faced sheep with matted grey wool nibbled at the fine grass on the roadside, baaing bleakly as he passed. Hunks of millstone grit, their surfaces blackened by centuries of smoke from the town below, towered over the purple-grey of the moor and a lone grouse scuttered up from the heather with a coarse 'go-back, go-back' and flew across the top of the thick mattress of crisp, coppery bracken.

He pulled up in a gravelly lay-by that commanded a fine view of the valley and got out to stretch his legs. The nip in the morning air almost took his breath away. Up here, amid the heather and the bracken, the troubles of the dale below seemed far away; they always did. He found it reassuring, and wondered if city folk ever had this opportunity to put their lives into perspective, to enjoy that feeling of being small and insignificant. Did they ever feel the need to?

From his lofty perch, the houses below seemed like specks of grit, and the mighty river was just a slender ribbon of silver grey, snaking its way between them.

Sweeping woodland, naked except for the deep green of Scots pine, furnished the slopes of the valley and beyond the far bend of the river lay Wharfeside Nursery, the glass of its small greenhouses twinkling like fragments of crystal in the early-morning sun. Further up he could just make out the black dot that was End Cottage and below him, larger due to its proximity, was Tarn House, whose sweeping lawns, banks of rhododendrons and curving hedge of lustrous laurel still showed signs of his activity with spade, fork and hoe.

He looked at his watch. Eleven o'clock. Coffee time at Tarn House. He thought better of it. Helena had listened to him enough of late. As his father had said, "We've had enough emotion over the last few weeks to last us a lifetime." But Sir Freddie would want an answer, and he would want it soon.

"When you're dry you can have a Bonio, but until then you lie in your basket and don't interrupt while Daddy's thinking." Bertie stopped towelling Pally's muddied feet and plopped her with her sister in the blanket-lined basket under the mahogany writing table in his red-walled, theatrically festooned study.

Gilt-framed photographs of George Robey and Bud Flanagan watched him disappear as he walked through the red-plush curtain, held back with a fat golden tassel, and took the towel into the kitchen. He dropped it in a wicker linen basket then washed his hands at the sink, using his soap-on-a-rope in the shape of a carrot. He looked out at the February garden for inspiration. "Dear God!" he said to himself. "I wish I were a fairy with a magic wand. Well, I wish I had a magic wand. Snowdrops, a few clumps, winter-flowering irises without flowers, a witch hazel, a mahonia and what else? Winter jasmine on its last legs. Oh, well, I suppose I can cobble something together out of that little nosegay."

He made himself a coffee and noticed that, as usual, Terry had methodically laid out on the worktop all the cooking utensils he would need to prepare their supper when he returned from the restaurant that evening. Just for once it irritated him. He moved a few of the things around. Put a knife back in a drawer. He didn't really know why: he just felt a need to interfere. Then he walked back down the Indian-rugged hall to his study and took down a fat book from the middle shelf. *Exotic Water Gardens*, it said, in gilt letters on the spine. Bertie laid it on his desk and opened the cover. Then he turned to page forty-three, took out the little bottle of whisky that nestled in a cut-out compartment and poured a generous tot into his mug. Ally and Pally looked up, showing the whites of their eyes. Bertie noticed. "Just Daddy's medicine. No need to look so disapproving." He took a gulp of the enriched coffee, said, "That's better," and put back *Exotic Water Gardens*, complete with its secret. He took down another volume: *The Year In Your Garden*. It was a pity that the section for February was so thin; it wouldn't help him much with his column for the *Sunday Sphere*. Still, tired old tarts couldn't be choosers. As he thumbed through the half-dozen pages looking for inspiration the phone rang.

"Honeysuckle Cottage," Bertie answered, his rustic tones in operational mode.

"Bet you haven't got any in flower, though," replied the voice at the other end.

"Mr D'Arcy." Bertie dropped his Mummerset burr and carried on, "I bet *you* haven't got any in flower either at this time of year."

"Never heard of winter-flowering honeysuckle, Bertie? Call yourself a gardener? Try saying *Lonicera fragrantissima*."

"Don't be so cheeky. What can I be a-doing for you?" asked Bertie.

"Very little, judging by yesterday's fiasco."

"Yes, that was a turn-up for the books, wasn't it?" said Bertie, nonplussed.

"What went wrong? I thought you reckoned Freddie Roper was going to be all over me?"

"Oh, no, I didn't. I just said that what he was looking for was a young, thrusting type and that you should make yourself available. It seems as though he must have found another available thruster."

"Has he asked Rob MacGregor to front the campaign, then?"

"I wouldn't know, though judging by the time they spent closeted together I wouldn't be at all surprised. I'll try and find out tomorrow. It's programme day and Mr Smarty-pants'll be in the studio most of the time. I'll get it out of him."

"Well, I shall be deeply pissed off if it's him and not me."

"You're not worried about sullying your reputation by advertising, then?"

"Can't afford principles, Bertie. Too expensive. And with that amount of money in my pocket I wouldn't have to worry about them."

"I see." Bertie smiled to himself.

"There must be some way I can get in there."

"Well, you haven't got much time. You know how fast these advertising types move."

"Yes. Faster than greased lightning. Want everything done yesterday." Guy sounded a touch impatient, as if he wanted to move on to more important things. "By the way, Bertie, who was that woman sitting at the top table at the press do?"

"Which woman?"

"Well, there was only one. Plump piece. Hair like a Barbie doll. Sitting next to that PR bloke, Clay, or whatever his name is. The woman in the red suit."

"Oh, her," said Bertie, sniffily. "She's Simon Clay's boss. Head of PR. Rather a bolshie bird. Claudia Bell. Right old bag. Can't think why they keep her on. Puts everybody's back up. I think she must have something going with Freddie."

"Married, is she?"

"Divorced. Several times. Why are you asking?"

"Oh, just curious."

"And is that what you're ringing about?" asked Bertie, getting impatient.

"Not really. It's just that I did have one piece of good news yesterday," said Guy.

"Oh, yes?" asked Bertie, his ears pricking up.

"They've asked me to present the Chelsea Flower Show programme this year. Not bad, eh? Bit of prestige at last. That should make Mr MacGregor look to his laurels."

"Ooh, I'll say," said Bertie, with a touch too much relish. "Am I allowed to drop it into the conversation tomorrow?"

"Not likely. I want the pleasure of telling him myself."

"You're really not a fan, are you?" mused Bertie.

"Not much, no."

"Why not? Why's he put your back up? I mean, he's pinched my programme from me, but what's he ever done to you?"

"Got in the way, Bertie. Smug bastard. He can't be for real, he's too good to be true. And, anyway, he's too much of a son of the soil for my liking. Just find him a pain in the arse, frankly. The ladies seem to quite like him, though. Speak to you soon. Pip-pip." And Guy rang off.

"That's all it is," said Bertie softly, replacing the receiver in its cradle and looking under the table at the two King Charles spaniels. "Just two pretty boys as jealous as hell of each other. Well, we wouldn't know anything about that, girls, would we?"

Mrs Ipplepen was the reason why Rob found himself sitting at the kitchen table at Tarn House drinking coffee. He'd intended to go straight back home and finish his piece for the *Daily Post* but she'd spotted him driving along the road, as she was on her way to make Lady Sampson's lunch, and flagged him down. How was he? How was his father? Wouldn't he come in and have a quick coffee? Lady Sampson would love to see him. He felt relieved that he had been bullied into it.

Helena was, indeed, pleased to see him. Fresh from the hairdresser, her hair an immaculately coiffed silver grey, she looked bright-eyed and almost young in well-tailored black trousers and a roll-necked sweater of charcoal grey.

They talked of the nursery's recovery and of Wayne's gilt-edged worth, and Helena asked after Harry and how he had taken the shock of it all. Rob had been about to get round to the subject of Harry when Mrs Ipplepen, a symphony in turquoise nylon, rustled her way into the kitchen bearing a quiche from the freezer.

"Vera," said Helena, "do you think there's enough for two?" And then, to Rob, "You'll stay for lunch? Or are you in a hurry?"

Before he had time to answer Mrs Ipplepen was in like a shot, "Ooh, yes, Mr Rob. It's a very big kweesh. It'd be a shame to de-thaw it just for one. An' I've got some running beans and some of Cyril's taters from the allotment."

"Well, if you're sure it's no bother?"

"No bother at all," said Helena, a relieved look on her face. "Lovely. A glass of sherry?"

"Well, I have to go back and write my Saturday piece," he offered feebly.

"A small one, then. Bound to make it flow better. I'll get it, Vera, you carry on with the quiche," and she left the two of them in the kitchen.

"I'm glad you came in, Mr Rob," said Mrs Ipplepen, speaking conspiratorially and looking over her shoulder to check that the coast was clear. "I thought she needed a bit of company. It would 'ave been Sir's birthday today."

"Oh, heavens, yes," said Rob. "I'd forgotten. Is she OK?"

"She's fine, really," replied Mrs Ipplepen. "Just a bit intraflective, if you know what I mean."

"I know," said Rob, smiling gently.

Helena came back with a sherry bottle and three glasses. "A new bottle. Jumbo's favourite. Rather appropriate today," she said brightly.

Rob crossed the kitchen to intercept her. "Here, let me," and he took the bottle from her, pulled his budding knife from his jeans pocket and began to cut away the plastic seal.

"Ah, that's what I like to see," said Helena, "a real gardener who always carries his knife in his pocket. Very impressive."

"Yes, but it's not as sharp as it should be. When I worked on Dad's nursery I could sharpen it every day on his whetstone. Now I have to do it when I call in, and when I remember, and I forgot this morning."

"Oh, so you've been in this morning?"

"Yes."

"Ooh, I bet it's a right mess," said Mrs Ipplepen, looking up from the bowl of beans she was topping and tailing by the sink.

"Glass of sherry for you, Vera?"

"Oh, no, thank you, your ladyship. If I have a drop while I'm topping and bottoming these beans I'll lose a finger."

Rob pulled out the cork and poured two glasses of the tawny liquid.

Helena raised her glass, Rob raised his, and they both said, "Cheers," quietly. Nothing more. Mrs Ipplepen busied herself with her beans.

"Vera's got some news, haven't you, Vera?"

"Ooh, 'aven't I just."

"What's that, Mrs Ipplepen?" said Rob, trying to stop his mouth from turning up at the corners.

"It's my Tiffany, Mr Rob. She's expectant."

"Oh, well done, Mrs Ipplepen. I *am* pleased for you."

"Well, it was nothing to do with me, though I did offer 'er plenty of encouragement. Eight years it's been, but that 'usband of 'ers finally got his finger out at last."

"Er, yes," said Rob, not knowing quite where to look. Helena averted her eyes, for fear of meeting his.

"Yes, you can just see the bump," Mrs Ipplepen went on.

"It must make you feel very proud," offered Rob.

"Ooh, yes. Every time I look at 'er I feel quite nocturnal."

"Vera, it was the other bit of news I was thinking of," said Helena, speaking louder than normal to drown the laughter in her voice.

"Other news?" asked Mrs Ipplepen.

"About Mrs Wragg."

"Oh, *her*," said Mrs Ipplepen, disapprovingly.

"Mrs Wragg? Gladys Wragg?" asked Rob.

"Yes, Old Glad-rags," confirmed Mrs Ipplepen, warming to her subject. "Bumped into 'er at the 'airdresser's – you know, Sharon's by the station," she said, patting her cerulean curls into shape. Rob noticed that both hair and overall had changed from shades of pink to shades of blue, but that the two were still a million miles from matching. The spectacles remained pink.

"She was cookin' under the drier and goin' on about 'er Dennis and 'is plans for expansion. Said that the nursery down by the river was their next priority and that now that it 'ad been flooded they felt as though it were an act of mercy to take it off old Mr MacGregor's 'ands."

"Did she, now?" said Rob.

"Yes. Well, I told 'er to keep 'er nose out of other people's business an' that we didn't want another big garden centre in the dale. One was quite enough."

"Good for you, Mrs Ipplepen," said Rob, raising his glass to her.

"I thought it'd stop there," she continued, "but then when she came out from under 'er drier she came over to see me under mine and gave me a right earful. No class, that woman. Flaunts 'erself around as though she's aristocratic, begging your ladyship's pardon." She nodded in the direction of her employer and flashed her a Clara Bow smile. Orange lips. "Any'ow, she starts goin' on about 'er Dennis and about 'ow 'e was a fillinfropisist for bein' considerate an' all that. Said that the land was 'ardly big enough to be worth 'is botherin' with but that 'e felt sorry for Mr MacGregor an' wanted to 'elp 'im out."

"Cheeky blighter," said Rob, and then, turning to Helena, "You see, that's what I've always found difficult to understand."

"What's that?"

"Dad's nursery is tiny. Two acres at the outside. It's not nearly big enough for Dennis Wragg to be interested in. There's no access, except for a country lane, and there's certainly no room for a car park. There's nothing I know of that would conceivably make the plot in any way desirable to an investor. Added to which it's just been flooded."

"And still he wants to buy."

"What is it about this small patch of riverside that makes Dennis Wragg so keen to have it? I just can't understand it." Rob's brow was furrowed and his sherry glass nearly empty.

"Another one?"

"No, thanks."

"Do you suppose there's some sinister reason, then?" she asked, helping herself to another half glass.

"Like what? Buried treasure?"

"I don't know. What an exciting thought! But it could be something like that."

Rob laughed.

"Oh, I know it sounds silly, but there has to be a reason why this dreadful man is determined to get his hands on Jock's nursery, and if it isn't for the obvious reasons then it has to be for hidden ones. So what are they?"

"Blowed if I know," said Rob, draining his glass.

"Maybe I'll make some enquiries," said Helena, with a sparkle in her eyes. "Jumbo had plenty of good contacts in all the right places and it's a shame to let them go to waste. Perhaps I'll be able to find out something. Anything. Anyway, I'll try. It's quite exciting, really."

"I'm glad you think so," said Rob, puzzled.

"Come on, then," said Helena, putting down her glass. "You've just time for a quick garden tour before lunch." And then, under her breath as they walked out into the hall, "We'll have to make it a quick one or those beans will be cooked to death. As far as Vera's concerned *al dente* is some kind of American gangster. Ha-ha. That was rather good, wasn't it?"

"Don't call us," said Rob, chuckling, "and we probably won't call you."

*

It was eleven thirty before Rob tramped his way up the stairs to bed at End Cottage. He looked at the clock by his bed and sighed. Half-ten was his normal turn-in time on the day before a programme, but since he'd been waylaid by Mrs Ipplepen he'd spent the rest of the day trying to catch up with himself and failing. By the time he'd brooded about his father, rung the studios and ordered the props he needed for *Mr MacGregor's Garden*, brooded some more, put away a poached egg on beans on toast, spoken to Katherine on the phone (being careful not to say anything about Jock) and completed his piece for the *Daily Post*, the day had all but gone.

He could have killed a large Scotch but thought better of it. Dumping his clothes in a heap in the corner of the bedroom and stretching his whole body so that his hands almost touched the ceiling, he walked to the bathroom to get ready for bed and found himself wishing he could slide under the duvet with Katherine again tonight. She was working late. She wouldn't want to disturb him when she came in and would sleep at Wellington Heights. But how warm she had been, and soft, and fragrant. As he lay alone in the centre of the double bed, hovering between sleep and consciousness, another figure came into his mind and his body stirred. He did his best to banish the fluttering in his stomach before finally falling into a deep sleep.

He failed to hear the telephone ring at ten to twelve, and it wasn't until early the following morning that he listened with rising panic to the single message on his answering-machine: "Hi, it's Lisa. Just to say . . . I'm missing you. And your body. That's all. Lots of love. See you soon. Ciao."

There was no message from Katherine. But then, she hadn't wanted to wake him when she got home from a frustrating day at the office at half past midnight.

Chapter 15

"Close those barn doors a bit on number twenty-four, Jeff" came the shouted instruction across the studio floor. Jeff, a tall, lanky, acne-covered lad wielding a long aluminium pole, poked and prodded at the floodlight high above him, clouting the two metal doors that acted like blinkers on either side of it until the fat man with the glasses and the light meter seemed satisfied.

Ten o'clock in the morning. The cavernous drama studio at Northcountry Television echoed to the sounds of carpentry and shouted instructions as the set for *Mr MacGregor's Garden* began to grow out of nothing. The green plastic lawn was rolled out and secured in place with stage weights. A noisy dumper truck ferried in mountains of compost to act as flower-beds and give rise to yet another fusillade of sarcastic letters asking Rob if he got his soil from Fortnum and Mason.

A potting-shed interior – or three sides of it – was being erected in one corner, and a white-raftered greenhouse, without any glass, was already complete in another, its slatted staging waiting for the primulas, the alpines and the pots of spring bulbs that would make up one of Rob's items this week.

Hefty stage-hands in grey overalls lumbered in, cradling in their Popeye arms huge rhododendrons and spotted laurels, the background shrubs that would be 'planted' in front of the trellis fence that marked the perimeter of Mr MacGregor's studio garden.

Behind it curved a cyclorama of pale blue sky which, within half an hour, thanks to Jeff's ministrations with the pole, would be free of shadows.

Four grey cameras skulked silently on their own in the centre of the floor, each pointing at a rectangular board covered in a black, white and grey pattern. They crouched there, hunched and still, like four old men in the public library intent on reading the newspaper for free. It was something referred to in reverential tones as 'line-up'. In two years Rob had never properly fathomed what it meant.

A pony-tailed props girl busied herself at the back of the rustic-toned shed, hanging up old sieves and stacking flower-pots of warm terracotta on the shelves. A skein of raffia dangled from a hook on the back of the potting-shed door, and the battered brown potting-bench, carried in by two panting men with rivulets of sweat running down their foreheads, was positioned to one side.

Another commotion and shouts of, 'Watch those lights,' heralded the arrival of a fifteen-foot evergreen tree that would be positioned somewhere between greenhouse and potting-shed to give the garden a feeling of 'real lived-in permanence', according to Edgar Prout, the set designer. He bobbed between the bushes in his faded denim smock, looking angst-ridden, and danced, like a mayfly, among the mayhem that would become, he hoped, in the fullness of time – well, in the next half-hour actually – a delightful English country garden in the Rosemary Verey mould, even if most English country gardens were, at this time of year, drowning under a deluge of drizzle, and Rosemary Verey probably was enjoying warmer climes.

It mattered not to Edgar. He sucked at his forefinger, nervously ran his fingers through his thinning hair and pointed here to direct the planting of a spiky holly, there to indicate the position of a diaphanously draped concrete nymph, all the time wearing a preoccupied look as though he were searching for something he couldn't find. It was probably perfection.

Rob pushed open the heavy swing door from the outer corridor and walked into the studio. He liked this time of day, the feeling of anticipation, the nerves gripping the stomach. The only other time he had felt a sensation remotely like it had been when Helena had taken him to concerts: when the orchestra began to tune their instruments from the oboist's A it made the hairs on the back of his neck stand on end. It was the same now.

He stood quietly for a few moments just inside the door, looking up at the bright lights that shone down from the blackness of the studio flies to cast their brilliance on the blossoming rural scene below. He half smiled, half winced at the phoniness of it all, and heard his producer Steve Taylor's voice in his head: "It's only to get a bit of colour into the programme in winter. You'll be outside again in a couple of weeks, back in the muck where you belong."

A trim youth with a shaven head perforated by one earring came towards him. "Hi, Rob. Are they in your dressing room?"

"Yes. It's the blue and green rugby shirt and the 501's. OK?"

"Fine. Do they need pressing?"

"No. I think they're OK, thanks. As long as you're happy with the colour."

"Sounds fine to me. Nothing there to strobe and we're not using CSO so you won't disappear!" The youth from Wardrobe gave Rob a friendly pat on the shoulder and disappeared into the shadows, having satisfied himself that the costume requirements were as disappointingly minimal as usual. Shame they weren't doing *Martin Chuzzlewit*.

Rob was aware now of what he could and could not wear on the programme. Small checks tended to flicker and flash in front of the camera so he stayed clear of them. If Steve Taylor wanted to do something clever – make a plant appear and disappear, or stand Rob in front of a scene that didn't really exist in the studio – he would use CSO, Colour Separation Overlay. Rob would stand in front of a plain blue background which, thanks to electronic wizardry upstairs, could be turned into any chosen background on the screen. The only problem was that if any part of Rob's clothing were blue that, too, would soak up the scene.

He moved towards the frenzied activity to check that his props had arrived and that everything was being placed where he would need it, and as he did so Steve crossed the studio floor with a beaming smile. "Hi, sunshine. You OK?" he asked.

"You're very chirpy this morning," said Rob.

"You'd be chirpy if you'd just had two days on News and been released into the pastoral beauty of an English garden," he said, making a sweeping gesture in the direction of the horticultural panorama unfolding before him.

"Yes," said Rob, sardonically, and then, "Everything OK with the stuff I asked for?"

"Yep. No probs," said Steve, his lank black hair falling in front of one of his eyes. He began to roll up the sleeves of his pale blue shirt and slackened the knot in the floral tie at his neck. "Like it?" he enquired.

Rob looked closely at Steve's tie and shook his head. "Botanically inaccurate. Single roses don't have six petals. They have five."

"Smug sod! I thought it was just the job. It cost me thirty quid!"

Rob laughed. "Well, you've been done, but it's nice to know you care."

"I do! I tell you, a few days in the newsroom among those back-biting buggers and you realize that there's more bullshit on the second floor than there is in your compost heap."

"Oops, sorry." A cameraman wheeling his equipment across the studio floor missed Steve by a fraction of an inch, and a rigger whipped the cable from around him.

"Right," said Steve, recovering his balance. "Let's give 'em hell today, shall we? What have we got?"

He cast his eyes down at the bright yellow script handed to him by the floor assistant. Each programme's content was agreed in advance, but the basic blocking – deciding on the positions of cameras and presenters – was finalized on the morning with a kind of good-natured horse-trading. Steve, as producer/director, would have his own idea of how the programme would look, and Rob would know how he could make each item work best for himself. The morning involved compromise on both sides. Usually it passed without acrimony, unless Bertie started playing the prima donna.

They had come to the part of the programme that involved the son of the soil. They were standing in the potting-shed where a sack of seed potatoes had materialized on the potting-bench, but where Bertie had not materialized to go with them.

"Anyone seen Bertie?" asked Steve. There were a few mutterings from cameramen but no positive identification.

"No sign yet," said the robust girl in Doc Martens, who was the floor assistant.

"The old bugger's probably slept in," said Steve, looking at his watch. He caught the eye of a young body-building type in his early twenties, with close-cropped hair, black T-shirt, black jeans and sandy-coloured Caterpillar boots. Looking between him and his watch he said, "Twenty minutes OK for you, Rory?"

"Yeah, fine, Steve, fine." Rory Watson turned to address the floor. "Coffee break, then, chaps. Back here ready to block in twenty minutes, please. Not half an hour, twenty minutes."

There was a good-natured 'Oooooh' from the cameramen and floor crew and Rory turned a delicate pink, before shrugging and walking off the floor.

"It's his first show as floor manager," confided Steve. "AFM until yesterday, but I think he's ready for it. Reliable as the smile on your face," he said, in the direction of Rob, who was gazing transfixed across the studio floor.

"I said, reliable as the smile on your face," repeated Steve, pointedly, and Rob came partially down to earth. He had noticed a female face peering in through the tiny window in the studio floor. She waved to him, and smiled. His mouth had gone dry and his stomach had executed a back flip. Lisa Drake disappeared from view and Rob tried to concentrate on what Steve was saying.

"Coffee, I think. Yes?"

"Mmm? What? Oh, yes, coffee." Rob flashed a bright but nervous smile at him and they walked across the studio floor in the opposite direction to the door that had reminded him of another door in his life which was, as yet, not quite closed.

"Where the hell is he?" Steve Taylor's voice boomed across the studio floor. *Mr MacGregor's Garden* was broadcast live at 7 p.m. It was now 6 p.m. and there was still no sign of Bertie. Calls had been made during the morning to his house; there was no reply. In the afternoon a taxi from a Bradford company had been sent round to his cottage to pick him up. He wasn't there. All obvious avenues had been explored and Bertie was nowhere to be found.

"Right, sod it." Steve Taylor turned to Rob, who was standing in the middle of the studio lawn, surrounded by banks of rhododendrons and a selection of mowers. "Let's think this thing through. You start off with the welcome and the menu from under the tree, right?"

"Right," agreed Rob, clamping his thumbnail between his teeth and concentrating hard.

"We come out of the graphics to find you here on the lawn and you launch into Bloomer of the Week which is that rhododendron behind you. Then you walk forward and go into the piece on selecting a mower. Right?"

"Yep," confirmed Rob. "And then we go into the snowdrop VT from Pencarrick."

"We come out of that and find you in the greenhouse for your flowery bit and then you link into the VT piece about what's on this weekend."

"Fine."

"Now, during that VT you'll have to move while you're doing the voice-over and end up over there in the potting shed to do Bertie's bit on seed potatoes. Do you know what he was going to do?"

"Not exactly but it's no problem; I can go through all the usual things with the props that Bertie's ordered – you know, how to choose your variety, what makes a good seed potato, how many you'll need for a ten-foot row, and then show folk how to sprout them. He's ordered egg boxes so they'll be fine for standing them in. How long do you want on that?"

"Three and a half minutes. OK?"

"Yes, just get the PA to give me really clear counts in my ear and I should be able to pace it. Do you want to block it now?"

"Good idea." Steve turned from Rob to address the assembled company. "Cameras, we'll block the spud bit in the shed – the bit that should have been Bertie's – with Rob, and we'll have to go without the old sod, even if he does turn up. It's too late to rehearse him now."

They walked towards the potting shed, and as the cameras waltzed across the smooth studio floor in front of the green plastic lawn, Steve went through the rest of the programme with Rob. "There's the final VT which is your choice of this year's best seed varieties with music and voice over, and then we come out for your final piece on turfing over there by the shrubbery. Then it's into next week's trail and goodbye. The PA will give you a hard count but you can't skip anything on the VT, so if you need to shorten your ending I suggest you do it once we've come out of the pictures. Have you got about thirty seconds worth of words you can keep for the end so that we can chop them if we need to?"

"I'll think of something. It shouldn't be a problem."

"Right. OK cameras let's get this last bit sorted; we're on air in half-an-hour. God! And I thought the newsroom was hair-raising. Are you OK?"

Rob nodded.

"It's a hell of a lot to carry on your own. They'll probably be bored rigid with you by the end of the half hour so keep it perky. Only joking, you'll be great. I'll kill the bastard for this. Anyway let's crack it and give the lads a ten-minute break before we go on air. I'm off to the gallery. Good luck."

And he was gone. Rob fiddled about on the potting bench with his potatoes, egg boxes and assorted props and muttered to himself as he laid them out in order, going over it rapidly in his head so that the props led him through the story.

146

"Ready to rehearse, Rob?" asked Rory, a look of mild panic on his face.

"Yes; ready when you are."

"Quiet, studio!" yelled Rory, as though he were trying to quell a riot. And then, more quietly: "When you're ready, Rob."

Rob picked up out of the imaginary voice-over for the 'what's ons' and launched into his piece on potatoes. The count from the PA was loud and clear in his ear but there was a lot to cram in and he came out fifteen seconds too long. "You'll need to chop it by fifteen," said Steve, a touch tartly in his ear.

"OK. I'll have it sorted by the time we do it," Rob responded. "I'll drop a couple of the varieties.'

He knew by now that when a piece had to be shortened there was no point in trying to go faster and cram everything in. The piece would look rushed and sound gabbled. Something nearly always had to be cut out.

It was now half past six and the atmosphere in the studio was noticeably tense.

Rory was listening intently to his earpiece and muttering replies to the voice he was hearing in the walkie-talkie on his chest. "Right, studio, a fifteen-minute break, please. No more. We're up against it tonight so can you please make sure you're back in here in fifteen minutes. Thank you."

He turned to Rob. "Makeup, Rob, please."

"On my way," said Rob, wiping his hands together to rub off the earth that had clung to the potatoes.

He pushed open the door into Makeup and sat down in the chair next to Lisa Drake.

Only her head was sticking out above a pale blue nylon cape, which was more Mrs Ipplepen than Miss Drake, and her eyes were closed as the makeup artist applied eye-liner to her upper lids. But she had heard him come in and knew he was there without opening her eyes. "I hear you've a bit of a panic on," she said quietly.

"Yes. No Bertie."

"Will you be able to cope?" The voice sounded genuinely concerned.

"I think so. I'm just wondering what's happened to him. I hope he's all right. Not gone under a bus or anything. What are you doing in here? I thought News had its own makeup room upstairs?"

"We do, but it's being renovated so they're sending us down here to share yours. I hope you don't mind?"

"Don't be silly." Rob's eyes, too, were closed now as Josie Peart, the makeup girl, sponged tawny-biscuit foundation on his face. It suddenly struck him that it was like being in bed with her again – both of them lying back with their eyes closed and communicating naturally, relaxedly, easily. He felt the fluttering again in his stomach but took comfort in that he could put it down to nerves rather than the proximity of Lisa Drake. At least, that was what he told himself. He didn't believe it.

He heard the rustle of the nylon gown as she got out of the chair, but saw nothing – his eyes were still closed. Josie continued dabbing. Lisa picked up a comb and ran it through her hair, checked her lip gloss in the mirror and brushed specks of dust from her deep green jacket and skirt.

"Must dash. I've a recording in two minutes. Good luck." He didn't see her, but the peck on his cheek burned like fire, and the fragrance of her skin made his heart leap.

The door closed with a heavy clunk, Josie finished powdering his eyelids and Rob opened his eyes to discover a small envelope with his name written on it on the worktop in front of him, and a pink flush on Josie's cheeks.

"Ten minutes, Rob." Rory's head bobbed around the makeup room door.

"Fine. I'll be there in a minute." Rob checked his appearance in the mirror.

"Batteries, Rob," said another voice, and a lumbering untidily dressed middle-aged man with a beard came into the room with a small screwdriver in his hand and a couple of batteries.

"Oh, God!" said Rob. "Why do you guys always leave it until the last minute? I've just tucked my shirt in."

"It's all right, I can do it without taking your shirt out." The soundman walked behind Rob and pulled, with some effort, the small metal transmitter from his back jeans pocket. He prised off a small panel, flipped out the old battery with his screwdriver and pushed in a new one. He clicked the panel back into place, tucked the transmitter into Rob's pocket and checked that the short black aerial was dangling free.

Then he came round to face Rob and spoke into his chest. "This is Rob's mike, one-two-three, one-two-three. OK?" A voice in the soundman's ear told him that it was, indeed, OK, and he bumbled out of the makeup room with muttered apologies, scattering old batteries and Cellophane wrappings as he went.

"I wouldn't mind," Rob confided to Josie, "but they have bloody hours to change your batteries and they choose to do it about five minutes before you go on air."

"Perhaps it's because they've been in a bit of a rush tonight," she offered, as unflappable as ever.

"Yes, I suppose so. Anyway. Done now. Better get out there."

"Good luck, I'm sure you'll manage." Josie was already tipping a plastic bagful of soiled makeup sponges into a sink to soak. She'd seen it all before, and they usually did.

Rob patted his microphone to make sure it was comfortable, fluffed up the front of his hair, checked his flies, said, "Thanks, Josie," and pushed open the heavy door into the studio, sliding the small envelope into his empty back pocket.

Chapter 16

"Quiet, studio!" Rory's command was uncompromisingly authoritative, even if it was his first live programme as floor manager.

"Very impressive," said a growling voice behind him, and Rory jumped as he noticed Frank Burbage, sleeves rolled up, tie slackened at the neck, script in hand, surveying the sylvan scene. "Mind if I watch?" asked Frank, in a stage whisper.

"No, not at all."

"Bugger all else to do," mumbled Frank. "Madam's recording her bit so I can't crack on for half an hour. Thought I might kill a bit of time in the garden. Sure he won't mind?" Frank nodded at Rob on the other side of the studio floor.

Rory, torn between the etiquette of informing Rob that he had a professional onlooker, and the desire not to break his concentration that such an interruption would cause, shook his head and motioned Frank to join the other hangers-on who stood silently in a dimly lit corner, then crossed the floor towards his presenter.

Mr MacGregor's garden positively shimmered under the lights. Candy-floss clouds sauntered nonchalantly across the azure sky, and the damp earth below released its sweet fragrance into the warm air of the studio.

The set designer's hopes had been realized: the once bare

concrete floor of this cavernous aircraft hangar of a studio had blossomed under Edgar's influence into an English garden – banks of gloriously verdant shrubs luxuriated under the majestic tree that now looked as though it had been growing there for years. A few coppery fallen leaves were strewn here, terracotta flower-pots slithered on to the earth there, and a white-painted bench on which Rosemary Verey would have been proud to recline was enveloped by the sparkling emerald leaves of laurel. The whole confection was embellished by potfuls of brilliant flowers in the white-raftered greenhouse. The dusty, russet-toned potting-shed, hung with the impedimenta of a century of horticulture, looked venerable enough to have been used by Adam.

On the Regency-striped lawn in the middle of this televisual Eden stood Rob MacGregor in navy blue and bottle green rugby shirt, blue jeans and black wellington boots, his hair shining under the lights like amber, and his clear complexion pretty well composed, bearing in mind the events of the day. A phalanx of lustrous lawn-mowers cut an arc to his left, his green eyes shone, and the once ordinary if good-looking guy seemed to take on an extra dimension, infused with a new power that switched itself on only moments before the programme began.

There was no falseness about his demeanour, just an enhancement of his natural characteristics. It was, as one prominent television executive had remarked, "as if someone had turned up the knobs marked 'colour', 'contrast' and 'brilliance'". Some called it charisma. Others called it star quality. Whatever it was, Rob MacGregor had it, rather fittingly for a gardener, in spades.

"Good luck, Rob," Rory whispered in his ear, and gave his arm a squeeze.

"And you," said Rob. Their eyes met for a moment, their smiles flickered and then Rory took the reins. His words quelled the final studio mutterings: "Counting to titles in five, four, three . . ." The 'two' and the 'one' were counted out silently with a show of fingers, and on 'zero' Rory gave a downward wave of his arm as the signature tune engulfed the studio.

151

As it approached its coda, Rory's voice broke in once more, "Coming to you in five, four, three," again the fingers, and then, as the graphics sequence mixed through to a wide but steadily tightening shot of Rob in the centre of his floral paradise, Rory's eyebrows were raised, his hand was lowered, and Rob kicked off the programme with a cheery "Hi!"

A fly watching these goings-on from high up on the wall would have been impressed by what he saw. The man in the rugby shirt and the four grey objects around him seemed to be engaged in some kind of courtship ritual. They appeared to dance with one another. First the rugby-shirted figure would pay attention to one of his suitors, and then to another. You could always tell which one had attracted him at any given time, for a little red light would show that he had won its undivided attention. As he moved across the floor from one place to another the grey objects would follow him like sheep, and every now and again, pictures unrelated to anything going on in the studio would come up on a large screen and they would all relax for a while and the little red lights would go out. People would talk during these sequences, until silenced by the man with the clipboard who kept counting backwards. Then the little red lights would come on again and the courtship would be resumed.

The opening had gone smoothly. Frank Burbage was impressed at the way Rob had worked neatly through the lawn-mowers and linked in and out of the first film on snowdrops. The greenhouse piece on winter flowers had passed off well, with only one messy close-up thanks to a careless cameraman bumping his equipment into the front of the staging.

Rob was now moving across the studio, speaking the words he could see on the autocue of the retreating camera. These made up the voice-over to the short film of this week's 'what's on' sequence. Rory, walking backwards to one side of the camera so that he was still in Rob's eye-line, counted him silently out of the commentary using his fingers, and the voice of the production assistant counted him out through the earpiece in his left ear so that there could be no doubt as to when he was back in vision for the sequence on potatoes in the potting-shed.

It was at this moment that he heard a voice in his other ear which momentarily threw him. The doors at the corner of the studio burst open just before the 'what's on' film came to an end and the little man they had given up for lost almost fell in. His hair, normally so neat, was tumbling over his left eye, his clothes were in disarray and his nose was the colour of beetroot. His voice, though the words were indistinct, was loud. Bertie Lightfoot was not a happy man. He was also rolling drunk.

After a brief silence, perhaps half a second, but in Rob's mind half a lifetime, Rob began the introduction to the seed-potato sequence.

Bertie, recognizing that the programme had reached his spot, was having none of it. He toppled towards the set with every intention of reclaiming his potting-shed. Half-way across the studio floor, he tore off his coat and let it fall to the ground. Five seconds later his body followed it as Frank Burbage executed the quietest rugby tackle ever seen outside a Trappist monastery. As Bertie hit the deck, Frank's hand hit Bertie's mouth, preventing the expletives, for which he was already drawing breath, from reaching the ears of the nation.

Up in the gallery Steve, who had glimpsed the fracas on a fortunately untransmitted wide shot, said, "Shit!" The production assistant, who had been nudged by Steve's flailing arm, dropped her stopwatch and also said, "Shit!" Then, regaining her composure, she grabbed her spare timepiece and said into Rob's ear, "Three minutes left on this item."

Rob tried hard not to look to where Frank was now sitting on top of Bertie, who was beginning to sob through Frank's smothering hand. Rory looked from one scene of activity to the other, aware of his responsibility in both areas. But Frank seemed in control of the fallen body so he stuck with the one that was still vertical. Rob motored on, trying to look relaxed and trying, also, to make sense of the words coming out of his mouth.

Bertie's face was turning the colour of his nose. Two riggers had now stepped in to relieve Frank of the hysterical heap, from which strangled cries were emerging. Rob raised his voice a little as the burly men tried to manhandle Bertie from the studio floor. It seemed as though they were having some success – supporting him under each arm as though he had lost the use of his legs, which he almost had – when Bertie finally shook his head free. He looked back at Rob and half shouted, half sobbed, "It's not fair. It's not bloody fair. I didn't do anything wrong. I bloody loved him." And then he was gone, and his voice was no more than an echo.

For a split second the studio was enveloped in an almost sepulchral quiet, but Rob battled on, did his best to brighten the tone and see the programme through to its end. He could not remember laying the turf, though at the end of the programme he could see a small lawn, so he guessed he must have done it. His pay-off seemed, to his own ears, to have a hollow ring, and as he reached his final words in time with the tense production assistant's count, the relief in his voice was almost tangible. He had never been so glad to say goodbye in his life.

The final notes of the play-out music hung in the air for a few moments until Rory said, with more than slight relief, "Thank you, studio." A brief pause and then a booming "Well done, lad!" from Frank Burbage was followed by a cacophony of raised voices as everyone, from cameramen to floor assistants, riggers to sound crew, swapped reactions to what they had just seen.

Steve burst through the studio doors, his floral tie streaming behind him like the tail of a kite, raced over to Rob and threw his arms round him. "Are you OK?" he asked, as he straightened up.

"I think so," replied Rob, dazed. "What happened?"

Just what had happened became clear over the next half-hour in the makeup room. Bertie had been carried there and dumped in a high makeup chair, where he sat looking as crestfallen as a child at the dentist's.

Rob and Steve stood in front of him as he sobbed uncontrollably, his nose running and his eyes streaming. His anger had gone now; all that remained was misery and exhaustion. Josie pushed a mug of black coffee into his hand, which he occasionally sipped, as he regaled them bit by bit, with the events of the last twenty-four hours.

For several months now, relations between Bertie and Terry, his companion of more than twenty years, had become progressively more strained. Terry, worried about Bertie's drinking habits, which had waxed at the same rate that his career had begun to wane, had tried to persuade him to ease off the bottle. Bertie had told him to mind his own business, so Terry had turned for solace to the young chef at his restaurant. What had begun as a friendship had developed into love. Last night Terry had not come home. This morning he had rung to tell Bertie that it was all over. He would be collecting his things at the weekend.

Bertie sat in the makeup chair in an untidy heap, the picture of a broken man, with tears and saliva running down his face and his eyes as rheumy as those of a bloodhound. Steve and Rob listened attentively as he recounted his sorry tale in fits and starts between wiping his eyes and sniffing. Over the past few weeks he'd driven Rob to despair; now Rob felt only sympathy for the pitiful man in front of him.

"What do you want to do?" asked Steve, gently.

"Just go home," said Bertie, quietly. "Just go home." He blew his nose on an already soggy red spotted handkerchief and tried to pull himself together. "I'm sorry I've let you down and caused all this trouble. I think perhaps I'd better give the programme a miss for a bit. Sort myself out."

"Whatever you think," said Steve. "We'll do whatever you want."

"I think that would be best," said Bertie, as he eased himself out of the chair. He looked at the floor and said, almost to himself, "I really loved him, you know. Really loved him. Stupid old fool." And then he looked up at Rob. "I'm sorry I messed it up for you. Bit of a day, though. Just blame it all on a tired old queen."

"Don't be daft," said Rob. He watched as the normally dapper Bertie pulled on his now bedraggled mac and tottered, unsteadily, towards the door.

He heaved it open with some effort and then turned back for a moment. "Well, you've got the programme now, so good luck. I hope it goes well, I really do. Just a shame about the Chelsea Flower Show." He wiped his nose on his sleeve. "I gather they've given that to Mr D'Arcy. Ta-ta." His valediction delivered, the door swung closed and he was gone.

Rob gazed after him, puzzled and saddened in equal measure.

"Well, that's that, then," said Steve, scratching his head. "I'd better get Lottie to book him a cab home or he'll probably start walking."

"The poor old sod," said Rob, reflectively. "I wonder what he meant about Chelsea?"

Steve looked up from dialling a number on the phone in the corner of the makeup room. "Yes, the poor old sod. But it does leave us in a bit of a spot, old son. With the best will in the world I can't really see you doing this entire series of programmes on your own. We'll have to find you a co-star. Any ideas?"

Chapter 17

Katherine sat on the end of her bed at Wellington Heights with her legs crossed underneath her. Wrapped in a fluffy white towelling robe, she listened, wide-eyed, as Rob, standing naked in front of her, towelled dry his mop of curls and recounted the events of the evening.

"Wow!" gave way to "Oh, God!" as the sorry tale of Bertie's fall from grace was related.

"It sounds as though Frank Burbage was a bit heavy-handed," she observed.

"I guess it was a spur-of-the-moment thing."

"I thought football was his speciality, not rugby."

"It seems he's quite keen on both. Mind you, I think he knocked the wind out of himself as much as Bertie."

"Have the papers got hold of it?"

"Thankfully, no. Apparently Bertie was far enough off-mike for his words to be indistinct. It just sounded like some kind of technical gaffe."

"You did well to keep going," she said, looping a stray strand of jet black hair around the watercolour brush that held the rest of it in a knot at the back of her head.

"Oh, I felt a bit stupid and useless, really. There's old Bertie falling to pieces in front of me and all I do is carry on regardless and let other people do the mopping up."

"Well, there wasn't a lot else you could do. It would have been far worse if you'd just stood there gawping."

"I guess so." He let the towel drop and sat beside her on the bed. "So what will happen to Bertie?"

"Steve reckons he needs a rest. I feel really sorry for him. He really loved that guy he lived with, you know. He looked completely empty, drained. As if his world had ended. He looked a bit like Dad." Rob gazed reflectively into the middle distance, as if seeing Bertie's breakdown all over again.

"Poor old man," said Katherine softly. "I hope someone keeps an eye on him."

"Me too. You know, he did say one strange thing."

"Mmm?"

"He said that Guy D'Arcy was presenting the Chelsea Flower Show programme."

"I thought it was you."

"Well, it is."

"Odd," she said. There was a momentary lull in the conversation. "Anyway, in the meantime what's going to happen on your programme?" she asked brightly.

"Steve asked me if I had any ideas."

"And have you?"

"Well, not really. I guess he would be happy if I could get some tasty babe to front it with me."

"Clean out of tasty babes, then, are you?" she asked, running her hand up his naked arm. "I know what you could do. You could get Guy D'Arcy to make a guest appearance each week and they could rename the programme *Me Oh My It's Rob and Guy*."

"You little swine! Just wait till I sort you out." He pushed her back on the bed and dug his fingers into each side of her waist.

She shrieked at him, "Don't you dare touch me there or I'll scream," and then began to giggle loudly as he continued. "Stop it, stop it!"

He slipped the belt of her towelling robe undone, and the shrieks became murmurs of pleasure as he stroked the curve of her hip, enfolded her in his arms and kissed her. "You smell wonderful," he whispered into her ear.

"Mmm. Not as wonderful as you." She ran her hand down his back towards his firm bottom, then slid from the bed and stood in front of him. He rolled over on the white duvet and gazed up at her through a fringe of damp brown curls.

"You look lovely in your eye-liner," she said softly, slipping the robe off her smooth white shoulders and letting it fall to the floor.

He gazed at her. "Could you ever see yourself making love to a man who wore makeup?"

"Only one particular man." She pulled the paintbrush from the back of her head and shook out the knot of shining black hair, which fell half across her face. Then she walked towards him, conscious that he was drinking in her every move.

"I love your body." He sighed.

"And I love yours."

She trailed her index finger slowly from his heel up to his shoulder as she walked beside the bed, then lifted up the duvet and slid in. "It's cold out there. Don't you want to come in?"

"Oh, yes, please." He sprang up and all she saw was a flash of freckled flesh and taut muscle before she felt him nuzzling up to her under the crisp, white linen. He pulled her so close that she felt she might almost be a part of him, and as he wrapped his body around hers it seemed as though they could never again be prised apart. She hoped it might be true.

The glint of early-morning sun through muslin and the smell of bread reminded Rob that he was waking up in Katherine's bed. She was still beside him, lying with the side of her face against his shoulder and her arm across his chest. He listened to her relaxed, regular breathing and smiled contentedly at the thought of their gentle lovemaking after the traumas that had gone before. Maybe now they could get their act together again and rediscover the closeness they had enjoyed before the pressures of their jobs had pulled them apart. Stupid, really. At moments like this he knew they were soulmates; it was only the mechanics of their daily lives that had got in the way of their relationship. Absence, he had discovered, made the heart grow fonder . . . of somebody else. It was time they made more of an effort to be together. He pulled a wisp of her shining hair from her warm, pink cheek.

It was only now that he remembered he had not yet told her about Jock's financial problems. He would wait a while before he did. It was ages since they'd had a relaxing weekend together, and he didn't want to spoil it. As Steve Taylor had once remarked, "A trouble shared is a trouble dragged out till bedtime."

She stirred and sighed, then, her eyes straining to open, asked what time it was. Rob glanced sideways at the clock on the bedside table. "A quarter to nine."

"Mmm. Coffee time," she murmured. "Are you going to make it or shall I?" still with her eyes tight shut.

He grinned and stroked her hair. "I'll make it, you stay there." He slipped out of the bed and picked up the towelling robe that lay where she had dropped it on the floor. He put it on, even though it barely came half-way down his thigh, and ambled towards the kitchen, rubbing his hands through his tousled hair and stretching.

He noticed his shirt and jeans tossed over the back of a chair, and saw something square and white on the floor below them. Still trying to focus, he bent down to pick it up. It was a small envelope with his name written on it in stylish fountain-pen script. He slid it into the pocket of the towelling robe and went into the kitchen.

He filled the coffee-maker with water, plugged it in and reached for a couple of mugs from the hooks over the worktop. As he did so, two arms slid around his waist from behind and he realized that Katherine had slipped from the bed as soon as he had left it, pulled on his old shirt and wandered blearily into the kitchen.

"I was getting cold," she murmured, stifling a yawn and nuzzling him between the shoulder-blades. As she did so, she slid her hands down into the pockets of the towelling robe to hold him closer.

"What's this?" She pulled her right hand from the pocket. In it was the small white envelope.

Fear leaped like a tiger into Rob's stomach. "It's nothing. Just a card. Give it here." He spun round and tried to snatch the envelope from her.

She grinned and danced backwards over the floor, holding it out of his reach. "Not so fast, Mr MacGregor. What is it?"

"It's nothing. Just a card from a fan. Give it to me."

"Oh, goody. I wonder what it says." She tore open the envelope and took out the small card, which bore an illustration of a man with a beard and glasses planting out cabbages, watched by a small rabbit in a blue coat. Rob's heart was pounding. Time stood still. The coffee-maker seemed to be dripping in slow motion.

Katherine opened the card and read out loud the message inside:

Dear Mr MacGregor,
Thank you for the most wonderful time.
    Perhaps next time we can meet in your garden rather than mine.
    With love,
    Lisa.

The butterflies in Rob's stomach turned into vultures.

Katherine's face paled. She let the card drop to the floor.

"I'm sorry." His words hung lamely on the air.

"Sorry?" She looked at him quizzically, not knowing what to say. Then, almost to herself, she murmured, "Lisa Drake."

Rob blurted out, "I didn't know what it said. She gave it to me last night, before the show. I didn't even think about it."

"No. Obviously." She sounded stunned, but quite calm. Rob looked at her, standing on her own in the middle of the kitchen floor, tiny inside his baggy shirt. She folded her arms and looked at him. "How long has this been going on?"

"It hasn't. I mean, it was just once."

"Just once?" Katherine's face hardened and the colour started to come back to her cheeks. Her eyes did not leave his. "When?"

"The night you went out with Charlie Wormald."

"Oh, please! We're not talking about a fit of jealousy because of Charlie Wormald, are we? Please tell me we're not!"

Rob floundered and felt himself awash with a sickening mixture of shame and agony. "I didn't know – I mean – I thought . . . When I saw you in the restaurant with him and he was all over you . . ."

"You saw us in the restaurant? You saw us . . . *in the restaurant!* You mean you followed us there? What is this?" Her face was red now, and her voice raised.

"No, I didn't follow you deliberately. Lisa and I dined there, too, we were over in a corner. I worried that you might see us but -"

"I bet you did – 'Lisa and I . . .'" She half turned and put her hand to her forehead. "I don't believe I'm hearing this. Tell me I'm dreaming." She turned back to him, incredulously, half laughing as the words tumbled out. "You dined with Lisa Drake in the same restaurant as me and then you took her home and –"

"No. I didn't take her home."

"Oh?"

"We went back to her place."

"Oh. Well, I suppose I should be grateful for that."

"I was confused. You'd said that you were going out with your boss and his wife. I was fed up. I'd been looking forward to a weekend on our own. We've hardly had one lately. Then Lisa rang and asked me out for a drink. What could I say?"

"How about no?"

"OK, so I said yes because I was pissed off at the thought of you preferring to go out with your boss than me. But then when I saw you two sitting together and him all over you, I thought –"

"You thought I was having an affair with Charlie Wormald?" Tears were now hot on the heels of her anger and she began to shake. "Charlie bloody Wormald. You stupid, stupid man. There's only one man I care for and that's you – Well, it was." The tears rolled down her cheeks and she swept them impatiently aside with the sleeve of his shirt.

"You bastard!" She almost spat the words at him through the tears. "How could you? I suppose you slept with her?"

Rob could not bear to look at her. He turned away and put both his hands in the pockets of the robe, gazing at the floor. "Yes." Never in his life had he felt so wretched or such a cheat.

"Oh, God! And are you seeing her again?"

"No."

"And am I supposed to believe that?"

"I can't expect you to believe anything, I suppose."

"Dead right you can't."

"I'm sorry." Rob looked at her. "I'm so sorry. I feel so ashamed. I didn't mean to let you down."

He crossed to her and put his arms out to hold her. She stepped back. "No. Please don't. Please."

She sidestepped him and walked quickly to the bedroom.

"I'm sorry," he said, as she disappeared around the corner.

He walked slowly after her, not sure what to expect. She met him at the bedroom door, her eyes red-rimmed and her nose running. In her arms was a pile of his clothes. She pushed them towards him. "Just go. Please."

He opened his mouth to speak.

"Just go." She turned away and closed the bedroom door quietly behind her.

Rob could hardly believe it had happened. One minute they were lying in bed next to one another, as close as it was possible to be, and the next he was standing outside her front door on a chilly pavement watching busy shoppers coming out of the baker's with loaves of bread wrapped in white paper bags.

He felt a mixture of helplessness and anger, frustration and stupidity – stupidity that had resulted in him losing the one woman he really cared about. Why was it so easy to see that now, when it had been confusing before? As a chill breeze blew across the pavement he felt deep sadness at his folly.

He pulled his jacket around him and walked around the corner to his car, uncertain of quite where he was going.

Chapter 18

When Guy D'Arcy lifted his head from his pillow that bright Saturday morning he remembered he was alone. Normally he would look upon such solitude as failure, but this morning immense relief surged over him. He had discovered from a brief phone call the previous evening that he had lost the contract to design Sophie's father's stately acres in the heart of the British countryside. Losing it had been, indeed, a blow, but losing Sophie was not. He had had no compunction in giving her the riding boot as soon as he knew that her father's preferences lay in the direction of Edward Siggs-Baddeley. It did not come as too much of a surprise. Sophie's father had always been an ardent royalist.

She had wailed inconsolably when he packed her off, mascara coursing down her plump cheeks, Prada bag slung over her arm, but he felt thankful that he would no longer have to wake up next to a girl he considered marginally less attractive than Red Rum.

He hobbled over to the window, recovering from a partially celebratory, partially consoling hangover, and hauled back the curtains to gaze at the morning.

"The middle of February, D'Arcy, and where are you? Time for a stock-take, old boy," he said aloud, pulled on his bathrobe and headed downstairs to the kitchen. He lifted the left-hand lid of the Aga, filled the kettle and slapped it on the middle of the hob.

Pulling back the kitchen curtains, he gazed on the frosty scene before him – a small garden, fenced with willow hurdles that seemed strangely out of place in Fulham. They protected the plot from the prying eyes of its neighbours, but in spite of the garden's tasteful appointments – a small rostrum of timber decking, a pale ochre Cretan pithoi and a path of old bricks – little seemed to flourish in the grey, silty earth.

He turned his back on the bitter scene and sat at the kitchen table while the kettle sighed on the hotplate. "What have we got at the ripe old age of twenty-nine? No girlfriend. No roof, except one that's auditioning as a colander, and no money to pay for its repair, thanks to too many expensive meals with too many expensive women. The *Sunday Herald* is getting tetchy and may give you the old heave-ho sooner rather than later, but at least you have the Chelsea Flower Show to look forward to, and that might be a bit of useful street cred as far as the paper's concerned.

"Freddie Roper, whom God preserve, preferably in aspic, would seem to have passed over you in favour of the northern oik when it comes to impressing his customers with your charms, but who knows? Maybe fate will smile upon you soon." He picked up a business card from his AAC press pack and stared at it: Amalgamated Agricultural Chemicals, Claudia Bell, Public Relations, with a telephone number. He smiled to himself.

His musings were interrupted by the kettle, and he poured its contents into a large cafetière. He collected another pile of post from the doormat, along with *The Times* (he might write for the *Herald* on a Sunday but that didn't mean he had to read it on the other six days of the week), sauntered back to the kitchen table and poured himself a large mug of coffee.

He dumped the post on a chair, then opened the paper and turned first to the obituaries. None of his father's contemporaries appeared there today, only an octogenarian circus acrobat, who had perfected the forward double somersault on a slack wire, and a Master of Foxhounds who had ridden to hounds until, at ninety-four, arthritis had confined her to one of those all-terrain vehicles. In this she had apparently made herself a nuisance to one and all by regularly following the hunt until she ended up in a ditch, calling for help through yards of bombazine, top-hat and veil. Guy smiled at the thought of the indomitable old biddy. Rather like Granny, he thought.

The weather forecast offered more of the same – crisp and bright – and the arts pages seemed to be full of plays by Strindberg in Islington. A sod of a day for anything remotely amusing. And then on page four (he had started at the back of the paper as he always did) he saw a small item at the foot of column three: 'By Our Media Correspondent', was the byline, and the brief piece was headed 'FRESH FRONT FOR FLOWER SHOW'.

Guy read on:

The highlight of the gardener's year, the Chelsea Flower Show, will this year have a new look on television screens. Presented for the last fifteen years by an assortment of current-affairs presenters, the show is now to be fronted by two of the small screen's most popular gardening gurus, Rob MacGregor and Guy D'Arcy.

A spokesman for Unicorn Television, the independent production company responsible for the Chelsea Flower Show coverage, said: "Rob and Guy are phenomenally popular with viewers and we hope the combination of the two will bring the world's best flower show to a wider audience."

Chelsea Flower Show runs from 19 to 22 May.

"Bloody hell!" exclaimed Guy, hurling the paper on to the kitchen table, and knocking over a bowl of sugar. "Oh, buggeration!" And then the phone rang.

"Yes?"

"It's me . . . Bertie," said a rather weak voice at the other end.

"Why didn't you tell me about MacGregor, you old sod?"

"What about him?"

"He's presenting the Chelsea Flower Show programme."

"I thought you were," replied Bertie.

"According to *The Times* we're doing it together, which the bastards never told me when they asked me to do it."

"So are you going to decline?"

"I've a good mind to. Bloody MacGregor. Gets everywhere. But no, I'll give him a good run for his money. It's about time the show had a bit of class."

"Mmm," said Bertie.

Guy detected the absence of Bertie's usual bounce and asked if anything was the matter.

"Just a bit down. I've decided to go for a little holiday. Take it easy for a while."

"But what about the programme? Are you leaving MacGregor to his own devices?"

"Oh, I think he'll cope. They'll probably find somebody else to make a guest appearance. I don't really care."

Guy recognized that this was not the usual Bertie by a long chalk. "What's happened? What's wrong, old love?"

Bertie told him of Terry's departure, but said nothing of his embarrassing performance at the studio.

"Oh, God, I'm sorry," said Guy, "really sorry."

"Me too," muttered Bertie. "So if I'm not around for a while you'll know why."

"You take it easy, you old bugger. I'll speak to you when you get back. Oh, by the way, I don't suppose you know Claudia Bell's home number, do you?"

"No, I'm afraid I don't. Sorry."

"Not to worry . . . it's just that it being Saturday . . ."

"Sorry?"

"Never mind. You take care of yourself. Goodbye."

"Goodbye." Bertie put the phone down.

"Bugger," muttered Guy under his breath.

Chapter 19

The shrill clarion of the copper alarm clock heralded Rob's reluctant entry into Monday morning. The weekend had passed for him in a sullen blur. He'd wandered around End Cottage in a kind of low-key trance, uncertain of time, and dabbled outdoors in the damp earth around his plants as the river ran relentlessly by. From time to time he stretched upright from the spade and looked towards the moor, but he lacked the energy to scale the heather-covered peaks where, as before, he might have been able to rise above his troubles and see them with a clearer eye.

He slammed a hand on the clock to silence it, and tried to divine, from the chink of light sneaking between the bedroom curtains, just what kind of day it was. The curtains gave little away and he slid his aching, naked body out from beneath the covers, idly tugged back the curtains and gazed out on a pale, watery sky.

It struck him that whatever his mood, and whatever happened to him, his one overriding interest each day was the state of the weather. Pathetic, really, but understandable. He'd spent so many years of his life being governed by the sun and rain that the habit of looking up at the sky and listening to every available weather forecast was not something he could shake off.

He wondered what Katherine was doing now, and wished, whatever it was, that she were doing it with him. He wished so much he could speak to her, but fear of upsetting her more, and shame at his fall from grace, kept him from the phone. The depth of this emptiness was something he'd never felt before. Sadness, yes, and frustration. But never this bottomless hole.

He sighed a deep, sorry-for-himself sigh and hauled on yesterday's clothes. What was it she had said to him on their last evening together? "Clean out of tasty babes, then, are you?" They had been talking about a new co-presenter. Never had he been cleaner out of tasty babes. Bar one, of course. Perhaps he should give her a ring. The more he thought about it, the more sense it made. Why hadn't it occurred to him before? The perfect co-presenter for *Mr MacGregor's Garden* was Bex Fleming.

Jock MacGregor had been at work an hour by the time his son surfaced. He, too, was not feeling very chipper, but he knew that after a while among his plants his mood would improve.

He carried a tray of Victorian gold-laced polyanthus plants into the potting-shed, having fetched them from the cold frame attached to the greenhouse, and picked his way through the last of the flood-borne mud that Wayne and Harry were still attempting to clear. By the end of the week the place would be ship-shape again. Jock was relieved – he had begun to find the disorder wearing.

Placing the plants on the old stone bench, he took down a dozen four-inch clay flower-pots from the wooden rack at the back of the shed. A mound of compost, like a miniature Everest, was piled in the centre of the cold, hard bench and he took up a handful and rubbed it between his fingers, grunting appreciatively. Then he sniffed it, enjoying the cool, organic aroma that reached his nostrils. Satisfied that the hand-mixed concoction of loam, leaf-mould and sharp grit would suit the plants in question he began to prise the young clumps from their seed tray and pot them up.

It was a satisfying job, sullied only by the faint noisome smell that emanated from Wayne and Harry's handiwork. He watched them working together – Wayne like an eager young pup, scooping up the mud at the rate of three shovelfuls to Harry's one. He smiled to himself and looked beyond them to the beds, now freshly forked over and newly lined out with plants. In spite of the flood they looked as full of promise as they always did at this time of year. The window was fringed with the white blossom of Japanese quince, and by the path he could see the amethyst spears of *Crocus tomasinianus*, planted thirty years ago as a handful of dry bulbs. Even the flood waters had not managed to dislodge them, and now they had grown into a long ribbon of blooms which, if the sun came out later in the day, would turn into pale purple stars. Jock took the trouble to pot up a few dozen of them each autumn, knowing that, come late winter, they would sell on sight to anyone with an eye for quiet beauty and an easily grown plant.

He glanced at the clock. Almost nine. He'd better open the gates. Wayne had left Harry to his shovelling and was down in the far corner of the nursery getting together an order of hardy perennials and shrubs that would be collected later that day. Jock took the bunch of keys from his pocket and strolled down the path.

A gentle breeze ruffled the leaves of a row of mixed evergreens down the side of the gravel walk, and he noticed, at the end of the row, the three rose-bushes that had been given to him by the late Professor's wife. Wayne had retrieved them from the flood waters and planted them in the first available patch of ground. They were beginning to break into bud; their crimson shoots defying the chilly late February air. He smiled again. Spring couldn't be far away.

At the gate he pushed the stubby key into the padlock, turned it, released the chain and noticed a Land Rover Discovery coming down the lane. It drew to a halt, and Jock recognized Lady Helena Sampson. She locked the car and walked down the lane towards him.

"Good morning, Mr MacGregor."

"Good morning, Lady Sampson, how are you?"

"I'm well, thank you, and you?"

The preliminaries over, Jock opened the gate and invited her into the nursery, curious to know of the reason for her early-morning visit but too full of Scots circumspection to ask.

She did not keep him waiting long. "I hope you don't mind me calling so early but I have to go out later this morning and wanted to leave Makepiece something to plant."

Makepiece was the old gardener who had replaced Rob. His specialities were salvias and grumbling, but Helena tried, each year, to ensure that he also planted things that she wanted.

"Have you any hellebores?"

"We've only a few left," Jock told her, "but you're welcome to have a look."

He walked her to the cold frame adjacent to the greenhouse and pointed to a couple of dozen plants at one end, their stout stems topped by a range of flowers that varied in colour from white and pale yellow to pink and deep crimson.

"Oh, aren't they lovely?" she exclaimed, with genuine pleasure.

"Aye, they're not bad. It's taken years of selection to get such a good colour range and I'm quite happy with them now. They'll do."

As Jock helped Helena to pick out half a dozen plants that suited her, she asked him about the early years at the nursery, and about Fred Armitage who had owned the place before him. She talked fondly of Rob, and Jock felt that ripple of pride at his son's achievements as she sang his praises. "I'm sorry to hear that Mr Wragg seems determined to continue being a nuisance."

"Aye, a nuisance he is," replied Jock. "He's like a dog with a bone. I don't know how we'll shake him off. Or why he wants the place. I just can't fathom it."

"I was just wondering," said Helena, "did you know that Mrs Wragg was an Armitage before she married?"

"I'm sorry?" Jock looked puzzled.

"Gladys Wragg. Her maiden name was Armitage. She was Fred Armitage's niece – the man who owned Wharfeside Nursery before you did."

"Was she now?" said Jock, his brow knitted and his thoughts scattered to the wind. "D'you think they want the nursery for sentimental reasons, then?"

"Oh, it doesn't strike me that Mr and Mrs Wragg have enough sentiment between them to write a birthday card, from what I've heard from Mrs Ipplepen. I just thought that it was a strange coincidence."

"Very strange." Jock rubbed his whiskery chin thoughtfully. "His niece, you say?"

"Yes, she was Fred Armitage's brother's girl."

"I wasn't aware that he had a brother."

"Well, apparently he did. Not at all like Fred, I'm told. Black sheep of the family. I think he went to prison for a while. Bit of a wide boy. Mrs Ipplepen says Fred never spoke about him. Wouldn't even admit to having a brother. Sad, really."

"Well, well." Jock was lost in his thoughts, trying to work out the significance of what he had just learned when Helena brought him down to earth.

"Well, I must be going. Can I pay for these, Mr MacGregor?" She looked at the labels, swiftly totted up the prices and placed several notes in Jock's hand saying, "I think that's right."

Jock touched his cap, pushed the notes into his apron pocket without looking at them and walked towards the potting shed with Helena to find a box for her plants. But all the time he was thinking about Fred Armitage and his brother.

Rob had thought of ringing Katherine every ten minutes from the moment he had left her flat, but her words – "Just go" – kept echoing in his ears, and he lacked the courage to phone and put matters right in case they went even more wrong.

He'd thought round and round it, determined to come up with some way of making her understand how bad he felt, how much he wanted her, but knew in his heart that it was too soon, that Katherine's wounds would be too raw, as were his own.

He flopped in the spoke-backed chair by the table in the small back room he used as a study, and looked out over the top of the word-processor at the river and the moors beyond, seeking inspiration.

He scanned the list of things to do that he'd jotted down on a primrose-yellow Post-it pad:

–Ring Sir F. – Yes to advert.

He would have to say yes, even if it meant that Katherine would be even angrier with him for abandoning his principles. He could no longer risk his father having to close down the nursery. It would break Jock's heart. Just like Rob had broken Katherine's heart. At least this way he could help one of the people he loved. He should have been pleased at the prospect of such a lucrative deal. He wasn't. He cast his eye further down the list:

–*Daily Post* piece.

–Ring Bex Fleming.

–Sort prog ideas.

–Mail.

As his hand reached for the phone, it rang.

"Hello?"

"Can I speak to Rob MacGregor, please?"

"Speaking."

"Hello, Mr MacGregor, it's Simon Clay's secretary here from Amalgamated Agricultural Chemicals. Mr Clay would like a word. Will you hold for a moment, please?"

"Yes, of course." A sharp click and then a small but fully orchestrated chunk of Vivaldi's Four Seasons – Spring – before Simon Clay, the arty PR man of AAC who had been so full of himself at the press briefing, came on the line with a distinctly apologetic tone. "Rob? Simon, hi! I'm sorry to bother you . . ."

Rob was about to apologize for not having got back to the company sooner with his affirmative reply, but Simon Clay pressed on.

"Look, I'm dreadfully sorry but there's been a bit of a cock-up at this end as far as the BLITZ thing is concerned."

"Sorry?"

"Well, it's just that it's usual for the advertising and PR department to sort out the personnel for advertising campaigns, but it seems in this instance that the chairman wanted to involve himself as well. I gather Sir Freddie asked you about fronting the new campaign?"

"Yes. He did."

"Well, look, this is dreadfully embarrassing, but I'm afraid the PR department had actually decided to go in a different direction. I do hope you won't mind, and I can only apologize for the inconvenience we've caused you but . . . I'm afraid we won't be able to use you. So sorry. I do hope you understand."

"Yes, fine. No problem. These things happen. Do I need to ring Sir Freddie?"

"No. No need. I'll explain and say that I've spoken to you. OK?"

"Yes. Fine. Er . . . fine."

"By the way, very pleased to hear that you and Guy D'Arcy will be presenting the Chelsea Flower Show programme this year."

"I'm sorry?" Rob was puzzled.

"Yes, saw it in the paper. I think it will be a really great combination. Anyway, must dash. Cheerie-bye then." And he was gone.

Rob replaced the receiver, calmly and thoughtfully. Two bombshells in one phone call. He felt he should have been hugely disappointed at the loss of the advertising campaign and the subsequent windfall. But he wasn't. He was relieved. The money would have been useful, particularly as far as his father was concerned, but how could he ever have squared it with him? Or with himself. Or with Katherine. He'd like to talk to her about it now. And about Guy D'Arcy. Why hadn't his agent mentioned that he was to co-present? Liz Cooper was up-front about such things, as a rule. Maybe they hadn't told her in case he declined. Not that he would have done. It might add a bit of sparkle to the proceedings.

He took a sharp pencil and crossed 'Ring Sir F. Yes.' off the list. How the hell was he going to help his father now?

He skipped the next instruction to write his *Daily Post* piece and came to 'Ring Bex Fleming'. The image of the fresh-faced girl swam into his mind and made him feel marginally better. Only one snag here: he didn't have her number. He dialled the Birmingham television company. The call was answered by a telephonist, who recognized his voice and said that OK, she would give him Bex's home number and the number of the garden centre where she worked, "Although I shouldn't really, but as it's you, Mr MacGregor, I'm sure it will be all right," followed by a girlish giggle from the fifty-something voice.

He dialled her home number first. No reply, just an answering-machine saying, in that bright voice he remembered, "Hi, this is Bex. I'm not in, but please leave a message after the tone and I'll get back to you when I can. Thanks for calling." He decided that before he did he'd try her at work.

The phone at the garden centre was picked up by a clueless youth who said, vaguely, that Bex was around somewhere. When Rob asked if he could locate her, the youth reluctantly agreed to try. The phone was laid down and Rob listened for what seemed an age to general garden-centre noise, magnified by the evidently cavernous selling area where punters were probably milling around buying artificial flowers, jam purporting to be made in country cottages and expensive watering-cans. He was glad his dad just sold plants.

"Hello?" The voice broke his train of thought.

"Hello? Bex?"

"Yes?"

"It's Rob MacGregor."

"Hi! How are you?"

"I'm fine. Look, I'm sorry to bother you at work but I wondered if you fancied coming on the show?"

"What?"

"Well, it's a long story but I need a new co-presenter."

"Me?"

"Well, why not?"

"But you don't know what I'm like. I might be useless."

"I don't think so.'

"Well . . . when?"

"Er . . . how about this Friday?"

"*This Friday?*"

"Yes. Do you think you could?"

"Well, yes – if I can arrange it with my boss I'd love to . . . but why?"

"Oh, I'll fill you in on the details later but basically Bertie can't do it any more. My producer asked me if I had any ideas so I thought of you. He'll have the final say, of course, but I just thought I'd sound you out and see if you fancied it."

"Well, I do. I'd love to. But what do you want me to do?"

"Oh, we'll work all that out later. As long as you can do it, that's great."

"Shall I wait to hear from you, then?"

"I'll get Steve Taylor to give you a call, if that's OK. He's the producer. He really ought to sort it out, not me. I'm just glad you're keen and I hope your boss doesn't mind."

"He's usually OK about it – sees it as a way of promoting the business. Just one thing."

"Yes?"

"How did you find my number?"

"I got it from an extremely helpful telephonist at your studios."

"Well, you were lucky. Normally it's easier to get eggs out of a cockerel than it is to get phone numbers out of Brenda. But I'm glad she recognized your voice."

"Yes, me too. Well, I'll see you later, then, I hope. And thanks. I'm really pleased."

"Me, too. Speak to you later. 'Bye." Before Rob hung up he heard her whisper softly to herself, "Oh, *yippee!*"

Chapter 20

"You were brilliant, simply brilliant!" Steve Taylor bestowed a large kiss on Bex's left cheek. Her soft, peachy makeup failed to disguise the rosy glow that suffused her face, and the warm hum from the technicians around the studio floor left her in no doubt that she had done all right. She looked over to where Rob was standing behind the potting-bench at the far corner of the set and blushed again when she saw the warm smile that greeted her.

He ambled over and put an arm around her shoulder, looked her in the face, grinned and gave her a hug.

"Wow!" he said, quite softly. "You were terrific. Really cool."

"Thank you. Are you sure?"

"Is *he* sure? Never mind him – I'm sure and that's what matters." Steve, black hair flopping over his horn-rimmed glasses, turned to speak to Bex once more, having thanked his minions. "Are you ready for this on a weekly basis, then?"

"Me?" Bex couldn't believe her ears.

"Yes, you," he answered. "I knew that one day I'd see a bit of UST in this programme and now I've found it I'm not going to let it go."

"UST?" enquired Rob.

"I'll tell you later," said Steve, already retreating. "Look, I've got a news bulletin to sort out but I'll be in touch with you both in the next couple of days. Bex, can you come up with an item for next week? It's our last studio day and after that we'll be on location now that the weather looks like getting better. Don't agree to do anything else on TV for the foreseeable future. OK?" The door swung to and he was gone.

"OK," muttered Bex. "Well. There we are, then." She looked up at Rob. "He seemed quite happy with that, didn't he?"

"Yes. Especially the UST, whatever that is."

"You mean you really don't know?"

"No."

"You clearly don't read enough teeny girls' magazines."

"And you do?"

"Well, I did once."

"So what does it stand for?"

"Unresolved Sexual Tension."

Rob was disconcerted. "Ah. I see."

"It's all right. We just have to make sure it stays unresolved."

There was a pause. Rob looked at Bex, and then she burst out laughing.

Katherine tapped the top of her pencil impatiently on her desk and gazed at the ceiling of her office at the *Nesfield Gazette*, the telephone clamped to her ear. The late-afternoon sun glinted in through the tall bay window of the Victorian building, past the gilded old-fashioned lettering whose shadow printed the newspaper's title across her desk. On her notepad she saw: 'Est. 1843'. At the other end of the line her boss Charlie Wormald, Est. 1943, was in full flow.

"Fine. Yes, Charlie, I will. Fine. No. Yes . . . yes, I will. Goodbye." She dropped the handset back into the cradle and muttered under her breath, "God, that man." And then her eyes glazed over. She thought of another man. The one who, in spite of her efforts, was occupying her mind every moment of every hour of every day. Anger mixed with pain and love in equal measure until she found herself running round in emotional circles.

It had been like this since she'd asked him to go, almost a week ago now. Her anger kept her cool to start with, but it subsided regularly and she found herself wallowing in the fact that she missed him. Missed his clothes on the floor. Missed his toothbrush in the mug. Missed his touch. Missed the smell of him. She had never liked to feel dependent on any man but in the case of Rob MacGregor she had failed. Damn him! She'd thought he was different from the rest. He was no different at all. Just as responsive to flattery as any of them. At the centre of her life now was a big black hole, and she felt empty. She pulled a large handkerchief out of the sleeve of her black jumper and blew her nose on it. It smelt of him and she bit her lip.

There was a light tap on the glass of her door and Nancy Farrer, the well-preserved secretary who manned the phone in the lobby next to Katherine's office, turned the knob and put her head tentatively round the door.

"Lady Sampson's here to see you, Katherine."

Katherine wiped her eyes quickly. "Fine. Tell her to come in." Surprised at this sudden interruption, she stuffed the handkerchief back up her sleeve and got up from her chair, smoothing down the black corduroy mini-skirt over her black tights.

Muted thanks could be heard outside the door, and then Helena, smartly turned out in a well-tailored tweed jacket, cream turtle-neck jumper and dark brown trousers, her hair pinned back with a tortoiseshell comb, came into Katherine's office and greeted her warmly. "Katherine, how are you?" She shook her hand and Katherine motioned her to sit down.

"Oh, no, I won't if you don't mind. I'm dashing off up the dale for supper with one of Jumbo's old partners," she glanced at the large man's watch on her wrist, "and I mustn't be late. It's just that I wanted to ask you something."

Katherine found herself wondering if Helena knew about her and Rob. Perhaps Rob had told her. She decided that from her manner he had not. She would say nothing.

"It's about Dennis Wragg – you know, the man wanting to buy up Jock MacGregor's nursery?"

Katherine nodded and gave a brief sniff.

"I know this sounds dreadful of me but I thought I'd try to look into the background of it all. I don't want to do a Miss Marple or anything but I just have some kind of feeling that there might be an ulterior motive."

"I think you're right there," Katherine agreed.

"I wondered, does your newspaper have any kind of indexed archive?"

"We do have back numbers – why?"

"Well, I want to try to find out a bit more about the Armitages. Fred Armitage, who used to own the nursery before Jock did, had a brother who was a bit of a bad 'un, according to my daily, Mrs Ipplepen. Gladys Wragg happens to be his daughter."

Katherine's journalistic instincts went into overdrive. "Really?" She came round to the front of her desk and perched on the corner.

"It seems to me to be a bit of a mystery. Why is Dennis Wragg so keen on such a small piece of land which has no real value to him except that it once belonged to his wife's family? I wondered if the paper might offer any clues."

Katherine reached over the desk for her notepad. "When was this black-sheep-of-a-brother last heard of?"

"Somewhere about the nineteen forties, I think."

"And his name?"

"Reggie. Reggie Armitage. Younger brother of Fred. Nearly went to prison, apparently. Don't know why. Am I being a frightful old busybody and wasting your time?"

"Not at all. I'm as curious as you. Leave it with me and I'll see what I can come up with. Nancy loves raking through the old copies of the paper in the back room. They go right back to . . ." – she glanced at the shadow, which had now moved to the corner of her desk ". . . 1843." It faded before her eyes as a cloud obscured the weak, setting sun.

Helena watched Katherine lose herself in her thoughts, thanked her and took her leave. The purple-grey evening enveloped her in a gentle sadness as she headed off up the dale for supper.

*

Guy had never seen so much flesh, except on a Sumo wrestler. Great folds of it enveloped him, pure white and oozing, so that he could hardly move. He forced his head back on the pillow of the ornate, lace-encrusted bed, and tried to breathe in air that was not laden with Estée Lauder Youth Dew.

"I know exactly what you're thinking, you know," said the voice of his companion.

I bet you don't, thought Guy, who was imagining what it would be like to be a baker suffocating in dough.

"You're a calculating little bastard and I know exactly why you're here and exactly when you'll give me the old heave-ho."

"So why don't you throw me out?" Guy heaved his naked body as upright as was possible thanks to the constraints of the too, too solid flesh beside him. He'd thought that Sophie's thighs were hefty but they were put in the shade by the monstrous limbs he gazed upon now, which made the Michelin man look anorexic.

Claudia Bell was fifty-something and well preserved facially, but her figure in the red suit at the press conference had clearly owed a good deal to the art of Rigby and Peller, the Queen's corsetiers.

"I don't throw you out, you dreadful little boy, because you're fun. Wicked, but fun. And you're better in bed than anyone I've ever known." She giggled girlishly and then added, with a rueful note, "I only hope I don't lose my job."

"Now why would you do that?" asked Guy, forcing himself to stroke a relatively inoffensive stretch of flesh on her forearm.

"Because Freddie is a jealous man and likes to think I'm his and his alone."

"And aren't you?"

"Not now, you vile boy. Not after last Saturday. And certainly not after tonight. Come here and let me smother you!" Guy gasped for breath as, once more, a tidal wave of quivering carnality threatened to engulf him.

He screwed up his eyes as Claudia clenched him in a leg and armlock that squeezed out of him every last drop of breath. It was agony, as he gulped at the perfumed air through the lacquered blonde locks, but it had been worth it. This temporary discomfort was a small price to pay for the glittering prize. BLITZ was his, thanks to Claudia, and Rob MacGregor was history.

Rob had wanted to ask Bex out for supper, to celebrate her success, but she'd said she had to be at work early the following morning and must catch her train. She was sorry, but she really couldn't stay. They agreed to speak soon and parted at the studio doors.

As he walked across the darkening car park towards the battered Fiesta, he was conscious of footsteps behind him. He turned, expecting to see Bex again, but found himself looking into the eyes of Lisa Drake. For a moment he stood quite still, surprised by her sudden proximity and aware that his mouth was open and that no words were coming out.

"Hi," she said, smiling.

"Hi."

"Did you get my card?"

"Card. Yes. Card. Thank you. Yes, I did." He was speaking as if programmed by computer and heard words coming out of his mouth that seemed nothing to do with him.

"So when are we going to do it again?"

She quite took his breath away, standing there in her well-tailored bottle green suit, the hem of her skirt a full hand-span above her shapely knees. And those legs that seemed to go on for ever. And her wide eyes. And the scent of Chanel. Already he felt the customary churning of his stomach that occurred whenever she came close. His mind ran through the alternative replies, all in a split second. Should he say 'tonight', or 'tomorrow night' or 'never'? Should he treat Katherine as a thing of the past? Was she a thing of the past? Should life move on? His mouth and some distant part of his brain took over as he heard himself say, "Lisa, I'm sorry, but I don't think we can do it again. I had a wonderful time, and I think you're great, but it's just that I'm already in a relationship that I don't want to give up."

She smiled a disbelieving sort of smile. "What?" She almost laughed, looking at him as though he were teasing her.

"We can't do it again."

"You're not serious, are you?"

"'Fraid so." He said it softly and with feeling, hardly knowing where to look.

Her face registered the incredulity of one not used to being contradicted. "You're prepared to throw away terrific sex just for old-fashioned loyalty?"

"Yes."

"But why? I thought you felt the same as I did. I thought this was something special." She smiled an encouraging smile. A smile that a black-widow spider probably smiles at a fly. She was not going to give in easily.

"It is. It was. I just can't go on leading a double life." It hurt him to say so. Even now, the evening they had spent together was replaying through his mind. The ecstasy and the complete losing of himself in her, and now the knowledge that she had felt the same. He had never experienced sexual attraction on this level before. Probably never would again. The combined feelings of danger and passion were a heady brew. He could hardly bear to look at her. When he did look up, the first signs of anger were beginning to spread across her face.

"Well, this is a first," she murmured. She half laughed and looked away. "Right. Well, I'm sorry I got it wrong. I only hope she realizes what she's got." She looked back at him, trying to hold his eye, but Rob could only gaze at the ground.

She carried on, "OK. Have it your own way. I'll let you get on with your life. And if you don't mind, I'll get on with mine." She raised a hand and quickly stroked it down his arm. "Goodbye."

She paused, about to say something else, then thought better of it. Turning away smartly, she pressed a button on her key-ring to open the door of the charcoal-grey BMW, slid in and roared out of the studio gates, her rear tyres kicking up chippings like the hooves of a galloping horse. In a few seconds, the throaty growl of her 325i was lost among the general hum of traffic.

"Fuck," he said slowly, under his breath. "Oh, fuck." And as he pushed the key into the lock of his car he noticed that his hand was shaking.

Chapter 21

"Gone? What do you mean she's gone?" Frank Burbage's voice boomed across the desk at Steve Taylor at a decibel level that was uncomfortable at any time of the week, but especially so at ten o'clock on a Monday morning. "Gone to her bloody hairdresser or gone for good?"

"Gone for good, I'm afraid."

"But she can't just bloody well up and leave. Who the fuck's going to do all her bulletins?"

Lottie Pym raised her eyebrows as she passed on her way to the photocopier with a P.45.

Steve endeavoured to placate him. "We'll appoint a replacement as soon as possible. Some time this week, I hope. Tomorrow we'll get a stand-in, but for today you'll just have to do the bulletins yourself."

"Fucking hell!"

Lottie Pym raised her eyebrows again on the way back to her desk. She was used to the language but not the volume.

"But she seemed fine on Friday. Positively buoyant," said Frank Burbage, with a note of bewilderment in his voice. "What the hell's happened since then?"

"She was made an offer she couldn't refuse, apparently."

"What sort of offer?"

"The only offer that Lisa would consider unrefusable. An offer to work on the network bulletins in London."

"Bugger me!"

"And me for that matter. It's not going to be easy to find a replacement."

"But had anyone any inkling that she wanted out? And, anyway, hasn't she got a contract to keep her here?"

"'No' to the first and 'yes' to the second, but the powers-that-be felt that the month left on her existing contract wasn't worth making a fuss about. The boss reckoned that it would reflect badly on the station if we tried to hold on to her and we'd come out of it better if one of our newsreaders was seen to be doing well on the network."

"But how come none of us had any idea?" asked Frank, settling himself into a chair opposite Steve Taylor and leaning forward on his desk. He rested his large chin on his hands and began his interrogation. The initial anger was gradually being replaced by curiosity and an appetite for gossip.

"None of us had any idea because I don't think Lisa had any idea herself. I know she had itchy feet – what young regional newsreader with any intelligence doesn't? – but I didn't realize that her departure would be quite as sudden. But then, to be fair to Lisa, I don't think she did either. I think it came like a bolt out from the blue and she was given twenty-four hours to make the decision."

Frank Burbage pushed his ruddy face nearer to Steve Taylor's pasty one. "Who by?"

"The Beeb."

"Oh. Well, that's it, then. Look out Jill Dando and Anna Ford, Lisa Drake is about to leave you standing."

He slouched back in his chair. "I wouldn't mind but she never even whispered anything to me. Three bloody years and she never breathed a word. Taught her all she knows and what thanks do I get?"

It was Steve's turn to raise his eyebrows.

"Oh, all right, so she was bloody good, but you've got to let me have my moan. Is she coming back for anything?"

"No. Wardrobe are sending her clothes direct to Telly Centre. Lottie's cleared her desk for her and boxed up her stuff – that's going off today by carrier. I am a bit surprised. I thought she might want to say goodbye but she said she'd rather not."

"You've spoken to her, then?"

"Yes, she rang me last night, about elevenish. Said it had all happened suddenly on Friday night. She'd been invited to London on Saturday morning, met the head of News who said he wanted an answer by Sunday morning and could she start on Monday. Said she'd rather just slip out quietly. Didn't want a fuss. Sounded a bit upset, actually, rather than elated. Odd, really."

"Bunch of bastards. They don't hang around, do they? Not like it was in my day. Gentlemanly, it was then. 'Come to my club and have lunch, old boy, and we'll make you an offer you can think about.'"

"Mmm." Steve took off his glasses and rubbed his eyes, replaced them and looked back at Frank, who was now launching into a reflection of his own halcyon days at the BBC.

Frank had never made the top flight of newsreaders, but had been sufficiently close to let a note of wistfulness creep into his voice. "You know, in those days they had career plans for you. I remember talking to a senior executive who said, 'This year we'll keep you in Industry, then next year we'll give you a stint as junior Court Correspondent' – you know, descriptions of Princess Margaret's dresses on visits to the poor in Nigeria – 'and then we'll give you a diplomatic stint in Paris or New York and when you've gained your street cred there' – except that in those days they didn't call it 'street cred', they called it 'experience' – 'we'll bring you into the studio as anchor.' Had it all mapped out for me, they did."

"So what happened?"

"Buggers changed their minds. Took on Martyn Lewis instead. Left me in Industry with a Saturday football match to keep me sweet. I never got so much of a sniff at Princess Margaret's skirts, let alone Nigeria. So I buggered off up here."

"Very much after the fashion of Lisa buggering off down there."

"Except that I did have the good grace to work out my contract."

"Well, there we are." Steve adjusted his body to indicate to Frank that this conversation had better come to an end as he had a lot to sort out. Frank took the hint without offence and pushed back his chair.

"You going to say anything to the viewers?" he asked, as he retreated towards his own desk by the window.

"Not sure yet. They'll know soon enough. We're putting out a statement to the press today about how delighted we are that Lisa has done so well – that sort of thing. We might not need to mention it on air."

"You'll have all the little old ladies writing in. And the dirty old men. They'll miss their early evening bit of fluff," said Frank, mockingly, as he pushed on his gold half-moon spectacles and began sifting through the sheets of paper on his desk. He picked up a scrap torn from a spiral-bound shorthand pad and read out loud: 'Dear Mr Burbage, Could you please ask Lisa Drake if she could send me a signed photograph for my bedroom. I am a big fan of hers and it would give me great pleasure to see her in front of me when I wake up.'"

He grunted, tore the sheet of paper into tiny pieces and dropped them like confetti into the round grey litter bin by his desk. "Well, you'll have to tune into the Beeb now, you little pervert."

The news spread round Northcountry Television faster than a flu epidemic. The talk in the canteen and in Makeup, in the car park and the loos was of nothing else. The station had lost its pin-up. Who would replace Lisa Drake? Junior female reporters began to smarten up their appearance. By Tuesday lunch-time Next and Principles had reputedly sold out of tailored two-piece suits.

Rob had heard about it on Monday afternoon during his conversation with Steve about Friday's programme. The news left him stunned. As stunned as Frank Burbage, but for different reasons. Should he tell Katherine? She would probably know by now, anyway, and it was not a piece of news that he felt comfortable breaking to her. He would leave it a while.

Several times during the last week he had dialled half her number. Once he completed the sequence and the phone began to ring at the other end but he lost his nerve and hung up. As long as he didn't speak to her there was still hope that she would take him back. He was too frightened of ringing her and discovering that she wanted nothing to do with him. But he could not keep on like this for much longer. That much he knew.

He needed a day out. A day away from the dale. He looked at the papers on his desk at End Cottage, among them a calendar of Royal Horticultural Society shows. The Early Spring Show at Westminster opened the following day. He hated London, but he would go. Just to get away. Then he remembered that London was where Lisa had gone, but he told himself that London was a big place and that there was no chance of them encountering one another and, anyway, if he were presenting this year's television coverage of the Chelsea Flower Show he ought to put in an appearance at one of the smaller shows. His reasoning ended there, which is why, on a sunny Tuesday morning, he found himself standing in one corner of the Royal Horticultural Society's lofty hall in Westminster rather than on the banks of a clear Yorkshire river.

The words 'cat' and 'cream' came into Rob's mind. A few yards away, between the stands of flowers and trees that proved spring really had arrived, he could see the figure of Guy D'Arcy, lording it over the ladies of the Trust Fund.

In navy blazer, grey trousers, sky blue shirt and pale yellow tie, Guy, with his easy aristocratic charm, was the sort of chap with whom Felicity Fortescue, the doyenne of Dickers in Devon, and the dumpy, tweed-trousered Emma Coalport – the Sackville-West disciple – felt comfortable.

"It's good news that you're doin' Chelsea," said Felicity, perforating the parquet with the spike of her battered shooting stick. "Time the programme had a bit of quality about it. Not that I ever watch the box meself."

"No. Never have time," snapped Emma Coalport, her beady eyes raking the stands of early herbaceous perennials. With any luck there would be some that she might be able to snaffle at low prices if she were to squash against some poor nurseryman with her cottage loaf of a figure and beat him into submission with her halitosis.

Rob smiled to himself and walked towards a long, low table covered in dark green hessian where a young nurseryman from Scotland had arranged a miniature landscape of rare Petiolarid primulas of the kind that folk south of the border could only dream of growing. He bent down to look at them closely, their leaves dusted with white flour and their blooms a soft azure blue. How his father would love them. He should have brought him, but then, Jock would never take time off from the nursery at this time of year.

He stood up and looked at the layout of the hall. For all the fact that he hated London, he did like coming to the monthly Westminster flower shows once or twice a year. What gave him a buzz was the smell of leaf and flower and rich earth that hit your nostrils as you left the exhaust fumes of the London traffic outside. The flashing of the press pass and the clicking through the turnstiles took him into a towering grey hall with high windows and a dark wooden floor that seemed as large as a football pitch. All over it, like small gardens, stood the raised wooden-sided stands draped in dark green cloth, each replete with flowers, fruit and vegetables of the highest quality, and all manned by some of the country's finest nurserymen.

At the top of the wide flight of steps at one end of the hall was a sort of loggia equipped with rows of chairs where old ladies would park their weary bodies, knees apart, showing off to all below the salmon sheen of their directoire knickers. Rob tried to avert his eyes, not always successfully.

He always took a notebook with him, and found it hard to resist coming home without a couple of RHS-crested carrier bags holding new treasures to try in his own garden or to give to Jock. He was just convincing himself that he could not grow the Scottish primulas in his riverbank garden when he recognized the voice at his elbow.

"Rob, how *are* you?"

He looked up from the miniature Caledonian landscape and found Guy D'Arcy beaming at him and offering his signet-ringed hand. Rob shook it firmly and smiled.

"I gather we're going to be working together again," said Guy, positively oozing bonhomie.

"Yes, so I hear." Rob did his best to keep an even tenor in his voice.

"Should be fun."

"Yes. Great fun." Rob tried to sound keen.

"I've been thinking about the programme quite a lot, and I think we should be really careful to make it a class act, don't you?"

"Sorry?" Rob was unsure that he had heard correctly.

"Bring a bit of class to the whole thing. I mean, Chelsea is a part of the Season, isn't it? Along with Ascot and Wimbledon. You know the sort of thing."

"Er . . . yes."

"It seems to me that we need to emphasize that. It would be very easy to let the programme slide into a sort of matey gardening show, but I think that would be a mistake, don't you?"

"Well, I'm not sure I quite see -"

"You have a great touch, I know, but I think this show probably calls for a different sort of style. I hope you don't mind me mentioning it?"

Rob found himself unable to answer, taken aback at Guy's brass neck.

"Oh, and have you heard about . . ." Guy looked over his shoulder to left and right in too theatrical a way for it to be kind. Satisfied that they were not being overheard, he continued *sotto voce*, "Have you heard about BLITZ?"

"Well, yes, I was at the press conference."

"I know. But no. I mean, have you heard about the advertising campaign?"

"No." Rob thought it best to admit nothing.

"Oh. I thought you might have done. Confidentially, of course . . ."

"Of course."

"They've asked me to front it. Rather good news, isn't it? They seemed to think I had the right kind of image for such a product. You know – a bit classy and go-ahead, I suppose. Not for me to say, but it's rather good to inspire such confidence, isn't it?"

"Very. Er . . . good luck with it," Rob said, pleasantly.

Before he had time to say any more, Guy brought their conversation to an end. His arrow having struck home, he had no further need to stay in the company of this populist man of the soil.

He was about to turn on his heel when he was almost bowled over by a little old lady in a grey mac, laden down with carrier bags, out of the top of which poked leaves and flowers in amazing diversity. She ignored Guy and turned her kind but myopic gaze on Rob. "Ooh, hello! Goodness! It's Mr MacGregor, isn't it?" she asked, with a genuine thrill in her voice. "Well, I never. I've been coming here for years and I've never bumped into you before. Great fan of yours, I am. I'm a member of the RHS, you know. I know a lot of folk think it's snobby but I like the plants and I like the nurserymen." She beamed at him from under her transparent rain hood, her wire-rimmed glasses framing pale blue rheumy eyes. "Well, I just can't believe it." She smiled at him and seemed to be examining him, like a keen butterfly collector taking pleasure in spotting a rare species. "Wait till I tell my sister. She thinks you're wonderful, too. It's so good to see a really young gardener who knows his stuff and who gets his hands dirty. I've been following your advice ever since you started and I've learned all sorts. Look. Would you mind? Just a minute . . ."

She thrust her overflowing carrier bags – all eight of them – into Guy's hands and delved into a large brown handbag for a battered envelope of photographs. "Here we are. This is my garden. We live in Cambridge, me and my sister, and this is what we had when we started."

The old lady went painstakingly through the two dozen photographs that illustrated the progress of her garden in Proustian detail, while Rob listened attentively and Guy, horrorstruck but unable to extricate himself gracefully, stood by holding her bags.

"Oh, now, look, I'm holding you up. I'm sorry to go on about it. Daft old lady that I am. But, you see, you've helped Esmé and me so much with our little garden that it's nice to say thank you in person, so to speak. I'll let you get on. And good luck."

She turned to Guy and took back her carrier bags. "Thanks ever so much. It's just that we're great fans of his, see. Sorry to interrupt your conversation. Goodbye." And then, to Rob only, "Lovely to meet you."

She bustled off into the crowd saying, "Goodness me," to herself, leaving Rob trying hard to suppress a smile, and Guy, for one rare occasion in his life, totally speechless.

Chapter 22

Two more weeks elapsed before Rob plucked up enough courage to dial Katherine's number, and even then he felt nervous. Supposing she refused to answer? Supposing the answering-machine was switched on: should he leave a message? What if she answered and then put the phone down on him? Having gone through a seemingly inexhaustible list of pessimistic permutations he eventually found his index finger punching out her number on the phone in his kitchen at seven o'clock one evening.

He heard the engaged tone at the other end and replaced the receiver. She was in. Either that or somebody else was leaving a message.

He poured himself a glass of red wine – Fleurie, they'd always drunk it together. He took a sip, and another, waited a few minutes, then dialled her number again.

It rang at the other end. Apprehension oozed from every pore. Then a small voice answered, "Hello?"

"Hello," he said, softly.

There was a pause. Then, "Hi. How are you?" Non-committal.

"OK. How are you?"

"Oh, you know."

"Yeh. Guess so." There was a longer pause. Then he said what he really wanted to say. "I miss you."

"I miss you, too." She sounded measured, unemotional.

"I'm sorry about everything," he half muttered, half blurted. "I'm sorry I cocked it up."

"Me too." There was more of a hardness in the voice now.

He was uncertain whether this was a motion of censure or simple agreement. "I just wanted you to know that I've explained to – the other person – that there's no chance of anything happening. That's all."

"Oh?"

"And I'd love to see you some time."

"I see."

"If that's all right."

"I'm not sure. Look, I'm sorry but I'm still hurting. I wanted us to be together because we *wanted* to be together, not because we thought we *ought* to be together or because it had become a habit."

"I know."

"What are you doing?"

She asked the question matter-of-factly, but Rob thought he detected a softer note in her voice. "Having a glass of wine."

"What sort?"

"Guess."

She paused for a moment. "Fleurie."

"Yes."

She paused again. He could hear her breathing. Then, hesitantly, she said, "Our wine."

"Yes. I only wish you were drinking it with me."

"Look, I'd better go."

"Do you have to?"

"I think so, yes. Thanks for ringing me."

"I'll speak to you soon, then?"

"Why?"

The question took the wind out of his sails. "Because I love you."

Silence, and then softly, "Do you?"

"Yes."

The pause seemed to last for ever. "I must go. Mamma's coming round. You take care. 'Bye."

"'Bye."

And she was gone. He held the receiver to his ear a little longer to make sure she had rung off, and then, aware of the loneliness of the moment, when one caller puts the handset down and the other still holds it to their ear, he replaced it smartly in the cradle and took another sip of wine. Somehow it didn't taste like it used to.

Chapter 23

God, it felt good to be outside. Good to feel the sun making you squint. Good to be rid of the studio and making programmes in real gardens. Rob looked across to where Bex Fleming was standing among a sheet of daffodils, talking to the camera as though it were an old friend. He watched her from his perch on top of a flight of stone steps at the side of the Old Manor House in Nidderdale from where *Mr MacGregor's Garden* would be broadcast this week.

Behind the house the hills rose towards the soft blue sky and were now flushed with fresh green as the buds began to break. Rooks cawed in a clump of poplars alongside the tumbling beck that argued with the rounded boulders in its path. Now the scent in his nostrils was of pollen and unfurling leaves, not of baby wipes and Max Factor.

Location filming meant that the programme would no longer be live but recorded. Despite his love of the adrenaline that only came with live broadcasts, the change was something of a relief in the wake of Bertie's outburst.

He watched Bex pick her way among the nodding blooms, talking to the camera as she did so. She would stoop now and again to caress a flower, and pause occasionally to make some point more forcefully.

He watched quietly, and at a distance, admiring her skill and her rare ease with the camera. He had forgotten about his own technique, it was now so much a part of him, but he had seen enough people pass through the studios as guest presenters to know that her combination of horticultural knowledge, ease with the camera and a pleasant personality was unusual. Couple them with blonde good looks and the mixture was irresistible.

And yet he watched Bex going through her paces with a brotherly rather than a lecherous eye. It surprised him a little. She was stunning to look at, had a personality that he found hugely attractive, and yet right now he felt that nothing intimate would come of their friendship. Odd. But thank God for that.

"And cut." Steve's voice sliced through the spring morning. "I think that's lunch."

He walked over to where Rob sat on the old stone steps. "All right, sunshine?"

Rob smiled at the spring in his step and the colour that was beginning to appear in his normally sallow cheeks. "I'm surprised you can cope with it," he said.

"What?"

"The air. I'd have thought it would have been much too strong for you, an indoor type."

Steve pushed his horn-rimmed glasses back up his nose and inhaled deeply, smiling beatifically as he did so. "You know, I think I could get into this gardening lark. Wonderful life. No worries, leisurely pace, meeting other delightful men of the soil. It's a recipe for a ripe old age, I reckon, rather than being stuffed into a newsroom with all those jaundiced journos."

"You coming out here for good, then?" Rob asked.

"I wish," replied Steve, his smile disappearing like the sun behind a cloud. "I wish."

"That's a definite maybe-not, then?"

"That's a definite no, I'm afraid."

"Shame," said Rob.

"It's all down to Miss Drake, I'm afraid."

Rob was conscious of the flush rising in his own cheeks now and did his best to arrest its development. "Oh? Why's that?" He rose from the step, brushed down the seat of his jeans with his hands and looked out across the valley.

"We need a replacement before the week's out, so I've auditions to organize for the next couple of days and then I'll be studio-bound getting the new girl into the swing of things."

"Well, you'll enjoy that."

"Yes. But it'll be a bit of a slog, and the prospect of all those babes making eyes at me and offering me their beds in return for a job will be a real strain."

"Oh, I bet," said Rob, turning round to look at him and see just how straight he had been able to keep his face.

"It's true. The sexual appetites of female newsreaders are known to be voracious.'

"Really?" Rob turned his back on his producer once more.

"You mean you hadn't noticed?" Steve queried.

Before Rob had time to reply, or even to turn round, Bex interrupted.

"Did somebody say lunch?" she asked, flashing a smile at the two men.

"Yes." Steve pointed in the direction of an old stone barn. "The lady of the house has knocked up some home-made soup and rolls. Help yourself. We'll be over in a minute, I just want a word with Rob."

Bex smiled again, said, 'OK,' and sauntered off.

"That sounds ominous," said Rob.

"No, not really. It's just that we've been looking at the way you two have been getting on on screen."

"Mmm?" Rob raised his eyebrows.

"You and Bex."

"And?"

"You must have noticed how well it's been working? And the ratings have been going through the roof."

"I know." Rob wondered what was coming.

"It's not that we want to reduce your content in the programme, but just that we think it would be a good idea if Bex had fractionally more to do, rather than just a single item. The programme would still be called *Mr MacGregor's Garden* and you would still have all the links and the lion's share of the work, but Bex's presence would be rather larger than Bertie's. What do you think?"

Rob was not sure how he felt. Disappointment was the first emotion to flood through him. Then he paused, remembered what he had been thinking about Bex only moments previously, and realized that there was only one reaction he could voice without being either vain or hypocritical. "I think it's a great idea. She's great. We get on well. It's fine. I'll just put my enormous jealousy on the back-burner."

Steve smiled. "Good man. We're not pensioning you off, you know, just making you even more sexy by pairing you with a fanciable co-presenter." He watched Bex walking into the barn below them, her corn-coloured hair glinting in the spring sunlight. He shook himself out of his temporary reverie. "Anyway, think what Lisa Drake did for Frank Burbage's reputation. Everyone thought he was a tired old warhorse until she came along to liven things up. I'm not suggesting you have an affair with Bex or anything. Of course I'm not. Having nursed Frank and Lisa through theirs I've had quite enough of that sort of thing."

And he got up from the step and walked towards the barn for his lunch.

"Could we do that just once more, Guy darling?"

Two girls descended upon Guy D'Arcy, one with a powder puff, the other with a can of hairspray, as he stood beneath the mouth parts of a gigantic plastic greenfly wearing a white tuxedo with a red carnation in his buttonhole, a black tie, black trousers and patent-leather shoes.

Under the arc-lights of the massive studio he stood square on to camera, legs slightly apart, in classic James Bond stance, his left hand tucked into his right armpit, and his right hand grasping a weapon, which rested on his left cheek after the manner of the Ian Fleming hero. Admittedly, he looked slightly less macho than Sean Connery, Roger Moore or Pierce Brosnan, but that was probably because the Beretta normally used in this classic pose had been replaced by a hand-sprayer filled with pesticide.

Three more young women stood on the sidelines in the half-light, clucking about the jacket, the buttonhole and the state of Guy's eyeliner, while the hero of the piece continued to reduce to jelly any of them who came within breathing distance of him. He did look good. He felt good, too. And the prospect of not having a leaky roof any more, or even of moving upmarket from Fulham to Chelsea, cheered him no end. His thoughts never turned to Rob MacGregor. Not once. And even thoughts of Claudia Bell were, mercifully, receding into the depths of his memory. Lovely lady. Large lady. But very grateful.

"Just once more, darling, if we could," came the disembodied voice of the director over the studio PA. He would be happy to do it as many more times, darling, as the director of the commercial requested.

"Thank you, studio," said the voice, and the floor manager, a girl with short dark hair and a crisp white T-shirt that emphasized her figure, raised her eyebrows at Guy to check that he was happy before saying firmly, "And cue . . ."

Thunderous music in pseudo-Bond style boomed out from vast speakers at the edge of the studio floor. As it reached its crescendo in the short cadenza it paused. Guy looked into the camera at his most appealingly macho and said, "The name's BLITZ. Licensed to kill." Then he spun round on his heel and aimed the spray gun at the massive greenfly. It exploded in a coruscating shower of sparks and flashes, while brilliant spotlights beamed through white smoke to put our hero in dramatic silhouette.

"And cut. Lovely, lovely. I'm coming down."

And I'm coming up, thought Guy, conscious that over the past week his career had taken a much more promising turn.

It had been a spectacular shoot. A week on location with

helicopters, filming dramatic aerial sequences in Italy where things looked greener at this time of year, followed by two days in the London studios for the dramatic dénouement. The theme of the piece was a James Bond chase in which the villains were not Spectre and Smersh, but greenfly, whitefly and scale insects. Our hero triumphed in the end, thanks to his trusty spray-gun filled with BLITZ, which put paid to the lot.

Two more girls came over to tend Guy; one offered him a chamois leather dampened with eau-de-Cologne to dab on his temples, another helped him out of the white tuxedo.

The director, a grossly overweight man with a pink shirt, yellow bow-tie and rosy cheeks, waddled out of the gloom and across the studio floor as the smoke began to clear to offer his congratulations. "Wonderful. Absolutely lovely. I'm very excited about it. Guy, you were just what we needed and I'm sure the campaign will be a huge success. Go home and put your feet up, you're a star."

Guy thanked him politely, shot his cuffs and left the studio floor with a bevy of attentive girls in his wake. He could get used to this, he thought. He could very easily get used to this.

Helena Sampson's day had not been nearly so fulfilling. She had spent several hours thumbing through back issues of the *Nesfield Gazette* in the dimly lit storeroom at the newspaper offices and come up with little. What she had discovered was the death notice of the wayward Armitage brother in the Hatches, Matches and Dispatches column during the December just gone – Katherine had remembered having seen it. Strange that he should only just have died. But it was the sole indicator of his passing and offered no clues as to the character of the man:

Armitage, Reginald Steadman, aged 77 years, on 23 December, in Devon, after a short illness. Husband of the late Susan Armitage and brother of the late Francis (Fred) Armitage. Beloved father of Gladys. Private funeral. No flowers.

Not the kind of announcement that would have made Miss Marple sigh one of her inscrutable sighs.

She asked Nancy, Katherine's secretary, if it would be possible to have a photocopy. The copy was taken and the large, dark green linen-bound volume of the *Nesfield Gazette*, July–December 1997, was returned to the grey metal shelves of the storeroom until some other curious researchers needed to delve within its covers.

Helena folded up the piece of paper, put it in her handbag and blinked as she left the gloom of the storeroom for the sunlit street.

Chapter 24

Rob was deeply pissed off. For several days after the revelation of Frank Burbage's affair with Lisa Drake, he had alternated between feeling angry and stupid, sorry for himself and annoyed at his folly. Where once he had felt the excitement of having a new lover, he now felt the sensation of crushed pride. Clearly he had been just another amusing conquest along the way. It irritated him that he was so affected by it. Saddened him that he had been so taken in.

He forced himself not to think of her, to concentrate, instead, on Katherine. Katherine, who'd seemed reluctant to talk when he'd rung her. So what was the point? He would wipe both of them from his mind, for a time at least, and concentrate on his work.

It wasn't easy. He messed about in the garden at End Cottage. He wrote his pieces for the paper and soldiered on with his weekly sortie into *Mr MacGregor's Garden*, happier now that it was being recorded in the great outdoors and with someone whose company he enjoyed. He picked up the *Daily Post* one day and discovered, on page seven, an article about Bex Fleming. They'd given her a make-over, to prove that this girl with the T-shirt and jeans who wielded a spade with Mr MacGregor on Friday nights could look surprisingly glamorous when she let down her hair, put on some makeup and showed off the legs that were normally encased in denim and wellies. They were not bad legs at all, thought Rob, gazing at the full-length photograph and trying hard not to feel like yesterday's man.

He folded up the paper and sighed. He didn't enjoy these gnawing feelings of jealousy and rejection. From riding the crest of a wave just a couple of months ago, he now found himself in the Slough of Despond. The programme was doing better than ever; he and Bex had been offered a two-year contract, which he had been pleased to accept. But Jock's financial problems had not gone away and neither had Dennis Wragg. What *had* gone away was the imminent possibility of having enough money to sort things out. What had also gone away was love.

Guy D'Arcy could not have felt better as he sauntered around his garden in Fulham spraying the promising young shoots of roses and shrubs with his trial sample of BLITZ. Young greenfly were already beginning to show on the fresh green growth, and Guy hummed the Bond-like music to himself as he sprayed here and there, using his spray-gun like a pistol and providing his own bullet-like sound-effects. "Pow . . . pow-pow!" He checked over his shoulder now and again to make sure that the neighbours were not watching him, then went indoors to wash his hands.

It was funny, he thought, how when one thing went well, everything seemed to go well. It was almost the end of April. BLITZ would be launched in a couple of weeks' time and the *Sunday Herald* had been happy to promote the fact that their gardening correspondent was about to launch something that would change the face of gardening for ever. Then there would be the Chelsea Flower Show programme to look forward to. He'd probably take a holiday after that. And he knew just the person to go with him.

Since the heavy-hocked Sophie had cantered out of his life, and he'd given Claudia the old heave-ho, he'd been happy to resort once more to the little black notebook from Smythson in Bond Street – the one labelled 'Blondes, Brunettes, Redheads'.

He'd needed to go no further than the first page of the section labelled 'Brunettes' – thoughts of Claudia's blonde, lacquered hair still sent a shiver down his spine, and the merest whiff of Elnette or Youth Dew was enough to make him break out in a cold sweat. He needed someone young and fresh, and nearer to featherweight than his conquests of late.

He had a 'yes' to his first phone call the night after Claudia bustled back to Sir Freddie. The new girl in his life was Serena Clayton-Hinde – legs up to her aristocratic armpits, sleek black hair that flicked up above her shoulders, the impeccable voice and manners that came straight from South Kensington and a sex drive that came straight from *Farmer and Stockbreeder*. Serena's appetite between the sheets, Guy discovered, was on a par with his young nephew's appetite for chocolate Hob-Nobs.

Serena had class and good looks in abundance, but no money to speak of (Daddy had been a Name at Lloyd's). Still, now that Guy's fortunes had changed, and the cheque was already in the bank, that didn't seem to matter. She knew all the people he knew, looked great on his arm and made no excessive demands on him, except when she was on her back. It was time, he thought, to start looking for some kind of permanent relationship, and Serena had all the makings of a suitable spouse.

Guy smiled to himself as he dialled the number. The phone rang just three times at the other end.

"Hello?"

"Serena? It's Guy."

"Sweetie, how are you?"

"I'm fine. Look, I was wondering if you fancied dinner tonight."

"Mmm. I'd love that."

Guy adored the husky aristocratic tones. He smoothed down the short hair at the back of his neck with the hand that wasn't holding the phone. "Shall I pick you up at around seven thirty? Then we could have a drink in Covent Garden before we go somewhere round there to eat?"

"Great. And what about afterwards?"

Good God! thought Guy. She's thinking about it already. "We'll come back to my place. You'd better bring whatever you need. OK?"

"Lovely, Guy. Lovely. See you later, then. I'll go and get myself ready for you. By-eee," and she chuckled, half to herself and half to him, as she put down the phone.

Guy shook his head. Serena's conversation wouldn't keep Stephen Hawking entranced for long, but for the brief history of time into which the evening would soon pass she would do very nicely. He whistled the Bond theme again as he climbed the stairs.

Helena Sampson never whistled. But she did hum to herself as she walked out of the front door of Tarn House, depositing her front-door keys safely in her handbag. They nestled alongside an envelope she had received that morning from Katherine Page.

Wharfeside Nursery on a spring morning, thought Wayne Dibley, was the best place on earth. He sat on a large, moss-encrusted boulder down by the river, eating a freshly baked pie that Harry had brought back from the local pork butcher. He threw back his head to drink the warm liquor through the hole in the top of the shiny crust, then crunched through the crisp pastry into the succulent meat inside.

It was lunch-time, and Wayne liked to leave Jock and Harry to their desultory old-men's conversation in the potting-shed and sneak down to the water's edge. Here he could have time to himself, to watch the minnows darting from pool to pool in small shoals, and speckled trout nosing upstream in the deeper water. If he sat quite still, a white-breasted dipper would sometimes appear and probe around in the rapidly running water that tumbled over pebbles at the edge of the stream.

Something caught his eye. A flash of blue-green. He sat still, his half-eaten pie in his hand, watching a hole in the sandy bank opposite. Moments later, a kingfisher skimmed low over the water then up on to the overhanging branch of an alder.

This, thought Wayne, was real living. He munched slowly on

the remains of his pie, watching the bird preen and ruffle its vivid feathers. He reached for the pint pot of warm, sweet tea at his elbow and, as he drained the cracked mug, he looked at his watch. Five to one. Better get going. Jock was a stickler for punctuality and the lunch-hour lasted an hour, not an hour and a minute. Wayne scrambled back up the bank with the empty pint pot in his hand. The kingfisher flew off, downstream.

Shading his eyes from the sunlight that flashed between the branches of the willows and alders that lined the bank, now speckled with the fresh, juvenile green of unfurling leaves, he ambled down the path, pushed open the nursery gate and strolled towards the greenhouses to check his watering.

After a few months of proving himself to Jock, the old man had finally conceded that Wayne could take charge of one of the ancient greenhouses and its plants, with the result that he had become so anxious to do the job properly that he checked his watering three times a day. A bit much, Harry called it, grumbling whenever Jock enquired as to the lad's whereabouts. Jock only smiled to himself, aware that Wayne was following in the steps of his own son, with his liking for moments of solitude. It was a rare tendency in a lad from Wayne's part of the town, where youths tended to feel left out unless they were roaming around in a gang.

Wayne pushed open the door of 'his' greenhouse, plonked the empty pint pot on the staging and set about scrutinizing the pots and trays of plants that sat, cheek by jowl on the damp gravel. There was no sign of dryness in the compost of any of them, even when he pushed his finger in to check for moisture. Jock had been insistent on this point: you could not tell how dry a plant was merely by looking at the compost, you had to feel it with your fingers.

Wayne's greenhouse contained bedding plants – antirrhinums and nicotianas, he had learned to call them, instead of snapdragons and tobacco plants. And pelargoniums, masses of them, not to be confused with true geraniums, which he now knew were hardy garden plants.

He wandered to the end of the stone-flagged path that ran down the centre of the greenhouse and looked at some shrubs that he'd dug up and put into large pots a few weeks ago. Jock had been talking about how the Victorians used to force them into flower early by growing them in pots and bringing them into a cool greenhouse in January. Wayne had asked if he could try it and Jock, not wanting to dampen the lad's enthusiasm by pointing out that it was now late February, had said that he could have a go with three or four, provided they weren't his best plants.

Wayne had potted up a lilac, a deutzia, a viburnum and several of the old Professor's rose-bushes that had almost been washed away in the flood. The deutzia looked a bit sickly, but the others were doing well and flower buds were clearly in evidence. The lilac was showing colour, and fat, promising rosebuds indicated that in a few weeks' time, all being well, Wayne would have succeeded in the task of encouraging his rose-bushes to bloom in May.

Satisfied that all was well, he picked up his mug, closed the old greenhouse door behind him and headed for the potting-shed, dribbling an imaginary football in front of him and singing under his breath the words of the latest bit of rap that had come his way.

Harry was at the white porcelain sink in the corner of the potting-shed when Wayne opened the door, washing mugs in the cold stream of water that trickled out of the solitary brass tap. He looked round and held out his hand. "Give us it 'ere an' I'll rinse it."

Wayne handed over the mug and Jock, already at the potting-bench, turned round to the lad.

"Everything all right down there?"

"Oh, yes, fine. I thought there might be something dry, what with the sun and all, but everything was fine. I'll check it again later. I saw a kingfisher down by the river. Brilliant, it was."

"Not here often enough, though. I think the bad weather must have brought it in. It usually likes smaller streams, but that sandy bank must be to its liking."

"I couldn't see a nest."

"No, you wouldn't. It nests in a hole – like a rabbit. Probably got a brood of chicks already. It has two broods a year, you know – one in April and another in June. Keep your eyes open and you might see more of them, unless it decides to move off."

"Do you think it will?" Wayne asked, concern in his voice.

"Difficult to say. You can't predict what birds will do, least of all kingfishers. They're getting rarer, I'm sad to say, but I hope this one stays. I watch it from the kitchen window most mornings now. Lovely bird -" Jock broke off from his musings at the sound of a car coming down the lane. He poked his head out of the potting-shed door and saw Lady Sampson's Discovery pulling up by the wall outside the nursery gate.

She got out, locked the car door, pushed open the gate and walked purposefully down the path towards the potting-shed.

"Good morning!" she hailed Jock.

"Good morning to you," answered Jock, stepping out of the potting-shed and raising his cap. "How are you, Lady Sampson?"

"I am *very* well, thank you."

"Well, that's pretty definite," countered Jock.

"Do you have a few minutes to spare, Mr MacGregor? I've got something to tell you. Is there somewhere we can have a quiet chat?"

"Aye, if you like. Over there on yon bench. Will that do?" Jock's face now showed a mixture of emotions – curiosity, bemusement and not a little worry.

Helena looked towards the green-painted, slatted Victorian bench at the far end of the path where it had been placed so that visitors to the nursery could pause for a while and admire the view of the river and the dale beyond.

"That would be fine," she confirmed, and the two of them set off down the path.

"This sounds a bit serious," ventured Jock.

"It is, rather. I was going to talk to Rob about it before I spoke to you, but he's not in so I've come to you first. I hope you don't mind. It's to do with Dennis Wragg."

"Oh. I hope you're not going to try to persuade me to part with the nursery. Everyone else is and I'm afraid I'm digging in my heels," said Jock, trying hard to remain polite in the face of what appeared to be more interference.

"Not at all. I think it would be a great shame if you parted with the nursery. It's the last thing I want to see."

Jock felt relieved that at least one person appeared to see his point of view.

"So what's to do with Dennis Wragg?"

"You remember the day I came to see you and said I'd discovered that Gladys Wragg was the daughter of Fred Armitage's brother?"

"Yes. Bit of a shock that was."

"Well, I think you should prepare yourself for another shock. Sit down."

Jock lifted his checked tweed cap, smoothed down his grey hair and replaced it before parking himself on the green-painted bench.

"It seemed to me just too coincidental that Gladys Wragg was the daughter of Reggie Armitage who, in turn, was the brother of old Fred Armitage, the man you bought the nursery from. I thought this must have something to do with why the Wraggs wanted the nursery."

"Aye. I can see that," admitted Jock.

"Well, being an old woman with far too much time on her hands, I thought I'd try to get to the bottom of it. And I think I might have done."

Jock sat up and turned his head towards her. "You have?"

"Yes. I hope you don't mind. Oh, goodness, you *don't* mind, do you? I hope you don't think I was just interfering?"

"Lady Sampson, you know me well enough to know that I would tell you if you had overstepped the mark. You haven't, and I'm flattered that you've taken the time. Go on."

"Well, although Vera Ipplepen might be something of a gossip, her grasp of local knowledge is usually based, to some degree, on fact."

"Aye." Jock smiled.

"Well, according to Vera, Fred Armitage's brother was a bad 'un. All she said was that Reggie was the black sheep of the family. I didn't want to pursue it with her so I went off and did a bit of research. I wasn't really getting anywhere until Katherine stepped in. She discovered that not only was Reggie 'a bit of a bad 'un', but that he only just escaped going to prison for armed robbery."

"What?"

"Katherine plodded her way through back issues of the *Nesfield Gazette*. That girl has even more staying power than I have. It must have taken her ages."

Jock looked reflective. "Aye, she's a grand lassie."

"I managed to discover that Reggie Armitage had died recently, but Katherine found out that he had been accused of being involved in a jewel robbery in Leeds in nineteen thirty-nine."

"But he didn't go to prison?"

"No. The evidence was too slight. Reggie was accused of being the driver of a van that he and his supposed accomplice used to make a getaway. But the prosecution couldn't make it stick. The man who was reputedly his partner was sent down but Reggie got off scot-free."

"His accomplice didn't shop him, then?"

"No. You see, they never found the loot. The accomplice, who was the Mr Big of the piece, probably reckoned that if he shopped Reggie they'd both lose the proceeds, whereas if one went to prison and the other guarded the loot, at least the one who was put away would have something to look forward to when he came out."

"But he'd be away a long time for armed robbery."

"If they'd been able to pin him down for armed robbery, yes. But they couldn't. All they could get him for was being in possession of a firearm without a licence."

"So what did he get?"

"Six months."

"And he claimed his share of the loot when he got out?"

"No. He never came out. He died in prison of a heart-attack a week after he was sent down."

"So Reggie had all the loot and was a free man?"

"If he *was* a part of the robbery, yes, but he would have known that he would have to be careful. He knew the police would be watching him like a hawk, so even if he converted the loot into a lot of money he couldn't do anything ostentatious in case he was found out."

"But how do you know all this? It isn't the sort of thing they print in newspapers, is it?"

"Well, the facts of the case were published, with quite a degree of speculation about what really happened. The feeling was very much that Reggie and his partner had done it but got away with it due to lack of evidence. They didn't say so in as many words but the implication was there."

"If they did commit the robbery, how much did they get away with?"

"Just a minute." Helena opened her handbag and withdrew a buff envelope from which she pulled several photocopies of news clippings. "Here we are. The jeweller's in the Headrow was robbed of uncut stones worth eighty-five thousand pounds."

Jock whistled. "That was quite a sum of money then. It's quite a sum of money now. And did they never get the stuff back?"

"No. Even though the getaway van wasn't exactly speedy, they somehow managed to spirit the loot away."

"So what happened to it?"

"Who knows? It could have been tucked away in a safe deposit box somewhere. But then there is always the chance – and I know this sounds a bit far-fetched and straight from *Boy's Own Paper* – that it could have been hidden somewhere. And with Reggie being the brother of Fred Armitage . . . Well, there's always the chance that it could have been hidden in the nursery."

"Get away!" Jock looked baffled.

"Well, that would explain why Mr and Mrs Wragg want to get their hands on the place."

"But that's just too ridiculous." He looked at Helena, who raised her eyebrows.

Jock continued, partly incredulous and partly embarrassed at not believing her seemingly ludicrous conjecture, "You don't really think the loot is here, do you? I mean, wouldn't he have given it to a 'fence' or whatever they call them? Or wouldn't he have collected it before? The robbery was – what? Sixty years ago?"

"Almost, yes. But Reggie was a teenager and he wasn't a big-timer. His accomplice was the real villain, and he wasn't someone Reggie mixed with regularly, according to the newspaper reports. They reckoned Reggie was well out of his depth. It's possible that he wouldn't have known how to find a fence."

"So when did Reggie die?"

"Just a few months ago, down in Devon. He was seventy-seven. 'After a short illness', the death notice said."

"And you think that he told Gladys Wragg about it on his deathbed and she's out to reclaim her father's ill-gotten gains?"

"It's certainly possible."

"But I still can't see why he didn't reclaim the stuff earlier. Why on earth would he leave a load of jewels anywhere, then tell his daughter about them sixty years later? It just doesn't make sense."

"Oh, it could make very good sense. I've been a magistrate long enough to know that people do the strangest and most unpredictable things when they're under pressure. There must have been times when he was tempted to use the loot, but there would always have been the risk that if he were shown to be worth a lot of money the long arm of the law would have noticed and come down on him like a ton of bricks. On balance, life would be less of a strain without it. To use it might also have been more than his conscience could bear."

"So presumably Reggie thought that, sixty years on, folk would have forgotten about the raid and he could safely tell his daughter where the loot was?"

"I'm only guessing, but it's perfectly possible. People often see things more clearly when they're facing death." For a moment, Helena was lost in her thoughts, and Jock in his. The river ran slowly by beneath them.

Then Jock broke into the stillness. "So the Wraggs are not likely to give up just yet, then?"

"On the contrary, I should expect a fair degree of activity over the next few months, and quite a bit of urging you to sell."

"But why do they need to buy the place? If they're just looking for loot they could simply do the place over." Jock's face darkened.

"Well, as yet the Wraggs have shown no signs of being into robbery or violence. Oh, maybe my imagination is just too well developed. But we'll see. There has to be some reason why the Wraggs want your nursery and this reason strikes me, fantastic though it might seem, as perfectly plausible."

"So I need to keep my eyes open everywhere for the glint of diamonds?"

"Yes. Though I doubt that they'll be lying around in full view."

"No," mumbled Jock. "No, I suppose not."

Chapter 25

Rob ran himself a deep, hot bath, and tipped in half a packet of pine Radox. After a morning chained to his word-processor he'd felt a burning desire to get out into the fresh air and work off his pent-up emotions. As a result he'd driven down to the nursery to offer his father his services for the afternoon. Jock regaled him with Helena's theory about why the Wraggs were so interested, and was not in the slightest bit surprised when Rob made disbelieving noises. He really did begin to wonder if she had flipped.

"Yes, I know it sounds far-fetched, but it is possible," his father insisted.

"Possible but hardly probable."

"That's what I thought at first. But the more you think about it, the more it makes sense."

Rob had become a little impatient with his father and had taken himself off to his old greenhouse, only to discover that it was occupied by Wayne. He should not have been surprised. He'd been gone for several years now and could hardly expect his father to regard it as his territory indefinitely. He smiled at the new occupant, exchanged pleasantries, then walked to the potting-shed, took down a well-worn spade from a hook and sauntered off towards the plot of vacant ground by the river.

The young trees that had been growing in this patch of black, crumbly earth had been sold during the winter, and Jock, Wayne and Harry had not got round to digging it over. Rob knew that this was where the wallflowers would be sown in May and set to, turning it over with his spade and pulling out the odd patches of chickweed, groundsel and annual meadow grass that had sprung up since the flood and hurling them into a barrow.

In just a few minutes he was into his rhythm, pushing the spade into the dark, yielding earth, lifting up a lump of soil, flicking it over and allowing it to fall back into the hole from which it had been removed.

This kind of exercise he found far more rewarding than anything on offer at the local gym. Spend an hour on a rowing machine or an exercise bike and what had you to show for it except a sodden T-shirt and a lack of breath? Here, as the sweat speckled his brow and ran down his cheeks, he could pause now and then to lean on his spade and look at the freshly cultivated soil appearing in front of him. He had always found it supremely satisfying, and every time he felt unsettled or agitated, a spot of digging would sort him out.

He stuck at it until the patch of ground was completely cultivated, free of weeds and even in its clod size. Then he trundled his barrow to the compost heap in the far corner of the nursery, cleaned off his spade with an oily rag and hung it up in the potting-shed before bidding his father farewell and heading for home.

Jock looked at the patch of newly turned earth and bit his lip. Father and son had exchanged few words since the conversation about Lady Sampson, but Jock felt a wave of emotion as he looked at the cultivated ground that bore the marks of his son's spade. He'd never met anyone who could turn over soil so evenly, but there it sat, the peak of each of its clods at exactly the same height, and all achieved so effortlessly, it seemed. He sniffed and shook his head, smiled and returned to the potting-shed, grateful.

Rob pulled off his damp rugby shirt and jeans, dumped his underwear and socks in the dirty linen basket and slid his aching body down beneath the fragrant suds with a sigh. He was out of practice, but the afternoon had been just what he had needed. He reached for the bottle of beer at the side of the bath and took a long swig before lying back and allowing the warm water to ease the stiffness of his muscles. "Oh, Katherine," he whispered, "where are you?"

Rob might have been facing the prospect of an evening alone, but Guy D'Arcy was not. He had taken his time in dressing for his evening out with Serena Clayton-Hinde, putting on the pale blue Turnbull and Asser shirt, the silver watering-can cufflinks, the understated soft lemon tie and the grey Ralph Lauren slacks and navy blue blazer.

He picked up Serena from her home in Chelsea and drove her first to a wine bar in Covent Garden then on to Le Caprice, where they dined at a corner table and enjoyed scallops and lobster and a modest amount of champagne before Serena hinted that she was ready for the rest of the evening's activities, and wasn't it time to go? Aware that he had put away more champagne than he should have done, Guy drove very steadily towards Fulham in his new black BMW and parked it a few doors down from his house, thanks to the extra cars that always seemed to be there nowadays due to partying neighbours. The sooner he moved to Chelsea the better.

Serena was giggling and pulled him in through the front door as soon as he had opened it and extracted his key. Guy was feeling in pretty good spirits himself and pinned her to the wall in the hallway, running his hands down the slender body, encased in a little black velvet number. Serena pushed her arms inside his jacket and pulled him towards her. "Oh, Guy, Guy." She sighed, pressing hot kisses on his lips, all the while darting her tongue into his mouth. Guy eased himself away from her, took her hand and led her upstairs, a lecherous grin on his face. Serena giggled again, "Where are you taking me, you naughty man?"

"I'm taking you exactly where you want to go," replied Guy, walking backwards up the stairs with practised skill.

"Mmm . . ." A wide and slightly drunken smile lit Serena's face as she kicked off her shoes and began to climb. The lack of footwear made her legs seem even longer in the short black dress.

She teetered up the stairs, led by Guy's outstretched hand, while he used the other to take off his jacket and tie.

Once inside the bedroom, lit only by a small lamp on a tall mahogany chest of drawers, they faced one another and began to remove each other's clothes, grinning and kissing as they did so. Serena popped the buttons on Guy's shirt, slid it from his shoulders then set to work on his belt. Guy reached around her back and found the zip of her dress, easing it from her shapely white shoulders and running his middle finger down her long, smooth back.

Soon they stood in front of one another, naked.

"Mmm . . . just look at you," purred Serena, holding both his hands in hers and eyeing him up and down.

"And you," replied Guy, taking in the endless legs, the slim waist and the firm, if slightly small, breasts.

Slowly Serena pulled him towards the bed, flipped up the corner of the duvet, then fell back and pulled him on top of her. She was all animal now, her hands roaming everywhere over his body, her limbs thrashing around and twining round his waist, his chest and his neck. She planted moist, hot kisses all over his body, her once-neat black flicked-up hair ever more wild and unruly, falling over her face as she abandoned herself.

Beads of sweat began to appear on Guy's forehead as he became more entangled in the lissome limbs of this human boa constrictor. For fully fifteen minutes their mutual passion heightened, with groans, sighs and liquid noises.

Then Serena stopped. She pulled away from Guy and leaned up on her elbows, a troubled look in her eyes. "What's the matter?" she asked.

Guy was lying perfectly still, on his back. "I don't know." He tried to speak calmly.

"Does this happen often?" The concern in her voice matched the crestfallen expression on her face.

"It's never happened before in my life."

"Perhaps you need a bit more help." Serena's face broke into a mischievous smile. "Let me see what I can do." She reached down and began to stroke Guy between his legs. He groaned with ecstasy and arched backwards with pleasure as Serena's gentle and caressing touch made his heart thump in his chest.

"Come on, baby," she murmured, running her tongue over his firm stomach and gradually working her way down. Her smile faded as her lips reached the objective of her anatomical quest. She raised her head and looked Guy sympathetically in the eye. "What's the problem?"

"I really don't know."

They both lay there silently, looking up at the ceiling, the picture of disappointment. Every few seconds their heads would turn, as if to convince themselves that it really had happened, in the direction of that which hung pathetically down between Guy's legs. For the first time in his life, Guy D'Arcy had been unable to get it up. It was doubtful that he would ever get over the shock.

Chapter 26

The month of May dawned, if not as brightly as diamonds then at least as sparkling as the dew that garlanded every blade of grass. Katherine sniffed at the keen morning air as she walked down the road from her flat towards the offices of the *Nesfield Gazette* in the centre of town. Although she had left home early, Nancy had beaten her to it. The gilt-emblazoned door had been unlocked and the smell of fresh coffee greeted her as she pushed it open and walked into the paper's small reception area.

"Morning, Nancy."

"Morning, Katherine," came the voice from the kitchenette behind the old mahogany counter. "Lovely day."

"Yes, lovely," replied Katherine, sounding less than convinced, as she slipped off her jacket and hung it on a tall Victorian hat-stand. She peered out of the window through the back-to-front copperplate script that decorated it and looked upwards towards the moor: a lush green sheen was beginning to take the place of the russety brown and purple rug that had been its winter livery. She sighed. Would she ever get used to being without him? She sighed again. Enough. To work.

Nancy bustled in with a tray of coffee and rich-tea biscuits. "Would you like it in here or in your office?"

"Oh, in my office, please. I've a lot to do this morning. Any messages?"

"Only from Mr Wormald, saying he'll call at some point today."

"Now, there's a surprise," muttered Katherine, under her breath. "Everything else OK?"

"I think so. The two lads are out covering the stories you talked about yesterday, and everything's fine with this week's issue down at the printers. Oh, and the member of the council planning committee called and said that ten o'clock this morning would be fine. Is that OK?"

"Yes, fine." Katherine looked at her watch. "A quarter to nine. I've time to sort out a few things here and then I'll nip over to the County Council offices"

"Ah. She said could she meet you somewhere else? She thought the Council offices might be a bit public."

Katherine immediately perked up. "Did she?"

"She did," replied Nancy, looking knowingly at Katherine. The two of them knew by now that meetings with councillors that were not held at the Council offices tended to yield more tasty titbits than those that were.

"She suggested the lay-by on the Myddleton road, just after the footbridge. Are you on to something, do you think?" Nancy knew when she could risk asking and when to leave well alone. On this occasion her curiosity had got the better of her.

"Rumours about a bypass again – and you know how excited people get about that."

"I certainly do," said Nancy, as she dispensed the steaming brew. "Oh, well, good luck."

"Thank you." Katherine took a mug of coffee and walked towards her little office at the side of the reception area with decidedly more spring in her step than she'd had on her arrival. Now it was not simply the smell of coffee in her nostrils but the smell of a story, too. Nancy watched her go. It was nice to see her sparkle for a moment or two. She hadn't sparkled much at all just lately. Nancy took a biscuit and dipped it in her coffee. She had just slipped the soggy half into her mouth when the phone rang.

"*Neshfield Gashette*," she spluttered.

"Nancy?"

Nancy managed to swallow the soggy morsel and clear her throat, putting one hand over the handset while she did so.

"Yes?"

"Nancy, could I speak to Katherine, please? It's Rob. Rob MacGregor."

"Rob! Hello, yes, of course. I'm sorry, I was half-way through a biscuit. Just a minute, I'll see if she's there."

Nancy pressed a couple of buttons on her phone and Katherine picked up the handset on her desk.

"Yes?"

"It's Rob for you," said Nancy. "Are you in?" She asked without any edge in her voice, years of training having taught her the knack of sounding detached.

"Yes. Yes, of course," though half of her wanted to say no to give herself time to think.

A couple of clicks and then: "Hello? Katherine?"

"Yes?"

"Hello, it's me."

"I know."

"Hi!" A pause while both of them got used, once more, to hearing each other's voice on the phone.

"I'm sorry to ring you at work. I tried you at home but you'd gone."

"Yes, I left early."

"It's just that I needed to speak to you. It's about Helena."

Katherine's heart sank a little. She'd hoped that perhaps he wanted to talk about other things. But he didn't seem to.

"Do you think I could come and see you at the office? It wouldn't take long."

Her heart beat a little faster. How could she say no? She had to be professional. "Yes – yes, of course you can." Why was she speaking to him as if he were just another person and not *the* person? "When would you like to come round?"

"How about this morning?"

"I can't do this morning. I've someone to see. But I could make it this afternoon."

"Fine. What time?"

"About three. Would that be OK?"

"Fine."

He paused and she listened. Then she said, "I'll see you this afternoon, then."

"Yes . . . 'bye."

"'Bye." She put down the phone and tried to concentrate on the work that lay on her desk. But she failed, and her eyes, again, rose upwards to the moors, though she didn't see them, only him.

A smart rap on her office door brought her down to earth. It was not Nancy's polite tap. The door opened and Charlie Wormald stepped into the room, beaming what he considered to be a lady-killer smile.

"Good morning, Miss P. How are you?"

"Charlie! I thought Nancy said you were phoning me later today?" She tried to hide her irritation, not entirely successfully.

"Well, I thought I'd call in person. Better that way." The sunlight beaming through the window glinted on the high forehead that had been browned by frequent visits to the sunbed.

"What do you mean?"

"Oh, just wondered if you fancied lunch?"

"No thanks, Charlie."

"Go on. Take an hour or two off – all work and no joy makes Kate a dull girl!" He moved around to her side of the desk and perched his nattily suited body rather too close to hers. "There's a lot to talk about and we haven't dined together for weeks. What do you say?" He reached out his hand to clamp it on hers but she was too fast for him, rising smartly from her seat and walking over to the window.

"Oh, come on, Charlie. You know it's a waste of time."

"Waste of time? What's a waste of time?"

"All this."

"All what?"

"Do you really want to know?"

Charlie Wormald looked at her as if he knew what was coming. "Can't think what you mean."

"I think you can. I've had enough of your games, Charlie. You're old enough to be my father and you're a married man. I'm not interested. I'm here to look after your paper, not your love-life."

Charlie looked surprised. "I see."

"I've got quite enough problems with my own love-life without getting mixed up in yours, so just back off and let me get on with my job."

Charlie was still perched on the edge of Katherine's desk. "Well, that's told me I suppose." Half of him didn't want to give in so easily. The other half reminded himself that sexual harassment cases were all too frequent nowadays, and spiky Miss Katherine Page was probably just the sort to rush into litigation.

"Don't look so worried, Charlie. I'll still run your paper for you. Just don't push me on any other counts, that's all."

"R-i-g-h-t. Well, I suppose lunch is out of the question, then?"

"For now, yes. You can take me out to lunch when you want to discuss business."

"Well, there is one bit of business I do want to discuss."

"What's that?" Katherine remained at a safe distance by the window, her arms folded.

"I've . . . er . . . had a few approaches about a new road. Something to do with a bypass. Know anything about it?"

"What sort of thing?" Katherine asked cautiously.

"Just this and that. Nothing definite. I just thought you ought to know that there are certain people who'd rather the paper kept a low profile on the subject. It might be a good idea not to stir anything up. Know what I mean?"

"I know exactly what you mean, Charlie, and the answer is no."

"What?"

"You promoted me to editor of this paper because you trusted my judgement. I seem to remember that you told me at the time I was the only person you couldn't imagine being corrupted by power, or was that just a chat-up line?" Charlie drew breath, but Katherine continued before he had a chance to speak. "If you want a yes-man in this job, or a yes-woman, you've employed the wrong person."

"Now, look here -"

"No, Charlie, you look here. I've already buggered up a relationship because you were over-friendly in a restaurant and someone got the wrong idea. That's something I've had to learn to live with. But I'm not prepared to bugger up my professional life as well. I'm having to learn to live with my first mistake, but there's no way I could live with myself if I started kow-towing to pressures from people who should know better. And that includes you."

"I see."

"Good. And now you probably want to give me the sack." She turned her back to Charlie and looked out of the window. She guessed she should have felt sick; instead, she felt strangely elated. If he sacked her now, she really wouldn't care. It had done her good to get things off her chest.

"No. I don't want to give you the sack. You're a bloody good editor. I've always admired your guts. That's half the problem, I suppose. I should have stuck to admiring them and not the rest of you."

Katherine suppressed a smile, relieved at Charlie's acceptance of her stance.

"Fine. Well, I'd better let you get on."

Katherine looked at her watch. "Yes. I've someone to see. I won't tell you what it's about. You might think it's rubbing salt in the wound."

A stiff, chilly breeze, not unusual for early May up in the dale, blew through the open window of Katherine's old Renault 5 as she waited in the lay-by as arranged. It was already ten past ten and there was no sign of the councillor. She wondered how long to wait before deciding that she had been stood up when a large, dark green Rover cruised in behind her. The door opened and

Councillor Mrs Gosport heaved her portly, plum-coated body out and slammed the door. She crunched in her sensible black court shoes towards the passenger door of Katherine's Renault and tapped lightly on the glass. Katherine leaned over and pulled on the handle to release the lock and Councillor Mrs Gosport ('Call me Molly') compressed her bulky frame into the modest amount of available space.

Molly Gosport was classic county councillor material. A no-nonsense woman with a strong sense of community spirit, she was, nevertheless, not averse to using the local paper to further her own ends – strictly for the public good, of course. She pulled off her black leather gloves, laid them in her ample lap and thanked Katherine for coming. "I'm sorry to have suggested such a covert meeting but I thought the Council offices might just be a little too public."

"I see." Katherine slid her hand into the pocket of her jacket and pulled out her shorthand notebook.

"Yes, you'll need that," confirmed Molly Gosport. She un-buttoned her coat, which eased itself open with a sigh of relief from every seam, and warmed to her story. "You've heard about the bypass, I presume?"

"Well, it's been off and on for years, but there's not much activity at the moment, is there?"

"More than you'd think. The original plans were thrown out but there are new ones afoot, though it's not generally known yet. This sort of thing happens now and again, but this time I think there are some parties involved who are in it to feather their own nests and that's really not on." Molly Gosport's chins wobbled in unison, like the wattle of a prize turkey.

"So what's the story?" asked Katherine, her ballpoint pen poised over her pad.

Half an hour later Councillor Mrs Gosport extracted herself with not a little difficulty from the Renault 5 and wobbled back to her own car, leaving Katherine alone with two things – the scent of a hot story and the acrid tang of mothballs. In spite of the chilly air, she wound down her window for the journey back, marshalling her thoughts as she drove alongside the river towards the centre of town.

To see Rob sitting in front of her almost took Katherine's breath away, until she reminded herself why they were no longer together. She must stay cool and not give in to her feelings. She tried not to sound too hard. "So what is it?" She hoped she had avoided coming across as an impatient schoolmistress.

"It's Helena. She's read all the clippings you dug up for her about Reggie Armitage and has come up with a scenario that's worthy of Agatha Christie."

"Oh, God!"

Rob filled Katherine in on the elaborate chain of events that Lady Sampson had envisaged, all the time just grateful to be in Katherine's company, and hardly daring to hope that she felt the same. Katherine watched him, drinking in every movement of his body, every flicker of his features, at the same time registering the absurdity of the complex scenario. At the end of his explanation, having managed, in spite of her feelings, to keep pace with the story, Katherine admitted that she had no idea that Helena would have made so many assumptions. "Do you think it's really possible?"

"Well, I suppose so, but it's hardly likely, is it? The only thing it would do is make sense of why Dennis Wragg wants the nursery, and there's no other plausible reason as far as I can see."

"Until this morning I'd have agreed with you," said Katherine.

Rob looked at her keenly. "What do you mean?"

"I've just had a meeting with Councillor Mrs Gosport, and the reasons for Dennis Wragg's interest in Wharfeside Nursery are suddenly crystal clear."

When Rob left the offices of the *Nesfield Gazette* at half past four his love for Katherine knew no bounds. The only trouble was, he was still without her.

Chapter 27

"You've probably just been working too hard." The Harley Street specialist washed his hands at the sink in the corner of his consulting room as Guy D'Arcy put on his shirt and tucked it into his trousers. "There's nothing obviously wrong. Your blood pressure's fine and so are your blood-sugar levels. I've checked your peripheral circulation and the neurological tests don't show anything. It's probably just a temporary thing. I should think it will pass. It happens to most men at some time."

None of which Guy found very comforting. His ability to pull anything was as important to him as his career, and the prospect of Serena spreading it abroad that, once between the sheets, he really wasn't up to it filled him with gloom.

He needed to take his mind off things. He walked from Harley Street all the way to Jermyn Street to buy himself a new shirt and tie for the Chelsea Flower Show. But even lunch at Fortnum's with an old school chum couldn't take his mind off his predicament. He kept putting his hand in his pocket to make sure that it was still there.

Frank Burbage was whistling "You're Gorgeous" to himself as he marked up the pages and shuffled around the rough draft of his script for the lunch-time news. He sat behind his desk, putting gold cufflinks into the starched cuffs of his boldly striped shirt and barking things at secretaries from time to time in between looking out of the window at the bright morning.

"Wonderful day," he hollered at Lottie Pym, as she passed his desk on her photocopying run. She looked at him and smiled nervously. She always preferred it when Frank was grumpy – at least then you knew where you were with him. When he was cheerful you wondered when the next flare-up was due. She pressed the buttons on the photocopier and waited while the machine spewed out the scripts.

Frank may have had one eye on the weather, but the other eye was on the clock. It had taken Steve Taylor longer than he had hoped to find a replacement for Lisa. Frank had had to sit next to a motley crew of temporary substitutes, many of whom he considered to be as ugly as sin or as useless as a chocolate fire-guard. Some had gazed at the autocue, transfixed; others had dried up altogether. But at last Steve had succeeded in his quest and was due, this morning, to introduce his news-star-in-the-making to her workmates.

Why her identity had been kept such a closely guarded secret was a mystery to Frank, but Steve had said that the station didn't want any leaks before the official announcement and photocall due at noon today. Frank adjusted the knot in his brightly striped tie, looking in the hand mirror he always kept in his drawer, and hoped that the lavish amount of aftershave he'd dabbed on earlier in Makeup was lasting well.

He checked his teeth for spinach (unlikely as he'd not eaten it for breakfast) and ran a steel comb through his wiry grey hair, wincing as a handful came away between the teeth. He pulled out the departing filaments and dropped them from a dizzy height into his litter bin, looking wistfully after them as they disappeared from view among the old scripts and envelopes.

Frank mused on the possible identity of Lisa's replacement. There had been rumours abroad for a week or more. Some put their money on a BBC name being wooed over to this side – a sort of tit-for-tat arrangement or, as Frank preferred to put it, tit-for-tit.

Others were convinced that the newcomer would be just that, an unknown plucked from journalistic obscurity and thrust into the limelight where she would either blossom or wilt and die.

Frank didn't give a bugger as long as she made him look good and wasn't averse to a bit of private tuition on the side. Or the back.

There was a brief commotion in the corridor on the other side of the pale, wood-grained door of the Northcountry Television newsroom. Frank Burbage slipped off the gold half-moon spectacles, which although they made him look distinguished also added to his years (his ex-wife had told him), and coughed to clear his throat. He stood up behind his desk, assuming that television persona of the wise but fanciable uncle his viewers had come to recognize, as Steve ushered into the room the tastiest bit of crumpet Frank had set eyes on since he'd interviewed Elle Macpherson nine months ago.

"Hello!" he whispered, under his breath. "Hello-ho-ho!"

Steve steered his new charge over to Frank, who thrust out his hand. "Hi! Frank Burbage." He took her right hand in his, covered it with his left and looked into her hazel eyes as if gazing into a crystal ball.

"Hi! I'm Jessica Swan." She firmly withdrew her hand.

"Really?" And then, half to Steve and half to his new potential partner behind the newsdesk, "Well, I reckon that swapping a Drake for a Swan can only be good news."

Jessica smiled a rather strained smile. "I hope so."

Steve butted in to smooth over the initial stickiness. "Jessica is from Suffolk. She's been working at Anglia for a while. But she can tell you herself. OK, folks, back to work." He shooed off the peering group of journalists and secretaries, who'd been hovering around Frank's desk, on the pretext of clearing some scripted item with him or asking him if he wanted a coffee, with the intention of getting closer to the station's new bit of glam.

He turned to Jessica. "I'll see you in my office in five minutes and then we'll go down for the photocall. OK?"

231

"Fine. Thanks." She smiled at Steve and watched him go.

"Sit down . . . please." Frank gestured to a chair alongside his desk and watched keenly as Jessica lowered herself into it and crossed her long legs, easing down the checked tweed skirt to cover at least half her shapely thigh. The neatly tailored matching jacket was open wide enough for Frank's all-invading eyes to notice that underneath her ribbed turtle-necked sweater was a perfect pair of breasts. Her hair was short and dark brown, perfectly framing almond-shaped hazel eyes, a dainty upturned nose and full, wide lips. He looked at her teeth, like a vet examining a filly, and gave her a clean bill of health. In short, she was a stunner.

"So . . . welcome to Northcountry Television," breathed Frank, leaning across his desk in his most avuncular and friendly style – and almost suffocating Jessica in a cloud of Listerine vapour.

"Thank you. It's great to be here." The voice was clear and confident with no trace of an accent, and although there wasn't a lot of warmth in it, thought Frank, at least she wasn't sounding quite as chilly as she had in her first greeting.

"Tell me where you've come from."

Jessica leaned back in her chair, looking round the office as she replied, not giving Frank the undivided attention he would have preferred. "Oh, you know, the usual channels. University, then local papers, then local TV. I thought it was time for a move so kept my ears open. When I heard this was up for grabs I got my boss to put in a word and . . ." having taken in the staffing, the seating arrangements and the colour of the walls, she finally brought her eyes back to Frank ". . . here I am."

"Which university?" asked Frank, now a little wary of Miss Cool-and-Confident.

"Cambridge. Newnham College."

"Ah, same as Joan Bakewell."

"Yes, and Germaine Greer."

"Mmm. Double first?"

"Yup. English."

"Good for you." Frank was wilting, but attempted one more

232

sally. "So, as I say. Welcome. And if there's anything I can do," here he leaned forward again and put his hand on her arm, "don't hesitate to ask. I always think that the relationship between the newscasters – and I always use the term newscasters, not newsreaders, just in case those bloody hacks over there," he waved an arm in the direction of his scribbling minions, "get too full of themselves – I always think that our relationship is a vital part of the programme. The viewers like to see us getting on. Know what I mean?" He raised his eyebrows and smiled across at her.

"Yes," replied Jessica. "I know exactly what you mean, Frank." She leaned across the desk so that her face was barely a foot from his. Frank could smell her perfume and something stirred inside him. "And if you make one false move, Frank, I'll cut your balls off." With that she rose from the chair, smiled the most glittering smile at him, and walked off smartly towards Steve's office.

Frank sat back in his chair, looking for all the world like a schoolboy who had just been beaten at conkers.

Jock MacGregor's relationship with Harry Hotchkiss was not something to which he had ever given much conscious thought. Harry had come as a fixture and fitting with the nursery, and the two men had always rubbed along fine. Jock felt responsible for Harry's welfare, as the episode over the rent increase proved, but the two men never socialized, and their conversation at work seldom achieved intellectual heights, Harry's main preoccupation being the British Legion, his cough and his bowels.

Although Jock's daily preoccupation was now the survival of his business, there was no way he could communicate any of his fears to Harry. He would have to live with them for as long as it took the business to get back on an even keel. He tried to rid his mind of depressing thoughts.

On this particular morning, as the two of them were in the potting-shed brewing up the PG Tips, Jock found himself wondering about Harry's relationship with his previous employer and, come to that, with his previous employer's brother. Wayne was down in his greenhouse, checking his watering again, and two customers who had come in to look for 'something unusual in the shrub line' were rummaging about among the viburnums at the bottom of the nursery. Jock, finding a window in Harry's bronchial and bowel activity, tentatively asked a question. "Old Fred Armitage . . ."

"Mmm . . . harrumph?" asked Harry.

"How long did you work for him before I came along?"

"Oh, let's think . . ." Harry gave a loud, rumbling cough that seemed to emanate from somewhere near his groin and then offered, "It would'a been about ten year. I started wi' 'im in nineteen forty."

"Did you ever meet his brother – Reggie?"

Harry paused with the grubby brown kettle hovering over the even grubbier teapot. He looked up at Jock, then down again, and carried on pouring the scalding water over the pile of brown leaves in the bottom of the pot.

"Aye. Just the once. He were a bad 'un. Mr Armitage'd 'ave nuthin' to do wi' 'im."

"So when did you meet him?" Jock carried on potting up young scented-leaf pelargoniums and trying to sound casual.

"Just after I came 'ere. Mr Armitage were raising 'is voice in't pottin'-shed, which weren't like 'im. I 'eard 'im across't nursery."

"Did you know why he didn't like him?"

Harry had another clearing of the tubes and fished out his packet of Capstan Full Strength. "'E were up to no good. 'E'd nearly been put away for summat and Mr Armitage were reet cross wi' 'im." Harry tapped the end of the cigarette on the packet and put it into his mouth, lighting it with a match from a packet of Vestas.

"Do you know what he'd done wrong?"

"Summat to do wi' a jewel robbery, though me mother din't reckon as 'e done it."

"Oh?"

"Nah. Said 'e were too thick. But then 'e only drove't get-away car."

"You think he did it, then?"

"Oh, 'e done it all right."

"But he didn't go to prison?"

"No." Harry drew heavily on his cigarette, filling what was left of his octogenarian lungs with the richly flavoured smoke. "'E goroff. Then 'e came 'ere to see if Mr Armitage would 'elp 'im out."

"And did he?"

"No. Told 'im to bugger off."

"So he went?"

"Not for a bit. I'd see 'im 'angin' round the gate of the cottage some nights when I went off 'ome. I think 'e were tryin' to squeeze some money out of Mr Armitage."

Jock paused before putting to him the sixty-four-thousand-dollar question. "So what do you think happened to the stuff that he stole?"

Harry exploded into a fit of coughing, a shower of grey ash tumbling from his cigarette and tears streaming from his reddened eyes. His body bent as double as his age would allow, and gradually worked its way upright again as the coughing spasms subsided.

"Oh, I know what happened to it."

Jock stopped his potting and quietly turned to face an exhausted-looking Harry, who was now pouring tea into two large mugs on the corner of the potting-bench.

"It were found a few weeks later."

"Who found it?"

Harry ladled four spoonfuls of sugar into his tea before handing Jock his own unsweetened mug.

"I did."

Jock nearly dropped his tea. "*What?*" He looked at Harry, who was now stirring the rich brown brew in his mug to try to dissolve the small sugar mountain that had just been added to it.

"Reggie Armitage 'ad been fiddlin' around 'ere for weeks after't robbery. I kept out of 'is way. Mr Armitage never talked to 'im an' I din't want to upset 'im. But I saw Reggie leavin't nursery one night when I were goin' past on me way to't Legion. When 'e saw me 'e chucked summat into't bushes by't river. In't mornin' I 'ad a look at wot 'e'd lobbed an' it were a builder's trowel. I couldn't work it out so I telled Mr Armitage."

"And what did he say?"

"Not much. 'E didn't seem to think nuthin' of it."

Harry paused.

"So what did you do?"

"I looked around't nursery for a bit of new brickwork."

"And did you find any?"

Harry took a swig of his sweet, tan tea.

"Yup."

Jock's heart beat faster. This was beginning to sound like the last chapter of the book written by Lady Sampson. "Where?"

Harry gestured sideways with his head, "In yon," tilting his flat-capped head in the direction of the lavatory next door.

"In the toilet?"

"Yup." Harry took another fag from the packet and lit up.

"So what did you do?"

"I got an 'ammer an' chisel and knocked out the bricks."

"And what did you find?"

"A biscuit tin with a black bag inside it an' some bits of glass. I gave 'em to Mr Armitage an' mended t'wall. 'E'd no right doin' that to somebody else's property."

"But why have you never told me this before?" asked Jock, pushing his cap on to the back of his head and scratching his pale forehead in disbelief.

"Because you've never asked me," replied Harry. "An' it's not something I've ever told anyone else. It were private. 'Tween Mr Armitage an' me."

Jock sat down on a slatted chair in the corner of the potting-shed, the wind temporarily knocked out of his sails. "What do you think Mr Armitage did with the bits of glass?"

"'E told me 'e was goin' to give 'em to't police."

"Do you think he did?"

"I don't know. Only I know that they never took Reggie away, an' I'd 'ave thought they would've done if they'd 'ave found the stuff. Funny, in't it?" He looked at Jock with an expression that was difficult to fathom.

"Yes, very funny." Jock sipped his tea. His legs, it seemed, had temporarily lost their ability to support his weight, which was a shame because right now he would have dearly loved a breath of fresh air.

Chapter 28

"Shine, Jesus, shine," hummed Mrs Ipplepen to herself, as she wiped over the worktops in the kitchen of Tarn House. "Fill the world, dah, dee-dee-dah-dum-dum . . ." She buffed up the chrome taps over the sink with her J-cloth, her squat frame swivelling from side to side and making whistling noises inside her nylon overall as she did so. She beamed like a Cheshire cat.

The front door slammed and her dumpling body lifted three inches from the floor. "Ooh! Who's there?" She spun round to look, her overall following a split second later.

"It's only me!"

"Ooh, ma'am, I was miles away, you made me jump!"

"Sorry, only it was rather difficult to shut the door quietly with my hands so full." Helena crossed to the pine table at the centre of the kitchen and dumped on it a wicker basket filled with food shopping.

Mrs Ipplepen gazed proprietorially at the freshly cleaned table. "Oh, and that reminds me, I'm almost out of polish." She crossed to the slate hung by the kitchen door to add to the catalogue of wants on her own shopping list for hygienic rather than gastronomic necessities. ANTIQUACKS, she wrote, on tiptoe. Spelling had never been Mrs Ipplepen's forte. She hummed as she chalked, and motes of white dust glinted in the shafts of sunlight slanting diagonally through the window.

"You sound cheerful."

"Oh, I am, ma'am," replied Mrs Ipplepen, lowering herself from the dizzying heights of her tiptoes and turning round to face her employer. "I can 'ardly retain myself. It's my Tiffany."

Helena slipped off her grey felt coat and laid it over the back of the chair. "Oh, goodness. Has she -?"

"Yes, ma'am. It came early, almost a month. They reckoned it was something to do with 'er being ultraviolated."

Helena, bewildered by her cleaner's meaning even after all these years, chose not to enquire as to the relevance of ultraviolation and instead rushed up to Mrs Ipplepen and threw her arms around her. They didn't quite meet. "Oh, Vera, I *am* pleased! But it seems like only yesterday that you told me she was expecting."

"Well, she'd left it six months before she told me an' Cyril. Didn't want to get our 'opes up in case anything went wrong."

"Very wise. And are mother and baby both doing well?"

"Yes, ma'am, except for a bit of trouble early on."

"Oh dear."

"The baby came out with its unbiblical cord wrapped around its neck. A bit blue in the face, but they soon put him right."

"It's a boy, then?"

"Yes, a bonny, bouncing boy," confirmed Mrs Ipplepen, pausing and wringing her J-cloth in her hands as the tears welled up in the beady little eyes that positively shone behind elaborate blue spectacles.

"Oh, how wonderful. And is Cyril pleased?"

"I'll say. 'E says that at long last 'e'll 'ave some reinforcements. Bein' surrounded by women for all these years."

"This calls for a celebration. I'll go and find a bottle of champagne in the cellar!"

"Oh, ma'am, I couldn't, it'll make me all tiddly."

"I think, just this once, Vera, that it really won't matter. And if you do get all tiddly I'll make sure you're driven all the way home."

Their conversation was interrupted by the ringing of the front doorbell and, once more, Mrs Ipplepen's body was elevated a few inches nearer to the ceiling.

"Ooh! Who could that be?"

"It's difficult to tell from here. You go and answer it, Vera. I'll get the bottle.'

Helena opened the door to the cellar and disappeared into the cool gloom, while Mrs Ipplepen bustled off towards the front door, where she found Rob MacGregor standing on the mat.

"Mr Rob, Mr Rob, you 'aven't 'eard!" and she flung her arms around him. Hers didn't meet either, but that was because they were short.

"Heard what?" asked Rob, laughing at her enthusiasm and excitement.

"It's my Tiffany. She's just 'ad a little boy."

"Wonderful, Mrs Ipplepen. Really wonderful!" Rob gave her a kiss on both cheeks, and she blushed like a schoolgirl.

"Oh, 'eck. You'll make me come over all unessential."

"When did it arrive, Mrs Ipplepen? I thought it wasn't due for ages yet."

"This morning. It was a month early. They had to introduce it because of complications."

"Who is it, Vera?" Helena came into the hall carrying the champagne. "Rob, hello! Perfect timing. You've heard the news?"

"Yes. It's wonderful. I'm really pleased for you, Mrs Ipplepen. And for Tiffany."

They walked through into the kitchen, Mrs Ipplepen bouncing along with all the excitement of a child on Christmas morning.

"Here you are, Rob. You can open this," said Helena. "A little celebration of – What's the baby's name, Vera?"

"Well, they can't decide at the moment. There's a few favourites but I don't like 'em all."

"So what are they?" asked Rob, removing the foil and unscrewing the wire around the champagne cork.

"Tiffany's keen on George and Henry, but I keep telling 'er to 'ave something unusual like Tarquin or Merlin. You know, make 'im stand out in a crowd."

"Ye-e-es." Helena and Rob were momentarily speechless, but the pop of the champagne cork broke the silence and the glasses were filled for the toast to Mrs Ipplepen's first grandchild.

"Here's to the new arrival," proposed Helena. "May he have a long and fruitful life."

"And here's to his grandmother," added Rob. "May she enjoy his company for many years."

"Ooooh!" said Mrs Ipplepen. "Cheers!" and sipped at her champagne, spluttering as the bubbles went up her nose.

Helena and Rob left her to her inebriated cleaning in the kitchen and walked through to the old conservatory at the back of the house, where the new season's leaves of an ancient peach tree provided shade from the bright spring sunshine.

"Bless her," said Helena. "She's so thrilled. I think I shall have to drive her home in an hour or so, if she isn't asleep!" She turned to Rob. "So how are you, this lovely spring morning?"

"Oh, I'm fine. Fine. I've just nipped in to pass on some information that you might find interesting – on the Dennis Wragg front."

Helena perked up for the second time that morning. "Oh, yes, what?"

"I think I owe you an apology."

"What on earth for?"

"I was a bit scathing about your dramatic reason for Dennis Wragg's interest in the nursery, and having spoken to Dad I don't think I should have been."

"What do you mean?"

Rob, having listened open-mouthed that morning as Jock recounted Harry's story, filled her in on the details.

"So, you see, you were right. The only trouble is that the treasure trove was discovered rather a long time ago."

"Oh dear." Helena's excitement at being proved right was replaced by disappointment at not having produced the real reason why the Wraggs were so keen to get their hands on the nursery.

"But supposing they don't know that the jewels were found? Supposing they think they're still there, simply because Reggie Armitage might have thought they were still there and told them so?"

"It's possible I suppose," admitted Rob. "But I think there's a more likely reason why Dennis Wragg wants the land. A reason that's rooted in the present, not the past."

"And what's that?" Helena lowered herself into a white Lloyd Loom chair underneath the overhanging boughs of the peach tree.

Rob explained about Katherine's meeting with Councillor Mrs Gosport and furnished her with the precise details of Dennis Wragg's involvement.

"It seems that the town's bypass was held in abeyance for a while. It's always been an on/off thing, anyway. But when it became a runner again, one or two people with their fingers in assorted pies saw it as a way of making some money. If they happened to own the land that would be compulsorily purchased for the building of the bypass, they would come into a tidy sum. The new route of the bypass is scheduled to go – guess where – right through Wharfeside Nursery. They were keeping the details of the route quiet for obvious reasons, including the fact that it would mean the acquisition and demolition of a couple of houses, too.

"Dennis Wragg has a friend on the planning committee who's clearly in line for a cut of the proceeds, and he tipped Dennis the wink, according to Molly Gosport – though she says that all this is quite off the record, for legal reasons – so he's after the land before the announcement is made."

"But this is dreadful," Helena exclaimed. "Does this mean that Jock will lose his land anyway?"

"Not now. Molly Gosport reckons that once the beans are spilled about the shenanigans that have been going on, there will be no way that the council will want to proceed. It's just too much of a hot potato, and they have enough on their hands already, what with by-elections coming up. She's convinced that the bypass idea will be dropped on the grounds of insufficient funding, and that Dennis Wragg will deny any knowledge of it."

"So what's Katherine going to do? What can she say?"

"Molly Gosport has told her the things she can say, and advised her on what would be libellous and what would be fair comment. She'll go into print on Friday."

"Well I never. What a story. It gets more and more amazing."

"You're telling me," agreed Rob, looking out across the garden at the rhododendrons, now in full bloom around the wide, curving lawn.

Helena watched him as he spoke. "That's not all, is it?"

"What do you mean?"

"Rob, I've known you for long enough to know when there's something wrong." She hesitated. "I saw Katherine the other day. She had the same faraway look in her eyes as you do."

"Did you say anything to her?"

"Of course not. It's not my place to interfere. But are you and Katherine . . .? Well, you know. Are you still having a bad patch?"

Rob looked up at the peach tree, bedecked with long green leaves and studded with small, green, downy peaches. He sighed. "'Fraid so."

"Can I ask you something?"

"Mmm?" He gazed, absently, at the young, ripening fruits.

"Is it the other girl?"

He came out of his reverie and turned to face Helena.

"Not any more. I was besotted for a bit but I managed to sort myself out. Realized I'd been stupid. I thought I'd got away with it and then Katherine found out about it and – Oh, it's hell being involved with two women."

"Were you in love with her? The other girl, I mean."

"No. At first I thought I was. Infatuated, more like it. A 'grand passion' – even if it was a brief one. Completely out of my head. I didn't guess how much it would affect my relationship with Katherine. Funny, really."

"No. I don't think it's funny at all."

"Oh?"

"No. This might not seem to have anything to do with it, but when you have your first child, you love it so deeply that you can't imagine loving the second one anything like as much. Can't imagine having any love to spare. But when the second one arrives, you suddenly find yourself with an increased capacity for love. Your love is somehow multiplied by two, and then by three, or as many times as the number of children you have." Helena paused, remembering her years as a mother of young children. "But when you fall in love it's quite different. If you fall in love with a second person it doesn't work out the way it does with children."

Rob listened intently. "No?"

"No. Somehow it divides into two, and each half is less than the whole. You end up not being able to love either party fully." She turned and looked out of the peach-fringed window. "Children multiply your love. Lovers divide it."

It was a few moments before she heard the door close quietly behind her. She turned to see the remains of his champagne still fizzing in the glass.

Chapter 29

At first Rob did not recognize the burgundy-coloured Jaguar parked in the lane adjacent to Wharfeside Nursery. It simply crossed his mind that his father could do with a few more such well-heeled customers. Then he spotted the number plate: 2429 DW and his heart leaped. The car belonged to Dennis Wragg.

Rob pushed open the green wrought-iron gate and walked down the nursery path. Two old ladies were cooing over some perennials in an open-topped frame, and Wayne stood by them with a small, wire-framed truck in which they were depositing their selection of plants. Wayne looked distracted and, on seeing Rob, pointed to the bottom corner of the nursery where he could see his father in conversation with two men, one in a short cream raincoat, the other with a briefcase and a navy-blue mac.

He strode purposefully towards them and, from a couple of yards away, greeted them with a firm "Good morning."

Jock, who was facing Rob, looked up, and the other two men wheeled round. One of them was Dennis Wragg, his balding, Brylcreemed head shimmering in the sun; the other was Stan Halfpenny.

"Good morning," they replied, almost in unison, clearly wrong-footed.

"All right, Dad?" Rob enquired of his father.

"Fine, thanks, son. I was just explaining to these two gentlemen that I still have no intention of selling the nursery, but they don't seem to believe me."

"Really?" Rob was surprised, and a little unnerved, to see Stan Halfpenny. "Stan, why are you here?"

"I came with Mr Wragg, who is my client."

"But Dad is also your client, isn't he?"

Stan shuffled a little and developed a sudden fascination for the gravel path. He looked up to reply. "Yes, he is. So that makes my position especially difficult. I'm just trying to act in the best interests of *both* my clients."

"But one of them is rather more important than the other, I guess."

"Sorry?"

"One client is, I suppose, rather more profitable than the other."

"That has nothing to do with it."

Dennis Wragg, who had been silent thus far, drew himself up to his full five feet four inches and addressed himself to Rob. "Look, sonny, this is between your father and me. It's nothing to do with you."

Before Rob could reply, Jock interrupted, "It's every bit as much to do with him as it is with me. I hope I've a while to go yet, Dennis, but when I do go then Rob will inherit this nursery and it will be his to do with as he wants."

Rob was taken aback. From time to time, he had wondered about the future of the nursery, and about his own future in relation to it, but his father had never mentioned it and Rob had not wanted to ask for fear of seeming as though he were either muscling in or pushing his father out.

Jock looked directly at Rob, but spoke for the benefit of the other two men. "So, you see, he has as much of a say in its sale as I do."

Dennis was clearly irritated. "Well, then, if he has any sense he'll see that now is a very good time to sell. And if he knows his stuff as much as the nation thinks he does, he will know that there is no future for small nurseries like this one that can't offer the facilities the punters want in this day and age."

Stan Halfpenny continued to be hypnotized by the gravel as Dennis Wragg warmed to his subject and turned on the charm. "Look, Rob, I don't want to sound like some prophet of doom, but you know as well as I do that this nursery, run as it is, just isn't profitable, even if it is owned by the father of a gardener who is a household name. It's a dinosaur. All I want to do is turn it into something more suited to the twenty-first century and give your father a decent lump of money to see him comfortable for . . . well, you know . . . in his retirement."

"And you think so, too, do you, Stan?"

Stan Halfpenny looked up, his forehead glistening with perspiration. "I think it makes great economic sense, yes. But the decision is up to your father. And you," he added, as an afterthought. "I'm just here to advise."

"And would the route of the Nesfield bypass have any bearing on things?"

The two men reacted as though they had been threatened with the same fate as King Edward II, but swiftly regained their composure. Or, at least Dennis Wragg did. Stan Halfpenny looked even more nervous.

"What do you mean?" asked Dennis Wragg, half smiling and at his most innocent and oily.

"I think you know what I mean," suggested Rob. "My father hasn't heard yet, but I have."

Jock regarded his son questioningly, but he did not speak.

"I've discovered, from sources that I'm not prepared to reveal, that the Nesfield bypass is on the cards again, and that the proposed new route runs right through the nursery. As a result of which, whoever owns this land at the time will come into a tidy sum courtesy of a compulsory purchase order. And if that person were you, Mr Wragg, you would make far more money than you would have paid my father for the land in the first place."

He turned to Stan. "And I suppose your commission, Stan, would be quite considerable?"

Stan reacted quickly. "It's not like that."

"Shut up, Stan!" Dennis Wragg shot Stan Halfpenny a look that could have turned him to stone, had he been looking in his direction. As it was, he seemed intent on locating the nearest exit, which was clearly too far away.

Dennis Wragg advanced two paces towards Rob, as Jock looked on with his mouth half open. "You have no proof of this. This is malicious gossip, and it's the sort of thing that gets people into deep trouble. There are laws against slander, and I'm not one to stand by and be slandered. This could cost you a lot of money, young man. And a lot of embarrassment."

"I know it could. If it isn't true. But, then, if it is true it could cost *you* a lot of money, not that I think you're capable of being embarrassed. So, for everybody's sake, it would be better if you took my father at his word and stopped harassing him to sell. And I think that, in the interests of us all, it might make sense, Stan, if you were to stick with one client in this case, rather than two. Don't you?"

Stan Halfpenny struggled with his feelings, then admitted that it would probably be a good idea.

"I suggest you go now. If you do as we ask, I've no intention of talking about this to anyone else, and as far as I'm concerned this conversation has never taken place. All right, gentlemen? Goodbye. Tea, Dad?" And with that Rob headed for the potting-shed, smiling cheerily at the two old ladies, who nearly fell over their trolley as he breezed by. Jock nodded absent-mindedly at the two raincoated men and followed in the slipstream of his son, wondering if there would ever be an end to the surprises that life seemed to produce with the frequency of a top-class conjuror.

Once inside the potting-shed, and while Rob filled the kettle, Jock found enough wind to ask about the bypass.

"Don't worry. It won't happen now, Dad."

"What do you mean it won't happen? Why not?"

"Because Katherine is about to blow the gaff on the whole thing in the *Nesfield Gazette* at the end of the week. She was tipped off by a disgruntled councillor, who smelt a rat."

"You don't think she'll mention Dennis Wragg? He'll sue."

"No, I doubt that she'll mention him by name – she's got more sense than that. All she has to do is hint at corruption and intrigue in relation to the routing of the bypass. The paper's lawyers will go over what she's written with a fine-tooth comb to make sure there's nothing libellous in it, but it will be such a can of worms that, with the by-elections coming, it's a safe bet that the whole thing will be shelved indefinitely. That's the inside knowledge."

"Well, I'll be blowed." Jock sat on the slatted chair by the loam-filled bench, leaning forward with his hands on his knees as though he had just run a marathon.

Rob poured the contents of the boiling kettle into the pot. "Dad?"

"Mmm?" Jock looked exhausted.

"Did you mean what you said about the nursery?"

"What?" He looked up at his son.

"That it would be mine when . . . well, you know."

"Of course it will. What else did you think would happen?"

"Well . . . it's just that we've never talked about it."

"I didn't think we needed to. You see, I didn't want you to think that you had to take it on. Why should it become a millstone round your neck? It's up to you to do what you want once I've finished with it." He looked up and smiled at his son. "I'll let you know when I have. Now then, is that tea ready?"

Rob began to pour the strong brew into two mugs. "Just about."

"Well, it'll have to wait for a minute or two, I've a customer to see to." Having watched the large woman in the plum-coloured coat bustle down the nursery path, Jock pushed himself up from the chair and crossed to the door. "She's one of my regulars. Very keen on old-fashioned roses."

He left the potting-shed at a brisk pace, knowing that Councillor Mrs Gosport did not like to be kept waiting.

Devon, thought Rob, was his second favourite county after Yorkshire: it went up and down and it had a dramatically rugged coastline. He couldn't stand the flatness of Lincolnshire and the fens, where the lack of hills to look up to made him feel uneasy, but Devon was almost like home, if a tad warmer. He dumped his overnight bag on the kitchen floor of End Cottage, and stretched to flex the muscles that had stiffened on the long train journey back from Totnes. This week *Mr MacGregor's Garden* would be broadcast from a garden near Salcombe that had been awash with rhododendrons, dogwoods and other spring-flowering shrubs. The place had seemed like the Garden of Eden and had given Rob a welcome break from the intrigues of Nesfield.

He picked up the post that he had stepped over so carefully on his way in and dropped it on the kitchen table. The local paper, folded up, sat underneath the small mountain of envelopes. He eased it out and unfolded it.

"BYPASS BLUNDER" trumpeted the headline. Rob raised his eyebrows, read the article and whistled through his teeth at what Katherine had been able to get away with. She had named no names, but reported more than enough to set this particular hornets' nest buzzing loudly. The locals would not be happy with the implications suggested by an "informed source".

Rob wondered whether to call Katherine and congratulate her on her scoop when the phone rang.

It was Bex. "Hi! Did you get back OK?"

"Yeh, fine, thanks. How about you?"

"Fine. No probs. Great garden, wasn't it?"

"I'll say." He wondered why she had called. She didn't normally ring him. He didn't have to wait long to find out.

"I tried to speak to you after we'd finished but I couldn't find you. I just wondered if you were OK."

"Sorry?"

"You seemed a bit down. I just wondered if there was anything wrong?"

"No. Not really. Just a bit of woman trouble."

There was a pause at the other end of the line. "I'm a good listener, you know."

"Thanks. You're very kind. But it's time I did something about it instead of just hoping that it will sort itself out. A bit scared to, I suppose."

"Come on, then."

"Come on then, what?"

"Tell me all about it."

"I don't know that I want to tell you all about it. Why should I lumber you with my problems?"

"Because I'm a mate. And I'm probably the only half decent girl you know who isn't madly in love with you."

"Bloody cheek." Rob smiled, relieved at her candour. "Why not?"

"Because I don't fancy you, that's why, but I'm incredibly fond of you. So there you have it. I'm a pain, I know. But I might be able to help. Have you talked to anyone else about it?"

"Only an old friend of mine – someone old enough to be my mother."

"No one who's your age and who knows what it's like right now?"

"No. No one." Slowly at first, he began to fill Bex in on the details of his love-life, unsure at first why he was doing so, but then, as she listened quietly, saying, "Mmm," at intervals, he talked more freely. He did not identify Lisa, did not go into the most intimate details, but by the time he had finished Bex was in possession of most of the facts.

"So where are you now?" she asked, sympathetically.

"In limbo. I want to get back together with her. I'm desperate to, but I'm too frightened that she'll say no and God knows what I'll do if she does."

"Well, she's not going to come to you, you know."

"You don't think so?"

"I'm sure so. And she wouldn't be much of a woman if she did. I'm sorry to sound harsh, but if you want her back you'll have to prove to her that you want her enough."

"I suppose so. I'll go and see her as soon as I get back from Chelsea."

251

"Look, I feel for you, I really do, and I'll do anything I can to help, you know that. But for God's sake stop being such a wimp! Go and tell her. Let her see how much you care, how much you really want her back. It's the only way you're going to get together. It's knight-in-shining-armour time now."

"You're right." Rob sighed. "Thanks."

"Oh, don't thank me. I'm great at giving advice but not so good at taking it. I spend every night with this square-faced fella in the corner" – and she flipped on the television with the remote control. "My love-life at the moment is about as exciting as – Oh, God! *No!*"

"What?"

"Turn your telly on – quick – ITV."

Rob reached for the remote control on the corner of the pine dresser and zapped the television standing on a worktop by the sink. Up came an image of Guy D'Arcy in a white tuxedo, spray-gun at his side, riding in a fast sports car, pursued by a gigantic whitefly, which cruised above his head like a pallid Stealth bomber. Rob watched, wide-eyed, as the voice-over, supplied in part by Guy D'Arcy, with expletives by Bex Fleming, provided a running commentary.

"The name's BLITZ – licensed to kill," and a huge greenfly exploded in a shower of sparks.

"Did you see that?" she asked incredulously. "What a load of crap! How does he get away with it?"

"I don't know," answered Rob, truthfully. All jealousy he may have felt towards Guy D'Arcy had evaporated and been replaced by relief that he, himself, had not had to play cowboys and Indians with an assortment of insect predators.

"Have you see it before?" Bex asked.

"No, that's the first time."

"But weren't *you* going to do it?"

"I was, but they changed their minds. Thought they'd use somebody who was a bit more cool and suave, I suppose."

"Well you're well out of it. 'Licensed to kill', I ask you! What a hoot! Mind you, I'm surprised his TV programme let him do it. The man has no scruples at all."

"From what I've heard he has very large scruples."

"Thank you, Mr MacGregor. That's more like it."

"And, anyway, you know we're beating him hands down – thanks to your good looks, charm and impeccable horticultural pedigree."

"Watch it, MacGregor!"

"It's true! Anyway, I'm just glad it didn't turn out to be me, even if it does make Guy D'Arcy a rich man. Hey-ho!" He chuckled. "Mind you, I might have looked quite good in a dinner-jacket."

"Yes, but not as good as you look in jeans and a sweatshirt. Anyway, that's enough flattery for one evening. I'm off to have a bath. You doing anything?"

"No, I shouldn't think so. A bath sounds like a good idea."

"Well, take care. I'll see you next week. 'Bye."

He put the handset down and opened the fridge to grab a cold beer, at the same time reaching for the remote control to switch channels to BBC 1 for the news. The trumpet fanfare blasted through the old beams of End Cottage, but it was the face that came into view immediately afterwards that made Rob start and almost drop the bottle of Black Sheep Ale. It was Lisa Drake's.

If Lisa's appearance on the BBC evening news had come as a shock to Rob, then Jessica Swan's appearance on Northcountry Television's news had come as a pleasant surprise to people in Yorkshire. All bar one. Frank Burbage drove home that night in a state of shock. He had read the news with his new co-presenter, and was still being careful not to overstep the mark on a personal level. But it would not be long, he thought, before he could start to be more familiar. Already Jessica was becoming more relaxed in his company. So much so that after the programme she had suggested they go for a drink. Frank tried hard to control his excitement and anticipation, but he did not have to try hard for very long. As they sat down at a corner table in the Dog and Fox, a pub suggested by

Jessica, the door opened and another customer came in, tall, good-looking and wearing a heavy coat.

"Frank," said Jessica, warmly, "there's someone I'd like you to meet."

"Who's that?" asked Frank.

Jessica beckoned over the customer who had just walked in. "This is my partner, Charlie Whitehead. Charlie's a doctor. We met in Suffolk and Charlie's just got a posting in the local infirmary. We're buying a house together up the dale."

Frank shook hands with Charlie in something of a daze. He thought he'd almost cracked it and now he knew he hadn't. What he also knew was that he'd never crack it. Charlie Whitehead was the prettiest female doctor he'd ever set eyes on.

Chapter 30

Saturday morning, 16 May, dawned with a diluted light that barely had the energy to squeeze its way between Rob's bedroom curtains. He swiped at the clanging alarm clock on the bedside table, then slid his naked body out from under the duvet and loped across the rough coir matting to the window. The curtains, pulled back, revealed a soft grey mist hanging like cows' breath over the water-meadows. Beyond them the sun, no brighter than a torch with a faded battery, was doing its best to burn off the vapour of the morning, and failing. Rob gazed on the pallid scene that seemed only to add to the draining sadness deep within him and sighed a long, soft sigh.

How tired he was of sighing. How tired of being tired. There were moments when his mind was occupied with other things and he could, for a while, forget Katherine. Well, not forget her, but at least put her from his mind. But then, when the writing finished or the programme was made, he looked ahead of himself at a pale emptiness that the early morning in front of him now seemed to personify. It was all so flat. So colourless. So hollow.

He stood for some minutes, mesmerized by the watery scene beneath his window, then shivered and hurried off to shower. At least for the next few days he would be fully occupied. The week of the Chelsea Flower Show loomed ahead. By nine o'clock he would be on a train speeding to London. There would be little time to mope. He had plenty to look forward to. Plenty to do. Just no one to share it with.

Katherine, wrapped up in a fluffy white towelling bathrobe, sipped her coffee in bed, the scent of freshly baked bread drifting upwards as it always did on a Saturday morning – as it always did every morning except Sundays – from the shop below. The previous day's paper had been a triumph for her. Charlie Wormald had told her so. She should have been pleased with herself. She *was* pleased with herself. Just low. And alone. And missing Rob. A watery May day stretched out in front of her. She reached for the television remote control that sat on the pine chest at the bottom of her bed. She pressed the 'on' button. Whatever her mood, she found it impossible to start the day without catching up on the overnight news. The fact that the morning bulletin was being delivered by Lisa Drake did nothing to dispel her gloom.

At half past ten Guy D'Arcy left Serena to the comfort of his bed. Only her tousled black hair was visible above the duvet as she lay spreadeagled beneath its warm, downy filling. The poor girl was exhausted, but last night had been especially frantic. Guy was back to his old self again. Serena had been well pleased with his performance, and he with hers. God, she had some energy. And thank God he had rediscovered his.

Wearing corn-coloured corduroy trousers and a navy-blue Guernsey, topped with matching Barbour, he slipped quietly out of the front door of the Fulham terrace house and pointed the automatic key at the black BMW nestling alongside the kerb a few doors away. The locks popped up, the hazard-warning lights blinked a morning welcome, Guy slid into the driver's seat and inhaled the rich aroma of leather upholstery.

He hardly noticed what a dull morning it was as he turned the key in the ignition. A few moments later the car purred away, and Guy purred almost as loudly as he and his motor cruised off in the direction of Chelsea. It would be the last journey they would make together, but at eleven o'clock on the morning of Saturday 16 May Guy D'Arcy didn't know that.

The traffic along the Chelsea Embankment was almost at a standstill, so Rob stepped out of the black cab and paid off the driver before walking the last few hundred yards to the Bullring entrance of the Royal Hospital. "Have a good week, guv!" shouted the taxi driver after him. "I'll be watching you!" Rob turned, smiled and waved as he lugged his overnight bag on to his shoulder and tried to remember which pocket contained the passes that would get him through the gates. This was a ritual he'd go through every morning between now and next Wednesday when filming would be finished.

He'd been to the Chelsea Flower Show several times, but never with so much anticipation – and never before the show's official opening day on Tuesday. Previously he had been a visitor. This year he was part of things. Through the railings he could see the vast marquee – said to be the largest in the world at three and a half acres – and behind the soaring off-white canvas, the roof of Wren's majestic hospital, the home of the scarlet-coated Chelsea pensioners.

Lorries jostled with one another at the main gate, ferrying their loads of plants and equipment on to the football pitches and tennis courts, lawns and shrubberies that for one week in every year became the most famous flower show in the world.

"Hello, Mr MacGregor!" A woman hailed him from across the road. He waved back. He remembered how his mother would always ask, "Who's that?" and then be embarrassed when her son confessed that he didn't know. He steeled himself for the week ahead, remembering that most people here would know exactly who he was, even if he didn't know them.

Gaudy banners advertising gardening magazines and newspapers were being strapped to the wrought-iron railings that curved inwards towards the entrance gates. The small roundabout outside them, encircled by slow-moving cars and trucks, was planted with bright bedding, and a motley assortment of people – each with their own part to play in this botanical extravaganza – came and went through the heavy iron gates. Rob found the appropriate pass, showed it to the peak-capped security man, who nodded him through, then began to take in the unready spectacle.

The tarmac drive that circumnavigated the grounds of the hospital was almost solid with vehicles, each displaying a sticker indicating to which stand it belonged. Some disgorged enormous steel trolleys packed with plants, which were wheeled into the marquee, others were being emptied of buckets of exotic flowers, stylish furniture or terracotta flower-pots. Many contained one person being shouted at by another person from behind, and occasionally a brief toot would indicate a blocked passage or an impatient dumper-truck driver – not so much road rage as road minor-irritation. But then this was the Chelsea Flower Show on a Saturday afternoon, not Briggate in Leeds.

Rob picked his way through the horticultural mayhem along the narrow asphalt drive that ran parallel to the Embankment where, beneath the towering London plane trees, a dozen spectacular gardens lay side by side. All over them, welly-booted gardeners were pushing in plants here, stemming a flood there, and scrubbing paths of sandstone and slate. Three weeks ago this patch of paradise would have been just a grassy slope; now it was becoming a floral wonderland where banks of trees and shrubs, border perennials and rare foreign treasures seemed to have been growing for years. Everywhere the sound of water met the ear – tumbling over rocks, squirting from fountains, skimming over plate-glass weirs and bubbling through rills.

Rob watched it all and lost himself for a moment, remembering the poem by Robert Southey that his mother had recited to him when he was a child,

'How does the Water Come Down at Lodore?
. . . shining and twining,
And rattling and battling,

And shaking and quaking,
And pouring and roaring,
And waving and raving,
And tossing and crossing,
And flowing and going,
And running and stunning . . .'

and that was as much as he could remember. His parents had loved the Lake District. His father would love the Chelsea Flower Show, but Rob had never been able to persuade him to leave the nursery and come and take a look. The prospect of coming to London had never tempted Jock, who found Nesfield quite busy enough for his liking.

Rob walked by the lavish gardens bearing the sponsorship signs of perfume companies and upmarket magazines, past smaller plots, designed and built by working landscape architects, that owed less to the chic London fashion houses of their neighbours than to the painting-by-numbers movement. Between them the twenty-odd gardens catered for all tastes, with varying degrees of success. What they all had in common was a breathtaking standard of finish.

Rob found himself staring at a perfect miniature of an old kitchen garden – the peeling, white-painted conservatory invaded by its ancient vine and spilling old clay flower-pots on to the worn flagged path outdoors. A cold frame alongside the greenhouse had lost its battle to contain the rampant, adventurous shoots of cucumbers that were making a bid for freedom. In the rich, damp earth, rows of cabbages and peas mingled with gooseberry and redcurrant bushes, half a dozen old-fashioned bell jars sheltered a crop of early lettuces, and a white picket fence separated the old-world garden from the admiring present-day audience who stopped to take it all in.

"You should be standing in the middle of all this, you know!" boomed a voice from behind him. Rob turned round to see Sir Freddie Roper advancing on him.

"What do you mean?" he asked.

"Haven't you seen the sign?" asked Sir Freddie, perching his all-too-solid frame rather too trustingly on a shooting-stick in the last stages of metal fatigue.

Rob looked at the corner of the garden where, below a scarecrow made of a blue jacket and some dangling shoes, was the sign "'Mr McGregor's Garden', sponsored by Amalgamated Agricultural Chemicals".

"Ah! Different spelling. I think that's another Mr McGregor."

"That's the trouble," replied Sir Freddie. "That's the bloody trouble. You see now why I wanted you to front the campaign for BLITZ, but the bloody ad-men thought they knew better. Wanted to give the product a more modern image – hence the bloody James Bond stuff and young D'Arcy. I told 'em it would fit in far better with our Chelsea garden if they'd had you, but would they listen? No. Daft buggers."

"It's hard to see how it fits in with BLITZ," admitted Rob, looking at the garden, which quite clearly owed more to Beatrix Potter than Ian Fleming.

"It doesn't fit in at all. That's what's so daft about it." At this point a figure came barging through the milling throng of workers and tradesfolk who were surrounding the garden and made a bee-line for Sir Freddie.

"There you are!" Rob recognized Simon Clay, the bespectacled PR man for AAC who seemed less cool than Rob remembered. He looked agitated.

"What is it?" asked Sir Freddie Roper, glumly.

"I need a word. Now. Over in the hospitality suite."

"But I was just having a look round," grumbled Sir Freddie, relieving the shooting-stick of his weight.

Simon Clay could barely bring himself to offer Rob a greeting. He took Sir Freddie by the arm and led him off in the direction of the gents' which led, in turn, to the small hospitality village. Rob watched them go, then turned to look back at Mr McGregor's Garden. It was pretty, and convincing – but down to the last pea in the last pod completely phoney.

*

The sleek black BMW 325i turned off Royal Hospital Road and into Burton Court where, for the duration of the flower show, the grounds surrounding the cricket pitch and tennis courts of this salubrious square in SW3 had been turned into a car park. Guy locked up and crunched his way over the gravel path, crossing the road to the side entrance of the Royal Hospital and passing, as he did so, the small military cemetery and several glossy black cannon mounted as if to repel boarders. He shuddered. His father had once suggested that Guy follow in his footsteps as an officer in the Guards before joining the family estate-agency business.

The prospect had appalled Guy, whose preference for manoeuvres of a different kind had led him in other directions. Then came 'The Big Row' and neither career had been mentioned again. He walked past the scarlet post box set in the pillar of the black iron gates and said, 'Good morning', to the peak-capped soldier on duty. A couple of Chelsea Pensioners in their navy-blue day-wear, were slowly making their way, with sticks, towards the flower show at the bottom of their garden. Guy overtook them and nodded a greeting. They plodded on, oblivious.

He checked his watch. A quarter to twelve. He had fifteen minutes before he was due to meet his co-presenter and the production team in their Portakabin on the other side of the showground; just time for a walkabout to see who was there and what sort of grisly things some of the garden designers had perpetrated this year. The more of these that he could foist on to Rob MacGregor the better. He had every confidence that he could commandeer the better ones for himself. Gardens sponsored by Cartier and *Harper's & Queen* would do him nicely; some modest little 'family' gardens and displays of vegetables should be more Mr MacGregor's bag.

Fifty yards past the newly erected turnstiles at the top of Eastern Avenue he turned right, leaving behind him the presently vacant trade stands covered in security sheets of nylon netting (their exhibitors would turn up and stuff their stands to bursting point on

261

Sunday and Monday). Ahead of him sprouted greenhouses and conservatories, from the humble to the luxurious. Guy peeped inside one octagonal summerhouse painted in *eau-de-Nil* and ivory, and discovered a confection of Colefax and Fowler, all deep-coloured chintz and mahogany, that would not have been out of place in the V and A – not so much a garden shed, more a garden château – and then looked upwards at the glazed tower of a conservatory-cum-pavilion, whose design had clearly been influenced more by Mad King Ludwig of Bavaria than Robinson's of Winchester. It was the kind of conservatory that should have been home to the Addams Family or Boris Karloff, but which would probably be purchased by a merchant banker or an Arab.

Guy mused on this. If he had been a merchant banker perhaps he would have got on better in the Royal Horticultural Society: so many of the council members seemed to be merchant bankers of one kind or another.

He looked again at his watch. Mustn't be late. A couple of minutes to twelve. He strode off down Mains Avenue to the Embankment side of the showground, returning the occasional greeting that came his way, though more of his acquaintances would be here on Monday afternoon during the exclusive Royal Preview, he reassured himself. Today the bodies milling around were mainly those of the workers, plus one or two freeloaders who knew somebody who knew somebody who was connected with the show.

"Guy, over here!" A tall man in a sheepskin jacket, his fair hair cropped as short as that of the shorn animal that had provided his clothing, waved a greeting as he walked over with outstretched hand.

"Tim Cherry, Unicorn Productions – I'm the executive producer of the programme."

"Hello!" Guy turned on the charm. "How nice to see you – and what an appropriately horticultural name." The two shook hands, Tim Cherry smiling good-naturedly but making no comment on Guy's observation simply because it must have been the twentieth time he had heard it that day.

"We're over here in the press tent – more room than in our Portakabin. I thought I'd stick my head out and see if you were around. Thought you might have got lost. Not that you're late or anything . . ."

"I hope not."

"No, no. It's just that the sooner we all say hello, the sooner we can all go off and do our own thing." He walked with Guy towards the steps that led to the press tent at the end of the Rock Garden Bank. "Now, you know from the schedule we sent you there's no filming today, just a recce. Hopefully there will be enough stuff finished to let you see what takes your eye, then you can decide what you might like to cover." He ushered Guy up the steep flight of steps that led to the pavilion-like canvas structure which, over the next few days, would house the world's press. Today it was empty except for a couple of dozen folding chairs, Formica-topped tables littered with shortbread biscuits and coffee, and about a dozen men and women chatting away with pink running orders in their hands.

Guy noticed Rob MacGregor sitting talking to a girl with a nose-ring and a black T-shirt bearing the legend 'Iron Maiden'.

Tim brought the meeting to order. "OK, folks, we're all here now. This is Guy D'Arcy. Guy, I think you know Rob MacGregor, your co-presenter?" Guy nodded across the table at Rob and Rob responded with a "Hi, hello."

"I'll just run round the table so everyone knows everyone," and Tim proceeded to supply a mini-CV of the assorted men and women, boys and girls, who peopled the tent and who would be, in various capacities, responsible for getting the televised version of the Chelsea Flower Show on to the screen.

Guy and Rob both concentrated on trying to remember who was who, so that a runner would not be confused with a director and a production manager with a researcher. Rob thought it wouldn't do to ask a director if she could toddle off and find you a cup of tea; Guy made a mental note not to bother about anyone less than a director.

Each of the presenters was given a director with whom they would work individually, Tim being the all-seeing producer. Rob was put with Rosie Duff, a middle-aged old hand who knew her stuff and brooked no nonsense from prima-donna presenters. Her dumpy figure supported a broad face framed by a bob of dense, silver hair and she carried herself in a way that defied argument. For all her matter-of-factness she seemed sunny enough, and Rob was relieved to be with someone on whose experience he could rely.

Guy was assigned to Oliver Shakespeare – hooked nose, a shaved bald head, an earring in the left ear, black leather jacket, motorcycle trousers and long leather boots. Ollie raised his right hand as though being sworn in at the Old Bailey – it was his customary cool greeting. He was usually a producer on *Clobber*, the fashion programme, but like most freelancers he took on other work when *Clobber* was off air because he needed a steady income. Added to that, the fashion scene at Chelsea interested him, and he was sure he could give the programme a more upbeat feel with shots at wacky angles and sexy close-ups of lilies and the like.

"Well, now that you all know each other we'll go through the running order – not that it's set in stone. I've put it together how I think it might work, but I'm happy to do a bit of horse-trading. Guy and Rob, if you're not happy with the items I've given you please say so and we can sort things out amicably, I hope."

They glanced at one another. Rob was determined not to be the one who was difficult but, at the same time, did not want to be lumbered with items that might be at best weak or at worst naff. Guy wondered how he was going to saddle his rival with items that were exactly that. At the moment the running order was vague enough to allow each man to feel reasonably confident.

"What I don't want," explained Tim, "is a programme that's too arty-farty."

Ollie perked up. "What do you mean?"

"It's Unicorn's first shot at this programme. I know it was getting tired but I don't want to go off completely in the opposite direction and make it look like *Gardener's World* meets *Eurotrash*, OK?"

Ollie shrugged. "OK, boss."

"People want to see the flowers and they want to hear good advice from Rob and Guy, so trust your presenters and believe that what you're looking at is interesting enough without having to turn your camera on its side, OK?"

Ollie shrugged again.

Various people chipped in with questions about this and ideas about that until, at last, Rosie pushed back her chair, rose to her feet and said, "Right. I think we should get on and have a look round, don't you?"

Tim hummed in agreement and Ollie gave his Shakespearean salute to indicate his compliance. Guy looked at him with an expression that seemed to Rob a mixture of incredulity and distaste. Then he left the table with the little posse that had gathered around Ollie and which, clearly, constituted his team.

Rosie smiled at Rob and muttered quietly, "Should be fun, this!" before turning round and instructing her own little coterie – the girl in the Iron Maiden T-shirt, who was the production assistant, a youth with gold-rimmed spectacles called Colin, who was their runner or general dogsbody, and Penny, a petite, dark-haired researcher, who had an armful of notes and a navy-blue cardigan full of holes.

Together they walked down the steps of the press tent and along the Rock Garden Bank in search of inspiration. The two groups had barely separated when Simon Clay, AAC's PR man, came bustling along the pathway, narrowly missing a collision with a dumper-truck in which, in spite of his cast-iron confidence, he would undoubtedly have come off worst. He hurried up to Guy, grabbed his arm and spluttered, "We need you for a moment."

Guy, looking a touch embarrassed, turned to indicate Ollie. "I can't come now, we're just about to go round the show for the programme. Can I come over later?"

Simon Clay looked deeply stressed, pushed his frog-like glasses further up his nose and ran his fingers through his thick brown hair.

"How much later?" he asked, anxiously, looking for a reply at both Ollie and Guy.

Guy looked at Ollie and Ollie looked at the black Rolex on his wrist and swung his head from side to side. "Ooh, a couple of hours. Say three o'clock to be safe."

"Oh, God!" Simon muttered under his breath. "Fine. OK. Three o'clock. We'll be in our hospitality tent – it's not finished yet but it's round the back, past the gents' loos. OK? Three o'clock. OK?"

"Fine." Guy watched him go, his mane of dark hair streaming out behind him. He looked extremely worried. And now Guy was worried, too.

Chapter 31

The sun had finally melted the early-morning gloom that had swamped the country from Penrith to Putney. By three o'clock it was a clear, still, sunny afternoon. Katherine had stirred herself from her morning torpor and pulled herself together. She had nipped downstairs to the bakery and bought herself a fresh wholemeal loaf. She could feel the warmth coming through the paper bag as she enfolded it in her arms, and back upstairs the two fat slices she cut from it tasted good, dipped in honey and washed down with fresh coffee.

She had showered, put up her hair in a mock-tortoiseshell clip and changed into a white Arran sweater and jeans, but when she found herself staring wanly at her conker-shiny floor she muttered, 'Damn,' pulled on a pair of dark brown suede boots and her woolly jacket, and took herself out for the day.

She shopped at first, but nothing seemed appealing. Either it was the wrong size or the wrong colour, too long or too short, or the fabric didn't feel right. So she walked down to the river, quickening her pace to force herself to breathe more vigorously and shake off her lethargy. Soon, the colour rose to her cheeks, the soft pink cheeks that Rob loved so much and which he had not seen for so long . . .

He thought about Katherine as he looked at the rosy-cheeked apples piled high on the National Farmers Union stand 250 miles from home. Thought about sharing one with her, along with a chunk of cheese. "Do you want to do something on this, then?" Rosie had asked him, breaking into his thoughts.

"Mmm?"

"Do you want to talk about the apples?"

"No, I don't think so. No, not really. Just looking." He smiled lightly, and walked on past the strawberries and some towering delphiniums, trying to bring his mind back to the matter in hand. But Katherine's face kept swimming into his head. How he wished she were here to share it with; to walk round together and point out her favourites.

The walkie-talkie strapped to Rosie's hip crackled into life. "Rosie? . . . Tim."

Rosie unclipped it from her belt, pressed the button on its side. "Tim? . . . Rosie."

"Rosie, we've got a bit of a problem. Can you get yourself over to the Portakabin. Bring Rob with you. The others can take half an hour for tea or whatever. As soon as you can, please."

"OK. Be with you in a couple of minutes."

Rosie looked at Rob, who returned her curious glance. "Sounds ominous," she observed.

Rob agreed. Tim's tone was more severe than it had been earlier in the day, and held an unexpected note of urgency.

"We're not late, are we?" he asked Rosie, looking at his watch.

"No, we're not," she confirmed, the two of them now walking through the Great Marquee as briskly as the clusters of unplaced plants and sacks of chipped bark would allow. "We're not due back for another half-hour. It's only four o'clock." They strode in silence towards the Portakabin and walked in to discover Ollie standing in a corner with his arms folded and Tim, sheepskin jacket discarded, sitting on a chair with his head in his hands.

"Hi?" said Rosie, half in greeting, half enquiring. "What's the problem?"

Tim looked up and folded his arms across his chest. "The problem is Mr D'Arcy."

"Being difficult, is he?" asked Rosie, as though she had suspected temper tantrums all along.

Rob wondered what had happened. All kinds of possible scenarios raced through his head in the few seconds that it took Tim to reply. Had Guy refused to work with him? Had Guy asked for a greater share of the programme? Had Guy made a pass at one of the girls?

"Guy's off the programme," said Tim, matter-of-factly.

"What? He's only been on it for a couple of hours," Rosie pointed out.

"Thank God. It would have been worse if this had happened half-way through the shoot – then we really would have been up shit creek without a paddle. As it is, we might just be able to stop this programme turning into a complete disaster. Rob, the girl you work with on *Mr MacGregor's Garden*, what's her name?"

"Bex Fleming."

"Is she free, do you think? Would she be able to co-present with you?"

"I don't know."

"Can she get a couple of days off? It'll mean her taking on board a hell of a lot of information very fast. We've lost one day, but with any luck she'll be able to pick it up quickly. We can brief her an item at a time – there's no other way of doing it. As far as her day job goes we should be through by Tuesday evening."

"I can give you her number and you can ring her and find out."

"Would you be happy to work with her?"

"Well, yes, of course. But why? What's happened?"

"A bloody disaster, that's what's happened. A bloody disaster. It's going to cost a lot of people a lot of money. But it's Guy D'Arcy I feel sorry for. Poor sod."

At three o'clock, as arranged, Guy D'Arcy had taken his leave of Ollie Shakespeare and made his way past the gents' toilet to the series of hospitality tents at the rear of the exhibitors' refreshment marquee. These canvas homes of the corporate beano would not be finished for a couple of days yet and were strewn with piles of white plastic chairs and small round tables.

Guy walked across a patch of grass enclosed by a white palisade fence at the front of the enclosure marked AAC and went into the small, taffeta-lined structure. In a few days from now, he thought, this would be the place where he would be able to hold court and sip champagne with his friends, courtesy of the manufacturers of BLITZ.

Inside the tent a handful of grey-suited men and one woman were sitting round a table engaged in low-volume but earnest conversation. As Guy entered they looked up and the conversation stopped. "Gentlemen," Guy said, breezily. Then he noticed their expressions and said again, "Gentlemen?" His eyes scanned the table. "And Claudia?" with less confidence and the merest hint of fear.

"Guy!" Simon did his best to sound normal, stood up and indicated that he should take a seat.

Sir Freddie Roper sat at the opposite end of the table, his face like thunder, but he didn't look up. His brow was furrowed, his lips pursed and his face the colour of the begonias Guy had noticed only half an hour earlier in the Great Marquee. Claudia Bell sat next to him, impassive.

Simon looked at Sir Freddie Roper and, when it became obvious that the chairman's silence was terminal, decided he'd better speak. All colour had gone from his cheeks. He looked as though he had just been sentenced to death and was about to make his last request. "I'm afraid we have a bit of a problem," he began, looking around him for support. It did not come. Claudia Bell gazed straight ahead. So he continued: "We have a bit of a problem with BLITZ."

"A problem?" asked Guy, disconcerted.

"Yes. Quite a big problem. We're going to have to withdraw it from the market."

"What?" Guy was baffled. "The campaign was OK, wasn't it? Didn't the adverts work?"

"Oh, yes. They worked very well. BLITZ has sold really well."

"So what's the problem?"

"The problem lies with our research department. I'm afraid the product didn't quite . . . well . . . It didn't quite . . . come up to scratch."

"It's a bloody failure!" Sir Freddie exploded, leaping to his feet, thumping the table and bouncing the grey suits into temporary animation. He was clearly unable to contain his anger any longer. "A failure that'll set the company back years. A company I've given the best years of my life to. A company in which I've sunk my reputation." He vented his spleen in the direction of all the grey suits sitting round the table, who now looked down as if in prayer.

Sir Freddie's eyes bulged and gobbets of saliva shot across the table like guided missiles as he continued his harangue. "Folly, bloody folly! I've banged on for years about the importance of research as well as marketing in this company. There are laws about what can and cannot be released. Laws! Not just recommendations but bloody *laws*. Laws designed to protect the public. They're even more strict nowadays than they were twenty years ago. The EU and all that. Why this didn't come to light earlier I just can't understand. What the fuck were you lot thinking about? Have you any idea what this is going to cost you? Cost the company? In reputation as well as money?"

The suits adopted a stillness more appropriate to Madame Tussaud's than the Chelsea Flower Show. Sir Freddie glowered at them. Claudia Bell picked a stray blonde hair from her sleeve.

Guy sat like a schoolboy hauled before the headmaster for a misdemeanour of which he was unaware. When, at last, Sir Freddie paused in his tirade and his colour had subsided to rich pink rather than deep crimson, Guy asked, tentatively, "Doesn't it work, then? BLITZ, I mean. Doesn't it kill the . . . baddies and not the goodies?" He sounded like a small child asking his father to explain the plot of the latest adventure film.

Sir Freddie, now spent of much of his energy, slumped back into his chair and took out a white handkerchief to mop his perspiring brow. "Oh, yes. It does all that. And bloody effectively, too."

"So what's the problem?" Guy dared to allow a flicker of a smile to cross his face.

Simon, seeing that Sir Freddie had expended more energy than perhaps was good for him, supplied the information Guy requested. "I'm afraid that BLITZ has a rather unfortunate side-effect."

"A side-effect? What sort of side-effect?" asked Guy, worry now etched clearly on his face.

"It's a side-effect that our research didn't reveal because it's not something that has happened with any of our chemicals before. Consequently, we were not looking for it. It's only since the product has been tested by our sister company in the States that this . . . er . . . unfortunate side-effect has come to light."

Guy looked bewildered.

"Go on, tell him," bellowed Sir Freddie.

"First of all the tests were carried out on rats."

"But rats don't use bloody insecticides, do they?" jeered Sir Freddie, in a voice heavy with sarcasm.

Simon continued, "Then it was discovered that when the chemical was used by gardeners some of them found that it gave rise to . . . similar problems."

"What sort of problems?"

Guy couldn't have been sure but he thought that he detected, on the face of Claudia Bell, the faintest glimmer of a smile.

"Well, it doesn't always happen, and it is only temporary – lasting a day or so after application. But, you see, BLITZ has been found, in certain men, to cause . . . impotence."

Chapter 32

Nobody seemed quite sure how Guy D'Arcy had left the showground, or where he had gone, but by the time the story hit the early-evening news he was 'unavailable for comment'.

Rob sat on the bed in the small hotel room off the King's Road, toying with a plate of pasta and watching the BBC bulletin. Had they no one else but Lisa Drake? he asked himself. He had turned on his television only a couple of times during the past week, but Lisa had flickered into view each time. It was as if she were getting her own back. His stomach tightened at the sight of her, and he would have turned off, had he not been anxious to see what was reported about BLITZ.

It was the lead item. "Chemical conglomerate AAC found themselves at the centre of a scandal today," intoned Lisa, "as their latest product had to be withdrawn from the market due to an unpleasant and unforeseen side-effect." Over Lisa's shoulder the commercial for BLITZ, with very low sound, was being screened to illustrate the point.

"BLITZ, the company's revolutionary new garden insecticide, was discovered, under certain conditions, to cause temporary impotence."

"Bloody hell!" Rob dropped his fork.

Lisa continued, oblivious to the interruption, "Sales of the product have been high due to a popular advertising campaign

273

fronted by television gardener Guy D'Arcy who was, this evening, unavailable for comment at his London home. Gardeners who have bought the product are being advised to return it to the point of sale where they will be offered a full refund, and anyone who has used the product is advised to consult their doctor. The manufacturers say that there is no cause for alarm as the side-effect of the chemical, discovered in tests in the United States, is only temporary and no long-term damage is evident. Our science correspondent Richard Soames reports . . ."

There followed a brief but authoritative report from the stern-voiced Soames, who explained the nature of the chemical and its side-effects. A spokesman for AAC was grilled about BLITZ and did his best to salvage the company's reputation. The item finished with the exploding greenfly, and Lisa Drake moved on to the latest news about a single European currency.

Rob switched off the set and got up, putting the tray with the unfinished plate of pasta on the table by the wall. He flopped back on to the bed and reflected that it might have been he who had had to do the disappearing act and not Guy D'Arcy, except that he knew he would have stayed and faced the music. Someone had clearly been watching over him. If they had not, it would have meant the end of his gardening career and, worse, still, probably the end of his father's nursery. He turned his eyes heavenward, muttered, 'Thank you,' then came back down to earth and thought of Guy D'Arcy. Nobody deserved that kind of luck.

"What a way to go!" he said to himself. "Poor Guy." And he tried very hard not to smile.

Bex had been stunned, not only by the news but also by having been asked to co-present with Rob. Shock was followed by surprise and then worry as she questioned her own ability to step into Guy D'Arcy's hand-made shoes. She need not have worried. As Rob knew she would, she took to it like a duck to water and rose to the occasion. Rob had greeted her at the show on the Sunday morning with a hug and a kiss, and assurances that she would be fine.

Bex changed into a pair of smart brown trousers and a tailored cream jacket, and put up her hair in a French plait. When she came out of the makeup caravan Rob gasped. She looked stunning. She smiled at him and asked, "Will I do?"

Rob flashed her his crooked grin. "You'll do." He put his arm around her shoulder and gave her a squeeze.

"You look nice," she said perkily, looking at him in his dark blue jacket, grey trousers and crisp white shirt with a floral tie.

"A bit smart for me," he claimed, running his index finger around the inside of his collar.

"No. You clean up really well!" She smiled at him again, and the dimples came to her cheeks.

"Watch it, Miss Fleming! Are you ready, then?"

"No, but never mind."

"You'll be fine, come on. Tim said he'd meet us by the water garden on the corner of Main Avenue. And, if it's any consolation, I hate this bit, too. I'm always happier when I've got the first piece to camera under my belt. At least you feel then that you've made a start."

They walked together down the avenue lined with gardens, unaware of the heads that turned as they passed, and found the camera crew set up and ready to roll alongside an enchanting water garden. Birch trees decorated the top of the slope, and between them and mounds of spring-flowering shrubs, a silvery ribbon of water tumbled over rocks and down into a pool fringed by primulas and flag irises. An old rowing-boat was pulled up on a shingle bank, and a length of rope held it fast to a weather-worn post.

Rob and Bex were positioned leaning on an old five-barred gate to one side, and the soundman fiddled with their microphones as they swapped lines with one another.

Tim instructed the two cameras: "OK, this is the opening piece to camera. We thought we might as well do it first as the garden's ready, so is everyone happy?" The two cameramen nodded. The soundman twiddled a few knobs, held up a long, fluffy sausage of a microphone and, after a few more seconds, gave a thumb's-up.

"OK, chaps. Do you know what you're going to say?"

"We think so," confirmed Rob. "We'll give it a go anyway and see what you think."

"Do you want a rehearsal?" asked Tim.

"No. We'll rehearse on tape – if that's OK with you?" He turned to Bex.

"Fine." She smiled.

Rob looked down at her. "Good luck!" he whispered.

"And you, Mr MacGregor."

He bent and pecked her on the cheek.

"If you're ready then?" There was just a touch of sarcasm in Tim's voice.

Rob and Bex settled themselves comfortably by the five-barred gate. Rob straightened his tie and Bex picked a piece of fluff off his jacket.

"And cue . . ."

Chapter 33

At 4.45 p.m. on the fine afternoon of Monday 18 May, the maroon Rolls-Royce Phantom VI bearing a silver maquette of St George slaying the Dragon atop its gleaming radiator swept silently through the gates of the Royal Hospital, Chelsea, and drew to a graceful halt outside the Great Marquee. The sky was duck-egg blue and so was the suit worn by Her Majesty The Queen as she stepped out of the shiny limousine to be greeted by the Panama-hatted president of the Royal Horticultural Society. Sir Ormsby Proctor had the appearance of our man in Havana in his cream suit and striped Eton tie, and he removed his headgear with practised swiftness as the door of the car eased open. Sir Ormsby bowed, then shook hands with his monarch, from his lofty height, and the line-up of Royal Horticultural Society luminaries were presented, in turn, to their patron.

"Isn't she small?" whispered Bex in Rob's ear. They were standing only a few yards away, behind the row of officials, all filming having been suspended for the duration of the Queen's visit, except for vital royal footage.

"Yes. But what a smile. She should do it more often. Her face really lights up." They walked, side by side, into the Great Marquee, gossiping like two old women over a garden fence, Bex forgetting all about the horticulture and eyeing the Queen's *haute couture* while Rob filled in his colleague as to the identity of the other members of the Royal Family who had preceded her. It was a good year – the Kents and the Gloucesters, Princess Alexandra, the Princess Royal and Princess Margaret were all now ruminating among the roses.

"I didn't know Princess Margaret was keen on gardening," confessed Bex, as the Queen's sister ambled by in pink only a few yards away, with Emma Coalport of the Trust Fund in tow.

"Mad keen on rhododendrons, apparently," whispered Rob. "I hope she doesn't get too close to Emma Coalport. That halitosis will fell her if she does."

Bex stifled a giggle. "I like the hat!" Emma Coalport, a woman with about as much fashion sense as a Bactrian camel, was wearing on her head what at first glance seemed to be an inverted waste-paper basket, but which, on closer inspection, proved to be a hat woven from palm fronds and decorated with dried flowers. The Princess seemed not to have noticed.

Bex looked around at the growing numbers of people, among whom the members of the Royal Family were gliding, quite unconcerned.

"What happens at the Royal Gala this evening? Do we get to stay?"

"Yes. Tim says he has some passes and we have to be there in case they want to film us hobnobbing with royalty."

"Oh, well, I'm sure the Queen will want to talk to me about her begonias," quipped Bex. "Do you fancy a cup of tea? I'm gasping."

"Yes, I do. Especially as Princess Michael is about to be buttonholed by Conrad Mecklenburg and I don't think I want to be splashed by the saliva. Come on."

They walked through the marquee in the direction of the Embankment, past the newly completed stands of flowers. Soon they emerged from the fragrant confines of the canvas into the clear May afternoon, but just as they were about to cross Main Avenue and head for the seclusion of their Portakabin behind the RHS enquiries pavilion, a voice boomed, "'Allo Mr MacGregor," in the rounded, Mummerset tones. "'Ow be ye doin' on this foine day?"

278

Rob froze in his tracks, looked down at Bex with a horrified expression, and the two of them turned round together.

Standing in front of them, his skin browned by the sun and with a twinkle in his pale blue eyes, was Bertie Lightfoot.

"Bertie?" enquired Rob, as if to make sure of the identity of his interlocutor.

Bertie grinned and dropped his false rustic burr. "That's right, luv. Fresh as a daisy and right as ninepence. Thought we'd 'ave a little day out."

"But . . . where've you been? How are you?"

"Been away for a bit, luv. Got meself in a right old state." The flattened camp northern vowels were still there, but the venomous sting had gone out of them. There seemed to be no acid left in the Queen of Myddleton.

"You look really well," Rob said, as yet unsure of how to proceed with the man, who, on last meeting, had been a sorry mixture of hatred and despair. Now, here he stood, in a pale grey suit and crisp white shirt, wearing a blue tie embroidered with golden palm trees. He looked the picture of health, and the epitome of contentment, too.

"Went abroad for a bit. Majorca. Lovely place. They know how to treat you there. Know how to live. I've rented a little villa. Thought it was time I treated meself so I've decided to spend part of the year out there now. Go into retirement. I should just about be able to afford it and I've 'ad a good innings."

Rob stared blankly at him, baffled.

"Oh, I know it's difficult to believe, duckie, and I'm sorry I was a bit of an old cow towards the end. Acid old queen, wasn't I?" Seeing that Rob was finding difficulty in summoning up a reply Bertie's eyes lit on Bex, who was standing silently by his side. "Is this your new co-star?"

"Yes. Er, Bex Fleming, this is Bertie Lightfoot."

Bertie shook Bex's hand. "Pleased to meet you, luv. Just make sure you keep him in hand and you'll be fine," he instructed, with even more of a twinkle in his eye.

Rob, at last, managed to speak. "I'm glad you're happy, Bertie."

"Well, it's all down to 'im, really." Bertie tilted his head in the direction of the show gardens and at a tanned young man walking towards them. "I'd like you to meet my new partner, Paolo. Paolo, this is Rob MacGregor, the lad I've told you about, and this is Miss Fleming, his new co-star."

Rob and Bex were silenced by the sight of the devastatingly handsome Spanish youth in grey slacks, grey polo-necked sweater and navy blue blazer with brass buttons, who politely shook hands with them and bowed. Bex blushed, Rob gawped, and the two of them listened rapt as Bertie told them, very simply and rather touchingly, how much he was in love, and how he couldn't see what someone as young and handsome as Paolo saw in him. They were still standing quietly together a few minutes later when Bertie and Paolo walked away from them, admiring the planting of a garden that had a tropical theme. "We could do something like that," were the last of Bertie's words that fell on their ears.

The Queen did not ask Bex Fleming about her begonias, but the Royal Charity Gala was an evening to remember. Society ladies in outfits that were clearly D & G rather than C & A wandered with their smartly turned-out squires among the flowers, fruits and vegetables of the Chelsea Flower Show, sipping a seemingly endless supply of champagne and nibbling exotic-looking canapés. Rob and Bex had done their best to abstain, in spite of regular approaches from guests enquiring why they did not have a glass. Rob explained politely that they had work to do, though he knew full well of Tim's concern that if his presenters were seen sipping champagne, questions would be asked about the licence fee. Tickets for the gala cost a three-figure sum, and Tim's bosses – some of whom had paid for theirs – would probably not be amused to see their employees getting tipsy in front of them, gratis.

At 8 p.m., an end having been called to the filming, Rob made a move to go.

"Oh, what a shame," sighed Bex, as he slid his jacket and tie on to a hanger in the corner of the Portakabin, "having to go and leave all this."

"It's all right for you," Rob complained. "You're not on camera until half past seven, and you're staying with friends. I have to be ready to go at six with only a grumpy hotel porter to wake me up."

"You poor old thing!"

"Save your sympathy!" he scolded. "If the Queen wonders where I've gone, tell her I had to go to bed early to keep up with my young co-presenter." He kissed her, flung a woollen jacket over his shoulder and headed off in the direction of the King's Road.

At five thirty the next morning, on the banks of the River Wharfe at Nesfield, Jock MacGregor was crossing the old stone bridge that linked his house and the nursery, listening to the sounds of the dawn chorus and the river running beneath his booted feet, just as his son was listening to the early-morning traffic clearing its throat as he walked down the tarmac drive to the Hospital Road entrance of the Chelsea Flower Show.

For Jock, this was the best time of day at the best time of year. Every leaf on every tree was clean and unsullied by weather. The water of the river tumbled clear and sparkling over the rounded boulders that tried to throw it off course, and the damp air smelt pure and clean in the nostrils of this connoisseur of early mornings.

He wiped the dew from the brass padlock with his gnarled thumb and turned the key to open the old gate, wondering how many more mornings like this his enfeebled bank account would enable him to enjoy. He paused to look around the neat nursery that was his life. Rows of trees and shrubs strained at their support wires, brimful of energy and raring to be free. Serried ranks of perennials lined the path, and underneath a long swatch of close-weave netting the bedding plants were now set outdoors in their trays, protected from the late frosts that could so often be treacherous in this part of the dale.

He mused on his good fortune at finding Wayne, who had brought to the riverbank a degree of energy and muscle power that he and Harry were no longer able to command. The nursery had improved its appearance as a result. He nodded to himself, a satisfied nod.

The winter had been perilously quiet, but this was the busiest time of year and the nursery would soon be alive with small groups of customers intent on buying their bedding plants, a necessary bread-and-butter line as far as Jock the plantsman was concerned. With any luck, those who came for something run-of-the-mill would go away with a treasure or two as well, if Jock managed to open their eyes.

He pocketed the old key and walked towards the potting-shed to begin another day, hoping with all his heart that this would not be his last spring at Wharfeside Nursery.

Rob showed his pass to the solitary security man on duty at the gate and walked through the deserted showground to the film crew's Portakabin. Here he put on a clean shirt, gasping as the chill morning air crept over his naked torso, and then the jacket and tie he had been wearing for the previous day's shooting.

It was a crisp morning, laced with a faint haze of mist, courtesy of the adjacent River Thames – a broad, lazy, dark brown motorway of a river, so different from the shimmering Wharfe at home. Where the Wharfe shone coppery in the Yorkshire dawn, the Thames glowed a dull bronze in the early-morning London light.

He looked at his watch. A quarter to six. He was early. No one else had arrived yet. The gardeners and nurserymen, the growers and landscapers were still tucked up in bed: having worked from dawn till dusk for three weeks they needed all the sleep they could get. It would be another hour or two before they stirred.

Rob walked from the Portakabin along the Rock Garden Bank, pulling his jacket around him to keep warm and looking at the gardens, whose waterfalls and fountains were stilled by the overnight lack of power. A blackbird broadcast its wake-up call from the branch of a maple that, just a couple of weeks ago, had not been there. Now the blackbird considered it a resident.

He turned left towards the Great Marquee, found the entrance and discovered that it was laced up, exactly like the big old bell tent they had used at Scout Camp in his youth. He looked round for help. No one was there.

He examined the rope fastening more closely and discovered that it was simply threaded through brass eyelets to hold the flap in place. Slowly he unpicked it until around four feet of canvas flapped free and he was able to duck underneath it and into the marquee.

What he saw took his breath away. Slowly he walked forward into the three-and-a-half-acre garden that had appeared as if by magic overnight. Gone were the champagne-sipping socialites; gone was the Royal Family. Now he had the place to himself and not another soul gazed on it with him. He stood alone in a floral paradise, the blackbird silent, the air still.

The feeble morning sun shone through the opaque canvas and released, in spite of its weakness, the fragrances of a spring garden. Scents met his nostrils in rich profusion – the heady perfume of lilies and narcissi, the fresh, light tang of sweet peas, and the sweet, cloying aroma of pine bark and crushed grass.

He wandered, like a small child let loose in a toyshop, among this creation of hundreds of gardeners, who had toiled night and day to bring together their object of floral perfection. Towering over him were royal blue spires of delphiniums and pastel pyramids of honey-scented lupins. Begonias from Bristol, their flowers like dinner plates, grinned their red and orange faces at him, and exotic blooms from Barbados erupted like succulent lollipops from fountains of juicy foliage.

Proteas and other spiky flowers from South Africa kept company with gigantic mounds of seemingly freshly lacquered strawberries, and roses in beds and borders, vases and urns, tumbled in indecent quantity into the botanical tapestry on which he gazed.

He stood in the very centre of the marquee like Adam in the Garden of Eden, and slowly turned around. Flowers met his eye whichever way he looked, and within a minute he could no longer see for tears. Here, in a corner of Britain's largest city, where smog and traffic normally reigned supreme, the best gardeners in the land had come together to show off their skills; gardeners like his father who had learned their craft over a lifetime and who shared it, each May, with an admiring and incredulous public. He felt a mixture of wonder and pride. Wonder at the impossible grandeur and size of it all, and pride that this was his job, these were his people, and this was what he had always wanted to do. He felt a burning desire to share it all. But Katherine was not there.

He took out his clean handkerchief, blew his nose, and went off in search of an early-morning cup of coffee.

Ollie Shakespeare, his glistening skull just visible over a long navy-blue greatcoat, had both hands wrapped round a polystyrene cup and was standing on the steps of the Portakabin. "There's a cup for you inside, if you want it, and a bacon roll."

"Great," said Rob. "Why are you here so early? I didn't think you and Bex were due to start until half past seven."

"Just been looking at the pieces I cut together last night." Ollie jerked his head in the direction of the video player in the corner of the Portakabin. "It's looking good. I think you'll be pleased. You and Bex work together really well."

"Thanks." Rob poured himself a cup of coffee and began to put himself on the other side of a bacon roll, the warm fat dripping down his chin. He staunched its flow quickly with a paper napkin, aware that if it got on to his jacket he'd be in deep trouble with Wardrobe.

"Come here," instructed Ollie, walking towards Rob with a fresh napkin and tucking it into his neck. "Better safe than sorry."

Rob grinned above the fresh white bib that now covered his jacket and asked, "Any news of Guy D'Arcy?"

"Not a word, except that everyone's fairly sure he's left the country."

Rob paused mid-chew. "How do they know?"

Ollie continued, warming to his subject, "Well, there's no sign of him at home and even his car was still parked in Burton Court until yesterday. The garage came to take it back. Really odd. He seems to have disappeared into thin air."

"Poor bugger."

"Yes, poor bugger," agreed Ollie. "He was a smug git, but it's a hell of a way to go. Did you see the news?"

"Yes. Has there been more?"

"Only about Guy. Saying he's disappeared without trace. I suppose he must be used to the publicity – I mean, all that stuff about him being a ladies' man, real gossip-column fodder. But I guess he thought all that had ended."

"Mmm," Rob mumbled, through a mouthful of bacon roll.

"The show was buzzing with it all yesterday. Folk going on about how daft the commercial was, but secretly dead jealous about the amount of money he must have made."

"I suppose that must be his only consolation," mused Rob. "I hope he got the money out of them before disaster struck."

"He insisted on it, apparently," said Ollie. "I heard him talking to one of those National Trust biddies on Saturday. She was giving him hell for mixing with trade but he said he'd needed the money and they'd paid him up front."

"I should think that went down well with the Trust Fund."

"Like a lead balloon. She told him he'd really let the side down. Guy just shrugged and said, 'I can't afford principles, darling.' I bet he wished he'd saved up a bit now."

Their ruminations were interrupted by Rosie Duff, muffled in a duffel-coat. "All right, my lovely?" she asked Rob.

"Fine, thanks. We were just musing on the fate of Mr D'Arcy."

"Ooooh. Now there's a story. Anyway, we haven't time for all that. Had your coffee? Good. Come on, then. The crew are there already. Off we go to the Big Top. It's time for the circus to hit town." She bowled off in the direction of the Great Marquee, with the bespectacled Colin and Penny of the perforated cardigan in tow. Rob plucked the napkin from his neck, wiped the bacon fat from his chin, waved a silent farewell to Ollie and tried to think what he was going to say about a display of cacti from Congleton.

By half past eight the Chelsea Flower Show had transformed itself from a tranquil, bucolic oasis into a bustling flower festival. Only thirty minutes after the turnstiles had opened, those people who could call themselves Members of the Royal Horticultural Society were allowed their special preview, which would last for two days, the general public being allowed in on Thursday and Friday.

Rosie had been wise enough to get her filming in the marquee finished by 8 a.m., knowing that the punters would make life more difficult as soon as they arrived. She was not wrong. Journeys across the Royal Hospital grounds that had taken two minutes on Sunday and Monday now took at least ten, thanks to the crowds. They were intent on seeing the exhibits, but also opportunist enough to stop Rob MacGregor in his tracks and let him know how much they liked his programme.

Rosie shepherded him from garden to garden, like a small but determined bouncer, amused at people's reaction to the man they felt they knew, even though they had never met him. She did her best to remain patient when they engaged him in conversation, and bit her lip when someone told him, "You're better-looking in real life than you are on telly."

More than one man had asked Rob, "Where's Bex, then?" and when they came together on a lavishly planted Mediterranean garden for the final pay-off, there was a cheer as Bex stepped over the swags of rope that separated the real world from that of horticultural make-believe.

"Where's Mr D'Arcy?" yelled a voice from the crowd. The brief, tense moment was short-lived.

Another voice shouted, "Nah, these two are better-looking," to a cheerful round of laughter.

"And they know their stuff," put in a little lady at the front.

Bex gave her a smile and then whispered to Rob under her breath, "Wow, it's like being in a zoo."

"Yes. But at least the natives are friendly. You OK?"

"Yeah. It's been great . . . and I've met this guy."

"What sort of guy?" asked Rob, thinking for a moment that Mr D'Arcy had returned.

"Grows begonias."

"Begonias!"

"Yes. Look, I know they're not exactly the height of fashion but he's great. He's got an earring, too, but he's really nice. Asked me out."

"You don't hang around, do you?" Rob was suddenly aware of his own loneliness.

"Excuse me." Ollie was fighting his way towards the garden with his camera crew. "Can we come through, please?"

The mass of bodies parted like the Red Sea, emphasizing Oliver Shakespeare's biblical appearance in a flowing greatcoat that was almost as voluminous as the robes of a prophet. Show catalogues were being waved by one or two people at the front of the crowd. "Autographs in a minute, ladies and gentlemen," instructed Rosie. "We've got to make them work for a living first."

Ollie and Rosie went into brief conference about the last shot and were joined by Tim. Rob and Bex turned their backs to the crowd and sorted out their words. Fifteen minutes later the filming of *The Chelsea Flower Shower Special* was finished and it was now up to Rosie, Oliver and Tim to turn the ragbag of disparate items into a cohesive whole that would please a gardening public unable to make the journey from their corner of the land to the riverbank of London SW3.

Rob zipped up the suit carrier and hung it on the hook at the back of the door of the Portakabin. He pulled on a white Arran sweater and sat down to tie the laces on his Caterpillar boots. That felt better. Better to be back in jeans and a sweater rather than a shirt and tie. He felt normal again.

A soft knock rattled the door. "Are you there?" It was Bex. She, too, had changed from her smart suit into jeans and a sweater. "I've come to say goodbye."

287

She stepped up into the Portakabin as Rob rose from the plastic chair in the corner. "And I've come to say thank you, too, for everything." She put her arms round him and gave him a hug, her head resting on his shoulder.

Rob heaved a sigh.

"What's up?" asked Bex, looking up at him.

"Oh, nothing. It's just nice to have a hug."

Bex paused and looked into his eyes. "You haven't gone and claimed her yet, have you?"

"No."

"Don't leave it too long."

"No."

They parted and Bex looked him in the eye. "She won't wait for ever." She rubbed her hand up and down his sleeve. "I've got some news for you. I've taken the plunge."

Rob looked alarmed. "Not -"

"No. Not the begonia man. That's just a bit of fun. I've handed in my notice. I'm going freelance. The *Sunday Herald* have asked me to take over Guy's column so I thought I'd bite the bullet and try to make my own way in the world. It's all thanks to you, really."

Rob smiled. "I'm glad. You're very talented."

"No." She gazed at him intently. "I've just been very lucky. Finding you." The smile that followed flickered a little. "Find her. Soon."

She walked to the door with her bag flung over her shoulder. She turned. "Silly man," she said.

And then she was gone.

Chapter 34

"I can't say I'm sorry, but it is a bit of a pain. He wasn't exactly my ideal gardener, although he just about kept on top of the weeds. Now heaven knows what will happen." Helena was at Wharfeside Nursery buying trays of antirrhinums and nicotianas and sharing her staffing problems with Jock MacGregor. Makepiece, the gnarled old gardener who had stepped in to fill Rob's shoes when full-time education lured him away, had finally decided that it was time to retire. He'd given a week's notice and thrown in the trowel.

"And at bedding-out time, too," groaned Helena. "Mrs Ipplepen says she'll send her Cyril round but I think he's a parsnip-and-potato man. He'll probably want to earth up the petunias in a few weeks' time."

Jock was loading her selected trays of summer bedding plants on to a low, flat-bedded trolley. "Have you said yes to him yet?"

"No. I thought I'd talk to you first, and see if you had any ideas. The trouble is that everyone who's available is old and grumpy and I'd far rather have someone young and lively." Jock looked up at her as he slid another tray on to the trolley.

Helena looked embarrassed. "Oh, sorry. Well, you know what I mean . . ."

Jock chuckled. "I know what you mean. A bit of youth makes a hell of a lot of difference." He surveyed the plants around him.

Helena smiled. "Well, at least I could bend a young gardener to my will a bit more than one who has, shall we say, set ideas about how things should be done. Jumbo and I never liked beetroot and Makepiece grows eight rows of them. Eight rows!"

Jock put down another tray and stood upright, rubbing his back. "You know, it's funny how things turn out sometimes. You can go through life just missing the boat nine times out of ten, but every now and then the timing of things turns out just right."

"In what way?"

"Have you thought about young Wayne?"

"Sorry?"

"Wayne Dibley – my lad. Have you thought about him?"

"I thought he was settled."

"He was. Had a lady on the far side of town that he used to work for on a Sunday but she's just gone into a home. He needs extra pocket money. Heaven knows, I can't afford to pay him more than the basic rate, and I'd have thought he'd be just what you need."

"Do you think he'd be interested?"

"Ask him yourself. He's coming over."

Wayne had just rounded the corner of the greenhouses and was making his way towards them. What became evident as he approached his boss was that he was not happy. He seemed pre-occupied. He stopped for a chat with a couple who were selecting a container-grown tree, but there was no sign of the flashing smile and the bright eyes that normally shone from his face. Having answered the shopping couple's question he continued his journey to Jock and Helena.

"You look as if you've lost a shilling and found a sixpence," offered Jock. "What's the matter?"

"Oh, just a bit fed up," answered Wayne, doing his best to offer Helena a smile.

"Well, Lady Sampson has some news that might cheer you up."

Wayne looked at the lady from the big house up at the top end of town.

"I wondered if you might be able to help me, Wayne."

"How's that?" he asked, hopping from one foot to another.

"My old gardener, Mr Makepiece, has just left me and I need someone to take his place. Not full time, just part time . . . with hours to suit. Mr MacGregor thought you might be interested. Would you?"

"Cor! Nor'arf!" Wayne's eyes lit up, the white teeth flashed, and his mood changed. "That would be really great." Then a little hesitation. "But only if you're sure I could do it." He looked at Jock and Helena, and received the confirmation he was looking for.

"I think you know enough to be able to cope," Jock assured him.

Helena was quick to take up his offer. "Wonderful. When can you start? I could do with these bedding plants being put in this weekend."

"Fine. This weekend, then. Great. Wow! That'll really get me out of a spot. Thanks." He was his old self again now.

"So what was the problem?" Jock asked.

"Problem?" asked Wayne.

"You looked miserable. What was wrong?"

"Oh, that. Just me roses. Something's gone wrong."

"Which roses?"

"The ones I was forcing. You know, the ones from Professor Wilberforce."

"I thought you were only forcing one of them?" There was an edge to Jock's voice. He had allowed Wayne to go ahead, on condition that he start off slowly by forcing one of this and one of that. This way, if things went wrong and the shrubs failed to respond or simply curled up their toes and died, Jock's losses would be minimized.

He had been particularly specific about Professor Wilberforce's rose-bushes, asking Wayne to force only one. He'd instructed the lad to leave the other bushes outdoors, fearful that he might lose them all if Wayne's growing skills were not up to scratch.

Wayne detected the disapproval in Jock's tone and began to defend himself. "It's just that I wanted it to work. I really wanted to prove that I could do it but it just seemed to go wrong." The lad began to panic and Jock realized that he had been a touch heavy-handed.

"Never mind, never mind. Did they all curl up and die?"

"No. Not exactly."

"What, then?"

"It's just that something seems to have happened to the flowers. They're a funny colour."

"Well, they shouldn't be. The flower colour will be exactly the same as it would be in the garden. It's only the timing of the flowering that will be different." Jock looked at Helena, who was wondering if this was the right time to make a quick, quiet exit.

"Come and look," suggested Wayne. "I did exactly as you said, gave them plenty of water when they needed it, and ventilation, and I fed them once a week. I just don't know what's up."

Jock followed Wayne back to his greenhouse, with Helena tagging along behind, unable to extricate herself without being ungracious. Wayne opened the door of the greenhouse, which was now almost empty, the bedding plants having been moved outside over the last couple of weeks. The pots of roses stood on the path at the very end of the house, which Wayne had begun to scrub out in readiness for its next occupants.

"Good grief." Jock looked at the rose-bushes from just inside the door and advanced on them slowly.

"I didn't give them anything I shouldn't have. I did exactly what you said," pleaded Wayne.

Helena followed in Jock's wake. "Oh, goodness me!" Her hand rose to her mouth.

The sounds of the rest of the world were blocked out from Jock's ears as he walked towards the three potted rose-bushes that stood on the old stone path at the end of the greenhouse. Their leaves were dark green and glossy, their stems rigid and strong, and the well-shaped flowers that had opened at their shoot tips were a pure, clear, unadulterated royal blue.

On the blue-painted verandah of the plantation house on the Caribbean island of Grenada, Guy D'Arcy put his feet up on the steamer chair and asked for another rum punch. He looked down across the slope of lush tropical foliage towards the turquoise sea below and reflected that it would take quite a lot of work to transform this patch of undergrowth into a paradise garden. Never mind. He had all the time in the world now. And quite a bit of money, too. Serena Clayton-Hinde, her tanned legs revealed at their full length in the cutaway black swimsuit, leaned over the back of his chair, kissed him full on the mouth and slipped the glass of punch into his hand. She ruffled the hair at the back of his head. "I'm going for a shower. Don't be long." She slinked into the cool interior of the plantation house and disappeared from view.

Ah, well, thought Guy, sipping the sweet, fruity mixture through a straw, life has its compensations.

Rob sat for a while on the riverbank watching a speckled brown trout nosing upstream through the dappled water, and then he lay back among the long stalks of foxtail grass, breathing slowly as their sweet odour drifted on the air. He closed his eyes to the bright gold of the early-evening sun and reflected on the events of the past weeks – the highs and lows, the revelations and the disappointments, the excitement and the underlying hollowness.

At least now his father would not have to worry about staying in business: the plant breeder's rights in 'Wharfeside Blue' would see to that. The royalties payable by nurserymen for propagating the plant and growing it under licence would yield a small fortune. A smile flickered across his freckled face at the name his father had chosen for the rose so generously bequeathed to him by the late professor of genetic engineering.

He'd read in *Scientific Horticulture* that plant breeders were boasting of being able to play around with genes and give scentless plants perfume and unusual colours. Disease resistance was regularly being bred into plants now, and scientists had indicated that it was just a matter of time before the blue rose was reality. It seemed that Professor Wilberforce had pipped everyone else to the post, and decided that his old friend Jock MacGregor was the man who should benefit.

He smiled again as he thought of Bertie Lightfoot, and of the young Paolo who had clearly endowed the old stager with a new lease of life. Then his thoughts turned to Guy D'Arcy and to the fact that, there, but for the fickle finger of fate, would he have gone himself. He shuddered as the first cool breeze of the evening rattled the leaves of the alders overhead.

And now here he was. Alone. He thought of Bex; of her kindness and concern. And her generosity. He liked her. A lot. He remembered what she'd said, just before they parted: "She won't wait for ever."

The scent of the grasses around him grew fainter in the cool air; their fragrance had changed now. It was some other perfume; a reminder of some other place. The scent of home.

He rose to his feet and dusted off his jeans, then strode over the grassy tussocks of the riverbank and up the lane towards the town. Towards Katherine's flat at Wellington Heights. He knew quite clearly now what he wanted to say. He rang the bell. There was no answer. Just the muted sounds of conversation from the bakery below.

He looked up at her window. It was slightly ajar, as it always was, and the curtain billowed gently in the evening breeze, but no sounds of occupancy came from within.

Sluggishly he retraced his steps towards the river. He would walk past his father's nursery and up the valley to End Cottage. There would be time for the half-hour stroll before it got dark. He was barely a hundred yards upstream of the nursery when he saw a small, familiar figure sitting down by the water's edge, gently tossing pebbles into the shallows.

He walked silently up behind her, stooped to pick up a pebble then threw it into the water in front of her. She started, then turned round and saw him, squinting as the sun caught her dark eyes. He stood and looked down at her, the evening light turning his hair to fiery bronze.

"Hello," she said softly.

He lowered himself on to the grassy bank beside her and looked, like her, towards the shimmering water. "I've been looking for you."

"Oh?"

"I couldn't find you."

"I was here."

"Why?"

"It seemed the right place to be."

They sat silently for what seemed, to Rob, an age.

"How are you?" he asked.

"I'm OK. How are you?"

"Better now," he said, looking upwards towards the moor. "I – I can't go on without you, you know. I was wrong to do what I did. So wrong. But I can't – I can't be without you."

She put her arms around her knees and pulled them up to her chest. "I see," she said.

"I've missed you so much." He put his arm around her and slowly, she leaned her head on his shoulder.

"I don't like it when you're not there," she whispered.

"Nor me."

They sat together, watching the water, mesmerized for a while by its music.

"Promise you won't go away again?" he asked.

She pulled away slightly and gazed at him, a hurt look in her eyes. "Only if you won't."

He cupped his hands around her face and kissed her gently, remembering the softness of her lips. Then he moved his head away from her a little and looked into her eyes. "I promise."

"You see, I try very hard to cope without you. I *can* cope without you. But I don't like it."

"I know. I know."

Tears filled her eyes. "When you're here I feel safe, and calm, and, well . . . just right. And when you're not . . ." She hit the rough turf with her hand and turned her head away.

Rob sank his face into the hair at the back of her neck. "Shh . . . Oh, my love, my love." He rocked her gently, and felt himself filling with warmth and love for her.

"How have you been?" she asked, almost whispering.

"Pretty rotten. When you're not here it's like being half a person. I so much miss sharing things with you. When you're not here it's like going through the motions. Nothing really matters. It's like marking time, just waiting to be with you again." He held her gently, and through his tears watched the river gliding by. "You see, I wasn't sure before. I didn't know whether it was just habit – just convenient and nice and cosy. I had to be sure."

"And are you sure . . . now?" Her voice faltered and a single tear coursed down her cheek. He turned back her head with his outstretched hand, intercepted the tear at her chin and licked it off his finger.

"Oh, I'm sure. I'm absolutely sure." He paused. "Can I ask you something?" He held her head against his cheek.

"Yes?"

"Would you mind very much if we sold your flat?"

"No."

"And would you mind very much moving in with me?"

"No."

"And . . . would you mind . . . marrying me?"

She opened her mouth to speak, but could make no words. The battle against her emotions lost, she began to shake with deep, silent sobs, looking first at the sky and then into his pale green eyes.

He whispered to her gently, "I'm here now. I won't go away again."

"Not ever?"

"Not ever." He put both arms around her and held her so tightly she felt the breath being squeezed out of her. It took all her effort, through the tears and the lack of breath, to say the words he had been frightened he would never hear again. "I love you, Mr MacGregor."

"And I love you, Miss Page, with all my heart."

They sat until the sun sank behind the alder tree. Then he helped her to her feet, dusted the grass from her bottom and put his arm around her shoulder. She leaned into him, put both her arms around his waist, and they walked upstream for home.